Twenty-Five

RACHEL L. HAMM

ISBN: Pick Up A Pen Books
ISBN-13: 978-0615822204

DEDICATION

For all girls who wish for love.

CONTENTS

Chapter One: A Birthday

Abigail

"Happy Birthday!" my family exclaimed, rushing into my apartment, arms loaded with all the essentials for a party: pizza, beer, gifts, and cake. I can't stand the taste of beer, but as it's the only alcohol my mother tolerates, I was happy to accept a bottle from the six-pack in my dad's hands. Because unlike most people, I do not look forward to my birthday. Nothing good ever comes of it. The day I turned five, my parents and I were in a car crash on the way to the zoo and I broke my leg. On my sixteenth birthday, the boy I had a crush on asked my best friend to the prom, and she said yes. And when my family barged into my apartment on the eve of my twenty-fifth birthday, my life was nowhere near where it should have been.

"What is this? I told you I didn't want to do anything for my birthday." I didn't try to hide the irritation in my voice or on my face; they knew I didn't want to celebrate. Apparently my frown wasn't as menacing as I hoped.

"Yes, well, you can wallow in self-pity later tonight. Seriously, Abigail, did you think we were going to ignore your birthday?" Anna laughed as she put the cake in the fridge and grabbed a beer.

"As the birthday girl, I thought you'd have some respect for my wishes."

"Since when have we respected your wishes?" Ashley demanded, encircling me in a tight hug.

Too true, I thought.

"I would've been happy to respect your wishes," Derek shrugged, "they told me we were going to a movie."

"Haha, very funny, D." I grimaced at my older sisters and younger brother in turn, but didn't have much time to complain because my mother was heading towards me.

"We won't stay long if you really don't want us here, but we wanted to have dinner with you." She kissed my cheek as she put a gift-wrapped box on my kitchen table. "After all, twenty-five years ago, I endured ten hours of excruciatingly painful labor so you could be standing here today. Don't I deserve a little bit of time with you to commemorate that occasion?"

"Nothing like a guilt trip to kick off the party," I groaned. Anna, Ashley, and Derek nodded in agreement and I knew I was defeated. "Alright, I give in. What kind of pizza did you bring?"

As we gathered around the table and everyone filled their plates with cheesy goodness, I couldn't help comparing myself with my sisters. A bad habit to be sure, but it was second nature from growing up in their shadows. By Anna's twenty-fifth birthday, she'd been married for three years and loved her job as a buyer for Macy's almost as much as she loved her husband. Ashley had been married for two years and teaching for three, she'd already been voted teacher of the year at the high school where she taught math.

Me, on the other hand. Well, I graduated from college three years prior to that dreaded day with good grades and excellent references from my professors. I even created a substantial portfolio of articles I wrote for the school's newspaper. But a year of job searching proved fruitless. The only job I found even remotely related to journalism was in the Subscriptions Department of the mailroom at the Boston offices of *Intuition* Magazine. Sure, Subscriptions is a step up from sorting and delivering, but it doesn't exactly get my creative juices flowing. My boss really liked me, or so she'd told me hundreds of times, but each piece I'd submitted to her was returned with a note stating, "Not *Intuition* material."

"Okay, Abigail, blow out the candles and make a wish!" My mother placed the chocolate and cookie crumble ice cream cake in front of me, twenty-five candles blazing away. I looked into the flames, trying to remind myself of what was going well in my life. The job I hated didn't pay a lot, but it paid enough that I was able to afford my car payments and rent a decent apartment. Okay, decent might be pushing it. My apartment was smaller than my freshman year dorm room. It barely held enough space for clothes and my mountains of books, let alone room to actually get dressed or complete other essential tasks, like sleeping. I wasn't living with my parents, though, so I still considered moving into it the best decision I'd ever made. And my family, they were always there for me, even if sometimes I wanted them to leave me alone.

The only thing left to wish for was love, but I wasn't that naïve. So I blew out the candles hoping only for a better year than the last. Mom sliced into the cake and handed me a plate.

"Do I get to open my presents now?" I asked, digging into my generous portion. The one good thing about birthdays, other than food and alcohol, is the presents.

"Absolutely. Here, open ours first." My father handed me a box and I ripped the paper off, revealing a state-of-the-art Single Serving Gourmet Coffee Maker.

"Wow, thank you!" I pulled my face into an oversized grin. "This is fantastic, I've been wanting one of these for months." I dug into the packaging and poured my eyes over the instruction manual.

"Oh good. I'm glad you like it. I thought it would save you some money, now you don't have to go to Starbucks so often, and you won't have to make a pot of coffee large enough for four when you're the only one drinking it." My mother's smile showed how pleased she was with the gift and I decided I would use it every day.

"This one is from all three of us," Ashley explained as she handed over the bag she had carried in. I pulled out the tissue paper and threw it on the floor, finding the bag held three envelopes and a wrapped box. I reached for the box first; inside was a charming, hand-carved, wooden picture frame. Initials on the sides represented the four of us.

I ran my fingers over the wood and looked at the picture. It had been taken at Christmas. Our father bought stockings with our initials sewn onto the toe. We were holding our stockings, with the toes clearly showing, and in addition to the four of us, Anna's husband, Will, Ashley's husband, Cain, and Derek's fiancé, Samantha, smiled for the camera.

"It's beautiful, guys, thank you." Setting it on the table upright, I grabbed the cards next and read them to myself.

"B, you may be 25 now, but that doesn't mean you're an adult or anything. You'll always be my baby sister. And I retain the right to belittle and berate you as much as possible. Love ya, mean it, N."

"Abigail, Happy Birthday. Mine's next month and I expect a jet ski. Thanks. Derek."

As I opened Ashley's, a slip of paper fell from the envelope onto the table. I ignored it while reading her handwritten comments, *"BB, I love you soooo much. Have the bestest birthday ever! Your favorite sister, S,"* then eagerly picked up the sheet to see what other surprise she had in store for me.

"Isn't that a riot?" Ashley laughed. "I found it a couple of weeks ago when I was helping Mom clean out her attic. It was mixed in with some of my old high school things."

"What is it?" Anna asked as Derek grabbed it out of my hand.

"*Twenty-Five Things I Want to Accomplish by Age Twenty-Five* by Abigail Bronsen," he read. Everyone cracked up, but I snatched the paper back, a deep blush spreading over my cheeks and neck.

"It was a project for English. We had to come up with a list, any list, and write an essay on why we included the items we did and why we left other things off. I think I was fifteen when I wrote this."

"What's on it?" Derek asked, trying to steal it again.

"Oh, just the usual fifteen-year old hopes and dreams. Marry Leonardo DiCaprio, own a Corvette, kill my younger brother, you get the idea." I folded the paper and stuck it in my pocket, my mind wandering to the few items I glimpsed, *learn how to surf, learn a foreign language, buy a house.* I tried to clear my head and pay attention to the conversation my parents were having about new windows in their kitchen, but every few seconds, my thoughts drifted back to the list. *Learn how to cook. Learn how to ski.* I shook each one out of my head, and wasn't surprised when Derek asked if I was having a seizure. Fortunately, everyone laughed at my stupidity and didn't question the reason for it.

Two hours of merriment and jokes at my expense later, I was ready to have the apartment to myself. My family had the uncanny ability to make me feel trapped in an elevator stuck between floors.

"Thanks for coming. I had a great birthday. I love you Mom, Dad," I ushered them out of the door with a hug and kiss. "I can't wait to use my coffee maker," I called after them. "Thanks Anna, Derek. I'll see you at lunch next week. Love you, Ash." I gave each a quick hug and watched as they filed down the stairs and flowed into the parking lot.

I secured the lock on my door and went back to the table, where my presents laid amidst torn and crumpled wrapping paper. I stared at the coffee maker and photo and pulled the list out of my pocket. Smoothing the folds and laying the paper on the table, I examined it. The gifts my family had so thoughtfully given me now seemed like instruments of mental torture, reminders of my failure in life. The first two items popped off the page, threatening to strangle me with disappointed hopes.

#1 Fall in Love

#2 Get Married

I tried not to think about the list or my lifetime membership in the Singles Club while I cleaned and straightened the apartment, but when every surface had been scrubbed and the last bit of trash stowed safely in the dumpster, there was little else to occupy my mind.

Well, happy birthday to me.

Chapter Two: An Accident

Ben

"Uncle Ben! Uncle Ben!" Joey ran towards me, slipping on the wet pavement and falling at my feet.

"Hey, buddy, careful!"

"Where's Mommy?" He stood unscathed and pressed his body against my legs, finding shelter from the thunder and rain under the massive umbrella in my right hand.

"She's at home with your sister."

"Why?"

I don't usually pick my nephew up from school, only on the rare occasion my sister had a photo shoot or client meeting and her husband had a surgery scheduled, but that day I'd gotten off work early and knew the rain would make it difficult for Tracey to get out of the house. "Because I thought we needed some Uncle Ben and Joey time. Whaddya say?"

"Can we get ice cream?"

"Sure thing, buddy, let's go." I took him to the closest restaurant and ordered a hot fudge sundae large enough for us to share. He ate most of it, or most of it ate him, I'm not sure. When the bowl was empty, his shirt and face were covered with sticky, sugary goo. He squirmed and giggled anytime I got close with a wet napkin to wipe him off and the waitress laughed every time she came by to check on us and found him even messier than the time before.

I tried to prolong the outing as long as I could, hoping the rain would lighten before we got back on the road, but when the storm grew worse, it seemed like time to return him to his parents.

Tracey greeted me, umbrella in hand, as I got out of my car and moved to the backseat to unbuckle a sleeping Joey. "Thanks Ben. I was not looking forward to taking Hannah out in this."

"Oh yeah, no problem. I remember the last time I tried to drive with her in the car while it was raining. The doctor was surprised how quickly I regained my hearing."

She laughed. "Yeah, the screaming isn't nearly as deafening when she's in the house, covering her head with a blanket to block out the scariness." She reached with one arm for Joey and I handed him over the best I could, soaking all three of us in the process by knocking the umbrella out of Tracey's hand. I picked it up and held it over them to walk inside the house. Tracey grimaced as she looked at Joey's ice-cream smeared face. "Have you ever heard of a napkin, Ben?"

"Hey," I put up my hands in protest, "I tried to clean him off, but he wouldn't let me. I'd say he's probably as stubborn as his mother."

"Shut up, jerk."

"Language, language, Trace. What kind of example are you setting for your children?"

"Get out of my house!" She grabbed the umbrella and shoved me out the door with it, but was laughing as I raced down the stairs and headed for my car. "Thanks, Bro!" she called as I unlocked the door and slid my soaked body into the driver's seat.

The highway was a mess. The rain fell so thickly it was difficult to see and none of the vehicles around me were taking any chances with speed. My frustration built slowly as I stared at the back of a red pickup truck for at least twenty minutes. Finally, a lane opened and I maneuvered my car behind a blue Nissan. It wasn't going any faster than the pickup, but at least it was something new to look at.

I took my eyes off the road for just a second to adjust the heat when my car lurched forward. Automatically, I gripped the wheel with both hands and slammed my foot on the brake, but still I propelled forward, the taillights of the Nissan coming closer and closer until I knew there was nothing I could do to stop from plowing into it. Instinctively, I relaxed my foot and shrunk back in my seat, preparing for impact.

"No!" the throaty growl escaped as I helplessly watched the Nissan skid on puddles of water drenching the road. The car spun four or five times but miraculously missed every other vehicle around it. Then, out of the corner of my eye, I saw some jackass gunning down the open lane beside me.

Do you not see what's happening! Before I could yell out, the Mazda smashed into the Nissan, sending it into the guardrail and ultimately stopping its frenzied spinning.

I threw open my door and jumped out, not thinking about the cars still moving down the road. Adrenaline pumped through my veins and my only thoughts consisted of *I hope they're okay, I hope they're okay. Please be okay.*

A seven-foot beast of a man got out of the jeep implanted in the tail end of my car. "Hey dude, you alright?" he asked.

"Are you kidding me? Call 911!" I scowled at him, running to the Nissan.

Water flew around me, making it difficult to see inside the car as I tapped on the glass of the driver's side window. "Are you okay? Are you hurt?" I cried out, praying there were no injuries, hoping for no passengers in the front seat. The impact of the Mazda would have killed someone sitting there.

The door creaked open and a petite young woman started to move her legs to get out, keeping her hands locked firmly on the steering wheel.

"Stay in your car," I placed a hand on her shoulder, "the paramedics will be here soon. If you're injured you shouldn't move." *Yeah, I read that somewhere.*

She slumped back into her seat as if she didn't have even the smallest bit of strength to resist me. "I think I'm okay. My neck hurts, but that's it." Her teeth chattered, making her voice break.

"You're shaking, can I get you a blanket, or a jacket?" There was something about the way dark, wet strands of hair fell across her forehead that caused my heart to beat faster.

"I'm not cold," she said; the chattering ceased.

I stood there, unsure what to do. I felt responsible for this and strangely, for her.

"What happened?" she asked after a few minutes, removing her hands from the steering wheel and wriggling them. I smiled at the daintiness of her tiny fingers, but shook my head to try and keep focus.

"This big guy in a jeep rear-ended me. I tried to use my brakes, but they were wet, and I couldn't stop. I hit you and you started flying all over the road, then this little Mazda came speeding down the lane and crashed into you and propelled you into the guard rail."

"Is everyone okay?"

Shit, I don't know. Well, I'm fine, that beast behind me was fine, and Mazda guy is out of his car, so he must be all right, too. "It looks like it."

"How did you see all that? Everything happened so fast, it's kinda fuzzy for me."

Oh God... "Did you hit your head? You could have a concussion." I leaned down, looking her straight in the eye. *Wow.* She had the most gorgeous green eyes I'd ever seen and my stomach literally did a flip as the overhead light in her car hit them and sent a twinkle my way.

"No, my head feels fine. I think I'm in shock."

I leaned even closer towards the sound of her voice and her eyes shifted so she was looking into mine as well. Fireworks exploded in my head. I was connected to this girl somehow. The pain shining out of those eyes struck me in the heart like an arrow and a strange urge to make her laugh filled me.

Sirens broke through my consciousness and I looked to them, breaking myself out of the trance her eyes pulled me into, but her voice threatened to pull me back, "Tell them to check the other cars first, I'm fine."

I wanted to protest. Her car had the most damage; I wanted to insist they look her over first. But I didn't. I didn't really seem to be in control of my actions as I walked away from her and headed back to my car.

Two police cars followed the ambulance and after the EMT's checked me over I gave my statement to the cops and collected insurance information from the other drivers, trying to keep my hands and mind busy so I wouldn't think about her.

What was it about the girl in the Nissan? Every time my brain paused from the task at hand it jumped right back to the moment our eyes locked together. She was young and pretty, for sure, but the pounding in my heart wasn't lust. I'm a guy, I know lust. It was something more. *You're ridiculous. You know nothing about her. You don't even know her name.*

I watched the paramedics lift her out of her car and onto a stretcher, then wheeled her to the ambulance. My heart constricted inside my chest, like a giant hand was squeezing it, fingers gripping, opening and closing; sucking the life out of me. The guilt was unbearable. She said she was fine, but they were taking her away in an ambulance.

My car wasn't really drivable, so I asked one of the police officers to give me a ride to the emergency room. I wanted to make sure she was okay. If I had any other motives, I wouldn't let myself think about them.

It didn't take long to get to the hospital and luckily my head cleared up in the waiting room. Whatever happened in the rain lost its effect on me. I called Tracey, asked her to bring me a car, and sat on a hard plastic chair. Mazda guy received his stitches and left. Beasty hadn't even come to the hospital. *Hmph. Go figure. The guy who caused the whole mess is fine. Bastard.*

As I waited, I couldn't stop wondering if the whole thing, the accident, was my fault. *What if I hadn't left work early? What if I hadn't switched lanes at the last moment? Maybe that poor girl wouldn't need to see a doctor right now.* I prayed she wasn't hurt.

"Ben!" Tracey came running into the waiting room, interrupting my guilt trip, Ike followed carrying Joey and Hannah.

"Hey, Sis."

"Are you okay? Oh my God, what happened?"

"Trace, calm down, I'm fine, see." I did a full turn so she could see I had no broken bones, no bleeding, but she still hugged me like I'd just returned from the dead.

"Really, I'm okay. I'm not hurt at all."

"What about the other cars?"

"The guy who hit me is totally fine. The girl I hit, well, I don't know, I'm waiting for her. But she seemed fine. I think the doctors are checking her out to make sure she didn't pull a muscle in her neck or something, at least I hope that's all it is."

"You're waiting for her?"

"Well, yeah. I need to make sure she's okay."

"Ah, my brother, the last true gentleman." She laughed, nudging my arm with her elbow.

"I don't think there's anything gentlemanly about it. I hit her. I have to help."

She raised an eyebrow at me. "Right, because that's what everyone would do?"

"Right."

"Then where's the guy who hit you? The one who caused the whole thing? And didn't you say on the phone that another car hit the girl? Where's that driver?"

"Um, they both left already."

"Exactly. See, you're a really good guy, Ben. Don't downplay that about yourself. Now. Let's sit down and you can tell me everything. Ike, hon, why don't you take the kids down to the cafeteria and get them some dinner." My sister certainly knew how to give directions. Ike didn't even question her, just set off with the kids.

We sat down and I gave her the full history of the last hour and a half. After ten minutes or so a door squeaked and I turned my body towards it as Nissan girl stepped into the hallway. Our eyes met. I felt like an idiot, but couldn't stop my mouth from stretching into an embarrassingly large grin as I hopped out of the chair, cutting Tracey off mid-sentence.

The girl's face blushed when I approached her. "You didn't have to wait for me."

"No, I guess not, but I wanted to make sure you were okay." Seeing her in the neck brace felt like a slap in my face. *I did that to her.*

"Oh, I'm fine, this is nothing," she pointed to the brace and shrugged, "just a precaution. What about you? I didn't even ask if you were okay."

"I'm fine. Not a scratch on me." She nodded and cast her eyes to the floor. I rocked back and forth on my heels for a few seconds, not really sure what to say next, but also unable to walk away from her. It was so weird, I wanted to help her, but she didn't really seem to need any of my assistance.

She looked up and seemed on the verge of speaking again when someone behind us shouted, "Abigail!" She stepped around me, looking for the source and waved to a taller woman with the same dark, wavy hair heading in our direction.

"My sister, Ashley, coming to take me home."

I nodded lamely. "Right."

"Goodbye, um, I'm sorry, I don't think I caught your name."

"Oh, probably because I never introduced myself. Sorry, I'm Ben. Ben Harris." I stretched out my hand. Her slender fingers slipped into mine and gripped firmly; I could feel heat building between our palms and wondered if she felt it, too.

"I'm Abigail Bronsen. It's nice to meet you, Ben."

"You, too, Abigail."

She dropped my hand and met her sister a few feet away. They hugged and I could faintly hear Abigail giving Ashley the same assurances I had given Tracey. She turned and waved as they headed for the exit. I tried to watch her walk away, but Ike was back with the kids and Tracey was thrusting a pair of keys in my hand so I had to pay attention to my family.

"Are you sure you're up to driving? We can drop you off and leave the car for you to use tomorrow if you need it."

"Yeah, I'm fine. Thanks, though. And thanks for the car."

"You're welcome."

We headed to the parking lot together, Joey tugging my hand to give him a piggyback ride. Usually I would have been more than happy to give in to him, but my body was starting to feel tense and sore.

"Drive safe, okay? And call me when you get home." Tracey hugged me tightly again, reminding me strongly of our mother. Kinda made me glad I hadn't called her, instead.

"I will. Thanks, Trace."

My sister's family piled into their sensible non-soccermomish van, driving onto the street first, with me following in Ike's car. The guy must really love my sister to let me drive his BMW. For some reason as I pulled out of the parking lot and headed home my mind flashed back to my last day with Rebecca. The contrast between her and Abigail hit me across the back of the head, but I don't know why one reminded me of the other. Abigail was beautiful while Rebecca had been only pretty; she seemed sweet while Rebecca had been bitchy.

My relationship with Rebecca was a mistake. Everyone realized this while we were dating. My best friends Matt and Trish hated her. She refused to play softball with us and that made the rest of the team hate her, too. Everyone knew we weren't going to last. Everyone but me. Until one day I walked into her apartment and found her having sex with another guy on her living room floor.

At least I knew why she always kept her apartment so clean.

Rebecca was the last person I wanted to be thinking about, but it was probably good she popped into my head. Thinking about her made me not want to think about women at all. My attraction to Abigail was absurd and I didn't want it to go any further. I barely knew her. I didn't know her at all.

Chapter Three: Twenty Questions

Abigail

I thought for a few days maybe the accident was an omen. A sign that things in my life were going to change. I kept replaying the moment when Ben leaned into my car and our eyes met. His were concerned, scared even, but so beautiful I gasped. All the chaos around me disappeared as I looked into his powerful gaze. As blue as the Atlantic Ocean and as gray as the storm clouds overhead, both at once, it penetrated me. I tried to break contact, wanted to break contact, but my heart wouldn't let me. Then he looked away.

I felt a spark with him and that sort of thing never happened to me. I should have known, though - because nothing good happens on my birthday - that it wasn't real and a month later I'd find myself immersed in the same boring routine.

6:30 AM: Alarm. *UGH! Why did God create a 6:30 AM? Snooze, please.*

6:45 AM: Shower.

8:30 AM: Arrive at Work. *Hello coworker, how was your evening, blah blah blah. Oh me? I'm doing great today, thank you for asking. blah blah blah.*

10:00 AM: Coffee Break. *Oh, thank you God for coffee.*

1:00 PM: Lunch. *Hello ham and cheese sandwich on white bread!*

4:30 PM: Leave Work. *The most exciting part of the day.*

4:45 PM: Coffee, Library, or Errands. *I know what you're thinking, woohoo, slow down party animal.*

6:30 PM: Arrive at Home.

7:00 PM: Dinner. *Give me something frozen and a microwave, please.*

11:00 PM: Bed. *Well, sometimes I stay up and watch Jon Stewart, but let's not split hairs.*

I knew my lack of an exciting social life was mostly my own fault for not putting myself out there, but it's hard. I've never been outgoing and unfortunately my financial situation didn't really allow for a lot of club and bar hopping.

It was a Wednesday afternoon, but it could've been any other day of the week. I left work at 4:30, as usual, and headed for Starbucks. A new girl working the cash register and taking orders didn't know what the "Abigail Special" was, so I ordered a simple mocha and headed for my favorite armchair.

The store was quiet, only a few other people were sitting at tables sipping their coffee. A young couple sat in the furthest corner away from me holding hands and whispering quietly to each other. I watched them for a minute and wondered what their story was. How had they met? Were they in love? Not that it mattered, but they looked happy. So unlike myself. I focused on my book and my coffee and the next time I looked up, the couple was gone.

I sat reading and sipping for another fifteen minutes, when a voice coming from the front of the shop caused me to look up. A young man talking on a cell phone and searching through a stack of newspapers near the exit was the source of my confusion. Though his voice sounded familiar, I didn't recognize the back of his head, so I returned to my book.

A few minutes later, after selecting a paper and ordering a drink, he took the armchair opposite mine and began reading. I glanced at him, but he looked down and I couldn't see much of his face. I decided he must sound like someone from work and that's why his voice sparked my attention.

I turned my concentration back to my book and for another ten or fifteen minutes read peacefully while the after-work crowd wandered in and out of the store. A loud ringing startled me out of my trance and the young man with the newspaper pulled his cell phone out of his pocket.

"Ben Harris," he answered. Dizziness engulfed me. I recognized the name and the voice at the same moment. *How did I not recognize it before? Oh right, because I was daydreaming about his face, not his voice.* I looked up quickly to confirm and he noticed the sudden movement. With his phone still at his ear, our eyes met. The blue stare pierced into me: definitely the same guy. I could tell he recognized me too. Goose bumps formed on my arms and I rubbed them fervently, trying to kick-start my blood flow.

He finished his call and we sat looking at each other for what felt like an eternity, but must have only been a few seconds. I wanted to speak, to acknowledge everything I felt, all the gratitude developed since the accident, but my voice seemed temporarily disabled.

Maybe things were looking up.

Ben

In my peripheral vision I saw a flash of dark hair and turned towards it. *Holy Shit.* I almost dropped the phone. It was HER. Abigail. As much as I'd been trying NOT to think about her, there she was, right in front of me, and I couldn't have been happier to see her.

Finishing my call as quickly as possible, I stuffed the phone in my pocket, refocusing on her pretty face, studying the way her eyes lit up when she smiled, and noticing a cluster of tiny moles on her right cheek at the jaw line, the cute kind, Cindy Crawford-esque. I remembered thinking how gorgeous I found her the day of the accident, but seeing her there was different. I realized she wasn't even my normal type - I'm usually attracted to athletic-type girls: tall, toned, no makeup, hair in a ponytail - but Abigail took my breath away with her more elegant simplicity. She looked put-together, like she cared what she looked like, but only to the extent that she be taken seriously, and she didn't flaunt her good looks, no eye batting or hair flipping or repositioning in the chair to show off her best angle. I had a feeling then that she had no idea how attractive she was.

Stop staring and say something to her! "Abigail." *That's it? That's the best you've got? Her name? Keep talking.* "I didn't realize… you look so different. You're so dry!" *Okay, maybe I should practice talking in a mirror before I have actual interactions with other people.*

She laughed and folded her hands in her lap. "You look different, too. Good, different, though."

"Really? Oh, well, thanks, I guess. You look good, too. I mean good different. Not that you didn't look good when we met before. Or now. You looked good then and now. Sorry, I'm not usually such an idiot." The words just tumbled out of my mouth, I couldn't stop them. And then I realized I was *still* staring and averted my eyes back to my paper. *What the hell is wrong with me? I'm never such a dork around hot girls.* Luckily, she laughed again and after my embarrassment subsided, she asked about my car and I reciprocated. I managed to pull myself together enough to carry on a conversation, but I don't really remember the beginning of it. At least not the actual dialogue.

The way her words just seemed to flow out of her mouth, the way her breath caught slightly when she laughed, she was just adorable. And intelligent. And funny. I was hypnotized. Everything she said made me want more. And then she THANKED ME! Thanked me for helping her! I hit her and she thanked me! Surely there aren't such generous-spirited persons in the world.

"Don't even think about it. What else could I do? I felt so terrible, causing your car to spin out of control like that. You can't even imagine how terrified I was watching it and praying you weren't hurt and didn't cause anyone else to get hurt. I wish I hadn't been driving so close to you, maybe it wouldn't have happened." As I finished speaking she leaned towards me and took my hand. She applied light pressure and forced me to look her in the eye.

"You have nothing to feel guilty about. Honestly, I know it wasn't your fault, and I can't begin to tell you how much I appreciate you coming to check on me and waiting for me at the hospital. There aren't many people who would have done that." The gentleness in her tone and words touched my heart. She smiled and I couldn't take her gratitude. I did feel guilty, because I was thankful for the accident. Thankful it gave me the opportunity to meet her. My cheeks burned with embarrassment. I broke our eye contact and stared at the hardwood floor, trying to think of something else to say. But she spoke before I could.

"Was that a business call earlier?"

"Huh? Oh, just now? Yeah. A potential investor wants to come down and take a look at my business."

"You own your own business?"

"Yeah."

"That's so cool. What kind of business is it?"

"It's kinda boring, I mean, boring for a girl."

"Hey! You don't know - I could be the least girlie girl you've ever met. I don't even like the color pink."

I laughed, I couldn't help myself. She was so freaking cute. "Oh really? Are you into sports?"

Her face broke out in a widespread blush as she answered, "Um, no."

"See, I told you!"

"Just because I'm not into sports doesn't mean I won't find your business interesting!"

"Well, I guess not. Okay, I own Inner City Sports. Have you heard of it?"

"I think so. I think my brother-in-law plays golf there. It has all kinds of athletic fields, right? Like tennis courts and basketball courts and a baseball field."

"Exactly. It's right across the street, actually."

"Really? Hmm, I wonder why I've never run into you before now. I'm in here all the time." She took a sip of her coffee and closed the book on her lap.

I wanted to smack my head against the fireplace for not being a coffee drinker. *You mean I could have met you months ago? Damn it.*

She continued before I could answer, "I don't know why you think I wouldn't be interested in that, it's incredibly interesting. Tell me more."

I told her about all the little ins and outs of ICS and about how I was lucky enough to get the start-up money from my trust fund and some very brave investors. She kept her eyes and attention focused on me the entire time. I'd never met a non-sports nut who wanted to hear so much about the complex before, but she appeared genuinely interested. She made me want to talk to her. But I wanted her to talk, too.

"Okay, so now I've told you about my business, what about you? What do you do?"

For the first time since we started talking, she looked away from me. She gazed intently at her fingernails and didn't answer.

"Abigail?"

"Sorry. My job isn't nearly as exciting as yours. It's pretty boring, actually."

"I'm sure it's not."

"Oh yeah it is. I work in a mailroom."

"It can't be that bad."

She shrugged and continued to study her nails. "It's not forever."

"Well then, what do you want to be when you grow up?"

She laughed again and met my eye. God, she had a great laugh. "I think I'm already grown up."

"You can't be too grown up. You're what, twenty-two? Twenty-three?"

"Twenty-five, actually. Last month." She grimaced; I could tell her age was not a favorite subject. I couldn't understand why, though. She looked fantastic and who really wanted to go back to their early twenties or teen years? Not me.

"And you?" she asked.

"I'm twenty-seven."

"And you already own your own business? I'm even more impressed."

"Well, like I said, I was lucky to have the start-up money pretty quickly. But don't change the subject. You said the mailroom is temporary, what do you really want?"

"To write. I have a journalism degree and I work at *Intuition* magazine right now. There are rumors of a column in Europe that I've been working towards. I'm constantly writing articles and turning them in to the editor, but she hasn't been interested yet."

"She will be one day."

"Yeah, sure." Her smile dissolved and she stared at the huge book in her lap. It was massive. Had she been reading it when I sat down across from her? *Okay,* I made a mental note, *age and job are touchy subjects. Get her laughing again.*

"Favorite movie?"

"Oh, goodness, are we going to play twenty questions?" She didn't laugh, but the smile returned.

"Yes. So, question number one: what's your favorite movie?"

"Um, that's a hard one. You're going to make fun of me."

"I won't, I promise. Scout's honor." I crossed my hand over my heart and made my face as serious as I could.

She laughed! "Were you a scout?"

"No, actually I wasn't."

"So you can't be trusted at all, can you?"

"I guess not."

She laughed again! "Okay, my favorite movie is *When Harry Met Sally*."

"I've never seen it. Why would I laugh at that?"

"You've NEVER seen *When Harry Met Sally*? Oh my God, Ben! You have to see it."

"Why? What's it about?"

"Harry and Sally. And friendship. And falling in love." She blushed and turned her eyes away again. *Damn, I really wish she'd stop doing that. Although she's absolutely gorgeous when she blushes.*

"Oh. So a chick flick?"

"Yeah, I guess. That's why I thought you'd laugh. But honestly, it's not like chick flicks they make nowadays. It's smart and funny and incredibly insightful about relationships. At least, I think it is."

"Then I guess I'll have to see it someday." *Preferably with you.*

"Yeah. So what's your favorite movie?"

"*Office Space*," I answered immediately.

"That movie is hilarious! The stapler guy is my favorite."

"Mine too! I didn't think you'd know it."

"Why not?"

"I don't know, most girls I know aren't into it."

"Really? My sisters and I love it."

Oh, now we're getting somewhere, her family seems like a good subject. "Sisters? How many do you have?"

"Two. And a brother."

"Wow, four kids. I feel bad for your parents."

"Don't. They loved having a noisy house when we were growing up. I'm lucky."

"I'll bet. I just have one older sister. I always wanted a brother though. Are your sisters and brother older or younger?"

"My sisters are both older, my brother is younger."

"Ah, so you're a middle child?"

"Yeah. Why, is that a bad thing?"

"No, not at all. It just makes me think of the *Brady Bunch*."

"Oh, you mean the whole Jan, and Marcia, Marcia, Marcia, thing?"

"Yeah."

"Yeah, I guess there's a little of that." She grew silent.

Way to go, Ben. Now you've basically insulted her and told her she's probably jealous of her siblings. What the hell were you thinking? She doesn't seem like that at all. Stupid! Talk about something else.

"Okay, question number two…"

"Wait, don't how many siblings I have and if I'm a middle child count as questions two and three?"

I laughed and breathed a sigh of relief, *Whew, she's not holding my stupidity against me.* "You're right. Question four: last concert you went to?"

"Hmmm, I'll have to think about that for a second. It's been a long time since I went to a concert. Oh wait! I took my brother to see Third Eye Blind for his birthday last year."

"Really? I didn't know that band was still together."

She shrugged her shoulders, "I guess they were when we saw them. Derek loves them. Your turn."

"My friend, Matt, and I went to see The All-American Rejects a couple of months ago."

"Oh, I like them. Their second album is really good."

"The second one? No, the first one's the best."

"I never like freshman albums as much. I always think the sophomore attempt is better."

"That's crazy! The freshman album is always better!" We both grinned. It was so refreshing to have an easy conversation with a woman. My phone rang again, interrupting our perfect flow. I shouldn't have answered, but I did.

Abigail

When he hung up, he looked at me and started to speak, but stopped himself.

"I didn't realize how late it was," I ventured, figuring he was looking for a way out of the conversation. *Man, he's probably been looking for a way out forever now. Just make it easy for him.*

"Oh, yeah, it's almost dinner time."

"You probably have somewhere to go, someone to meet?"

"No, actually, I don't. But if you have somewhere to go…" He stopped himself again.

"I don't have any particular plans, but I should probably get going."

"Of course."

I put my books into my bag and pulled my jacket on. "This was fun, I'm glad I ran into you."

"I'm glad, too. We should do it again. Dinner maybe?"

"Dinner? Sure. I'm free tomorrow night to grab a bite." *Holy crap, what am I saying?!* I tried to look away to hide the fire burning on my face, but he held me in his gaze.

"Really?" His eyes brightened and he flashed perfect white teeth at me. "Okay, that's great. Should I pick you up?"

"You don't have to - that'd be weird. It would feel like a date or something. No, I can meet you somewhere." He looked away for a moment and hesitated. And then I realized why. *Shit.* "Ben, I'm so sorry. Were you asking me on a date?"

"No, it's cool. Just a friendly dinner. How about that new place on South Street? Seven o'clock?"

"Seven it is." We shook hands quickly. "I'll see you tomorrow."

"Bye, Abigail." His hand withdrew and he used it to ruffle his hair. I nearly tripped as I stepped back to leave. He held back laughter, but I could see the corners of his mouth twitching.

"Bye." If my cheeks were on fire before, the blaze now spread down my neck and over my collarbone and chest. I put my purse on my shoulder and smiled at him as I walked towards the door.

I got into my car, thinking about what an idiot I was. A handsome, chivalrous man showed interest in me - actually asked me out on a date - and I didn't even realize it. And I liked him. He was nice, he seemed interesting, and I gave him the idea it would be weird to date him. Though part of me DID think it was weird; we only met because his car crashed into mine, so I was glad I kept it casual. But another part of me wanted to walk back inside and tell him I would love it if he'd pick me up for our date. I don't know why I let the situation cause me such mental anguish. We would have dinner as friends and he would be thankful I made the distinction once he realized how boring and uninteresting I actually was. A slightly comforting thought. I would be spared the sting of rejection, which would certainly come from him if it were a date. I enjoyed his company; maybe we would be friends. Yeah, he'd be a friend. A friend with sparkling blue eyes…

I reached this conclusion just as I arrived home and stopped overanalyzing the situation long enough to make myself dinner. I only pictured his gorgeous eyes once or twice before calling it an evening and heading to bed. Okay, it may have been three times, but I wasn't really keeping track.

Chapter Four: Ah, the First Date?

Abigail

I made it clear to Ben we were not going on a date. Yet, as I dressed to meet him, I realized what a huge mistake I'd made. Sure, he probably wouldn't like me. Sure, he probably would never ask me out again. But there was something about him. I wanted the experience of a date with him. How would he act? Would he hold open doors, pull out chairs? He seemed like that kind of guy.

The first two outfits I tried on looked horrible. I stripped down and threw my blouse on the pile of clothes forming on my bed. I hated myself for acting so stupid. I told him it wasn't a date, what did it matter what I looked like? I pulled my lavender sweater and black pencil skirt out of the closest and refused to look at myself in the mirror after putting them on. Grabbing my favorite black Mary Jane heels and making my way to the door, I caught my reflection in the window and the outfit didn't look bad. Good thing, because if I hadn't left then, I would've been late.

On the drive I tried to calm my nerves by singing along loudly to the radio. Singing always had a soothing effect on me. I didn't even know why I was so nervous. Okay, maybe I did. Those eyes, that smile, the successful business. This guy was completely out of my league, but I still wanted him to like me.

He greeted me with a grin and a wave as I pulled up to the restaurant. Leaning against his car, wearing black slacks and a light blue button down, he looked even better than he had at Starbucks, if that was possible. His light brown hair, styled to give that "just tousled" look, and his smooth shaven cheeks told me he'd taken just as much consideration getting ready as I had. I parked beside him and slyly, I hope, checked my reflection in the mirror to make sure my hair and makeup looked okay before getting out of the car.

"Good evening, Abigail. You look nice."

Great, I'll add polite to the never-ending list of his good qualities. "Oh, um, well… you look great. How are you?" As he stepped towards me, the wind picked up and his scent drifted into my nostrils. *Mmmm, mint, grass, fresh baked sugar cookies. Okay that's a little weird, but it still smells good.* I breathed in heavily, trying to memorize the smell by holding it in my lungs as long as possible.

"I'm good. Hungry, though." He smiled again.

"Yeah, me too. Let's eat." I was right about one thing: he did open the door for me as we walked into the restaurant. And the way he lightly placed his hand on the small of my back as the hostess showed us to our table gave me hope he didn't take me seriously the day before when I said it wasn't a date.

The restaurant was dimly lit with candles and white roses on every table. Dark red tablecloths and black napkins gave the room a warm and charming aspect. Our waitress appeared right after the hostess seated us; I ordered a glass of white wine and he ordered a beer.

"This is a nice restaurant," I started as soon as she left, "I've never been here before, though. Is the food as good as the atmosphere?"

"I like it. So, I have a random question for you."

"Okay, shoot."

"What book is it today?"

"Huh?"

He grinned at my puzzled expression and leaned forward in his seat. "The day of the accident, I noticed a pile of books in the backseat of your car."

"Yeah…"

"And yesterday, at Starbucks, you were sitting by yourself in the corner, reading a horrendously large book."

"I like to read." *Duh. Maybe he isn't as smart as I assumed.*

"So, my original question was, what book is it today?"

"You're just assuming I brought a book with me on our date?"

"This is a date now, is it?" A smile played on his lips, but he held back, producing the most adorable look I'd seen on his face so far.

"I'm sorry, you're right, this isn't a date." My cheeks flushed and I snatched the menu. I opened it in front of my face and scanned through the entrées. He reached over and pushed it down with his index finger.

"I never said it wasn't a date. You did when you agreed to come." When he released his smile, it made me blush even deeper.

"Oh, right. Well, I think I'm going to have the chicken cordon bleu. How about you?" I prayed he would drop the subject.

"I'm going to have the sirloin, it's the best in the city. But, don't change the subject. What book did you bring?"

It took me by surprise. I was still laughing when I realized he honestly wanted to know the answer to the question. I reached into my purse, pulled out my tattered copy of *Pride and Prejudice,* and laid it on the table.

"Ah, a classic." He chuckled and picked the book up. "I guess I shouldn't be surprised you're a Jane Austen fan."

"What's that supposed to mean?"

"Nothing bad. She seems to be the only author every woman I've ever met has read. My sister loves her."

"Well, she was a brilliant writer. She related to women during her time and women still relate to her today."

"Why do you relate to her?"

"I could answer that question, but I don't think we've known each other long enough for you to not be freaked out by the answer." This time he was the one taken by surprise. He laughed and his eyes danced in the candlelight.

"How long do I have to know you in order to not be freaked out? Two dates? Ten dates?"

"I don't know yet, but I'll let you know when I do."

"I could be wrong, but I think you just acknowledged this is a date."

"I guess it is." We were both smiling now.

The waitress came back with our drinks. As she placed mine in front of me, she noticed my book.

"I love *Pride and Prejudice*!" she gushed, "Jane Austen's my favorite author!"

"I told you so." He took a sip of his beer. I felt myself blushing once again as I slid the book off the table and back into my purse. The waitress looked from him to me, confusion spread across her face.

"Are you ready to order?"

Talk about a perfect date. Ben charmed me with witty conversation, hilarious jokes, and delicious food. The way he talked about his sister and his niece and nephew was adorable. A family guy - so cute. And whenever I felt embarrassed or unsure, his smile gave me confidence. He walked me to my car after dinner and we stood talking for another twenty minutes.

"Would you like to do this again, sometime? And we can call it a date from the start?" he asked after we said goodbye for the tenth time.

Oh my god. "Yes, I'd like that."

"How about this weekend? Saturday night?"

Oh my god. "Saturday sounds good, I don't have any plans. What would you like to do?"

"How about a classic - dinner and a movie?"

Oh. My. God. "Sure, I haven't been to the movies in months. What time?"

"I'll pick you up at seven."

OH MY GOD! "Okay. I'll see you then."

"Goodnight Abigail." He leaned forward and kissed my cheek, then stepped back as I got into my car and closed the door. He stood in place while I reversed and pulled out of the parking lot. Through my mirror I could see him slowly walking backwards to his car, hands in his pockets, eyes glued to my taillights.

My mind raced and soared as I drove home. I was officially a cliché. The first thing I learned in my college writing classes was to avoid clichés at all costs, but the butterflies in my stomach and the weakness in my knees were real. So real. That's how clichés are started, after all. I kinda liked the thought that I was experiencing the same giddiness as millions of love-struck women before me. Okay, love-struck is cliché too. And not completely accurate. I liked the guy, but I barely knew him!

Apparently he liked me, too. He liked me enough to ask for a second date, at least. I could still feel his hot breath on my cheek where his soft lips brushed against my skin. Unconsciously, my fingers grazed the spot.

I couldn't stop thinking about him. His eyes laughing in the candlelight, his brilliant smile. Everything we talked about blurred together. I could only remember the way he looked at me, like I was the most beautiful woman in the world.

This is crazy. How could a guy like that possibly want a girl like me?

Ben

Damn it. Why didn't I just go for the kiss? A kiss on the cheek? Really, Ben? That's the best you've got? As I watched her drive away, I replayed the evening in my head. The way her eyes changed color in the dim light. Her smooth, airy laugh. The brilliance of every word she said. And the cherry on top of the sundae, I stored her phone number and email in my Blackberry and secured a second date.

When her car turned the corner and disappeared from sight, I unlocked mine and slid into the driver's seat. Scrolling through the contacts on my phone, I found Matt's number, and hit 'Send.'

"Hey man, what's up?" he answered after three rings.

"Just calling to say I can't do dinner on Saturday." I turned on my lights and fastened my seat belt.

"Why not?"

"I have a date."

"Oh really? I thought you were celibate."

Ugh, I hate him sometimes. "Celibate's the wrong word. I was on a hiatus."

"A hiatus from sex?" He laughed as if taking a break from sex was the most ridiculous thing he'd ever heard of.

"From women." Drumming my fingers on the steering wheel, I wished I'd called Trish instead.

"Isn't that the same thing?"

I groaned, "Come on, man. Don't give me a hard time. I met a really cool girl."

"A really cool girl? High praise coming from you."

"Can you just tell Trish I can't make it and I'm sorry?" I put the keys in the ignition and started the engine. Pulling out of the parking lot, I waited for Matt's next round of mockery.

"Yeah, although I'm sure she'll forgive you for blowing us off since there's the possibility of you getting some."

"It's just a second date, I don't know about getting any. But you don't need to worry about that, my sex life is officially none of your business."

"Sorry, man. Just trying to help you laugh at yourself a little. You've been moping around the past six months since that bitch, but now, well, you sound different."

"Um, okay. I'll see you at softball Saturday morning." *Different? What the hell does that mean?*

"You sure you want to play on Saturday? You want to make sure you have plenty of time to get ready for your date."

"Shut up." I clicked 'End.' Was Matt right? Had I been moping around? Probably. Rebecca chewed me up and spat me out like a tough piece of steak. Tonight was the first date I'd been on since we broke up. *Am I on the rebound?* Matt's comments rattled the memory in me I'd been trying to repress for months.

"What do you want from me, Ben? You acted like I was the plague. I practically had to force you to sleep with me. I have needs. Juan has been taking care of those needs." Rebecca folded her arms across her chest and rolled her eyes at me.

I nearly exploded, "HAS BEEN? You mean this has been going on for a while?"

"Yes, for a couple of months."

"I can't believe this Rebecca. I tried to show you respect. I wanted us to have an emotional connection. I thought I loved you."

"But you didn't. And I didn't love you either. And I didn't want an emotional connection. I wanted a good, hard, long fuck. So I went and found someone able to give that to me."

"So, the past six months have meant nothing to you?"

"Not nothing. We had fun. You're a sweet nice guy. But did you honestly think this was going to last forever?"

As she asked the question, I realized my answer was different than I'd assumed. No, I never expected to be with Rebecca forever. She wasn't the one. I wanted a woman I could love with fervent passion. Rebecca didn't want to be romanced. She didn't want to get married, to have a family. Somehow I'd become the girl in the relationship.

I left without saying another word. She didn't try and stop me.

A loud blast from a car horn stirred me from the memory and I swerved just in time. Another accident was the last thing I needed. I tried to pay better attention but my thoughts seemed determined to wander. As soon as I stopped focusing on Rebecca's coldness, Abigail's warmth came into the foreground. If I *was* on the rebound, I liked the idea of her catching me.

Chapter Five: Insecurities

Abigail

Our second date went just as well as the first. We both enjoyed the movie and talked for over an hour at the restaurant after finishing our meals. We spent the drive back to my apartment discussing the film and the possibility of a sequel. When we reached my building, he immediately got out of the car to open my door for me.

"Thank you," I said as he took my hand to help me out. He walked me up the stairs; I loved the feeling of having him walk beside me. It's hard to describe, that feeling. Almost like safety, but not quite. More like possibility. "I had fun tonight," I said when we'd reached my door, pulling my keys out of my purse and putting them into the lock.

"Me too. Do you have plans for tomorrow?"

"Tomorrow? You haven't had enough of me yet?" *He can't be serious.*

"Nope, and I have a great idea for something to do tomorrow."

Did he hit his head during the accident? He must be suffering from a brain injury. "Tomorrow's Sunday. I usually do my grocery shopping for the week and clean my kitchen."

"Seriously? You'd rather clean and go to the grocery store than spend time with me?"

Hell no. I'd rather go to Vegas and marry you with only Elvis as a witness. "That's not what I meant."

"Good, I'll pick you up at three." He pecked me on the cheek, turned, and darted down the stairs.

"Okay," I called after him, but he didn't hear me. My voice hadn't gotten louder than a whisper.

Ben

Abigail was an enigma. A complete mystery to me.

I pulled into her apartment complex at twenty til three on Sunday and took a spot in the front row. Turning off the engine, my mind ran through our first four encounters at warp speed. I couldn't figure her out.

She acts like she's into me, but when I try to make plans she hesitates. Am I reading her wrong? I don't want to force her to keep seeing me, but I can't just let her go either. When she's with me, really with me in the moment, we can talk forever. She's completely confident and sexy when we're having a conversation about movies or books or our families. But as soon as I try and show her I like her, she retreats into a cocoon and suddenly she's, what? Protecting herself from me? I don't know.

As I got out of my car and closed the door, I came to the conclusion that today would decide things. If she didn't like me, I wasn't going to keep putting myself out there. This wasn't going to be a repeat of Rebecca.

"You're early!" she exclaimed as she opened the door, wearing sweatpants and a white tank top. Her thumb hitched back towards the clock on the wall. Only 2:45? I'd only wasted five minutes in the car over-thinking the situation?

"Well, my mother taught me that ten minutes early is actually five minutes late. Punctuality is an important virtue to have." *What the hell am I saying? I'm such an idiot.*

"Your mother should've clarified, for meetings, appointments, school, things like that, it's great to be early. But for a date! Give a girl an extra ten minutes!" She grabbed my arm and pulled me into the apartment. I laughed out of relief; she wouldn't be joking so early in the date if she weren't interested, right?

"Your kitchen looks very clean and smells lemon fresh," I teased, turning to face her.

"Oh, be quiet. Here, sit down for five minutes and then I'll be ready to go." She dashed into what I assumed was her bedroom before I could respond. Instead of sitting, I circled the living room, trying to discover more about her.

She liked Van Gogh, four prints of his hung above her couch. Beside the TV stand, an enormous case stuffed to the gills displayed her collection of books. Most were tattered, the bindings broken with pages spilling out. More books littered the coffee table. I finally sat on the couch, but only to get a better look at the picture frame on the end table. Abigail as a little girl, holding out a flower to a silver-haired man. Her dad, maybe?

"Okay, I'm ready." She stepped out of the room and smiled at me. I swear my heart stopped beating for a second. She looked stunning in a simple blue t-shirt, black leather jacket, and jeans, her cheeks glowed, and her lustrous brown hair bounced as she walked towards me

"You look great," I breathed as I stood up.

"I'd look better if you hadn't been so early."

"I doubt that." She couldn't look any better than this.

"Please, I'm a mess. Let's just go." She led the way out the door and down the stairs to the parking lot. I opened the car door for her and silently got in the driver's seat. It didn't make any sense. Did she not see the same girl I saw?

A few blocks away, I turned off the radio. "Why do you do that?" I asked.

"Do what? What did I do?"

"Refuse to accept a compliment."

"What are you talking about? You haven't said anything since you got in the car."

"No, I mean back at your apartment."

"Oh. I guess I thought you were just being nice. I don't know. I mean, I don't think I look great." She stared at her hands in her lap and I felt guilty for bringing it up, but I couldn't let her think like that. I faced her once we arrived at our destination.

"Well, you do. Don't assume the rest of the world sees you the way you see yourself. Maybe if you start believing compliments instead of dismissing them, you'll start to see yourself the way others see you."

Her eyes met mine, but she didn't smile. Her mouth opened to speak, but nothing came out.

One more attempt can't hurt. "You look really nice today."

"Thank you, so do you."

"Thank you." I smiled and she finally did, too. "See that wasn't so hard. Now, are you ready for something incredible?"

"Absolutely," she laughed, "what?"

"This." I pointed straight ahead at the building in front of us. She turned her head towards it, but then quickly back to me.

"And what is this?"

"We'll have to go in to find out." I opened my door and got out to get hers, but she was too quick for me.

Abigail

He took my arm lightly by the elbow to lead me inside. As he pulled open the door, I heard the cling of a bell, and stepping inside I saw a large, bright room filled with bookshelves.

"This is the best bookstore in the city." He continued guiding my arm and led me to the closest set of shelves. "The owner is a book collector and she loves tracking down rare books. She always tries to keep a collection of first and second edition copies of classic books on display. I thought you'd like to see them. Here, take a look." He pointed to a row of books behind a glass case. I didn't look immediately; instead I stared into his face.

"Thank you. For bringing me here."

"You're welcome. I thought you'd like it. But, you're missing the best part - look." He grasped my shoulders and spun me around so I was directly in front of the glass case. The first title my eyes fell on was *Pride and Prejudice*.

"Did you say the owner collects first editions?'

"Yes, I did."

"And this case is her collection of rare books? Of first editions?"

"Well, it isn't her whole collection, but basically, yes."

"And that," I pointed, "is that a first edition of *Pride and Prejudice*?"

"Yes it is," a woman's voice answered from behind me. I turned around and a cheerful little woman of about forty stood there. "Hello, I'm Nancy. I own this store. Are you an Austen fan?"

"You could say that. Austen-obsessed is more like it. Oh, sorry, I'm Abigail."

She laughed, shook my hand, and gestured back towards the case. "You'll also be interested in the first editions I've collected of *Sense and Sensibility*, *Emma*, and *Persuasion*. I'm still in negotiations with another dealer for *Northanger Abbey* and *Mansfield Park*."

"I can't even believe it. I've always dreamed of owning a first edition of *Pride and Prejudice*, but I never honestly believed I'd see one."

"Would you like to see it more closely?"

"Oh my God, yes!"

"Luckily, the volumes are in excellent condition, though still fragile, so you'll have to be gentle. And you can only see one at a time. I'll take the first over to one of the couches for you and you can sit and read for a little bit. I'm leaving in about an hour, if you finish beforehand, Ben can come and find me."

"Thank you so much! I promise I'll be extremely careful."

"You're welcome dear, I know you will. From one Austen lover to another, I don't like to keep these books locked up in a case. She would've hated that. She thought books should be read and loved by all."

"Yes, she did."

Nancy left us with *Volume I* at a plush couch in the center of the store. A few other customers were quietly reading and seemed completely oblivious to the treasure in front of them.

"Ben, I can't even find the words to tell you how much this means to me."

"That's pretty much what I was going for. Sit and read. I'm going to go and browse through the sports section."

I did as he suggested, carefully running my fingers over the cover and gingerly opening the book to the title page. I had to fight back the tears that came to my eyes.

An hour later, Ben's hand on my shoulder, heavy and firm, roused me from my trance.

"Nancy's about to leave for the day. She needs to put the book back in its case."

"Of course." Closing the book, I profusely thanked Nancy, then handed it to her.

"Don't worry about it, dear. I'm happy I could do this for you. Ben told me how much you love to read and that makes you a kindred spirit." We followed her to the front of the store and she placed *Pride and Prejudice* into its case.

"I'll let you know when I have the whole set," she said to Ben as she closed and locked the glass door.

"I'm sure we'll be back before then," he replied.

"Absolutely," I agreed. He beamed at me.

"It was lovely to meet you, dear." Nancy squeezed my hand, turned, and walked away from us.

"Do you want to look around?" Ben asked once she was out of sight.

"Not today, but we'll come back soon."

He smiled again and we made our way to the exit. Our hands brushed each other's briefly and sent a shock through me - literally. He jumped, too. The store's carpet must have caused static electricity. *Is the universe trying to tell me something?* I folded my arms across my chest so we wouldn't accidentally shock each other again, but he just laughed at me.

"Don't be silly," he said, stopping and facing me. He unfolded my arms and firmly took my hands in his. We stood still for a minute, looking at our intertwined fingers. He dropped them after another minute and we were walking side-by-side again. This time when our fingers brushed together, there was no spark, but his hand closed around mine. I couldn't believe this beautiful man wanted to hold my hand.

We walked this way out to the car. He followed me to the passenger side, but didn't unlock and open the door. Instead, he leaned towards me and I thought he was going to kiss my cheek like he had before. He hesitated for a moment, his eyes darting to mine, his hand reaching up to my cheek, and then kissed me.

His lips were soft and gentle. They parted and his tongue gently traced the opening of my mouth. I let him in, shocked at how good it felt. He pulled his mouth closed, covering my bottom lip, and shifted to my upper one, each move deliberate and precise. After a few more seconds of ecstasy, I opened my eyes and looked into his face. *Oh god, what are you doing to me?*

I'd kissed guys before. Guys had kissed me before. But never like that. Ben's kiss: Wow. Where'd he learn to kiss like that? Completely perfect, from the softness of his lips, to his minty fresh breath, to the way he delicately held my cheek. He knew exactly what to do.

He gazed into my eyes as I pondered how it was possible that this gorgeous man might actually like me. He seemed too good to be true.

Chapter Six: Knowledge

Ben

"Tell me more about yourself." I took a sip of beer and met her eye across the table. We were sitting in my sports bar after a Red Sox game and tour of my complex, finishing up a late dinner. She only held my gaze for a few seconds before picking up her own glass, laughing, and looking down at her empty plate.

"What do you want to know?"

Everything. I literally wanted to learn everything there was to know about her. It amazed me how much I'd learned and yet how little I knew. I'd learned her favorite color was blue and she met her siblings once a week for dinner. But I didn't know her parents' names or how she took her coffee.

I settled on a question quickly, though. "Why do you like to read so much?"

"I don't know how to answer that." She frowned and set her glass down. Her eyebrows scrunched up and I loved that I recognized her thinking face. I waited while she gathered her thoughts.

"I guess I like it because it gives me the opportunity to experience different things, see different people and places. Books help me understand the world. You can learn about the best and worst of human nature from a good piece of literature."

"Is that why you became a journalist? To learn about human nature?"

"Well, I'm not exactly a journalist. I don't get to write anything yet. But, yes, I think that's what made me want to be a writer. What made you want to own your own business?"

"I didn't like working for other people, I guess."

She laughed and her eyes twinkled in the soft lights around us as she lifted her face and smiled at me.

"Okay, well, Inner City Sports," I waved my hand around, indicating the painting of the complex hanging on the wall beside the bar, "was the product of trying to make my parents happy with my life choices." Abigail's smile faded slightly and she reached for my hand.

"When I was in college, I had a tough time picking a major. I guess you could say I didn't know what I wanted to be when I grew up. I was young, younger than my friends because I finished high school a year early, and I just wanted to have fun. My parents, well, they didn't really understand because they're both such driven people. My dad's a judge and he was a prosecutor for twenty years at the beginning of his career and my mom is a doctor, a pediatrician."

She nodded and waited for me to continue.

"More?" I asked.

"More."

"Well, they harassed me to follow in their footsteps for a while until they realized I had no interest in law or medicine. Then they said they didn't care what I did as long as I got an advanced degree in something. So I chose business. It was the most generic thing I could do and it got them off my back. They thought an MBA would lead to great opportunities." I rolled my eyes and the right corner of her mouth twitched up for a second.

"So anyways, that's why I own my own business. I had a business degree, I had to do something with it."

"I don't think that's the whole story."

"Oh, you don't?"

"You obviously love this place. Your face lights up when you talk about it."

"I guess you're right. I do love this place and a lot went into building it."

"I'd like to hear more about it."

"Really? Okay. Well, again, back in college, I used to volunteer for the Big Brother program at the local YMCA, as part of the philanthropy hours my fraternity had to put in. There was one particular kid I worked with. Dejuane. He loved basketball more than anything else in the world, but his mother wouldn't let him play on the courts in his neighborhood because of the gang and drug activity surrounding them. The Y was too far for him to go alone, so he only got to play when I could pick him up." I paused to take another sip of my beer and make sure she was still paying attention.

"Anyways, so I built this place. I wanted there to be a safe place for kids like Dejuane to go to play and have fun being kids. Initially, I only planned the courts and fields, but realized pretty early on I couldn't make a living, or keep it open, if I didn't find some way of making money, so a couple of friends suggested adding the bar and gym and my brother-in-law suggested the memorabilia store to bring in revenue." I took another breath and grinned.

"Dejuane is sixteen now and works part-time in the store. He's doing great in school and plays for the varsity basketball team."

Abigail put both elbows on the table and rested her head in her hands, glowing at me. "Ben, that's amazing."

Not as amazing as your smile. "I see what you're doing. You don't want to talk about yourself so you've got me talking about the complex."

"It's not that I don't want to talk about myself, but I don't have anything interesting to tell you."

How can she think that? "I don't believe that."

"Honestly, I think you know everything about me there is to know."

"I know that's not true. There's still so much I don't know about you." Moving to the chair beside her, I took both her hands in mine.

"Like what?" she asked.

"Like why you don't want to talk about yourself."

She pulled her hands away and looked at the tablecloth. She started tracing the circular pattern with her fingertips.

"Abigail?"

"Ben, really, I just can't. I'm sorry."

"You can't what?"

"Tell you about myself."

"Why not?"

"Because I don't want you to disappear," she spoke so quietly I almost missed it. It took me off guard. I had no clue where she got the idea I was going to disappear, but it gave me hope that she must like me a lot, otherwise she wouldn't be worried, right?

"I'm not going to disappear." I leaned forward, reaching to her face and tilting her chin back towards me. Her bottom lip quivered as I gently kissed her.

"You can trust me," I whispered against her mouth.

"I want to," she whispered back.

Chapter Seven: Number 24

Abigail

I should have felt uncomfortable, vulnerable, but Ben put me at ease somehow. I don't know how we got to that point, usually the guy lost interest around date three, but Ben stuck around for over a month.

When he dropped me off at my apartment that evening, he kissed me, made plans for the next night, and said, "I love your smile." He'd gotten into the habit of telling me random things he liked about me at the end of each date: *I like that you always smell like vanilla, your laugh is the best sound I hear all day, I love that you are willing to work your way from the bottom, up - that shows courage I've never had.*

With such encouragement, how could I not be falling for him? I still questioned his sanity sometimes, after all, he seemed to really be into me, but if he was insane, I was ready to follow him straight to the looney bin. So the next day, I dialed his number, deciding to stop being the girl who couldn't believe what was happening and start being the girl who showed the guy she liked just how much she liked him.

"Hey, what are you doing tonight?" I asked.

"I don't know. I don't have any plans."

Wow, do you realize your voice makes me melt every time? "You do now. We're going out."

"We are?" The surprise in his voice was unmistakable. My excitement increased.

"Yes. I feel bad that you're always the one putting in the effort, so tonight I'm doing everything."

"Oh, really?" Laughter danced in his tone, "Well, don't I feel special to have a beautiful woman making plans for me. What're we doing?"

"It's a surprise. I'll pick you up at nine."

"You'll pick me up? You're going to drive? You never want to drive."

"I think that might have to do with the recent traumatic car accident I was in, but yes, I'm driving. And you aren't allowed to argue."

Ben chuckled. "Yes, ma'am. What's gotten into you?"

"Honestly? I don't know. You, I guess." *You, definitely.*

"I tend to have that effect on women." He spent the next several minutes trying to coax the surprise out of me, but when I refused to budge, he left me with, "I like this stubborn side of you."

Snapping my phone shut, I began tidying the living room in an attempt to work out some of the nervous energy pulsing through my body. No guy brought on the butterflies like Ben did.

Sweeping a stack of magazines and junk mail into my arms, I headed to my bedroom and dumped the pile onto my bed. A single sheet of notebook paper fluttered to the ground. Bending over to pick it up, I recognized the words staring up at me and froze.

The list. I hadn't thought about it at all since my birthday, yet there it was. I smoothed out the folds and stumbled into the living room, falling onto the couch. I read each item carefully.

"*Learn how to ski.* Nope. Haven't done that. *Get a tattoo.* Nope. *Have a column in a national magazine or newspaper.* Most definitely haven't done that." I grew more disgusted with myself at each item. What had I been doing the past ten years that I hadn't accomplished anything?

So much for the new me.

* * * *

"Are you okay?" Ben asked, sipping his beer and glancing around the bar. I looked around, too. The bar was full, but it was dreary and noisy. We had to yell to hear each other, and the "Grade A" sign from the health department hanging behind the bartender looked suspiciously like it had been printed from the internet and not filled out by an inspector.

"Yeah, of course. Why?"

"You were so excited this afternoon on the phone, but now, I don't know, you don't seem like you're having a good time."

"No, I am! I am, really, I had a rough afternoon."

"Oh, I'm sorry…" His voice got drowned out by the cackling of a couple of girls hanging onto the bar beside us. Apparently they were attempting to score free drinks from the bartender even though he'd cut them off twenty minutes ago.

"Huh?" I leaned into him and he put his arm around my waist to pull my ear closer to his mouth.

"You wanna talk about it?" His breath tickled my neck.

"Um, no. I'm fine."

"Oh. Okay." He released his hold and turned towards the stage at the front of the bar. After a few painful seconds of silence he tilted towards me again and asked, "Hey, what's going on up there tonight?"

"You'll see," I responded. At that moment, a curly-haired man jumped onto the stage and brought a microphone to his lips.

"Ladies and gentlemen," his booming voice broke out over the rumble in the bar, "welcome to Karaoke Night! We've already got some singers signed up, so let's get the party started with Miss Abigail Bronsen singing 'Girls Just Want to Have Fun.' Give it up for Abigail everyone!"

"Karaoke? That's the plan?" Ben stared at me as if I'd just announced we were sealing a murder-suicide pact.

"That's the plan. If you'll excuse me for a few minutes, my fans await!" I kissed his cheek and shoved through the crowd, taking the mike from the emcee and positioning myself on stage so I could watch Ben's dumbfounded expression.

The music kicked in and I danced around the stage, catcalls and whistles from the audience fueling me into a frenzy as I picked up speed, swung my arms around my head, and sashayed my hips back and forth. I let the music fill my head, pushing out all thoughts of the list and my incredibly uneventful twenty-five years on earth.

"I come home, in the morning light/ My mother says when you gonna live your life right/ Oh mother dear, we're not the fortunate ones/ And girls just wanna have fun…" My voice rang out loud and clear, drifting to the far corners of the bar. At the first note Ben's jaw dropped in surprise, then adjusted into a cheesy grin.

"Woohooo! Go Abigail!" he yelled, holding his phone up and snapping a few pictures. He continued hooting and waving his phone in the air, the little screen glowing green and illuminating his hand as it swayed to the music. The rest of the crowd cheered and sang along with me by the final chorus.

"Oh oh oh, girls just wanna have fu-unn!"

Applause erupted around me as I stepped off the stage and made my way back to Ben.

"Wow! Way to kick things off, Abigail! Let's hear it for her one more time," the emcee shouted into the mike and more cheering and applause broke out.

"That was amazing!" Ben pressed forward and shouted in my ear.

I shrugged. "I was just having a little fun."

"You're a natural performer. Why didn't you tell me you could sing?"

"Everyone can sing."

"I can't."

"We'll see about that."

"Huh?" His eyes lost their spark as it dawned on him what I meant, "Abigail, you were great, really, but I'm terrible. You don't want to hear me sing."

"It's too late now." I pointed to the emcee, who brought the mike to his mouth.

"Alright ladies and gents, our next victim is Mr. Benjamin Harris, singing 'I'm Too Sexy.' Ladies, I guess you'll have to be the judge of that. Come on down, Benjamin!"

I clapped my hands together enthusiastically and let out a "Woohoo!" while nudging Ben forward. "You're up!" His face became so white, it was almost translucent, his Adam's apple bobbed as he gulped several breaths in, but then he walked determinedly to the stage.

"Yeaaahhh Ben!" I yelled after him. Several girls right in front of the stage mimicked my calls and Ben's face blushed deep red as he grabbed the microphone.

"You're going to pay for this, Abigail," he threatened, waiting for the music to start. The first verse was TERRIBLE! He missed half the words and sang so quietly it was hard to hear, but roaring and support from the crowd encouraged him and he laughed his way through the rest of the song, good humouredly dancing off the stage at the end.

"Of all the songs in the world, that's what you picked for me?" he accosted as soon as he broke through the throngs of people congregating around the bar.

"I thought it was appropriate. I didn't want you to take yourself too seriously. And, come on, those girls up there *did* think you were too sexy for your shirt!"

Laughing, he asked, "How bad was I?"

"Awful! But adorable." He grinned and kissed me, then sat back on his stool to watch the next performer, wrapping his arms around my waist and pulling me against him. My head rolled back and rested on his shoulder while we enjoyed the rest of the singers. The list was nowhere on the register of my thoughts at that moment.

"Is that all you had up your sleeve?" he asked, opening the car door for me after closing time.

"Yeah. Did you have fun?"

"I did." He got into the passenger seat and buckled up, looking thoughtfully out the window instead of at me. Something wasn't right.

"Are you sure? You're quieter than normal."

"No, I did. I had a great time. I just thought…" he let his voice trail off and ruffled his hair.

"What?"

Shifting in his seat, his breathing got heavy, "When you said you wanted to plan everything… well, I thought, nothing, it's stupid."

"What? I'm sure it's not stupid."

"I thought you meant you were planning something, um… uh, something more intimate."

Huh? "Oh?" *Holy crap.* "Ohhh."

Oh God, what do I do now? Shit, of course he's thinking about sex, he is a guy, Sex is the last thing I want to talk about. "I'm sorry, Ben, I didn't mean to give you the wrong impression," I stammered, "but I'm not ready to talk about THAT. We've only known each other a little while. I don't even know what this is that we're doing, I…"

Shit, just tell him the truth, "I… I…"

You can do it. Just spit it out. "Ben, I'm..."

He interrupted, placing his hand on my arm, "Hey, no need to explain. I shouldn't have presumed. We'll take it slow. To be honest, I'm not exactly sure what we're doing either. But I know I want to spend more time with you."

Thank God. "I want to spend more time with you, too."

Chapter Eight: Define the Relationship

Abigail

Why rock the boat? Ben didn't mention sex again after the karaoke night so neither did I. A week later and yet, nothing. I knew it would come up eventually, but until it did, I was going to ignore the voice in my head nagging me to come clean with him about my sexual experience, or lack thereof.

A knock at the door alerted me to his arrival and when I opened it, Ben's smiling face made that nagging voice disappear. I hugged him as he stepped into the apartment and he kissed my cheek.

"I ordered a pizza," I said as we headed to the couch.

"Awesome, I'm starving. Is *The Office* new tonight?" He picked up the remote and flipped through a couple of channels. It didn't take long for the pizza box to empty, our show started, and we settled on the couch together, his arms curled around me in a firm hold. I liked the way he gently shook when he laughed at the stupidity of Michael Scott and Dwight onscreen; I could feel the rumble in his chest on my back.

As soon as the show ended, Ben rose from the couch to stretch. Circling around the room, he paused to look at a few of the framed photos on the bookshelf in the corner. "Who are these people?" he asked, pointing at the picture of my brothers, sisters, and I at Christmas.

Joining him in front of the bookcase, I pointed to each person, "My oldest sister, Anna, and her husband, Will. My other sister, Ashley, and her husband, Cain. Me. My younger brother, Derek, and his fiancé, Samantha."

"What's with the letters on the stockings?"

"Those are our initials."

"No, they aren't. You're holding a 'B'."

"We consider that my initial."

"I don't get it, why?"

"When we were little, my mother had a hard time telling apart our clothes and our toys, and we used to fight over everything because it was hard to have anything that was our own without a brother or sister stealing it. So she started marking everything. She tried using colors at first, but that didn't last long because we all wanted to be the same color, so she turned to initials. Anna, Ashley, and Abigail all start with 'A' so to prevent us from fighting over who got to use 'A' as their initial, she used the second letters of our first names. Thus, Anna's initial is 'N,' Ashley's is 'S,' and mine is 'B.' Derek didn't have the same problem, so he got to use his actual initial."

"Is that why they're carved into the frame?" He picked up the wooden frame and traced the outline of the 'B' on the right-hand side.

"Yeah, they gave it to me for my birthday. We've called each other by those initials for a long time now. It's sort of become tradition, or a family joke."

"Wait, what did you say her name was?" He indicated Derek's fiancé.

"Samantha."

"Why does she get an 'A'?"

"Well, 'S' was already being used by Ashley. And we all figured we're old enough not to get upset if someone had an 'A' and…"

"The second letter of Samantha is 'A.'"

"Exactly."

"Can I call you 'B' too?" He laughed and put both arms around my waist, hugging me from behind.

"I don't know. I think that would be a little weird. Ashley, Anna, and Derek are the only people who call me that. Will, Cain, and Samantha don't use our initials. The stockings were just a joke my dad came up with. My parents haven't even called me that since I was in high school."

"Okay, how about Abby?"

My heart leapt, *he wants a nickname for me!* "No one calls me that."

"But can I?" He squeezed me a little tighter, resting his chin on my shoulder.

You can call me anything you want. "I don't know. Say it again."

"Abby," he whispered it in my ear.

My stomach flipped. "I like the sound of that."

Ben

"Abby, I have a favor to ask of you." Gathering my jacket and keys from the kitchen counter, I joined her at the front door.

"Okay. Shoot." She smiled and ran her hand down my arm. *God, if only she knew what touching me like that does to me!*

"I'm playing softball with some of my friends this weekend and I'd like you to come with me." I pulled my jacket on and waited for her reaction. It took a few seconds.

She spoke cautiously, as if she hadn't heard me correctly. "You want me to meet your friends?"

"Yes." *Deep breath, Ben.* "And I want to introduce you as my girlfriend."

"Is that what I am?" She turned her eyes up and looked into mine. Was she searching for the truth? Couldn't she hear the sincerity in my voice?

"I've been thinking a lot about it since the karaoke night and that's what I'd like you to be. What do you want?" We stood about a foot apart, but she took a step back, increasing the distance.

"I don't know."

Liar. "Well, let me phrase it differently. Do you want me to be your boyfriend?"

No response. I tried to keep my frustration to a minimum. I knew she liked me. She wouldn't keep hanging out with me if she didn't. She wasn't Rebecca who didn't care one way or another who she spent her time with. I meant something to Abigail. *Why won't she just admit it?*

I tried that approach. "Do you enjoy spending time with me?"

"Yes."

YES! "Do you want to continue spending time with me?"

"Yes."

Thank you! "Do you want to date anyone else?"

"No."

I knew it! "Do you enjoy this?" I cupped her face with both hands and lightly touched my lips to hers. A sigh escaped her throat.

"Yes."

Hell yeah, you do. "And this?" I moved my hands to the back of her head and held her mouth to mine, bruising her lips with force and passion. Her fingers dug into my back as our tongues effortlessly waltzed around each other. When I finally released her, she kept her eyes closed and pressed her fists into my chest, a smile plastered across her pretty face.

"I know you liked that," I whispered.

"Oh yeah."

"So, what's the problem, Abby?"

Her eyes popped open and found mine, "There's no problem."

"Saturday, you'll come and play softball with me and my friends?"

"Absolutely."

"As my girlfriend?" I qualified.

"Absolutely."

Finally! Now we're getting somewhere.

Chapter Nine: Play Ball!

Abby

When I looked out my window Saturday morning I was half-disappointed to see the sun shining brightly and cheerfully. *I guess there's no getting out of it.* Though excited to meet Ben's friends, I found myself less than enthusiastic about letting him see what a terrible athlete I am.

I pulled my hair into a ponytail and located a pair of old sneakers in the back of my closet when Ben knocked on the door. Amazed at how good he looked in his plain white t-shirt, grey sweatpants, and Red Sox baseball cap, I fumbled grabbing my sunscreen and keys off the kitchen counter.

"Are you sure you want someone so spazzy to play with your friends? I could knock one of them out with an ill-swung bat."

He laughed, catching the sunscreen bottle before it hit the tiled floor. "I'm sure. You aren't getting out of this. I want to show you off. And if you do knock a couple of the opposing team out, well, then that's a bonus. Just stay away from our team and you'll be good. Enough stalling - let's go." He put the sunscreen in his back pocket and took my hand to lead me to his car. Before getting in, he stopped to kiss me; his hands lightly tickled my arms as his lips caressed mine.

"What was that for?" I asked, pleased.

"Well, the guys don't tolerate a lot of PDA, so I thought I would get it out of my system before we got to the field."

"I see, anything else I should know before we get there?"

"Nope. Just be yourself and have fun."

"Sounds easy enough."

It took twenty minutes to get to the field Ben and his friends reserved for us at a park downtown. The closer we got, the more tangled my nerves became. *What if Mr. Sports Nut realizes he can't date a girl who doesn't know the difference between a fastball and a curveball? What if his friends don't like me?*

"Why aren't we playing at the complex?"

He pulled the car into a gravel lot and switched off the engine. "We never play there if we can help it. I like to leave the fields free for the kids." Ben waved to a group of young men and women converging on the edge of the parking lot and my nerves calmed down. It consisted of at least six girls and none of them looked like spectators. I didn't care if I was the worst girl on the field - I just didn't want to be the only girl on the field. *Surely at least one of them will be as horrible as me.*

He twisted in his seat to face me, "I got something for you." He reached into the backseat and brought forward a cardboard box. Seeing the look of trepidation on my face he quickly reassured me, "It's nothing special, just something you can use today for the game."

I took the box from him and burst out laughing once I saw the contents: a pink baseball glove and a pink Red Sox baseball hat.

"They make *pink* baseball gloves? I can't believe it! Your friends are going to think I'm a huge bimbo when I walk onto the field with this. Softball Barbie, anyone?"

"Nah, they'll think it's funny. But if you don't like it, I'm sure Madelyn or Trish will trade with you."

"No, no, I like it. Just promise me it's the last pink thing you ever give me. I'm more of a blue kind of girl."

"No sweat. Alright, let's go." He climbed out of the car and I scrambled after him. He waited until I reached his side and then took the hat out of my hand and adjusted the strap around my head, expertly pulling my ponytail through. Hand-in-hand, we joined the group waiting for us.

"Hey everyone - this is Abigail," he shouted.

"Hi Abigail," the group chanted back. I waved awkwardly. A few of the girls smiled at me, but for the most part everyone returned to what they were doing before we joined them. Twin blondes in matching red gym shorts and wife-beater tank tops scrutinized me up and down and rolled their eyes as Ben pounded his fist into my new glove. Woman's intuition told me they didn't appreciate my presence.

"Hey Ben!" A lanky man slapped Ben on the back and gripped his hand. "Is this the beautiful Abby we've heard so much about?" He smiled in my direction, thin lips revealed small teeth. He was the most disproportionate man I'd ever seen - long limbs yet short torso and tiny hands - but his smile was so warm, I found the awkwardness endearing.

"Yes, it is. Abigail - Matt. Matt, this is my girlfriend, Abigail. Matt and I've been friends since Little League." My hand involuntarily squeezed his as he introduced me; I'd never been anyone's girlfriend before, the words sounded both foreign and wonderful to my ears.

"Young Ben here is a horrible softball player, I hope you came prepared to be humiliated." Matt slung his arm across Ben's shoulder and grinned at me.

"I don't think I'll need him for that. I'm generally considered the world's worst athlete."

"Well, that's a relief, we needed someone at Matt's level to even out the teams." Ben smirked and the two boys continued their jabs at each other for several minutes as even more people gathered and teams began to form. Ben and I joined one and I listened during the huddle as my new group created a game plan. I asked them to put me in the place where I could do the least damage, so they put me in the outfield behind first base and in the lineup to hit right after Ben.

Luckily, the other team tended to hit straight to centerfield and I didn't have to field the ball very often. Unluckily, I struck out every time I went up to bat. I was having fun, though, and pretty proud of myself that I'd managed to avoid cracking anyone's skull open with my wild swings. Ben played shortstop and proved instrumental in getting outs for our team. Our strongest hitter, he didn't seem to care whether he scored or not. Though no one said it, everyone looked to Ben and Matt as the leaders of the group.

During a break between innings, Matt's girlfriend of six years and the smallest player on the field, Trish, approached and accosted me with a hug. "Abigail, it's so nice to meet you. Ben's told us a lot about you."

"Don't believe everything you hear," I laughed, slapping Ben's arm.

Trish laughed, too. "Don't worry. I always make my own judgments."

Ben nudged me closer to Trish before walking off to consult with our team's pitcher. She took off her hat, revealing dark red, curly hair cut at the nape of her neck, took a seat on my team's bench, and waited til he was out of earshot to ask, "So, Abigail, how did Ben convince you to play?"

"Huh? He asked me to play, so here I am. And when I got cold feet, he tried flattery, saying he wanted to show me off!"

"Hmm. Looks like he found the right method of persuasion. None of his other girlfriends would play."

I gulped, I'd been dreading hearing about his past, but I couldn't ignore the statement. "Other girlfriends?"

"Yeah, Rebecca and another girl before her, Meg, I think. She was a piece of work. She'd sit in the bleachers and complain throughout the entire game. We were all thankful when they broke up."

Ben and Matt were heading in our direction; Trish jumped up, "We'll talk again soon, Abigail!" and ran to meet Matt. He scooped her into a hug and all of his gangliness disappeared, even though he was close to two feet taller than her. They fit together.

Ben entered the dugout and took his place beside me on the bench. My smile felt forced as he explained the game plan for the next inning. I wasn't sure what Trish's information meant to me. Should I be happy his friends didn't like his past girlfriends? Or be worried they wouldn't like me, either?

Ben tried to introduce me to everyone else throughout the game, but it was hard to keep up. However, I made sure to pay attention when he pointed out the blonde clones glaring at me from the opposite dugout.

"That's Madelyn and Carrie. We call them the Twin Terrors. Man, can they hit the ball!"

"They don't seem like the type of girls who'd be into sports," I said, trying to sound as nonchalant as possible.

"Yeah, you're probably right. Trish thinks they only play to meet guys. She's probably right, too, they've dated everyone on the team. Except me and Matt, of course," he added with a grin, noticing my scowl.

"Of course." I grinned back, feeling much better.

I didn't realize we were in the final inning until Matt called out to his teammates: "Last out! One more and this game is over!" Unhappily for our team, I was the next up to bat.

I adjusted my hat so I could see more clearly and stepped up to the plate.

"Wait, time out!" Ben called and running to me.

"What's wrong?"

"Are you left handed?" he asked.

"Yeah. So?"

"That's why you've been having trouble hitting, you're standing on the wrong side of the plate." He positioned me on the opposite side and put his hands around mine on the bat.

"Choke up a bit, like this," he moved my fingers away from the base of the bat, "and you'll have better leverage." He walked back to his base and the blonde bimbos looked ready to shoot fire from their eyes.

Taking a deep breath, I turned to face the pitcher. First pitch - wild swing - strike one. Second pitch - my arms swung the bat forward even though my head knew the ball was outside and should have been a ball - strike two.

"Damn it!"

"Calm down, Abby. You can do it!" Ben shouted. I took a deep breath and looked across the field into his eyes. I couldn't do it. But that didn't matter. He didn't care if I was good or not.

I choked up on the bat again and nodded to the pitcher. Third pitch - swing and *Holy Crap!* contact with the ball! It went soaring past Ben on third base and into the outfield. The opposing team was so surprised I made it to first before they went after the ball. I raced to second base on trembling legs. Ben smiled at me from his spot on third.

The next batter hit a double as well, sending Ben and I to home plate. I ran across it and jumped straight into his arms. He lifted me up as if I weighed no more than a feather; I wrapped my legs around his waist and clamped my arms around his neck. He twirled me around as our teammates cheered from the dugout. I hadn't had so much fun playing a sport since elementary school.

After the game ended, Matt and Trish walked to Ben's car and rode with us to Cask 'N Flagon to watch the Red Sox game.

"Hey, who won?" It dawned on me I hadn't been aware of winning or losing all day.

"Oh, we don't usually keep score. We just play for fun." Matt answered from the back seat.

"Yeah, if they kept score, I wouldn't be allowed to play," Trish added.

"Sure you would, baby, just not on my team," Matt taunted, roughly kissing her cheek.

"Is PDA allowed now?" I joked, lacing Ben's fingers through my own.

His thumb gently rubbed the back of my hand. "I think it's safe to say Trish and Matt are the reason for the 'No PDA' rule."

"And proud of it!" Matt exclaimed. "But don't you worry, Abigail, if you and Ben want to start making out while we're waiting in traffic, Trish and I completely understand. We'll even let you know when the cars begin moving again."

Ben snorted, "Unlike you, we can control ourselves."

Matt ignored him and leaned closer to me. "So Abigail, Trish and I have to produce a verdict on you now. We need to know you're good enough for our friend here. He's a delicate boy and from the way he talks about you, I'd say you're in a good position to break his heart into a thousand pieces."

Ben's smile hardened on his face, but he didn't say anything.

Matt continued his teasing, "What exactly is it about our young Ben that you like? I mean after witnessing his horrible performance today, it can't be his athleticism."

Ben let out a little chuckle, but still didn't contribute to the conversation. It wasn't like him to seem so… so embarrassed. Even at karaoke he'd managed to pull it together and sing. I didn't like it. I wanted to put him at ease, like he'd done for me.

"Hmmm, what is it that I like about Ben? Well, I like the way he kicked your ass out on the field today."

Ben nearly choked trying to hold back his laughter, but Trish let hers spring forth in a loud guffaw. "Matt, I think you've met your match baby!"

Matt and I continued sparring throughout the rest of the drive and had Ben and Trish in stitches by the time we got to the bar.

"Okay, I guess you're good enough for him, but I'm keeping my eyes on you." He made a 'V' with his index and middle finger and motioned from his eyes to mine.

"Oh, yes sir!" With the most serious face I could muster, I saluted him, and Ben cracked up again, grabbing me around the waist and hugging me to his side.

"Hey, where's the bathroom?" I asked when he was able to talk again.

"Um, around the corner on the left."

I thanked him and went to freshen up. When I found my way to the tables the team had claimed near the big screen TVs, Ben was sitting between the blonde twins who'd been starring daggers at me all day. Inhaling deeply, I took the empty chair at Trish and Matt's table.

"Do you mind if I sit with you?"

"Of course not. Beer?" Trish motioned to the pitcher and poured me a glass when I nodded. I tried to pay attention as they discussed the Sox game, but my eyes and ears kept wandering over to Ben laughing with the twins.

"I'll bet that's not even their natural hair color. Or their natural boobs," I muttered, a little louder than I intended. Trish stifled a giggle and patted my arm.

"Hey, don't worry Abigail. Ben is a one-woman kind of guy, and trust me, blonde bimbos are not his type."

"I thought blonde bimbos were every guy's type," I joked, trying to mask my jealousy and failing miserably. I couldn't tear my eyes off his table.

"I know they're my type!" Matt said. Trish punched his arm. "Ow! Baby, that hurt."

"You'll get over it." She poured me another beer and I sipped it slowly. Ben glanced up and smiled at me, before turning back to the girls beside him. My heart skipped momentarily when he was looking at me, but then beat ferociously when he started talking to the twins again.

Great, I thought, *he calls me his girlfriend then spends the evening talking to other girls.* "I'm getting something stronger. You guys want anything?" Trish nodded and followed me to the bar. We put the drinks on Matt and Ben's tab.

Ben

"You are so drunk," I laughed as I helped Abby up the stairs to her apartment. I didn't realize how many drinks she'd consumed until the bill came and by then it was too late to do anything except take her home and put her to bed. Helping her take her shoes and hat off, I stayed until she was safe under the covers with a bottle of water and aspirin on the nightstand beside her.

"I'll sleep on the couch in case you need anything," I whispered, bending down and kissing her forehead.

"Hey. Hey, why'd your friends think I'm gonna break your heart?" She grabbed my shirt and kept my face close to hers.

"Because I like you a lot. Probably more than you like me." I sat on the edge of her bed and stroked her hair, fanning it out across the pillow. She looked up at me with watery eyes and frowned.

"Yeah, you like me so much you spent the whole night talking to other girls."

What??? "Hey, I was just hanging out with my friends. You could've joined us."

"Right, like I'd want to sit next to the blonde goddesses and have you compare me to them." She pushed me off the bed and turned her face away.

That's ridiculous. I straightened up and glared at her. "You're drunk. I don't like the twins. You're beautiful, there's no comparison."

"Oh please. I watched you all night. You were flirting with them." She rolled onto her side, putting her back to me.

"Seriously, Abby? You've got to be joking. I talked to them, sure. But I was *not* flirting with them." She was starting to piss me off. I didn't do anything wrong.

"They were flirting with you."

"What exactly are you accusing me of?"

"Nothing. I just want you to be honest with me if you're having second thoughts about us. About calling me your girlfriend."

Really? More insecurity? "Abby, you've got to stop."

"What?"

"This, you acting like a crazy person every time I try to get close to you."

"I'm not crazy!" she shouted, sitting up and staring at me, eyes now bright forest green, not a tear in sight.

"I can't have this discussion with you right now. Not while you're drunk. Call me in the morning if you're ready to start trusting me." I didn't want to leave, but I didn't know what else to do. How could I convince her she was the girl I wanted when she refused to believe it? I made it all the way to the front door before her voice stopped me.

"Wait Ben! Please don't leave." She came running from the bedroom and stumbled straight into my arms. "I'm sorry. God, you're right. I'm acting crazy. I just got so jealous when I saw you talking to those girls. I mean, they're so pretty, and you were laughing the whole time. I just, I don't know, I thought, um..."

"You're a hundred times more beautiful than the twins." I coaxed her head up and forced her to look into my eyes, but she only held my gaze for a few seconds before burying her head in my chest.

"I'm being serious. Abby, you have to believe me." Gripping her shoulders, I marched her back into the bedroom and placed her in front of the full-length mirror.

"Look at yourself," I commanded. She didn't. "Abigail, look at yourself." I nudged her chin so she had no choice. Tears began streaming down her cheeks.

"You are beautiful. Do you know what I see when I look at you?"

"No," she croaked out.

"I see the most gorgeous green eyes in the world. And the softest, silkiest brown hair. And lush, kissable lips. And a smile that makes me weak in the knees."

"Really?"

"Really. Why can't you see what I see?"

"Because no one else has ever looked at me like that before," she sobbed softly.

"I don't think that's true. Maybe you never noticed them looking."

"Well, then they looked and moved on." Her anger and sorrow seemed to be sobering her up. "No one has ever made me feel pretty before. I'm twenty-five years old and no one has ever even... no one's ever liked me or cared about me. You're my first boyfriend."

What the hell? So that's why she's so closed off? She doesn't believe anyone's ever liked her before? I didn't know what to say to that.

Abby

He didn't say anything for a long time. So this was it. The end. I'd admitted what a loser I was and now he was going to walk out the door.

But he didn't. Instead, he moved in front of me, blocking the mirror and placing his arms around my neck and shoulders. He hugged me tightly and I let my face burrow into his chest again.

"I like you. I care about you," he finally said, as I continued to cry into his shirt. He let me pour out all the ugliness I felt. I cried for twenty-five years worth of unhappiness, loneliness, and dateless nights.

And Ben held me.

Chapter Ten: Confession

Abby

We were cuddling on the couch at his place, watching the end of a movie on a rainy Friday evening a couple days after the softball game; Ben's arms wrapped around me, my head rested against his shoulder, and his cheek rested on the top of my head. I knew the film was almost over, but I didn't want to move. I could have lain there with him for days. But it did end - and Ben loosened his hold on me.

"You seem sleepy, do you want to get going?"

"No," I hugged his arms to me, "I want to stay right here."

"That's what I was hoping you'd say." He settled into his original position and began kissing my neck. It felt so good I unconsciously arched my back and stretched my head out, exposing more of my throat to his mouth. Every brush of his lips against my skin sent shivers through my body. I wanted more and more of him. My heartbeat sped up and blood rushed to my head as his lips gently made their way to my ear and whispered my name.

I couldn't take it anymore; I shifted to face him, sitting up on my knees between his legs. Kissing his cheeks, his nose, his forehead, his neck, slowly I made my way to his mouth. I locked onto his lower lip, forced his mouth apart, and drove my tongue in to meet his. His lips moved with me, his tongue danced around mine. Pressing my hands into his chest, I experienced every beat of his heart, every breath he took in. His smell, his taste, overpowered me. His electric touch nearly drove me wild; his fingers lightly danced up and down my back, sending tingling sensations through my spine. My hands moved to clutch his biceps.

Suddenly he shifted, too. Now he knelt on the couch as well, bringing our bodies even closer. I felt dizzy, excited, confused. His hands traveled to my face, then into my hair, tugging and twisting it around his strong fingers. Our lips stopped working for a moment and I opened my eyes. He pushed several strands off my forehead; his fingers lingered on my temple for a few seconds, then traced the outline of my face. I mimicked his motions, using my fingertips to memorize the contours of his face. I paused brushing them across his lips and we were unable to resist each other any longer.

He pulled me tightly to his chest, standing up from the couch and sweeping me into his arms in one swift movement. Our bodies behaved like magnets, instinctively attracted to each other, glued together in an unbreakable bond. Safe in his firm hold, my legs dangled inches from the floor. After a moment my feet touched the ground, our bodies still locked together.

He leaned into me and I found myself moving backwards. He guided me until I lay back on the couch, my head resting on the throw pillow he sat against only a few minutes before. It was still warm from his body heat. Continuing to kiss me, he leaned over, letting his legs tangle themselves in mine. Intoxicated by the pressure of his weight on top of me, my breathing turned heavy and my hands shook as I caressed his face.

Part of me wanted nothing more than to have all of him right there, in that moment, but another part of me was scared and unprepared. His hands slowly moved up my stomach, lifting my shirt slightly. Heat tore through my thighs and snaked up my belly and into my chest. I didn't want to stop, but I couldn't keep going.

"Wait," I breathed, "I can't." He immediately stopped kissing me and straightened up. It took every ounce of self-control to not grab his shirt and pull him back. Instead, I sat up as well.

"What's wrong?" he asked, concern and bewilderment mingled in his expression.

"I'm sorry. I want to. I really, really want to, but I can't." I looked away, hiding my tears from his gaze.

"Why? Did I do something wrong? Did I hurt you?" He reached over and nudged my chin so he could look into my face. A tear broke free from my eye and dropped on his finger.

"No, no, no. You did nothing wrong. You did everything right. But I can't sleep with you."

"Abigail, we aren't going to do anything you aren't comfortable with." His tone told me he was exasperated and disappointed. I hated doing this to him. Why hadn't I just told him the truth from the beginning?

"I know. But, you don't understand. I'm…" I paused. I wasn't sure I really wanted to say these words. "I'm a virgin."

"What?"

"I'm a virgin."

"How is that possible?"

"I've never had sex."

"Yes, I know what it means. But how is it possible that you've never had sex?"

"I've been waiting. What I mean is I've always known I would wait until I got married. And when you don't have any temptation, it's pretty easy to stick to that. So, we can't go any further tonight, because if you tempt me…" I let the last few words drift off and looked into his eyes, trying to read his reaction, but I couldn't. I wasn't expecting his next question.

"You've never been tempted before?"

"Before tonight, no." Looking down at my fingers, I examined my nails and cuticles, anything to avoid his bewitching eyes.

"Why didn't you tell me all of this before now?"

I considered the question for a minute before I answered, trying to find the right words. But nothing seemed right, because I should have told him a long time ago. "I didn't tell you because I was embarrassed. And I didn't tell you because I was afraid, afraid you wouldn't want to be in a relationship that didn't involve sex." Stealing a glance, I noticed his face turn red.

"First of all, you have nothing to be embarrassed about. Second of all, is that really what you think of me? That I'm so shallow I wouldn't want to be with you if I couldn't sleep with you?" He looked so upset, I instinctively leaned over and hugged him, but he pushed me away.

"Don't take it like that," I pleaded. "That's not what I said. But I've been in this situation before. Guys don't tend to react well when I tell them."

"And you thought I'd act like all of the jerks before me?" he protested before I could finish explaining.

"No! Well, not really. Mostly, I was afraid you wouldn't look at me in the same way. That you would think I was a prude; that I thought sex was a bad thing or I was judgmental about others because they hadn't waited. And I'm not like that. I never wanted you to think I was. And I guess a part of me thought maybe you wouldn't want to be with me anymore. I was scared you would suddenly disappear, that you'd stop calling and I would never see you again. Can you blame me? The whole world tells me men only have one thing on their minds and past experiences haven't changed that perception."

I waited for him to answer, but he just sat there. He didn't look angry anymore, but he didn't look like himself either.

"I'm sorry. I shouldn't have led you on. I didn't do it on purpose, but I still should have known better. I'm really sorry. I'll go." I started to gather my things from around the room: my purse beside the couch, my shoes in the corner, my jacket hanging in the closet.

"Abby," his voice was soft, but strained, "I don't want you to leave. I just don't know what to say."

My keys were in my hand, but I didn't walk out the door.

"I don't understand," he began again. "Why couldn't you trust me? We've been dating for almost three months and I've never even tried anything before tonight. I never would've made you feel uncomfortable or wrong about your decision. I never would've pressured you. Don't you know me?" He hadn't moved from his spot on the couch, he hadn't even turned to look at me as he said this. I dropped my jacket and keys and sat down beside him, taking his hand in mine.

"I want to trust you. I'm getting to know you. But this is all so new for me. I've never been in this kind of relationship before. I've never had a serious boyfriend; I've never even gotten past date three with anyone else. I don't know what I'm doing. Please don't be upset. I didn't mean to hurt you."

"Let's get a few things straight. I'm not like every other guy. Sex is not the only thing I want from a woman. And I've never had a relationship like this either. I wake up in the morning and the first thing I want to do is talk to you. I'm not going to jeopardize that by moving faster than you. Do I want to sleep with you? Yes, of course I do. You're sexy as hell and I love spending time with you. But I have an even stronger urge to protect you. I'd rather spend a hundred years with you, without sex, than spend ten minutes with anyone else. Can't you see that?"

"Yes," I croaked.

"Then why do you refuse to believe it? Abby, look at me. I'm not going anywhere - stop trying to convince me to leave you. I'm in this for the long haul. I'm not giving up on you." With that, he pulled me close and hugged me tightly.

After a few minutes, he loosened his hold and sucked a gulp of air into his lungs. "Can I ask you a question?" He slid away from me. I nodded.

"Why are you waiting?" His eyes looked into mine, telling me his curiosity came from wanting to understand me, not from wanting to change my mind. Inhaling deeply, I decided he had a right to know.

"When I was thirteen, my mom gave me the whole birds and bees sex talk. Somehow she decided simple mechanics weren't enough, she wanted me to know about the physical and emotional consequences, so she told me about her first experience. She was a junior in high school and head-over-heels for her boyfriend, a senior named Jake. Jake convinced her that if she loved him, she would sleep with him, and she thought she loved him."

Stretching my arms and legs, I stood up and walked to the window. Rain fell softly and silently on the grass. The dreariness outside matched the story I was telling. "She got pregnant and he dumped her. He swore to his parents and hers that he couldn't be the father, that they hadn't done anything, that they'd been broken up for over a month. She was absolutely devastated, the stress caused a miscarriage, and she spent the rest of high school depressed and suicidal."

Turning back around, Ben's anxious eyes caught mine and held me in place. "She refused to let any man touch her for years, she couldn't bear the thought of getting hurt like that again. But then she met my dad. He loved her and he didn't try and use that love as a bargaining tool. He was patient. He waited for her. Though I didn't really want to hear about my parents' sex life, she said the first time they made love was the most amazing experience of her life, other than giving birth."

I paused again, making sure his eyes hadn't glazed over, but they were still locked on mine, so I continued, "Then she told me that she knew I was young and this was a lot of information to take in, but there would be times I was going to be faced with adult decisions and she wanted me to be prepared. The most important thing she told me is that sex is a gift you give someone and you should only give it to someone who loves you. She told me she didn't necessarily expect me to wait until I got married, but that she wished someone would have told her how much it hurt to give yourself to someone who had no intention of giving anything back. I thought about it for a long time. At thirteen I wasn't ready to make that kind of decision."

Ben patted the couch beside him, so I joined him. Taking my hands in his, he wordlessly encouraged me to go on. "In high school, one by one, all of my friends lost their virginity. They told me the stories: it was painful, they didn't have fun, they wished they hadn't done it. Don't get me wrong, there were a few who loved it, but they were all girls who'd been in long-term relationships before taking that leap. I never dated anyone seriously, so it was never an option for me. I never had to make the choice. When I was nineteen, Anna and Will got married. When she told Ashley and me about their wedding night, I made up my mind. He loved her and they bonded on an even deeper level than she could ever have imagined. I want *that*. I want sex to be an experience where I feel more than passion and pleasure, I want to feel wanted, beloved."

My hands trembled inside his; I'd never shared anything so personal with another person before. Ben's face was hard to read, he wasn't smiling, but he wasn't frowning either. A tear slid down his face and he swiped it away, then bent his head down and kissed my hand.

"You'll have that someday."

Chapter Eleven: Breakfast and Dinner

Ben

We fell asleep on my couch somehow and I woke up at five AM surprised to find her in my arms. What had I gotten myself into? A virgin. A virgin waiting until marriage. I can honestly say I didn't expect that.

It's not like I hadn't gone long periods of time without sex before. I didn't sleep around, though I'd been tempted to in the past. And in my last two relationships I was the one saying "Slow down, let's not go so fast." But this was different. This was me having to be okay with no sex at all, ever, unless we got married someday.

Married? Holy shit, it's really early to be thinking about marriage. I like Abby a lot, but this seems too hard. Is she worth it? I told her I could handle it, that I was in for the long haul, but am I really ready for that?

One look at her sleeping face told me the answer. *Yes.*

Wait - had I really fallen that hard for her? Was it that simple? She stirred and her arms stretched across my chest. She smiled, but remained asleep. My heart pounded against my ribs.

Yes. She was totally worth it.

I hugged her a little closer to me and closed my eyes.

When I woke a few hours later, Abby had rolled off my chest and curled up at the foot of the couch. I stood, kissed her cheek, and went to the bathroom. After brushing my teeth, I emptied the fridge and began making breakfast.

Another hour later and the table boasted a spread of my finest culinary efforts: two stacks of pancakes, a platter of scrambled eggs, whole wheat toast, a plate of sausage links, and a bowl of sliced fruit. I started frying a pan of bacon.

"Good morning?" Abby's voice floated into the kitchen.

"Hey, good morning. Are you hungry?" I stepped away from the stove to kiss her cheek again.

"Starving."

"Good, because I think I've cooked all the food in the house. Grab a plate. Juice is on the counter." Returning to the stove, I watched her out of the corner of my eye. She tried to straighten her wrinkled shirt and ran her fingers through her tousled hair. I almost wanted to ask her to stop, she actually looked beautiful with bed head, but I held my tongue. She poured herself a glass of juice and headed straight for the buffet.

"You cook, too?" she asked, surveying the feast.

"Um, yeah. I have a lot of hobbies." I laughed nervously, wiping my hands on a dishtowel and keeping my eyes on her face.

"Well, thanks. It looks and smells delicious." She sat down and helped herself to eggs and sausages. I took the bacon off the stove, blotted it, and added it to the table.

Taking the seat opposite her, I fixed my own plate. Abby remained completely silent while we ate and I found it difficult to begin the conversation. After twenty minutes of discomfort she put her fork down, leaned back in her chair, and sighed. It was now or never.

"About last night," I began, "um, I wanted to let you know I meant everything I said and I mean it even more this morning."

She smiled and cocked an eyebrow. "You're okay with things staying the same, exactly the way they are? No sex?"

"That's not what I said. I don't want things to stay the same."

"But..." she tried to interrupt, but I held up my hand.

"I want us to move forward. I want you to trust me, to know me. I want us to get closer, not physically necessarily, but emotionally."

"Are you sure that's enough for you?"

My mind chose that moment to flash the events of the night before. Her lips pressing against mine, her hands clinging to my arms, our bodies smashed together, the fire in my heart as I looked into her eyes. I shook my head to clear the memory and coughed to regain my composure.

"No, honestly, I'm not. But I think I can handle it. I'd like to try."

She smiled and her cheeks darkened slightly. "Okay, me too."

"Good." *Damn, this is going to be hard.*

* * * *

As soon as things with Abby seemed right on track, things with my business began falling apart. My accountant, Steve, accosted me the next week with financial reports from the last couple of months.

"You have to cut back on spending or the complex is going to go under, fast." He shoved a stack of papers at me and I spread them out on my desk, examining each document carefully.

"What are my options?" I asked.

"I'd recommend selling the vans, closing the courts earlier, and increasing exposure for the bar. That's where you have potential to bring in additional revenue and you aren't living up to it." Steve took the armchair in front of my desk and waited for me to finish reading.

"I'm not selling the vans or closing the courts earlier. The whole point of ICS is to be accessible to the community."

"The gas, paying drivers, and insurance for the vans are costing you almost $3,000.00 a week. And closing the courts just an hour early is going to save you $1,000.00 a week in electricity costs."

"No. The vans and closing early are off the table. We'll work something else out. Increasing exposure for the bar. Got it. I'll come up with theme nights and we'll spread the word."

"Ben, I really think you should reconsider," he pleaded.

"Off the table, Steve."

He left frustrated and I spent the next hour memorizing every penny spent. By five o'clock I wanted to gouge my eyes out. Three months before, on a day like this, the gym would be the only place on earth I could go to find peace, but as I closed and locked my office, I wanted to go somewhere very different.

Abby answered on the second ring. "Hey, you."

Her voice instantly calmed me. "Hey, I'm heading over."

"I thought we said seven."

"We did, but I got out of work a little early."

"Okay, well, I'm getting in the shower. I'll leave the door unlocked for you. Will you check on the lasagna when you get here?"

"Sure thing, see you soon." *The shower? Is she trying to kill me?*

"Okay, bye." She hung up and I sighed, trying to get the image of her standing naked under hot jets of water out of my brain. I sped on the way to her apartment and made it there in ten minutes.

I didn't knock. As soon as I stepped inside, I realized how natural it felt, just walking into her apartment. The shower was running, which certainly didn't help with my mental image situation. I checked on the lasagna and set the table. The water shut off as I took a seat on the couch to wait for her.

She hadn't appeared after ten minutes. I selected a book from the coffee table and flipped through the pages. *So this is what she reads.* It was about photography and Abby's handwritten notes filled the pages.

A few loose photographs fluttered onto my lap and I set the book aside to gather them. Mostly scenic shots, notations on the back of each identified the date and time the picture was taken. I picked up the book, opened it to the middle to replace the photographs, and found a sheet of loose-leaf paper. Something compelled me to read it.

Abby

By the time I finished getting ready, Ben was sitting on the couch, channel surfing the television. I sat down beside him, hugging myself to his chest. He draped an arm around me and lightly kissed my lips.

"Hello." He smiled at me.

"Hi." We sat gazing at each other for a few seconds and then I stood up, "Did you check on the lasagna?"

"Yeah. It's looking pretty good. Only a few more minutes."

"Then I'm going to make a salad and get the bread ready to go in the oven. Do you want a glass of wine?"

"Do you have beer? Oh, wait, you don't like beer, do you?"

"I don't, but you do." I grabbed one out of the fridge and tossed it to him, then began working on the salad.

"Thanks." He opened the bottle and took a long swig, staring at the television. Something told me he wasn't really watching it. No one was *that* interested in Downy Fabric Softener.

"How was your day?" I tried. He was never this quiet. Something was wrong.

"It was pretty rough. I'm glad to be here now, though." There was no animation in his voice. And he didn't elaborate.

"What happened?" I finally asked, trying to keep the concern in my voice to a minimum. Knowing him, he'd try to hide whatever was really bothering him so I wouldn't worry. I didn't want to give him any excuse to "protect" me.

"It's all these issues with the finances. My accountant is worried about the economy and he's been cracking down on spending. It's frustrating trying to build the business and not having the resources to do it."

"It sounds like he's looking out for you, making sure the complex doesn't fail because of overspending."

"He is and that's why I hired him. It was just a long day."

The oven timer dinged, so I took the lasagna out and put the loaf of garlic bread in. "Dinner will be ready, soon. I'm sorry you had such a rough day."

"It's alright." He reached his hand out towards me and smiled. "Being near you helps, though. Come sit with me."

I went back to the couch and sat as close to him as I could. He draped his arm around me like before and we just sat there holding each other. His silence and downhearted expression told me the situation with his business was worse than he'd acknowledged. I felt helpless. I knew he needed something from me, but had no idea what. He seemed to be on the verge of speaking, but the timer went off again and he appeared glad for the excuse not to talk.

Twenty minutes later, he cleaned the last morsel off his plate and helped me bring the dishes to the sink. "That was delicious. I didn't know you could cook."

"I can't really. My mother gave me the recipe. I figured after your breakfast feast yesterday I should try a little harder."

"Does that have anything to do with this?" He pulled a piece of paper from his pocket and held it towards me.

I recognized it immediately and grew strangely angry with him. It wasn't his fault the idiotic thing kept coming back to taunt me, but still, my blood began to boil as I spat out, "Where did you get that?"

"I found it tucked inside one of those books on your coffee table, while you were getting ready. I was bored and thought I would try reading what you read. But I have to admit, this was much more entertaining." His smile did not soothe me the way it usually did, instead, it only provoked my anger further.

"Look, I wrote that when I was fifteen. It was a stupid class assignment. I only have it because Ashley found it and gave it to me on my birthday." I tried to keep my voice steady, but I don't think I succeeded.

He ignored my tone, "You haven't checked anything off."

"I've done a few of the things, but like I said, it's stupid. A fifteen-year old has no idea what life is going to be like at twenty-five."

"You don't want to do this stuff anymore?"

I shrugged, "Some of it, I guess."

"Then why don't we do it?"

"What do you mean?" I knew what he meant.

"Let's cross everything off. You've still got time before you turn twenty-six. We'll change the title to 'Twenty-Five Things I'd Like to Accomplish at Age Twenty-Five.'" He placed extra emphasis on the words 'like' and 'at'.

"You're crazy."

"And *you* are scared."

He was right. I was scared, but I didn't exactly know why, or exactly what I was scared of. And that's when I realized the real reason I was upset. Not because he reminded me of all the things I hadn't accomplished, but because looking at that list, I realized why I'd been alone for so long. Why would anyone want to be with a girl who couldn't bring herself to actually live the life she wanted? How much longer would he be able to stand being around me?

I didn't answer him, so he got up from the table and went into my bedroom. He came back with a pen in his hand. He skipped the first two items and read, "Number three: Get my journalism degree. Well, we can cross that one off." And he did.

"Which of the rest of these can you cross off?" He handed the paper to me and I sighed as I took it. Glancing down the page, I automatically ignored the first eight items.

"Number nine. I went to Disneyworld for spring break my sophomore year of college."

"Excellent." He offered me the pen, but I didn't take it, so he leaned over and made a slash through the ninth item. "What else?"

"Number ten, and number twenty-two, and number twenty-five. I got my first brand new car last year - the one you totaled, by the way," I smirked. "I took a photography class as an elective in high school, and I cut off all my hair into a really short pixie cut right after I graduated from college."

He crossed them off one at a time then pointed to number seventeen, "Why was giving blood something you wanted to accomplish?"

"My parents have done it twice a year for as long as I can remember, and always told us when we were growing up that when we were old enough, we could do it too, save someone's life with part of our own. But I've always been afraid of needles and blood, so the very thought of it made me sick. And then, right before I made this list, Anna went for the first time and she passed out. I've been chicken ever since, even though I've always wanted to do it."

"Well, then you will."

"I don't think I can."

"Don't worry, I'll go with you. I'll do it too. And I'll hold your hand the whole time, I promise."

"Maybe we should start with something else."

"Okay, it's your list. Which would you like to do first?"

I looked over the list and wanted to smack my fifteen year-old self for all of the crazy things I had written.

"We can't do any of them right now. Let's just forget about it."

He looked skeptical. "If that's what you really want."

"It is."

"Okay, fine, I'll drop it. But I think it could be fun." He took the paper off the table, folded it, and put it in his shirt pocket. "Just in case you change your mind," he said, noticing me watching him.

"Do you want dessert?" I asked, moving to the fridge, praying he'd really dropped the issue.

"I'd love some."

Chapter Twelve: Number 13

Abby

My new ring tone for Ben, "I'm Too Sexy," cut into the silent serenity of my kitchen and I nearly hit my head on the ceiling jumping in surprise. The spatula in my hand flew to the ground, splattering sauce all over my recently cleaned floor and stove. *What's he calling now for?* I wondered, *he's not supposed to be coming over until after dinner.*

"I hope you're calling to tell me you plan on spending the evening scrubbing up the mess you just made," I answered.

"Huh?"

"The phone startled me and caused marinara to defile my spotless kitchen."

"Your obsession with the cleanliness of your kitchen is very weird, especially since it's the only room of the apartment you ever clean."

"Hey, my home is very clean. I vacuumed yesterday."

"Of course, my mistake. Hey, I called for a reason, don't distract me."

"Sorry. What's up?" Retrieving the spatula, I dropped it in the sink and pulled a clean one out of the utensil drawer to continue stirring.

"I need you to come outside."

"Are you here?"

"Yes, come outside."

"Why don't you come in? I'm making spaghetti."

"Turn off the stove, get your keys, and come outside right now!"

"You are unusually obstinate today, Benjamin."

"Just get your butt out here, Abigail." He hung up and I quickly did as I was told. I moved the pan of sauce to a cool burner, fished around in my purse for my keys, and headed out the door.

Bounding down the stairs, I scanned the parking lot for Ben's car, but didn't see it anywhere. I heard a motorcycle zooming around the building, but I still didn't see Ben. I was about to call him when the shiny red bike making all the noise turned the corner and stopped right in front of me. The rider put the kickstand in place and swung his leg around, taking his helmet off as he stood.

"Ben, what are you doing? What are you thinking? When did you get that? Wait - is it even yours?" I couldn't feel the expression on my face, but it couldn't have been good, because the smile on his faded almost instantly.

"Yes, it's mine. My parents and Tracey got it for me for my birthday. And I like it. It's fun."

"Your parents got you that for your birthday? That's crazy. My parents got me a coffee maker for my birthday." We stood there silent for several minutes, arms folded across our chests, staring at each other. I could tell I was not reacting very well, or at least not the way he wanted me to. I don't know why it bothered me so much. I guess it just seemed extravagant. Unfair, maybe. *What's wrong with me? Why should it upset me that his parents can afford such a nice gift?*

"I'm sorry, that last thing came out a little harsher than I intended. It's a really nice bike. You're lucky your parents have such good taste." His expression softened as my bitterness did and he took a step towards me.

"Wanna go for a ride?"

"On that? Are you crazy?"

"Come on, it'll be fun and I won't let anything happen to you. And look," he stepped to the bike and came back with a dark blue helmet, "Tracey got me an extra helmet."

I took it and looked from the bike to Ben and back to the bike. I knew the only way to experience the exhilaration of flying through the streets with the wind chasing me was to get on the motorcycle, but I was absolutely terrified. Ben didn't say anything else, just got back on and waited.

Over the past few months I'd experienced a life I never knew was possible. He made my stomach turn cartwheels and my heart ached when we were apart. He held my hand and listened patiently when I explained why sex wasn't an option. If I could open myself up to him in that way, why couldn't I get on the back of the motorcycle and experience that with him, too?

"You are too young to be so afraid," he said softly.

He was right.

I pulled the helmet over my head and jumped onto the bike behind him. I clutched him around the waist and he took off, soaring out of the parking lot.

Instantly, my hold on him tightened and my eyes squeezed shut, but after a few minutes, I began to pay attention. The air whipped past us and I wished the helmet were unnecessary: I wanted to experience the wind blowing violently through my hair. I could feel every muscle in Ben's back as he swerved in and out of traffic. My eyes opened of their own volition, adrenaline pumped through my veins, and the speed really was exhilarating.

Looking to my left, the cars passing in the opposite direction seemed to slow down in response to our presence, and to my right, house and store fronts came into sharp focus; all fear drained from my head and I loosened my hold on Ben's waist, but tightened my legs around the bike. Cautiously, I let my hands fall free and gave in to the ride. Splaying my fingers apart, I relished in the air soaring through my skin.

We continued racing through the city for another twenty minutes or so, but it seemed like only a few seconds before we arrived at my apartment. I gripped the back of his jacket to steady myself while he shut the engine off and put the kickstand into place. He got off first and easily lifted me off the bike. We removed our helmets simultaneously; he was grinning ear to ear so irresistibly I grabbed his face with both hands and kissed him.

"I guess that's your way of saying you liked it?"

"Oh, yeah. I really did."

"Good. I hope this teaches you to never doubt me again." We laughed and he pulled me into a tight hug.

Ben

Abby shared her spaghetti with me and after we were both finished, I helped her with the dishes. I couldn't decide the best way to bring up the offer I wanted to make. I wasn't sure how she'd react. Maybe it was too soon. But, I knew I'd regret not asking. And I didn't really think she'd say no.

The last of the suds slid down the drain, Abby handed me a towel, and I dried the plates. When I couldn't stall with the dishes any longer, I started with the obvious. "My birthday is this Friday."

"I know. The big two-eight. You're getting to be an old man, Mr. Harris," she teased.

I fixed my eyes on her as she moved about piling the dishes into the cabinet and packing up the leftovers. She buzzed past me on her way to the living room and I reached out and grabbed her around the waist, pulling her into a quick hug before holding her out at arms length.

"Matt, Trish, myself and some other people usually go down to Florida for a couple of days every summer and Matt has a client who's agreed to lend us his house this weekend…"

"You should definitely go and have fun," she interrupted. "You and I can do something to celebrate when you get back." Slipping out of my hands, she opened the fridge and kept her back to me as I continued.

"That's not what I was going to say. I was going to ask if you'd like to go down to Florida with us for the weekend, to celebrate my birthday."

She spun around, the fridge door still open, and looked straight into my eyes. Crease lines formed on her forehead, but I couldn't tell if she was confused, surprised, or scared. It might have been a little of each.

"Oh." She paused and shut the door slowly, then leaned back against it. Her eyes fell to the floor. "I don't know."

I don't know what I'd been expecting, but it wasn't that. *I don't know? I ask her to go away with me for the weekend and that's her only response? Isn't four months together enough for her to know what she wants?*

"You don't know? What kind of answer is that?"

She shrugged. "The kind you give when you need to think for a few minutes."

"I don't get it, what do you need to think about? Why does it always seem like I'm begging my girlfriend to spend time with me?"

"That's incredibly unfair, Ben. I love spending time with you. It's not about that and you know it."

"Do you want to go or not?"

"I don't know," she said firmly, crossing her arms across her chest. I clenched my jaw and tried to stay calm. We stood on opposite sides of the kitchen, staring at each other. She didn't speak again and I didn't know what else to say.

"Fine." Pulling my keys out of my pocket, I walked past her and opened the door to leave.

"Where the hell are you going?" She grabbed my arm.

"Home."

"I find it very interesting that you're allowed to go home in the middle of an argument but I'm not allowed a few minutes to gather my thoughts. So fine. You wanna leave, leave. Makes my decision really easy." She dropped my arm and turned to walk into her bedroom, but I crossed in front of her and blocked the opening.

"I'm sorry. For trying to leave. You're right, I overreacted. I just don't understand what you're thinking sometimes. To me it sounds like an easy decision, who doesn't want to go and hang out on the beach in Florida?"

"Hanging out on the beach sounds great, but you haven't given me any details. Do I need to take Friday or Monday off work? Are we flying or driving? I can't exactly afford a last minute plane ticket. And sleeping arrangements…"

"We'll leave after you get off on Friday and come back Monday morning. We'll fly, I'll buy the tickets."

"Ben, no."

"Why not?"

"It's your birthday and you're going to pay? I don't think so."

"I planned the trip and I'm inviting you. Besides it's practically free if I use the points from my credit card."

"It just doesn't feel right. You pay for everything."

"I'm the guy and I have the money to pay. I don't see why it bothers you."

"Of course you don't." She rolled her eyes and pushed past me into the bedroom.

"Hey, what's that supposed to mean?" I followed and sat beside her on the bed.

"Nothing, it means nothing. I'm sorry, forget I said it. You didn't answer the last question."

"Which one?"

"Sleeping arrangements."

"Oh. Well, it's a big house. You can have your own room, or you can share a room with Trish, or…"

"Or with you?"

"Yeah."

"Ben…"

"No funny business. But really it's your decision. The trip isn't about sex or trying to convince you to change your mind, I don't want you to ever think that. I just want to spend some time with you and my friends away from work and responsibility and life."

"That does sound appealing."

"Yeah, so what do you think?" I took her hand and she scooted closer to me on the bed, resting her head against my shoulder.

"I think I want to go, but let me see if I can get off work on Monday."

"Really?"

"Yeah."

The silence that fell around us this time was peaceful, comfortable. I wrapped my arm around her shoulder and we sat together in quiet contemplation for several minutes until Abby lifted her head and kissed my cheek.

"What do you want for your birthday?" she asked.

"World peace," I answered. She laughed and draped her arms around my neck, pulling my face to hers for a deep kiss. She continued laughing when she pulled away. I didn't think it was particularly funny, but I wasn't going to argue with anything that made her laugh like that.

Chapter Thirteen: Number 18 and Number 20

Ben

"Ben! Snap out of it! Did you hear me?" Abby waved her hand in front of my face, jolting me from my stupor.

"Oh, I'm sorry. What did you say?"

"I said, 'Happy birthday.' Sorry I didn't say it earlier, but I got caught up in the excitement of the trip." She unbuckled her seat belt and pulled her tray table down to set a notebook on it.

"Oh, that's okay." I closed my eyes and leaned back in the seat.

"Hey," she touched my arm, "what's wrong?"

I tried to lighten my grip on the armrests, but my brain and hands seemed to be having communication issues. Finally, I gave up trying and decided to answer her question, even if it did make me look like a wuss. "I don't like flying," I whispered.

I expected her to laugh, but she didn't. Instead she took my face in both hands and turned it so I was looking straight into her eyes. "There's nothing to be afraid of," she said. "Think about the thing in life that makes you happiest." She tilted her head and rested her forehead on mine. I closed my eyes again.

The thing that makes me happiest? A couple of months ago it would've been the complex, or playing softball. But today, at this moment, it's you. Your smile and your laugh and your touch. Everything about you makes me happy.

She pried my fingers off the armrests and kissed my hands before interweaving them with hers. She spoke softly about her day at work and the ideas she wanted to develop into articles to turn in to the editor and how frustrating it was to be stuck in the mailroom.

We were on the ground before I knew it.

Matt and Trish were waiting at the house for us when we arrived. Trish showed Abby around while I went to help Matt with the grill.

"Happy birthday, man," he said as I stepped onto the deck.

"Hey. Thanks." I grabbed a pair of tongs and flipped a steak.

"How was the flight?" he asked.

"Oh, it was fine, good actually."

"What's the plan for the weekend? You sounded like you had some stuff up your sleeve when we talked last week."

"For tomorrow I thought we'd go scuba diving."

"Sounds like fun."

"Yeah, but hey, I need you to do me a favor."

"What's that?"

"I need you to say it's your idea, that you planned it and hired the instructor."

"Why?"

"I'm trying to surprise Abby."

He flipped another steak before stepping back from the grill and leaning against the fence railing. Crossing his arms across his chest, his eyebrows knit together and he looked at me, puzzled. "That doesn't make any sense, Ben."

"I know."

"Care to explain?"

"Nope. Will you just do it? It can be your birthday gift to me."

"So I can take Trish to the Red Sox season opener then?"

"You got me Red Sox tickets for my birthday?! Holy shit, man, no, you can't take Trish!"

"Fine, but then taking credit for scuba is going to be your Christmas gift." Straightening up, he returned his attention to the food.

"That's fine with me. I'm pretty sure you didn't get me anything for Christmas last year anyways."

Matt added a couple of hamburgers to the grill just as Trish and Abby joined us. They sat on wicker furniture and drank lemonade while Matt and I finished cooking.

After dinner, Trish brought out a chocolate cake and forced everyone to sing 'Happy Birthday.' Abby's clear, sparkling voice carried high above the others as she sang the cheesy song. I couldn't take my eyes off her. The moonlight danced in her eyes and her wavy brown hair swung across her shoulders as she burst out the chorus.

At the end of the song, she hugged me around the neck and I caught a whiff of her sweet vanilla scent. I squeezed her and a heavy weight bore into my chest. *Oh my God. I'm in love with her.* I couldn't believe it. We'd been doing this slow dance of emotions and feelings and tiptoeing around all the serious issues, but there I was, completely and utterly in love with her. She released me and motioned to the cake.

"Make a wish and blow out the candles!"

I took a second and tried to form the wish in my head. *I don't think she loves me yet, but she's on her way. I don't want to push her. She needs things to go slow, I don't want to scare her off by telling her how I feel if she doesn't feel the same way. But I wish there was a way to make her feel about me the way I feel about her.* I kissed her cheek, then blew out the twenty-eight candles.

"So, Abigail," Matt began as Trish cut into the cake and handed out the slices, "you're still around, huh? You haven't realized what a horrible guy you've got there?"

"I guess I'm just a glutton for punishment," she laughed, shaking her head. My mouth stretched into a wide smile, I loved seeing her joking around with Matt.

"You must be," Trish chimed in, "look at that outfit! Did he get dressed in the dark this morning?"

"I think so. I tried to tell him before we got on the plane that I was embarrassed to be seen with him, but he didn't take the hint." Abby tugged on the sleeve of my shirt before snatching my Sox cap off and planting a kiss on my forehead.

"Hey!" I caught her wrist and took the cap back. "I think you picked this outfit out!" Instead of putting the cap back on, I dropped it on her head, it fell down over her eyes and she stumbled back, groping around like a blind woman.

"Now that's a good look!" Trish laughed.

"We all know Ben's got a big head," Matt added.

"Hey, okay, okay! Enough roasting. It's still my birthday, you're supposed to be nice to me!" I grabbed Abby's wandering hands and pulled her into my lap. Pushing the baseball cap up, I found her eyes and let the warmth shining out of them fill me.

"You're right. We'll all be nice to you for another, um..." she took my hand and turned my wrist so she could look at my watch, "two hours."

"So what, at midnight it's back to Ben trashing?"

"Exactly!"

We both chuckled, but the absence of Matt and Trish's laughter caused me to look around for them. They weren't there.

"Hey! Where'd they go?" I asked. Abby started and looked around, too.

"I don't know." She turned back to me and her smile faded, replaced by a look of softness and, I dared to hope, love. She placed her palm on my cheek and made eye contact.

I pulled her closer and whispered in her ear, "Maybe they thought we needed a little privacy."

"Maybe." She smiled and bent her head towards mine. I met her halfway and we spent the next fifteen minutes kissing, listening to the waves crashing in the background. When she finally broke away, her face was serious and she stood up.

"Ben, we need to talk about sleeping arrangements while we're here."

"Okay."

"Um, Trish showed me this really cute blue room and my stuff is there."

"Okay."

"I don't think we should share a room."

"Okay."

"It's not that I don't want to fall asleep and wake up in your arms, because I really do."

"Okay."

"And it's not that I don't trust you to behave or myself to behave or anything like that. I just don't think it's a good idea to create the temptation."

"Okay."

"Could you say something else besides 'okay'?"

"What do you want me to say? I told you before we came that whatever you wanted to do was fine. I'm okay with your decision. You're probably right, anyways. No need to put ourselves in that situation."

She smiled and sat on my lap again. "Where did you come from?"

"What do you mean?"

"You're perfect. Absolutely perfect. I don't understand how you exist or why you're with me."

"Remember on the plane this afternoon when you told me to think about what makes me the happiest?"

"Yeah."

"Do you know what I thought about?"

"No."

"You. I thought about you. That's why I'm with you, because you make me happy."

"You make me happy, too."

We made our way into the house soon after that and I walked her to her room. We kissed and said goodnight, then I moved down the hall. She waited until I opened my door before closing hers. As it shut I whispered, "I love you."

Abby

When I walked downstairs the next morning Ben, Matt, and Trish were already sitting around the kitchen table eating breakfast. I grabbed a cup of coffee, poured myself a bowl of cereal, and sat down to eat when Matt addressed us.

"Okay friends. The first thing on the agenda today is scuba diving! I've got an instructor meeting us on the beach in an hour."

"I've always wanted to scuba dive!" I told Ben.

"I guess it's your lucky day." He tossed a glance at Matt then finished his food. I drank the dregs of my cereal quickly and ran back to my room to put on a swimsuit and sunscreen.

I couldn't believe how clear and blue the water was. We practiced for an hour in shallow water before moving further off shore. We saw fish of every size and color, seahorses, coral reefs, even a few jellyfish. Ben and I posed for a photo as a sea turtle the size of my head swam by us. We stayed in the water until well past lunchtime.

After scuba diving, Trish and I laid on the beach while the boys raced around on jet skis.

"Things seem to be going really well with you and Ben," Trish said.

"Yeah, I guess. I love spending time with him."

"Well, he is head over heels for you."

"What?" I could feel my face burning and knew it wasn't from the sun.

"Don't pretend you don't see the way he looks at you." She laughed at my dumbfounded expression and leaned towards me, propping herself up on her elbow. "And you know you guys don't have to keep up the pretense of separate rooms, Matt and I don't care."

"Oh, well we, um, I mean…"

She didn't pay attention to my embarrassment. "I'll bet the sex is just fantastic. Ben has that whole 'Big Strong Man' persona, but he's so sweet and sentimental at the same time, I can only imagine what that translates to in bed."

"I wouldn't know," I said warily. "We haven't had sex."

Her jaw dropped and she sat momentarily silenced. "Why not?" she eventually asked.

"I'm waiting until marriage and Ben respects that."

"Wow. That's actually really sweet. I can't say I'd be able to do that, though. I can't imagine the kind of self-control you must have."

"I'm not going to lie, it isn't easy. I mean, just look at him." The guys started walking up the beach and Ben's shirtless torso glistened in the sun, literally glistened, every muscle taut and firm. Trish and I were still laughing when the men joined us. I sat up so there was room on my towel for Ben and he kissed my shoulder as he plopped down beside me. I imagined his conversation with Matt was very different than mine with Trish.

Ben

"You girls having fun?" I asked, sitting on Abby's towel and kissing her tanned skin. It was hot from the sun and perfect against my lips. Her smile as she scooted over to give me more room tugged at my heart. She was definitely right about separate rooms. The temptation would have been too much for me.

"We're having a blast." Trish said as Matt took a seat on her towel.

The four of us sat on the beach for a while, talking and joking, until Matt decided he wanted to head back to the house for a nap.

"I'm getting sleepy, too, and I want to shower. I think I'll go with you," Abby said, standing and brushing the sand off her legs. Her slender, smooth, tan legs. "You coming?" she asked, turning her eyes to me.

"Um, no, I'm going to stay out here for a while longer," I answered.

"Me, too," Trish added.

"Okay, see you in a bit." Abby kissed my cheek before following after Matt. I watched her leave - I couldn't help myself. Why the hell did she have to wear a bikini?

When I finally tore my eyes away, I noticed Trish grinning at me.

"What?"

"Nothing." She lay back on her towel and pushed her sunglasses down over her eyes.

"Trish…"

"So, Abby told me that she's, um, *waiting*."

Great. The groan escaped my lips before I could stop it. I did not want to have that conversation.

"Don't be like that, I think it's really sweet."

"I didn't say anything."

"No, but your grunt said it all."

"What do you want me to say, Trish? That it sucks? Yeah, it sucks."

"From the way you were just looking at her I'd call that the understatement of the year."

"I'm dealing with it." I stretched out on Abby's towel and covered my eyes with my palm. I wanted to shut out the rest of the world, forget where I was, and forget I'd agreed to wait for her.

"I'm sure."

"Don't tell Matt."

"Why not?"

"You know why not. He learns Abby and I aren't sleeping together and I'll never hear the end of it."

"I won't say anything to him. But I think you underestimate him. And for the record, I think what you are doing for her is amazing. Don't forget that." Her fingers squeezed my arm and I dropped my hand to turn and look at her.

"Thanks, Trish."

"You're welcome."

Abby

On Sunday morning, Ben knocked on my room and carried in a tray of french toast and orange juice.

"No one's ever brought me breakfast in bed before!" I said as he placed the tray in my lap and kissed my cheek.

"I have to admit, I have an ulterior motive."

"Oh really? What's that?"

"I want to butter you up so you'll agree to come surfing with us today."

"Surfing? Seriously? I don't know how to surf."

"But I do, and I'm a great teacher. Matt has an extra board you can use."

"Sure, why not? It's still your birthday weekend. But I'm warning you, I'm going to be terrible at it."

"Well, yeah, with that attitude!" He grinned and kissed my cheek again before moving to the door. "Enjoy your breakfast and get ready, we're heading to the beach in an hour."

It took two hours in the water to learn the basics. And another two hours before I was able to pull myself on the board and paddle and yet another before I could actually stand. The longest I rode a wave was about ten seconds, but it didn't matter. Ben and I had a blast and he really was a good teacher. He was incredibly patient with me and didn't seem to mind when I asked him to demonstrate over and over again. I probably didn't need him to show me the moves as often as I asked, but I just loved watching him - he was graceful and manly, and unbelievably sexy.

We finally left the water around five and joined Matt and Trish on the beach, where they had started a bonfire. We devoured hamburgers and hotdogs for dinner and s'mores for dessert while drying ourselves by the blazing logs. After dinner, we found a secluded spot and watched the sunset together, curled beneath a blanket.

We went back to the house around midnight. Matt and Trish headed straight for their room, Ben kissed me, and went to his. I got ready for bed, brushing my teeth, putting on a pair of pajamas, and washing my face. After pulling my hair into a ponytail, I grabbed Ben's birthday gift out of my suitcase and walked down the hall to his room. I knocked on the door and waited a few seconds. He answered, wearing nothing but a pair of boxers. A knot rose in my throat.

"Abby, you okay?"

"Yeah. Can we talk for a minute?"

"Sure, um, hold on a sec." He closed the door and came back a minute later wearing a pair of flannel pants and an old baseball jersey. He stepped aside and motioned me in. I took a deep breath and entered, clutching his gift to my chest and taking a seat on the edge of his bed. He sat beside me.

"What's up?" His eyes darted to the present.

"Thank you for this weekend, I had an amazing time."

"You're welcome. I'm glad. I had a good time, too. And so did Matt and Trish. Trish is thankful I finally have a girlfriend she can talk to." He laughed, leaned over, and kissed me on the cheek. I loved when he did that.

"I want to say something to you, but I'm probably going to do a bad job, so just wait until I finish before you say anything, okay?" I turned so I could face him comfortably, folding my legs underneath me. He copied my stance and placed both hands on my knees. I absolutely loved how he always had to touch me whenever we were within reach of each other.

"Okay," he frowned at my serious tone, but seemed content to let me speak.

"I know I'm not an easy person to get to know. I know I make this relationship hard on you. I don't do it on purpose, I swear, it's just, I never expected a guy like you to want a girl like me, and part of me keeps thinking we're going to say goodbye one day and I'll never hear from you again."

He didn't move a muscle, but stared me intently in the eye.

"You've done nothing to deserve that kind of thinking. You've always treated me with respect, you've always let me know you care about me, and I'm going to stop doubting you. I'm going to stop doubting this." I placed my hand on his heart, then moved it to my own.

He leaned in to kiss me, probably thinking I was finished, but I stopped him.

"Wait, one more thing." I held out his present. "I didn't forget to get you a gift, I was just waiting for the right time to give it to you."

He took the package from my hands and carefully removed the wrapping paper. A wooden box with detailed flowers carved onto the lid emerged. Ben slid his fingers over the walnut, lingering on the intricate 'B' in the center of the box.

"My grandfather made it for me," I explained. "He liked to make little boxes like that one, and shelves, and tiny wooden animals. He carved my initial on top and gave it to me for my sixteenth birthday. He passed away before my next one."

He looked truly moved, every muscle in his face relaxed as he examined the intricate details. Barely lifting his eyes from the box to look at me, he whispered, "I can't take this, Abby." He tried to return it to me, but I pushed his hand back.

"I really want you to have it. It's a sign of my good faith in you. But your real gift is inside. It's kind of cheesy and cliché, but I hope you like it."

He lifted the lid and pulled out a shiny silver key.

"Before you jump to any conclusions, I want you to know this doesn't change what I told you last month."

He held the key up to the light. "What does this open?"

"My apartment. I want my life to be completely open to you. I think for now that starts with my home. I want to come home and find you waiting for me. Obviously, it's not an invitation to move in or anything, but at least this way, you won't have to wait for me outside the door if you get there before me." Taking in a deep breath, I turned my eyes down and looked at the bedspread. His finger caressed my cheek then tilted my chin up until we were looking into each other's eyes. *Those eyes will be the death of me.*

"This is exactly what I wanted," he said tenderly.

I didn't stop him when he leaned in again to kiss me.

Chapter Fourteen: Number 17

Abby

"This is so damn frustrating!" Crumpling my boss's latest rejection note, I fell onto the couch and pulled a throw pillow over my face to muffle my dejected screams. The cushions sagged as Ben sat beside me and began stroking my hair. He didn't speak; there wasn't anything he could say to make me feel better.

Since my birthday I'd turned in at least one article every two weeks, but still had no luck getting published. I watched as assignments were handed out to writers new to the magazine, unable to figure out why they were chosen over me. My mother suggested revamping some of the articles that reviewed well in college, but after looking through them I realized there wasn't even a concept I could use in a fashion magazine.

My brother, Derek, suggested I send the ones my boss rejected to other magazines, and it was the best suggestion anyone offered, so I spent the first week or so of August carefully editing and arranging the articles into packages I mailed out to every fashion magazine in the country. I also created a few political pieces I sent to the *New York Times*, *Time Magazine*, and some local newspapers. Excitement about these new prospects consumed me for approximately a week.

Then the rejection letters and emails began pouring in. Ben held my hand as I cried and read each one, but he continued to encourage me, "Write from your heart. You have beautiful things to say to the world."

That day, as I screamed into the pillow, his words hit me. *Write from your heart.* That's definitely not how I'd been approaching the situation. I'd been writing what I thought other people wanted to read, not what I wanted to write, or even what I would want to read. Why would anyone else want to read it if I didn't want to read it?

I sat up and gave Ben a hug, silently thanking him for his support, and he squeezed back. A wave of peace filtered through my brain. I knew the problem now, I just needed to relax and let the solution find its way to me.

Ben

My accountant hounded me on a daily basis about the economy. He planned weekly meetings to go over the books and brought in dozens of financial planners. Every day he asked me to reconsider the vans and the operating hours. Every day I gave him the same answer: "Hell no."

Even though Steve refused to give up on what he thought was the best plan for pulling ICS out of the economic sand trap, he was open to trying other strategies. I brought in marketing and advertising experts and we continued our efforts to increase exposure for the bar. I hired a yoga instructor to boost gym membership and was always on the lookout for new investors.

"You realize the problems with these additions, right, Ben?" he asked one afternoon.

"What?"

"Right now, they're costing you money, but not bringing anything in. We're sinking further into the abyss."

"Why do you have to be so negative?" I laughed, but he continued looking at me gravely. "Okay, fine. What do you propose we do?"

"Well…"

"Other than getting rid of the vans and cutting back the hours," I interrupted before he could make the same suggestion again.

"Other than that, we can look into changing our distributors, see if we can't get supplies at better deals, but if you won't let me nix the vans and hours, other drastic measures are going to have to be taken."

"Like what?"

"Like cutting back on payroll."

"I'm not giving out paycuts."

"That's not what I meant."

"What do you mean?"

"I mean either you're going to have to lay a couple of people off or you're going to have to cut back your employees' hours."

"Seriously, Steve, those are my options? Get rid of the vans, cut back the operating hours, or fire my employees? What if I bring on some more investors?"

"Investors expect a return on their investment. The complex just can't give anything back right now."

I sank into my chair and tried to massage away the headache forming in my temples. "Give me a week to think about it. I'll go over all the performance reviews from last month. But if I can't find anyone who deserves to be let go, then we're going back to the drawing board."

He tried one last time, "If you would just let me shut down the vans…"

"I know! I know, God, I know. But that means at least four people are out of a job. Just give me a week and I'll let you know what I want to do."

"You have to make cuts, Ben. I know it sucks, but you have to if you want to keep ICS open." He left the latest financial report on my desk and walked out of the office. I wanted to throw my chair at him.

Abby

We both tried our hardest not to let our job problems affect our growing relationship, but couldn't prevent it happening. Sometimes he would miss out on plans we had with Matt and Trish because of unexpected meetings and sometimes he'd come over and I wouldn't say a word to him because I was busy writing while an idea was fresh on my brain.

It was the four-month itch. If there is such a thing. We were drowning. Both of us fatigued and despondent, we didn't put as much energy into the other as we once did. I worried everything had been too perfect, so we were destined for heartbreak and misery. But every time this thought crept into my head, I pushed it aside and remembered what I said our last night in Florida. I would not doubt our relationship anymore.

He noticed the itch too.

"We've got to get out of this funk!" he exclaimed one night after a silent dinner. "I know this isn't us."

I went over and sat in his lap, wrapped my arm around his shoulder, and rested my cheek against his, carefully massaging the knots in his neck.

"You're right. We've both been stressed. We need to do something fun together."

"That's exactly it! I know what we need to do. Can you get off work early tomorrow?"

"I don't think so, but I'll check with my boss. What do you have in mind?" Sliding off his lap and positioning myself behind his chair, I worked the tight muscles strenuously, hoping to give what little relief I could.

"There's a blood drive going on near my office. We can go down and donate together."

"A blood drive? That doesn't sound like fun at all, you know I can't give blood."

"I know you're too scared to even try. Come on, you've always wanted to do it."

"Is this about that stupid list? Because I told you I'm not interested in completing that thing." My hands fell to my sides as he turned in the chair to face me.

"It's about you facing your fears. You can meet me tomorrow at three at my office if you want, or you can live in fear. Your choice. 'Bye." He kissed my lips briefly and left the apartment before I could respond. I turned the idea over in my head, thinking about everything my parents told me about giving blood and how important it was to modern medicine.

Ben was right, as usual. He was always right. At first, it had been endearing; that day it was annoying.

I couldn't think about anything else the next day at work. To give or not to give… It shouldn't have been such a hard decision, but as I tried to engross myself in the subscription renewals on my desk, it kept creeping back up. The answer was never the same twice in a row. Finally, I pushed my work away and headed to the break room for coffee. I finished adding in a bit of skim milk when my cell phone started vibrating in my pocket, seeing the caller was Ben, I answered quietly.

"Hello, handsome."

"Hello, beautiful. Have you given any more thought to coming with me to the blood drive?"

Groaning, I slammed my mug down harder than I intended, spilling coffee all over the counter. "Damn it!"

"Geez, fine, you don't have to come."

"No, no, sorry. I spilled my coffee. I guess I'll come if I can convince my boss to let me off early." I crossed my fingers that Helen would desperately need me to remain in the office today.

"Great. I'll see you at three, then."

"We'll see. I can't guarantee she'll be cool with letting me off."

"I think you can convince her. See you later." He hung up and I went back to my desk.

At 2:45, I was in my car heading to Inner City Sports. Of course. I couldn't resist doing whatever he wanted.

At first, the nurse was hesitant about taking my blood. I looked so pale she thought I was sick. Ben explained my fear of needles, but she took my temperature and force-fed me a cookie just in case.

She took Ben's blood first, so I could see how simple it was, but I could only watch for a second before the stream of blood in the tubes attached to his arm made me nauseous. When she finished with him, he selected a neon pink band-aid, which made me smile after everything else he tried failed. He sipped a glass of orange juice and held my hand as the nurse prepped my arm.

The nurse pointed to a chair at the opposite side of the room. "Sir, I need you to move over there."

"If he's going over there, so am I," I hissed at her through clenched teeth. She looked taken aback at first, but Ben shrugged his shoulders at her and she chuckled.

"Alright, I won't make him move, but you need to relax your arm a little bit." Ben immediately switched hands and focused his eyes on me. I got lost in him and didn't even realize the nurse started. When she announced she was done, I gasped and broke our contact.

"I didn't feel anything!" They both laughed at me and she applied a matching pink band-aid to my arm while handing me a glass of juice.

"Sit here for a minute and rest. Don't stand up too quickly," the nurse instructed as she left the room. I could only giggle. I had no intention of standing up at the moment.

"You did it!" Ben whispered, kissing my forehead.

"Thanks to you. I don't know how you do it."

"Do what?" he asked.

"Get me to do things I normally would never do."

"You would've done this eventually."

"I don't think I would have," I sighed.

"I know you would've. You just needed someone to give you a little push."

"Or a big one."

"Okay, a big push." Ben brushed a few loose strands of hair off my face and tucked them behind my ear. A look of adoration shone from his blue-grey eyes. My heart felt full of… Full of… I don't know. Just full.

"Thank you for pushing me."

"You're welcome."

He returned to work when we left the blood drive and I went home. I locked myself in, blasted music from my stereo, and sat down at my desk. I wrote for the next three hours, only stopping when Ben came in with dinner.

"Nothing like Chinese food to get the blood flowing again," he called into my bedroom, setting a bag on the kitchen counter.

"I'll be out in just a minute." I printed the article and placed it in a folder.

It felt good. It felt right. *If I can't get this story published, I'll give up and look into other careers.*

Ben was already at the table opening containers of rice and noodles. I grabbed two pairs of chopsticks out of my utensil drawer, retrieved two plates from the cabinet, and joined him.

"Whatcha working on?" he asked, filling my plate with fried rice.

"Something from the heart."

Chapter Fifteen: Good News, Bad News

Abby

It was another exciting day in the mailroom. The day's "very important" project, putting together packets of information for potential advertisers, gave me a pass on subscription duty for once, *thank God.* The magazine employed a whole team dedicated to going out and meeting with companies and advertising executives, but it fell to me and the rest of the mailroom staff to mail out the hard copy of information before the meetings occurred.

The hours crawled by and even the strongest coffee in the office failed to perk my spirits. Every time I marked a company off my list, I got an email adding a new one. I pushed through it though, and by 12:30 optimism about my progress replaced the boredom threatening to send me to an early grave. I took lunch a half-hour earlier than normal as a reward.

When I got back to my desk, a post-it note resting atop my stack of envelopes greeted me. A momentary sense of dread pulsed through my head, but realizing it wasn't attached to the article I turned in the week before, I picked it up and read slowly:

Abigail, please come to my office when you get back - Helen.

I re-read it at least three times. Helen *never* asked me to come to her office. I couldn't decide if that meant good news or bad, but there was only one way to find out. I smoothed out my skirt and checked my reflection in a computer monitor, then turned and walked straight to her office.

I reached the door and hesitated, the nameplate in front of me, *Helen Watkins: Senior Editor*, caused another flash of anxiety. The door stood cracked open, so I timidly knocked and took a step inside. She spun around in her chair, the phone to her ear, and gestured for me to come in.

I took a seat in one of the stiff armchairs facing her desk and waited. Wiping my sweaty palms on my skirt, I tried to look casual, but it was difficult to get comfortable in the hard chair. The phone call only lasted another minute; when she hung up, she looked at me and smiled. I couldn't help but get my hopes up - her smile said "good news."

"Abigail, I read over the article you turned in recently." She stopped there and it took a few seconds before I realized she wanted me to respond.

"What did you think?"

"It was good."

"Really?" Goosebumps erupted on my arms and I resisted the urge to jump out of my seat and hug her.

"Yes. It showed a lot of potential. I sent it to our editor-in-chief in New York, and she liked it, too."

"Really?" *Stay calm, Abigail. Keep it together.*

"Yes, I'll work with you on editing it. We like the journal-ish style you've started with, but it needs to be tightened up a bit before publication. We want to put it in the big December holiday issue, so it has to be ready by the end of the month. Can you handle that?"

Oh screw it! "Absolutely! Oh my God! Thank you so much! This is the best news ever!"

"I want you to go ahead and begin working on a follow up piece. If we get good reader response and feedback, we'll want the second piece for the January issue. If all goes well, you'll have a series on your hands, titled *Facing Your Fears* by Abigail Bronsen. The first two articles will be an introduction to you and why you're writing this, along with the fears you're facing in your own life and then the series will be based on our readers and the fears they are facing. How does that sound?"

"Incredible! Helen, I can't thank you enough for this opportunity."

"No need. Here, I've made some comments on how to strengthen it," she handed me the folder I originally gave her with the article in it. I opened it while she spoke and found my pages covered with red ink and post-it notes.

She didn't notice my eyes widen in horror at the massacre of my work, but continued speaking, "I've also made comments on the number of words we want and it would be a good idea if you gave blood again sometime soon so we can get a photograph."

"I'm sorry, what?" I thought I misheard her.

"A photograph for the article. It will look great next to the title."

"Oh, of course. I hadn't thought about that. Um, I'll look at my schedule and let you know." *Well, I'll look at Ben's schedule. He's going to have to come with me again or I'll end up vomiting on the nurse.*

"Good. Let me know when you've re-written the article. We'll want to edit it as quickly as possible so that New York also has time to edit it before the mag goes to print." She started shuffling around papers on her desk, so I thought she was finished. I stood up to leave, prepared to continue my outbursts of gratitude.

"I'll have it done ASAP. Thank you so much, Helen."

"Sit back down, we aren't finished." She handed me several small stacks of paper. I took them and regained my seat. "These are releases and compensation agreements. You will need to sign over the first rights to the article to the magazine in order to be published. That's what this release is for. It outlines everything: you'll receive a byline credit for the article, but once it's published, *Intuition* has the ability to sell it to other magazines, publishers, etc." She referred me to the first mini-packet in my hands as she said this.

Flipping through the pages, I couldn't believe how much was involved in signing away the rights to your work. Still looking through the fine print, I realized she'd already moved on to packet number two. As she droned on my insides wrapped around each other and threatened to spill out.

Compensation.

Benefits.

Non-competition clause.

My head spun at each new document. Helen looked at me expectantly; my brain left with no idea of what she wanted to hear.

"Um, can I take these with me and have my lawyer look over them?" *Shit, I need to get a lawyer!*

She leaned back in her chair and studied me for a minute before grinning. "Smart girl. Of course. But I will need them signed before we can begin editing together."

"No problem. I just want to make sure I understand everything."

She stood up now and held out her hand to me. I shook it, then gathered up the folder and contracts.

"Congratulations, Abigail."

"Thank you."

I don't remember walking back to my station and sitting down, but the next thing I knew, I was there, crying uncontrollably into my hands. My heart beat so happily it was the only thing I could do. It took several minutes to pull myself together, but when I did, I immediately called my mother to tell her the good news. I also left messages for Anna, Ashley, and Derek. I wanted to call Ben next, but changed my mind. Picturing his sweet smile as I told him the good news, I decided to wait until I could share it with him in person.

I sent him a text instead: *Got great news today. Can't wait to see you!*

Happening to glance at my computer screen as I put my phone back in my purse, I noticed twenty new emails. Reluctantly, I got back to work, but smiled to myself, thinking *I may only have a few more months in this Godforsaken mailroom.*

* * * *

"Damn it!" Ben crushed his cell phone shut and hurled it at the wall as I walked through the front door.

Jumping back, my heart sped up as I watched it strike the brick and shatter into tiny pieces. Concern replaced anger in his gaze as he watched mine widen. I reached cautiously for his hand, but he wouldn't let me take it.

"Ben, what's wrong? What happened?"

He fell down on the couch and covered his eyes. Rubbing his temples, he ignored my pleas for information. Finally, not knowing what else to do, I made my way across the room and began collecting the shattered bits of cell phone.

"Just leave it, Abby." Bitterness cut into each word, he sounded like a completely different person. Picking up the remaining pieces and setting them on the coffee table, I cleared my throat and sat down in the recliner opposite him.

"Talk to me, Ben. What happened?"

"That was my accountant," he mumbled.

Oh no. "And?"

"And the complex is in trouble." His hand fell from his face and he briefly met my stare before looking down at the hardwood.

"What's going on?"

"There's been zero growth in the past couple of months and last month…" he stopped and covered his eyes again. I waited, but he didn't seem capable of continuing.

"Last month?" It only took a second to make the journey from the chair to the couch and take the seat beside him. I rubbed his back and massaged the muscles in his neck; they were knotted and tense, but his frame seemed to relax at my touch.

"Last month, we spent, well, I spent, more money than the complex brought in. A lot more. They're telling me that the only way to make up the deficit without increasing it is to either get rid of my employees' health care or lay some people off. And that will only put a band-aid on the problem, anyways. How do I make that decision?" A tear skimmed down his cheek and the moisture in his eyes reflected his pain as he searched my face for the answer.

"I don't know, Ben. I'm so sorry." Taking his head in my hands, I cradled it to my chest, rocking him back and forth. He wrapped his arms around my back and let loose a few sobs before trying to disconnect. I held onto him and he only resisted for a few seconds before lifting his head and pulling me even closer. Wiping away his tears, I stared into those gorgeous eyes and silently said a prayer for him. I didn't have a lot of practice with prayer, but hoped my sincerity would make up for lack of experience.

God, please help Ben. He needs you right now. He would be heartbroken if his business went under. Please, God.

As I brushed off the last tear, Ben caught hold of my wrist and kissed my hand. He kept his moist lips pressed into my palm for at least thirty seconds then began tickling my wrist with more kisses. His mouth continued up my arm and my body stiffened, but warmth spread through my veins.

Those lush lips persisted in their assault as he reached my sleeve, kissing my shoulder through the fabric of my shirt, turning the corner and nibbling on my neck. Each tender caress, each graze of his teeth against my skin increased the tempo of my heart. By the time he reached my mouth, my chest pounded so hard I expected it to explode.

His tongue met mine, and my fever rose. I entwined my fingers in his hair, holding him to me, afraid to lose this moment, afraid to lose him if I let go.

The hairs on my arm stood as his hands slid down the sides of my torso and reached around. My brain registered as they slipped underneath my shirt and lightly roamed over my skin, but instead of sending up a red flag, it silently urged me on. *Don't stop now, it only gets better.*

I listened, knowing better, but not caring, and continued to lavish his tongue with my own while massaging his scalp with my fingers. His hands brushed against the hooks on my bra and moved forward, following the cotton fabric to the cups in front. He hesitated, but my mouth was too busy in its gentle rhythm with his to speak, and his thumbs slowly tested the peaks of my breasts. My body trembled, but still he moved on, brushing against the fabric of the bra until my nipples were firm and poking through the cups. Heat coursed through my chest and stomach and pumped between my thighs. *Oh, God, yes…*

A guttural moan filled the air, and I don't know if it came from him or me, but his lips broke from mine and began a downward descent, past my neck and chest. Playfully biting at the shirt covering me, he kissed each protruding nipple.

Oh God. No, I can't. This can't keep going…

"Ben," I whispered, my breathing hitched, incapable of speaking louder.

I felt the vibration from his throat as he moaned in response to my voice. Faltering, a whimper escaped my lips. *Yes, keep going. Yes… No! No, stop it Abigail. You have to stop it.*

"Ben, please, you know I can't." I had to gulp for air in between each word. I couldn't seem to let go of him, to pull myself away. He didn't appear to hear me, his mouth still lingered on my chest.

"Ben. No!" It was harsh, I hated the way it sounded, but I had to stop him. If he went further, I wouldn't be able to stop myself. Immediately, his hands lost contact with my skin and his face turned away, sucking air into his lungs.

"I'm sorry." I scooted away from him, pulling my knees up and tucking them to my chest. I could still feel his fingers and mouth covering me with affection, and curling up was the only thing I could think to do to distance myself from our passion.

"You're sorry?" he asked incredulously, surprise lighting up his eyes. "What the hell do you have to be sorry for? I'm the jerk who was trying to, I mean, I know how you feel, and I know we can't… Agh!" he groaned in disgust and leapt from the couch, keeping his back to me.

"Abby, I think you should go home."

The words hit me like a slap on the face. He wanted me to leave? My cheeks burned and I fought back the tears threatening to roll down my cheeks. Shooting off the couch and out the door before he could say another word, I slammed it closed behind me.

How dare he! He told me he was different, that he wanted more from me than sex, but then this happens and he doesn't want me around anymore. Asshole. I was so angry I didn't even want to cry.

Before I reached my car I heard his front door open and running footsteps coming after me.

"Wait, Abigail! Please!" he yelled. "Abby, I'm sorry, that came out wrong." He grabbed my arm and spun me around. As if by reflex, my eyes found his. In the moonlight they were clear and blue, and sad. My rage threatened to slip away as those eyes pleaded with mine.

"I didn't want you to leave because I was mad at you, or because I wanted to end things, or because you don't want to sleep with me. I asked you to leave so I could cool down." Reaching for my hand, his expression softened even more. I didn't resist his fingers as they closed around mine. "I was afraid if you stayed, I would try again, and I don't want to pressure you, or force you into anything."

Relief flooded through me. I couldn't find words to speak, but managed to squeeze his hand in reassurance.

"Can I just have a little time to regain my self-control?" he beseeched.

My entire body relaxed, tension and anger slipped away. *He still wants me, he* is *different.* "Yes, of course. I'm sorry I overreacted."

"Stop apologizing," he scolded.

"Yes, sir," I replied.

He laughed, bringing the twinkle back to his eye.

"You know it's hard for me, too, right? I want you *that way* so badly I can't think straight when you touch me. But, it's just..."

"Hey, stop. I know it's not easy for you either. But there's no need for explanation. This decision, this part of you, is one of the things I like the most about you."

"Really?"

"Absolutely." He kissed me gently before taking a few steps back. "Hey, I almost forgot, didn't you have good news or something?"

"It can wait."

"No, tell me."

I couldn't bring myself to say the words. Not then. Not when his business was crumbling around him. It didn't seem fair. How could I expect him to be happy for my job success as his fell apart?

"Oh, it was nothing really. I got excited because, um," my mind searched for something that could be considered good news, "Trish and I are going to a concert next weekend. She got us tickets to see the Plain White T's."

"That sounds like fun. I'm glad you two are getting along."

"Yeah, she's great." We stood there for a few minutes, silent, unsure of what to say. He knew there was more I wasn't telling, I could see it in his eyes, but he didn't question me. Instead, he hugged me and kissed the top of my head.

"Goodnight, Abby. I…" he stopped short and turned his eyes down, "I'll call you tomorrow."

"Goodnight." *Why did he stop himself? What was he going to say? Was he going to tell me he loved me? Oh my God. I think he was. What if he had? Would I have been able to say it back? I don't know…*

Chapter Sixteen: Another Confession

Ben

"Yes!" I jumped from my seat and pumped my fist in the air as Drew tore the shit out of the ball and trotted around the bases, bringing in two other runners. Abby looked up from her book and raised her eyebrows.

"Sorry. Home run," I explained.

"It's okay, I'm used to your outbursts by now, I think." She laughed and turned her attention back to her book, shifting in her seat. But after another couple of minutes she closed and set it aside.

"Ben, I need to ask you something."

"Sure, babe, but can it wait a little bit? It's the top of the eighth and the Sox are winning." I didn't wait for her answer, just looked back to the game. Silence returned to the room.

At the end of the inning, she reached over and grabbed the remote, turning off the volume in one swift move.

"Hey! Just one more inning!"

"I know, I'm sorry." She did look sorry, hanging her head and turning the remote over in her hand. When she brought her head up, her eyes found mine and pleaded with me.

"What? What is it? Are you okay?" I grabbed her hands and moved closer to her on the couch.

"Ben, how many women have you slept with?"

Whoa. I was not expecting that. Holy shit. I can't answer that. She doesn't want to know. Why would she ask me that? I dropped her hands and faced the television, trying to figure out how to answer the question both honestly and painlessly. I realized after a while that the game was over and I couldn't stall any longer. Turning off the TV, I twisted to face her.

"Are you sure you want to know?"

"I think I need to know."

Shit. I took her left hand and turned it palm up, stroking the soft pads of her fingertips. "No matter what I say, you need to know that my past, my history, doesn't change anything about us." *At least it shouldn't. It doesn't for me. Please, don't let it change anything for her.*

Her face lost all color and she flipped her hand over to grip my fingers. "Oh God, is it that many?"

I tried to laugh, to smile, but it came out all wrong and the trepidation on her face deepened.

"I don't think it's a lot, but I think you're going to think it is."

She gulped and straightened her back. Her eyes never left my face. "I can handle it."

Can you? Really? I frowned and looked down at the couch. I really, really didn't want to answer, but she waited for me, her fingers tightening around mine with each passing second. I took a deep breath.

"Five," I mumbled, still refusing to meet her eye. Her grip loosened and she sighed, putting her free hand on my cheek. I finally looked up. She was smiling.

"That's not a lot at all. Can I ask who?"

Who? The number isn't enough for her? Now she wants to know who? I don't get it. I don't want to hurt her; it would kill me to think about her sleeping with other guys. "Abby, I don't think this is a road you want to go down."

"I need to know. I need to understand why you're okay with us not getting closer physically."

Ah. Of course. She wants to know why I'm still around taking a voluntary vow of celibacy to be with her. I laughed nervously and stood up. "That's what this is about? You want to know why I'm okay avoiding sex?"

She shrugged her shoulders.

"You think there's something I'm not telling you that makes me okay with waiting."

"I don't know. I don't think you're okay with waiting, not after last week. But you are, for me. Why?"

I groaned and started pacing around the room. She watched me with those bewitching green eyes. I didn't want her to look at me differently after this, but I also knew she wasn't giving up the issue.

"The first girl I slept with, Jennifer, was my high school girlfriend. I was 17. We broke up a year later, when we were at different colleges. She didn't want to continue long distance. The second was my college girlfriend, Dionne. We didn't have a future beyond sex, which is why we broke up after graduation."

I snuck a glance at her face, she continued to follow my steps back and forth across the floor. "The next person, I didn't know very well. It was a one-night stand. Her name was Kasey and she was a friend of Trish's. Trish was trying to help me move on from Dionne and I wasn't really ready. She still avoids me whenever we happen to be at the same party or bar. I've never been more ashamed of myself than the morning after that night. I'm surprised Trish ever forgave me."

I peered at her again, convinced her eyes wouldn't be able to look at me anymore, but she actually smiled, stood, and crossed to meet me. She took my hand and I found the courage to go on.

"Number four was a girl I dated for about a year, Megan. She told me she loved me, and I couldn't bring myself to say it back, so she broke up with me. And number five was Rebecca. My last girlfriend before you." My face burned as I made eye contact with her.

"Your mother was right, Abby. It hurts when you sleep with someone and they don't feel the same way about it as you do. I've been on both sides. Jennifer and I cared deeply about each other, but the relationship always meant more to me than it did to her. When she decided to end things, I was devastated. The long distance sucked, but I passed up opportunities with other girls because I was in love with Jen and didn't want to break up. We both should've known long distance wouldn't work, but we were young and naïve. It was agony, I'll never do it again."

Abby nodded and squeezed my hand.

"When I met Dionne, we had such a physical connection, I refused to let myself get connected emotionally to her. She liked things that way. She enjoyed the sex and that's really all she wanted from me. I tried to introduce her to my friends and family, but she always made excuses to get out of it, and I was always secretly relieved."

I led Abby back to the couch and we both sat, she kept her hand attached to mine.

"Kasey really liked me, and I took advantage of her. I was drunk and stupid and I hate myself for it. With Megan, I did care about her, and I tried to take things slowly, but she said she wasn't fragile; she could handle physical intimacy without emotional intimacy. And for a while, she was fine. But she got hurt. She fell in love with me, and I didn't feel the same way. I wanted to. But somehow I couldn't."

"And Rebecca?" she asked when I was silent for a few minutes.

"Rebecca. Well, with Rebecca, I didn't want to make the same mistake I made with Megan. So I took it really slow. We didn't sleep together until five months into our relationship, when I was very much emotionally invested in her. But, after our first time, I discovered she'd been sleeping around with another guy the entire time we'd been together and that hurt more than anything I could've imagined. It felt like she took a cheese grater to my heart." I turned my head away.

"Ben, I'm so sorry you had to go through all that," she whispered, hugging me around the waist. I wiped my eyes with my sleeve before spinning to face her.

"I'm not sorry. If I hadn't gone through each of those experiences I wouldn't have been ready for you. I would've been the guy who got up and walked away when I found out you wouldn't be sleeping with me. I had to go through all the pain and I had to cause some, before I could understand what you understood a long time ago, that sex shouldn't be taken so lightly. That every time you sleep with someone different, a little piece of your heart attaches itself to that person, and you can't ever get it back. So, I'm ready and willing to wait, even if that means we never have sex, because I don't want to hurt you, and I don't want to hurt myself anymore."

"Thank you," she said, moving her arms from my waist to around my neck. I pulled her close to me and buried my face in her hair. I opened my mouth to tell her all I'd been feeling since my birthday, but she spoke before I could.

"Hey, I have to tell you something."

I pulled back and looked into her eyes. "Hmm?"

"My boss really liked the last article I turned in. It might be published in the December issue."

"Oh my God!" I jumped from my seat and lifted her up, hugging her to my body and spinning around, her feet dangled off the ground and her hands clutched my shoulders. "Abby, that's so incredible! I knew you could do it! I'm so proud of you."

She laughed as we continued to twirl throughout the room. I wanted to tell her so badly, tell her how much I loved her. But something held me back and I didn't.

Chapter Seventeen: A Few Steps Forward

Abby

Three little words. How hard is it to say three little words? Apparently very hard. Neither of us seemed capable of just laying the truth out there. I thought hearing about the women he'd slept with would change how I felt about him. Which is probably why I asked in the first place. But it didn't. It told me what I hadn't fully understood until then. He was the one. I wanted to spend the rest of my life with him. And I was scared to death he didn't feel the same way. He looked at me like he'd never seen anyone so beautiful. He acted like he loved me. But he'd never said it. What if I were Megan? What if he wanted to love me, but couldn't?

As October began, Ben decided he wanted to celebrate my last month in the mailroom. I tried to explain I wasn't guaranteed a monthly column, but he insisted. "I have faith in you," he said. Not exactly "I love you," but so close.

I glanced into his kitchen, where he stood busy at the stove, cooking dinner for us. *Us.* A word I thought escaped my vocabulary long ago. I watched him for several minutes: chopping, stirring, tasting, and an entirely new sensation filled me - comfort. I felt at home. This was what I'd been waiting for. My whole life I wondered what it would feel like to find a person who I could trust, laugh with, cry with. I felt so blissfully happy in that moment, for once I didn't wonder what he was thinking. He hadn't said those three little words yet, but I could.

I walked into the kitchen and put my arms around his waist, resting my cheek on his shoulder blade. He automatically put his free hand on the two of mine.

"Careful, the stove is hot." His instinct to protect me caused my heart to swell and I could hear its rhythmic thumping in my ears.

"I love you," I said. The strength of my voice actually surprised me, I expected the words to come out in a whisper, but they rang out loud and clear. He dropped the spatula on the stovetop as he whirled around. Taking my face in his hands, he kissed me, his lips strong and intense. Our breathing in sync, we stood completely still, and I drank him in, the words threatening to ruin the perfect moment by spilling out again. *I love you, I love you, I love you.*

When he pulled his mouth away, his face remained close to mine. "Sorry," he began, "the normal response is, I love you, too." His cheeks flushed pink with pleasure and my heart nearly exploded from happiness.

"I think I liked your response better." I smiled.

"I love you."

"I love you, too."

I knew there was no going back.

Ben

"Dinner is served! Your table awaits, Mademoiselle." I held out my arm to Abby and she linked her hand in my elbow as we walked through the kitchen and into the dining room, which I'd decorated with candles Trish picked out for me. Housed in frosted blue glass, the votives cast a sparkling light around the room. I only set the table for the two of us, having hid the extra four chairs in the basement. A bottle of champagne chilled in a bucket on the center of the table, candlelight flickered off its shiny silver surface.

I pulled out Abby's chair and kissed her neck as she took a seat.

"This is beautiful, Ben, but you didn't have to go to so much trouble," she said.

"Thank you and of course I did." I filled her plate with salad and poured us each a glass of champagne. After handing her a glass, I raised my own. "To my gorgeous and talented girlfriend, who I love very much, for not giving up on her dream." Now that the "L" word had been spoken between us, I found I couldn't stop saying it.

We clinked and both took a sip, she giggled as the bubbles tickled her throat.

"I have to admit something," I started after a few moments.

"What's that?" she asked, then proceeded to take a bite of salad.

"I didn't plan the dinner just to celebrate your article."

"Oh?" She swallowed and speared another forkful of lettuce.

"I wanted to ask you something."

"Oh?" Her eyes widened and she set her fork down. I took her trembling hand in mine.

"It's my niece's birthday on Saturday. She's turning three and my sister is planning this elaborate Princess-themed party at my parents' house. Would you come with me and meet my family?"

"Oh." She took her hand away and covered her mouth with it just as she began to laugh wildly.

"What? What's so funny? I don't get it. Do you not want to meet my family?"

"No, that's not it, I'm sorry. You got so serious and you took my hand, I thought you were going to… I thought… oh my goodness." She started laughing again, nearly falling out of her seat.

"Abby, seriously, what's so funny?"

"Nothing, it's nothing. Sorry. Yes, I'd love to meet your family."

I raised an eyebrow at her, but her giggling seemed to be under control for the time being and she didn't seem to have any intention of filling me in on the joke.

"Will I get to see embarrassing photos of you and hear humiliating stories from your childhood?"

"Um, no."

"I'm sure Tracey has loads of funny Ben stories," she teased.

"I'm sure she does, but I plan on threatening her life if she divulges any."

"Ha! Little brothers always threaten, big sisters are never intimidated!" She leaned over and kissed me on the cheek before returning to her salad and polishing it off.

"I'm ready for the main course!" she announced.

Abby

"How long have you known?" I asked as he set dessert, strawberry shortcake with vanilla ice cream, on the table.

"How long have I known what?"

"That you love me."

"Well, how long have you known you love me?"

"I asked you first!"

"Yes, but I have the upper hand. You first, or it's no ice cream for you!" He snatched my bowl and I was laughing too hard to stop him.

"Okay, I surrender. I'll talk, just give me back my dessert."

He obeyed and the bowl appeared in front of me again.

"I think I've been falling in love with you for a long time, but realized it the other night when you were so open and honest with me about your past, when you were so excited about my article. Everything about you makes me love you. You make me laugh. You comfort me when I'm upset. You actually want to hear about my day. But it's more than the way you treat me. It's the way you treat everyone. You are so kind and sweet and incredibly open-minded and accepting of everyone. I love how you get so silent and focused when your favorite team is playing, but still yell at the umps when they make a bad call. I love that you talk during movies. I love your smell and your smile and the way you look at me. I love that you make me feel at home with you." I kissed him deeply and our hands locked together underneath the table.

"Your turn," I said, staring into his beautiful eyes.

"I don't know if I can follow that, but I'll try. I've known for a while, since my birthday. You and Matt and Trish sang Happy Birthday to me and then you hugged me and I knew right then, it just kind of hit me. You're unlike any other woman I've ever met. You're insecure in relationships, yet somehow completely confident in who you are. You aren't afraid to cry when you're upset. You laugh aloud when something is funny, even if you're all alone or the only one laughing. I love to watch you read because your face tells me exactly what you're thinking. You embrace the huge dork inside of yourself and make me feel like I can do the same thing - embrace my inner dork, not yours, although I like to do that, too," his eyes were twinkling and he squeezed my hand.

"I could look into your eyes forever. And when you smile," he brought our clasped hands to his chest and held them over his heart, "well, I can't even describe to you how it makes me feel, except that I want to be the one to make you smile. I've wanted to tell you all of this for months."

"Then why didn't you?"

"I don't know. I guess I was scared you wouldn't feel the same way." He paused to see if I had something to add, but I couldn't say anything, so he went on, "Tonight, when you told me you loved me, I was so happy my first instinct was to show you how I felt, rather than say it, because in my head I've said it so many times."

I leaned across the table and took his face in my hands, kissing him yet again, thanking my lucky stars he was mine to kiss whenever I wanted. When I pulled away, he smiled and tucked a piece of hair behind my ear.

"Do you remember our first date?" he asked suddenly, scooting his chair over and putting his arm around me.

"Yes, of course."

"I asked you why you relate to Jane Austen and you told me we hadn't known each other long enough for me to not be freaked out by the answer to that question, but you would tell me one day."

"Yeah."

"You never told me your answer."

"You really want to know why I relate to her? Why I love her writing?"

"I want to know everything about you."

I could hear the sincerity in his voice. He wouldn't laugh at me; he would only love me more. I began slowly; I'd never tried before to articulate what her writing meant to me. "She understood what it feels like to be alone."

He continued looking into my eyes, I cleared my throat and continued. "She lived in a time when being a single woman was the hardest role to have. People would have looked down on her for refusing a marriage proposal from a good man and she would've felt guilty for burdening her family, but she wasn't ashamed. She knew to ease her brothers' obligations she would have to earn some kind of living and she did it on her own terms. She wasn't embarrassed to be single, but in every one of her books, she wrote about love - she wanted to be loved and to love someone. She understood the fantasy of the perfect man and gave us many different versions. She could have wallowed in self-pity, but instead, she created the love stories she never got to experience."

I paused again, taking a deep breath before leaving his protective hold and walking to the sink. I couldn't face him as I said, "For a very long time I thought I'd end up like her. Single and alone 'til the end of my life, with nothing but my fantasies of the perfect man to comfort me."

I heard his footsteps and then his arms slipped around my waist, his breathe tickled my skin, "But not anymore?"

"No, not anymore."

He squeezed me and kissed my neck. "You will never be alone again," he said. And I believed him.

Chapter Eighteen: Family Time

Abby

"So, what exactly are three year-old girls in to?" I asked Ben as we walked up and down the aisles at Toys-R-Us.

"Hannah likes everything. I brought her here once when I was babysitting for Tracey and she went down every aisle, touching everything, and calling it 'mine,'" he imitated a high-pitched little girl's voice on the last word. "Needless to say, I learned shopping is something you do without the person you're shopping for." He grabbed a Barbie and examined the contents of the box.

"That's probably not a good idea," I said, taking it from him and putting it back on the shelf.

"Why not? She loves dolls."

"The box says ages five and up. Those tiny accessories are a major choking hazard."

"Wow, how did I ever buy Hannah a present before you came along?" he mocked, but walked away from the Barbies, so I knew he appreciated my interference.

"I don't know. You seem completely helpless. How 'bout this?" I seized a coloring book and pack of markers off the shelf as we turned into the next aisle.

"I don't know, Tracey has serious issues about her carpet and walls and furniture. I don't think we should get anything that could end up with her house as a blank canvas for Hannah's artwork."

"You doubt me. I'm disappointed in you. These are special markers and this is special paper. The markers will only work on this paper, they won't work on the carpet or the walls or anything else except the paper made for them."

"That's brilliant! Thanks! Now, what are you going to get her?"

"You can't steal my brilliant gift! I'm trying to impress your family, remember?"

"Okay, fine. Then help me find something else."

"Well, you said she loves dolls - how about a baby doll? Cabbage Patch Kids are a couple of aisles over."

"Works for me. Let's hurry, though. The party starts in like thirty minutes."

It took Ben all of five seconds to pick out the doll. He grabbed the first one on the shelf. Luckily, it was cute, so I didn't stop him from getting into the checkout line. Then he drove to his parents' house while I assembled our presents into gift bags in the backseat.

"I can't believe you waited until the last minute to get her gift."

He laughed, "So did you!"

"You just told me about the party last week! I kept saying, let's go shopping for her gift and you kept coming up with excuses to put it off."

He shrugged. "What can I say, I'm a day-of shopper. It prevents second guessing."

"It also prevents putting any thought into the gift."

"I'm offended. I put a lot of thought into that Lettuce Head Doll."

"It's a Cabbage Patch Kid."

"Oh right, yeah, that's it. If Tracey asks, I bought it weeks ago."

"Your secret's safe with me. There, done." I triumphantly held up the bags.

"What did you do to them?" He sniggered as he looked at the bags through the rear view mirror.

"What do you mean?"

"They look so frilly and girly!"

"It's called tissue paper and a bow. You're such a boy."

He stuck his tongue out at me, but didn't have time to tease me back because we had just arrived.

"Whoa, their house is so big." I instantly felt unprepared for the situation I was about to step into. I looked up and down the street; a beautiful neighborhood full of three-story homes confronted me. Brick houses with perfectly manicured lawns were guarded from outsiders by white picket fences - literally. I thought white picket fences only existed in the world of *Leave it to Beaver* and *Bewitched.* His parents' was a red brick, two-story, four-car garage beauty with pale blue shutters on the windows and an ornate mahogany front door. I didn't belong there.

"Hey, smile! They're going to love you." We got out of the car and he took both gift bags in his left hand. With his right, he grabbed me around the waist and pulled me close to him. He kissed my cheek and repeated his assurances, "Don't worry, this is going to be great. We're just here to have fun. Now, smile."

I couldn't disappoint him, so I gathered my courage and flashed him my biggest, goofiest grin.

"That's my girl. Let's go." He started walking towards the house, but I remained frozen on the spot. Laughing at my stupidity, he took my hand and led me to the front door.

"Deep breath," he whispered as he pushed open the door and finally a flutter of trepidation passed across his face. It was gone before I could say anything, though.

"Mom? Dad? We're here." He emphasized the word 'we're' and this effectually snapped me out of my discomfort. I realized it was not just about me. It was about *us*. Him and Me. I would pull it together for him. If he thought I belonged there with him, I wouldn't let him down.

Straightening my shoulders and standing upright, I followed him into the house and plastered a smile on my face for the flock of people who appeared to greet us.

"Hey Mom, hey Dad." Ben hugged each of his parents.

"Tracey, you look beautiful." He hugged his sister.

"How are you, Ike?" He shook hands with Tracey's husband.

"Joey, my main man!" He high-fived his nephew and deftly scooped up his niece and folded her into a bear hug, "Happy Birthday Hannah-Banana!"

She squealed with happiness and he kissed her forehead roughly before setting her down.

"Who's that?" Joey pointed at me and looked up at his uncle.

"This is my very special friend, Abigail. Abby, this is Joey."

"Hi, Joey. Your Uncle Ben has told me so much about you. He said you like trains, is that right?"

He looked from Ben to me and held my face in his gaze for a minute before ultimately deciding he could trust me. He took a step closer and nodded.

"That's good, otherwise I wouldn't have anyone to give this to." I pulled a little wooden train out of my purse and handed it to him. He beamed up at me for a split second, then ran from the group and plopped in front of the coffee table, making choo choo noises as he raced the toy over its glass surface. Tracey looked at me with a warm smile spread across her face.

Ben claimed my attention again, "Abby, this is my mother, Barbara, and my dad, Mike."

"It's so nice to meet you." I extended my hand to shake theirs, his mother's stiff smile threatening to loosen my resolve until she spoke with sweet enthusiasm.

"It's wonderful to finally meet you, dear. Benny has been talking about nothing but you for months."

"Yes, we were starting to think you were a figment of his imagination." His father shook my hand before slapping Ben on the back.

"Very funny, Dad," Ben groaned.

"I wouldn't place too much stock in what he says about me. He tends to exaggerate my good qualities."

"I just call things as I see them." He turned to his sister, "Abby, this is Tracey and her husband, Ike."

"Abby, I'm really impressed. It's Hannah's birthday but you thought to bring something for Joey, too." Tracey hugged me while she said this. I was feeling more and more comfortable - things were going great!

"I have three siblings and we're all pretty close in age. We have videos from birthdays where three of us would be throwing tantrums because only one of us was getting presents. I thought it might be hard for him meeting someone new and watching his sister get all of the attention."

"You were right, Ben. She's a keeper!"

Everyone laughed and I opened my mouth to thank them for inviting me just as the doorbell rang.

"That will be Hannah's guests. Hannah, are you ready for your party?" Tracey and Ike took Hannah's hands and went to open the door while Barbara ushered Ben and I further into the house.

"Ben, why don't you put those gifts in the dining room, and Abigail, dear, will you help me bring the snacks out of the kitchen?"

"Of course, I would love to help."

Ben squeezed my hand and turned to the right, leaving me alone with his mother.

"Mrs. Harris, you have such a beautiful house," I began, but she quickly stopped me.

"Dear, please call me Barbara, or Doc. Mrs. Harris is so formal."

"Doc?"

"I'm a pediatrician, that's what my patients and staff call me. Didn't Benny tell you that?"

"Yes, he did tell me," a blush spread over my face, "I mean, he told me you were a pediatrician, I guess I forgot. I'm sorry."

"No need to apologize, dear. I don't expect you to remember every little detail he's ever told you about us." She buzzed around the kitchen throughout our conversation, preparing plates and bowls of food. "Here, dear, will you grab a couple of trays?"

"Of course. Lead the way." I lifted the closest two and followed her out of the kitchen. Shouts and bursts of laughter filled the living room, Ben galloped around the group of children, giving Hannah a piggyback ride; Ike hung Joey upside down by his ankles; and Ben's father jogged slowly around the couch, chased by at least five different little girls.

"Those are our boys." Tracey grinned at me. "Is there more in the kitchen, Mom?"

"Yes, dear, why don't you and Abigail bring out the rest while I get these kids outside."

"No problem," Tracey moved towards the kitchen. "Do you prefer Abigail or Abby?"

"Everyone calls me Abigail. Ben's really the only person who calls me Abby. But I answer to both, so whichever you prefer is fine with me."

"We'll let Ben have the monopoly on Abby. So Abigail, my brother talks about you all of the time."

"I wish he wouldn't. There's no way I can live up to the hype."

She laughed and handed me a bowl of pretzels and a bowl of popcorn. "I don't think you have anything to worry about. Anyone who can make him this happy is a winner in my books."

My cheeks deepened to a shade of maroon. Clearing my throat, I attempted a change of subject, "You and Ben seem really close. He told me you're one of his best friends."

"I got really lucky with my little bro. We have a lot in common, plus, it was just the two of us a lot when we were growing up. We have fantastic parents, but they have demanding jobs, so we entertained each other most of the time. I taught him how to cook, he taught me how to throw a curve ball."

"It must be great, being so close."

"Yeah. I know I can tell him anything and we have so much fun together. And you can see how much my kids love him." Stepping back in the living room, we watched as Ben blew raspberries on Hannah's stomach with Joey clinging to his leg, begging for a turn.

"He's going to make a great father someday." She nudged me with her elbow and I nearly dropped the bowls in my hands. Fire shot up my neck and into my already reddened cheeks.

"Right, so um, what is it you do, Tracey? I don't think Ben has ever told me."

She laughed again - she sounded a lot like Ben when she laughed - but seemed to understand my desire to move on to new topics, because she answered with, "I'm a photographer and a mom. Mostly free-lance work; Ike's the breadwinner. He's a surgeon. I'm lucky he makes enough money that I only work when I want to. I like to be at home with Joey and Hannah."

As she finished, Ben joined us. "Having fun?" he asked, his eyes hopeful.

"You certainly are," I replied, "you fit right in with the three year-olds."

"I'm in touch with my inner child." He grinned and put his arm around my shoulder. "Tracey's not giving you a hard time is she?"

"No, not at all. We're just getting to know each other."

"Good. Trace, you don't mind if I steal her away for a bit, do you? I want to give her the grand tour."

"No problem, but don't take too long, we'll be opening gifts soon."

"Don't worry, we'll be back in a few minutes."

His tour consisted of pointing into a couple of rooms before guiding me into his old bedroom and shutting the door behind us. The room looked so much like him. Dark green walls adorned with posters of baseball players I'd never heard of, a bookshelf in the corner full of yellowed issues of Sports Illustrated and old high school trophies, and a massive black desk covered with dusty notebooks and pictures of friends made up the scene of his younger days.

"So, what do you think?" he asked as I sat on the bed.

"About your room or your family?"

"My family - do you like them?"

"Of course I do, but honestly, I haven't had much time to get to know them. I know I'm going to like them because they're a part of you. I'm more worried they aren't going to like me. I think you set the bar pretty high. I can't live up to their expectations."

"Hey, stop that," he knelt in front of me, beside the bed, placed one hand on my knee, and lifted my chin with the other so he could look me in the eye. "You are wonderful: that's what I've told them. There's no need to live up to anything because it's a fact. I love you. You're the best thing that's ever happened to me; they aren't going to be able to see you any other way. Okay?"

"Okay." I leaned forward and kissed him, but a knock at the door interrupted the moment.

"Come in," Ben answered, getting to his feet. His father's head poked in.

"We're starting. Do you want to watch Hannah open her presents?"

"Of course, Dad. We're right behind you."

Ben

After the ankle-biters went home, Tracey put Hannah and Joey down for a nap while my parents, Ike, Abby, and I sat down in the living room.

"Would anyone like a drink?" my dad asked, glancing around.

"I'm driving," I answered, "Abby?"

She fidgeted in her seat, looking unsure whether it was appropriate for her to drink around my family. "Um, no. I'm fine."

"She'll have a gin martini." If I couldn't drink, she might as well.

"Ben, I said I'm fine." She poked me in the side and glared at me.

I put my arm around her shoulder and bent my head towards her. "Trust me, you want a drink." I tried to say it jokingly, but the truth was, I wanted a drink. I knew what was about to happen. My parents were always perfectly polite and charming for the first few hours. They lured their guests into a sense of ease and comfort then pulled the rug out from under them. I'd seen enough of my ex-girlfriends go through the interrogation to know it was coming soon.

My father handed her the drink, passed Ike a scotch, and Mom a glass of red wine as Tracey entered the room and found a seat. Abby took a tiny sip then set the martini on my mother's end table.

"Hmm, um, coaster, babe," I muttered under my breath.

"Oh, sorry!" She snatched one and nearly spilled her drink lifting it to place on the coaster. "I told you I didn't want one," she grumbled. I checked my laughter.

"Abigail, I'm trying to remember, what's your last name?" my mother asked, smiling sweetly at us. *Great, here we go.*

"Bronsen."

"Oh! Are you related to Montgomery Bronsen?"

"Um, no, I don't think so."

"Are you sure? Monty is a surgeon, he goes to our country club."

Not the country club, Mom. Come on!

Abby looked sideways at me and I shrugged, not really sure how to help her. "Yeah, I'm pretty positive. No doctors in my family as far as I'm aware."

"Oh." Mom crossed her arms over her chest and leaned back, looking Abby up and down like she was assessing a piece of furniture, probably one from a discount store she couldn't believe she'd gone into.

My dad cleared his throat while I covered my face with my hands. I wanted to take Abby's hand and lead her straight out the door, but I knew the interview would just continue the next time they saw her.

"What do you do, Abigail?" Dad asked after a few moments of silence.

She hesitated and her voice wavered as she answered, "I work at *Intuition* Magazine."

My mother resumed the questioning, "What do you do there?"

"She's having an article published in their big holiday issue," I interrupted before Abby could speak. She punched me in the thigh and faced my mother.

"I work in the mailroom right now. If my article gets good reviews I'll be promoted to columnist."

"I see."

"What do your parents do?" Dad asked.

"My mom's a secretary and my dad works construction."

"Oh." Now Dad crossed his arms over his chest. Could it get any worse?

"Mom, Dad, can we talk about something else?" My parents were acting like snobs, Abby had to be feeling attacked and embarrassed.

"We just want to get to know this lovely girl." Mom stood and crossed the room, taking the seat on the couch beside Abby.

"You know, dear," Mom said, "Ben is a wonderful man."

"Yes, he is." Abby seized my hand and squeezed.

"We want to make sure the woman he loves and eventually marries is good enough for him."

I groaned. I'd heard the same line several times in the past, nothing good ever came from it. "Mom..." I attempted, but both she and Abby ignored me.

"Barbara, I can assure you that I'm not good enough for him. But I can also assure you that he does love me, I love him, and if we do get married someday," she turned to face me, "which I'm not saying we are," she swung around and addressed my mother again, "but if we do get married eventually, I'm going to spend the rest of my life trying to be good enough for him."

I swear my jaw hit the floor. How the hell did she know the perfect thing to say? Mom seemed shocked for a second too, but only a second, then her smile spread across her face. Her *real* smile. She leaned over and put her hands on top of Abby's, which still clutched mine, and said, "That's all I need to know."

I breathed a sigh of relief and Abby's shoulders relaxed as she leaned back against me. My family acted like human beings for the rest of the evening and Abby smiled all the way home. I couldn't believe they let her off that easy, but maybe, for once, they saw the same thing in the girl I liked that I did. Maybe I *hadn't* lied to Abby earlier when I said they wouldn't be capable of seeing her as anything but wonderful.

Chapter Nineteen: Facing Your Fears

Abby

I tore the plastic off the magazine and threw the wrapping to the floor. Ben stood at the door to his closet, rummaging through his wardrobe, completely unaware of my excitement.

"What should I wear to meet your parents?" he asked as I gazed reverently at the cover of the holiday edition of *Intuition*.

"It doesn't matter what you wear." Gingerly, I lifted the cover and flipped through the ads to find the Table of Contents.

"Of course it does. Too dressy and they'll think I'm an uptight snob. Too casual and they'll think I don't care or that I'm not good enough for their daughter."

"You obviously have not met my parents." I looked up to find him glaring at me. "What I mean is, how you dress is not going to tell them anything about you. They could care less about clothes. The only way your style of dress could possibly offend them would be if you weren't wearing anything at all."

He continued staring me down. "Please help me. I want them to like me."

"Everyone who knows you loves you, they're going to love you, too." *Well, my mom will, at least.*

His face still registered displeasure with me. Sighing, I threw the magazine aside, sat up and tried to assist. "How about that pale blue button-down shirt you have? The one you wore on our first date."

He raised an eyebrow at me. "You remember what I was wearing on our first date?"

I ignored the laughter in his voice. "It matched your eyes." He could tease me all he wanted; any woman who saw him in that shirt would remember it. He didn't say anything, though, as he grabbed a hanger and held the shirt out for my approval.

"That's the one."

He put it on and went back into the closet. "Jeans or slacks?"

"Um, your dark jeans."

Stepping out of the closet a few minutes later, jeans on, shirt tucked in, he looked amazing. "I shaved this morning, but maybe I should shave again."

"Ben, you need to relax. Don't shave again. You look very handsome."

"You're one to talk about relaxing. I practically had to drag you into my parents' house."

"That was different. I was intimidated."

"You think I'm not?"

"I think you have no reason to be. Your parents live in a mansion and went to medical school and law school. My parents live in a one-story, two bedroom house and didn't even go to college. I was going in unsuccessful and poor, a graduate of Boston College. You're going in owning your own business, well off, and a graduate of Harvard. Honestly, I don't see what you're worried about." *Unless you're scared my dad is going to come at you with a shotgun, because that's probably not far off.*

He sat on the edge of the bed and looked at me earnestly. "I wish you wouldn't think about us like that. I know you don't do it when we're alone together, but whenever we're around other people you bring it up - like you're hoping I'll realize you aren't in my league, or something. Yes, I grew up with money and had opportunities other people didn't; that doesn't make me better than anyone else. If anything, it makes me worse because I didn't have to work as hard. And you know the business isn't doing great right now, not exactly the way I want to go in and meet the parents of the woman I love."

He paused and rubbed his forehead before continuing, "You might not have grown up in the lap of luxury or achieved fame and fortune, but you graduated in the top of your class, your article is being published in a national magazine, and you've had to work your butt off to get there. And *that* is very intimidating."

"Ben," I found my voice, "I didn't mean it like that…"

But he didn't let me explain, his eyes had fallen on the magazine. I didn't notice before, but it must have opened straight to my article when I tossed it on the bed. "Abby, oh, my God. Is this it?" He picked it up and stared at the page.

"Yep, that's it."

"I thought it didn't come out until tomorrow."

"Helen gave me an advanced copy."

"Can I read it?" He tore his eyes away from the paper and arched his eyebrow.

"Of course you can!" I laughed and he repositioned himself on the bed, leaning against the headboard beside me, his arm around my shoulder. We read it together.

Facing Your Fears: by Abigail Bronsen

What scares you?

Everyone is afraid of something. Some people live with fear and don't even realize it is weighing them down, turning simple tasks into stressful ordeals. Some people know what they are afraid of, but don't understand the basis of their fear. And still others realize they are scared, but don't know exactly what *they are scared of* or why.

I was told, not long ago, that I was too young to be so afraid. I immediately recognized the truth of the statement and not just for me personally. When I think of how short life is, I can't believe how much of it is wasted being scared.

I was very close to my grandfather growing up. He taught me you only have one opportunity to live and you should make the most of it. He delighted in the unexpected. He would show up at our house with no notice and stay for a week, he learned to fly a plane at the age of sixty. He used to tell me stories about how he and his friends went skinny-dipping in every major body of water in the state of Massachusetts. He lived life like he had nothing to lose. He died when I was sixteen and the intervening years between then and now caused me to forget the lessons he taught me.

But just when I thought I'd live the rest of my life alone and unfulfilled, a friend came along who reminds me of my grandfather. He asks me to expect more from myself. He told me to stop holding back, that being scared was a waste of energy. He encourages me to be young, wild, and spontaneous. Something I'm also terrified of, by the way.

It took a large push from my new friend for me to realize I was missing out on life because of my self-inflicted and irrational limitations.

I grew up with a huge fear of needles and blood. I would kick and scream any time my parents took me to the doctor's office and would vomit any time one of my siblings scraped a knee or had a nosebleed. The fear stemmed from a traumatic car accident on my fifth birthday, but even after years of therapy, the fear remained.

Just as my grandfather taught me to live a life without regrets, my parents taught me how important each life is to every other life around it. They believe in the interconnectivity of us all and that each person has an obligation to help humanity in whatever way they can. In addition to charity and volunteer work, the best way to help our fellow man, in my parents' eyes, is to give blood.

The very idea of letting a nurse plunge a needle into my arm to extract my blood causes me to chug Pepto-Bismo. Yet, I know how important it is. I know millions of lives are saved each year due to blood transfusions that could only be possible with blood donors. I've wanted to donate blood my whole life, but have always been crippled by my fear. I told myself I couldn't do it.

My friend told me I could. He went first, showed me it was no big deal. Then he held my hand and I donated my blood. It didn't hurt at all.

Giving blood was a huge step for me, but my phobia of needles and blood is still a part of who I am. The fear doesn't go away just because you face it. But the more you face it, the less control it has on you. I have so many fears and I don't know if I'll ever be able to face them all, but I'm no longer scared to try.

My hope is that the readers of Intuition *will be willing to go on a journey with me. It's time that we stand together and tell ourselves that fear has no place in our lives. I want to help each and every woman out there as they face whatever it is that frightens them. Write in and tell me what fears you would like to conquer, and each month I'll showcase some of our readers as they go through the daunting task of overcoming the obstacles plaguing them.*

Because I'm just like you: I'm tired of being afraid.

Ben

Wow. I mean wow.

I could sense Abby watching my face, searching for a reaction, for my stamp of approval. And I was happy to give it to her, but I needed another minute to digest her written words.

It was my Abby on the page, but it also wasn't. The person who wrote it was still unknown to me. She'd never told me about being in a car accident when she was little or exactly how much her grandfather meant to her.

But still, I was a part of the person who wrote it. She quoted me. She called me a friend, a supporter, an inspiration. The article didn't call me her boyfriend or the love of her life or anything corny like that, but I knew that's what it meant.

Slowly, I closed the magazine and set it beside me on the bed. I turned to face her and smiled. She breathed a sigh of relief as I folded her into my arms and hugged her with every ounce of strength I possessed.

"Beautiful, babe. It's just beautiful. I'm so proud of you."

"Thank you," she whispered, her voice muffled as she pressed her face into my neck. Suddenly, the collar of my shirt felt wet pressed into my skin.

"Hey, are you crying?" I pulled her shoulders back and sure enough her face and eyes sparkled with tears. She lifted her hand to wipe them away and shook her head.

"I don't know, I don't know why I'm crying. I guess I was worried you wouldn't like it. I'm so relieved you do. And I'm so happy I've finally been published. It's a lot of stuff at once."

"I know." I pulled her into another hug and we rocked back and forth for a few minutes until Abby's sobs ceased. We stood up and I took her hand to walk out the door. Looking at my watch, I groaned inwardly, we were going to be late to meet her parents.

"Um, Ben…" she stopped short in front of the closet and tugged on my hand.

"Babe, we gotta go. We're running late!"

"I know, but I don't think you want to meet my parents looking like that."

"Huh? You said a few minutes ago that I looked very handsome!" I raced into the bathroom to look in the mirror and burst out laughing as soon as I saw my reflection. Abby's tears and mascara had created thick black streaks along the collar and upper left hand side of my shirt. She followed me in and grabbed some tissues to wipe off her face while handing me a new, crisp white shirt.

"You sure white's a good idea?" I teased. "What if the waterworks start again?"

"I'll use waterproof mascara this time!" She laughed and I began to change shirts so we could get going. I caught her staring at me in the mirror, biting her upper lip, so I buttoned the shirt as quickly as possible. Her cheeks blushed the brightest scarlet I'd ever seen.

"I'm sorry," she stammered, turning and dashing out the door.

"Abby, wait!" I sprinted after her and caught her by the arm before she could make it to the living room. "It's okay. You can look all you want." I wiggled my eyebrows and, if it were possible, her blush darkened even more.

"No, it's not okay. I'm standing there lusting after you while you've been so patient with me, for me."

"I do my own share of lusting after you, don't worry about that." I took a step back and leaned against the wall, covering my eyes with my hand. Before I knew it, Abby's fingers closed around it and pulled it away. She leaned into me and stood up on her tiptoes, planting a light kiss on my bottom lip.

"I love you," she said. "I love you for being nervous about meeting my parents and for reading my article and being proud of me and for not making me feel like a freak or a prude because we aren't having sex. I love you for loving me."

"I love you, too." I didn't know what else to say and we left the house without another word. We were fifteen minutes late by then, but it didn't seem to matter as much anymore.

Chapter Twenty: Interrogation

Abby

We pulled up to my parents' home at quarter to seven. Lights shone from the front windows and the lawn appeared freshly mowed. Parking my Nissan in the driveway beside my dad's rusty orange pickup truck, I observed my mother peeking out the front door. Before turning off the engine, I took in a breath. I loved this man, and he was about to be subjected to my family. *God help him.*

Ben unfastened his seatbelt and moved to open the door. I couldn't let him go in without a little encouragement. Or at least some warnings.

"Ben?"

"Abby?"

"Don't say anything about the car accident. And avoid politics. And my dad doesn't like a lot of PDA, either, so don't feel weirded out if I don't hold your hand or anything."

"Geez, Abby, anything else? Should I just not talk at all? Or touch you? Is three feet apart okay?" He laughed, but looked nervous, so I leaned over and kissed him before we got out of the car to walk to the house.

My mother waited on the front porch to greet us. I gave her a hug before pulling Ben forward. "Mom, this is Ben. Ben, my mom, Dee."

"Ben, it's lovely to meet you. Welcome to our home." She warmly shook his hand, led him inside, and I followed. "Phil, the kids are here."

Ben grinned at me on the word "kids," but my father stepped in the room, so he turned his attention back to my mother, who gave the introduction this time, and Ben and my father shook hands.

"Can I get anyone a drink?" Mom offered as we all sat down in the living room.

"I'll have a beer," I responded without hesitation.

Ben looked at me puzzled and asked for the same. My mother headed into the kitchen and he said to me in a low voice, "You don't like beer."

"No, but it's the only alcohol she'll have in the house." The room became silent while we waited for Mom to return. She took her sweet time about it, too. When she finally came back, I took a swig as soon as she handed a bottle to me. Sitting next to my father, Mom smiled eagerly at us, but Dad started the conversation.

"Ben, how old are you?"

Great, here we go. "Jump right in, dad."

"I'm 28, sir." Ben patted my arm to soothe me. *Why is he so calm and collected all of a sudden?*

"And what is it you do for a living?"

"I own a business, sir. An athletic complex. Inner City Sports."

"An athletic complex? What is that exactly?"

"Well, it has tennis courts, swimming pools, basketball and volleyball courts, an indoor baseball field, golf course, and it houses a sports memorabilia store, sports bar, fully functioning gym, weight room, and ticket office."

My dad looked impressed, but sounded nonchalant as he asked, "How did you get into that?"

"I've always been a sports nut. I got the idea to build it when I was in college, working with the Big Brother Program at the local YMCA. There wasn't a place that inner city kids could go, be safe, and have fun. So I created one."

"Ben actually bought vans and sends them around the city, giving kids a ride to the complex so they can play. And the kids don't have to pay a thing for it," I bragged, wrapping my hand around his arm and moving closer to him on the couch, keeping my eyes on Dad's face to gauge his reaction. His eye fell on my hand, but his expression didn't change.

"How do you afford the upkeep if you give things away for free?"

"Dad!" I gave him my best I-can't-believe-you-just-said-that look.

Ben ignored my indignation, "He's got a point, Abby." He flashed me a quick smile and returned his attention to Dad.

"Honestly, sir, it is difficult. Memberships to the sporting fields and courts are always free, so anyone can go and play, but I have a contract with the city that allows city-sponsored recreational and intramural teams to play and practice there. There's a monthly fee to become a member of the gym, and the bar, store, and ticket office bring in money as well. And with the economy tanking the way it's been, I've also begun looking into using the complex as a social event space for weddings, birthday parties, charity functions, etc. to offset some of the expenditures in other areas."

My father looked even more impressed now, but changed the subject, "So Ben, what are your intentions with my daughter?"

You've got to be kidding me! "Really, Dad? Don't answer that Ben. Mom, is dinner ready yet?"

Ben didn't ignore me this time, though he looked like he wanted to. Mom jumped up and led us into the kitchen. We sat around the table and she began passing mashed potatoes and pork chops.

No one spoke for at least five minutes until Ben cleared his throat and began, "Abby's told me a lot about your family. She's so lucky to have so many siblings. I just have one sister."

"Are you going by Abby now, Abigail?" My father asked, eyes focused on his food.

"Um, no, I mean, I like it when Ben calls me that, but um, c'mon Dad, take it easy will you?" *Why did Ben think this was a good idea?*

Another several minutes of silence followed until my mother asked Ben about his parents. They carried the conversation throughout the meal. They discussed his family, her job, his job, my job, the Red Sox, and a thousand other topics. I chimed in occasionally, but Dad ate wordlessly, attentively listening to everything Ben said.

Ben

The meal was delicious, but Abby's father didn't seem to have any intention of getting to know me. He barely spoke at all during dinner and when he did, his goal seemed to be to make me as uncomfortable as possible. He succeeded.

I took my last bite and set my fork down. I reached for Abby's hand underneath the table, but she withdrew it and leaned both elbows on the table before I could grasp it. Instead, I squeezed her knee. She tensed for a second, then cautiously brought her hands back under the table and covered mine. I felt better instantly. Until her father finally spoke.

"Dee, Abigail, would you girls mind taking care of the dishes so I can have a chat with Ben?" he asked gruffly, standing and heading towards the living room.

"Um, Dad…" Abby tried, but her mother interrupted.

"Of course not, Phil. You boys go on. We'll clean up and join you in a few minutes."

My insides felt like they were going to shoot out of my mouth at any moment, but I got up with feigned confidence and smiled in Abby's direction as I followed him out of the kitchen.

"I'm sorry," she mouthed. I just shrugged my shoulders.

Her father stood at the mantle when I walked in the living room, holding a picture frame in his hand. The frown lines on his forehead deepened with each passing second. What was that description I'd read a million times? Impenetrably grave. That's exactly how he looked.

I stuffed my hands in my pockets and rocked back and forth on my heels, waiting for him to say something. Anything. Eventually he set the frame on the mantle and faced me, but still didn't speak. For lack of something better to do and out of plain nervous energy, I glanced at the photo.

"Oh! Abby has that same picture in her apartment." I stepped forward so I could take a closer look and realized the man in the photograph wasn't Abby's father, like I'd always assumed.

"Abigail's grandfather," Mr. Bronsen said, anticipating my question.

"That explains the flower."

"I'm sorry?" He crossed his arms over his chest.

"The flower Abby, er, Abigail, is holding in the picture. She gave me a box with that flower carved on the lid. She said her grandfather made it."

"She gave you her grandfather's box?" His mouth closed tightly after the question and I immediately regretted saying anything.

Gulping back my reluctance, I replied, "Um, yeah, for my birthday." Bringing my hand to my neck, I tried to rub away my embarrassment and avoided meeting his stare. I focused my eyes on little girl Abby.

"So…" he paused and something in his silence caused me to glance up. Looking into my eyes he continued, "this relationship must be pretty serious, then."

"Yes, sir."

"I see. How serious?"

We continued looking at each other in the eye while I tried to figure out how to reply to the question, but after a few seconds a smile threatened to break through his cold, hard mask. In that moment we both knew the answer.

I was going to marry his daughter one day.

He started over, "She'll always be my little girl. If you have a daughter someday, you'll understand what that means."

I nodded, unsure what to do or say next.

He took a step closer and put his hand on my shoulder. "I can tell you love her. I can tell she loves you. But I swear the moment she comes to me in tears over you, you won't live to see another day."

Abby burst through the door at that exact moment carrying a couple of beers. She looked like an angel coming towards me, preparing to rescue me from my personal hell. Handing one beer to Mr. Bronsen and the other to me, she grasped my hand and stood by my side, glaring at her father.

"Are you being *nice*, Dad?"

"Of course." He removed his hand from my shoulder and took a seat on the couch.

Abby stood up on her tiptoes and whispered close to my ear, "I'm so sorry that he ambushed you like that, I got out here as fast as I could. Was he horrible?"

"Not at all," I whispered back, squeezing her hand for reassurance and praying I'd never hear a repeat of the "if you ever hurt her" speech. She cocked an eyebrow in disbelief, but what did she expect me to say? *Um yes, in fact, at the moment you came in, he was threatening to tear me limb from limb if I ever make you cry.*

Luckily, a group of people charged through the door and prevented me from having to elaborate. The storm that was Abby's family thundered and stomped their way into the living room, initially oblivious to my presence.

First one tallish brunette woman, then another turned to face me, and my brain reeled as their resemblance to Abby struck me.

"You must be Ben. Oh my goodness, B, he's gorgeous." The tallest stepped towards me and held out her hand.

"You must be Anna, nice to meet you." I shook and she smiled. Her hair was exactly the same color as Abby's and they had the same deep green eyes, but she was almost half a foot taller.

"How'd you know?" she laughed.

"Your sister talks about you all the time. I probably know you better than I know Abby."

She laughed again and Abby rolled her eyes at me. The other woman stepped forward. "Ben, what's taken you so long to come and meet us?"

"Nice to meet you, too, Ashley." Ashley and I shook hands as well and her smile lit up her face. It was almost identical to Abby's, except Abby's lips were a little fuller, and Ashley had a faint scar below her bottom lip.

Her three brothers stepped forward next. I knew immediately which was Derek. He looked exactly like Abby's father, with dark hair instead of silver. He thrust out his hand and we shook as well. My palms were starting to grow sweaty, but I just had a few more people to greet.

"Ben, you should have gotten out while you still could." Derek grinned and Abby punched him in the arm. "OW! Jesus, B. I was just joking."

Abby ignored him as he rubbed the tender spot on his bicep and she introduced me to her brothers-in-law and her brother's fiancé. When the introductions were finally complete, her mother pulled several board games out of a hall closet and all ten of us sat in a circle and began to play.

Her father didn't speak to me again until the end of the evening as I was helping Abby put her coat on.

"Ben, will you be joining us for Thanksgiving?"

I was not expecting that. "I'd love to, sir."

Abby beamed at her father and ran to give him a hug. She kissed his cheek, then came and took my hand to walk out the door.

"It was great to meet everyone. Thank you so much for having me." I said to her mother at the edge of the driveway. She gave each of us a hug.

"We're so glad to finally get to know you, Ben. Abigail has been engrossed by you the past couple of months! We've barely seen her since she met you. But now that we know you, she doesn't have any more excuses!" Her mother looked triumphant and Abby rolled her eyes again.

Derek came up behind their mother and slung his arm around her shoulder. "So, Ben, are you coming to mine and Samantha's wedding next month?"

Abby poked him in the stomach and answered before I could, "I didn't have *And Guest* on my invitation."

"We'll send you a new one." Samantha appeared on Mrs. Bronsen's other side.

"I love weddings," I teased Abby.

"Great! We'll see you there!" Derek punched Abby lightly in the arm and smirked as he took Samantha's hand and walked her to their car.

I chuckled watching them walk away and Abby folded her arms over her chest. "Great," she said sarcastically.

"What?" I opened her car door for her and waved to her departing family members as they pulled out of the driveway.

"You fit right in!"

Chapter Twenty-One: A Wedding

Ben

Thanksgiving came and went. I spent it with Abby's family at her grandmother's house while my parents drove up the coast to visit my mother's old college roommate and my sister's family flew out to California to see Ike's family. It was an experience. Abby's family is big. I mean super big. I think there were twenty-five people in the house at one time. Aunts, uncles, cousins, plus her parents, siblings, and grandmother. All talking and fighting and eating at once, no one seemed to care if they could hear themselves think.

It was fun, but I'd never felt so out of place in my life.

Abby

I don't know how Ben did it. He got along with my crazy uncles and brothers at Thanksgiving and my dad even went so far as to say, "Ben might be an okay guy." High praise, indeed.

Ben just seemed to belong with us. With me, I guess.

The next thing I knew, we were a week away from my brother's wedding and my family was so in love with Ben, they included him in every invitation. To the couple's shower, the bachelor party, the rehearsal dinner. The only problem was he hadn't planned on being in Springfield, an hour away from Boston, for all these events and when he went to book a room, the hotel where the wedding was being held was full.

"I could just stay in your room," he suggested after the third hotel we'd contacted was booked, too.

"Why did my brother have to choose the week before Christmas to get married?" I groaned in response.

"Abby, listen to me. We're both adults. We've been controlling ourselves for the past seven months. I think we can share a room for a couple of nights without dire consequences."

Silence hung around us, suffocating me. I walked to the window and stared out at the snow falling. Ben's heavy footsteps approached and his hand closed around mine. I forced myself to face him again.

Get a grip, Abigail! It's not a big deal.

"Abby, you trust me, right?"

"Yes." *I do, but I don't. Really, I don't trust myself.*

"Nothing's going to happen."

Riiiiight. "How can you be so sure?"

"Because I love you."

"That's why I'm not so sure. I love you so much. I don't know if it's safe for me to share a room and a bed with you for a whole week. I might not be able to control myself." *And I don't know if I want to.*

He chuckled and his fingers tightened around mine. "All the more reason!"

"Ben!" I slapped his shoulder, but he only laughed for another few seconds.

"I'll have enough control for both of us, I promise. No funny business. Don't you want me to come with you?"

"Yes." *I really, really do.*

"Then it's settled."

"Yeah, I guess so." My thoughts flew all over the place as I looked deep into his eyes. *Do I really want to keep waiting? Are we going to get married someday? I want him to be my first, but what if something happens and we break up? I want to make love to him. What am I waiting for, really? What difference does it make if we have sex now or later? No. You made the decision to wait. And you're right. And Ben understands it. You've already waited twenty-five years. Why ruin it? Our wedding night, if we get married one day, is going to be amazing.*

Ben

For the first couple of nights in Springfield I slept in the right-hand bed and Abby slept in the left one. We were lucky her room had two beds, I guess, because being so close to her every night and not making a move was probably the hardest thing I'd ever done.

She was so damn cute at bedtime. It was the first time I'd been witness to her nightly routine. When she started getting tired she'd immediately brush her teeth and wash her face, afraid she'd fall asleep without doing it. She hummed while she brushed her hair and her pajamas looked like they belonged to a twelve year-old. My favorite pair was covered in teddy bears. Not sexy in the least, but her confidence was. She didn't seem to care at all when I laughed at them.

The night before the wedding, after we both crawled under the covers and I shut my eyes, her voice broke through the darkness.

"Ben, you awake?"

"Mmhmmm."

"Okay."

I opened my eyes and stared across the room into hers. She smiled.

"What?" I asked.

"Nothing."

"Go to sleep," I tried to scold her, but like I said, she was too damn cute.

"Do you believe in God, Ben?"

"Yes, I do." I have no idea where the question came from, but she rolled over and focused on the ceiling. My answer seemed to rattle her. "Do *you* believe in God?"

"I don't know. Sometimes." She pulled the blanket over her head and sighed loudly. "Sometimes I feel like there's too much crap in the world, too many people suffering, for there to be a God."

I sat up and leaned against the headboard of my bed, looking at the lump on hers indicating she was under the covers, wishing I knew what she needed from me. It had to be something, why else would she bring up God at midnight the night before her brother's wedding? "A lot of people feel like that."

"Yeah, but then, well, then I look at you, and I know only God could have created someone so wonderful and caring and I can't believe I ever doubted. And I watched Derek and Samantha tonight at the rehearsal. They really love each other. Could love even exist without a God?"

Wow, uh… "No, I don't think it could."

"Yeah. Okay, sorry. You can go to sleep now." Her head popped out from under the blanket and she turned onto her side, putting her back to me.

"Wait, now I have a question for you." I swung my legs off the bed and stepped softly around hers, kneeling so our faces were level with each other's. She reached her hand out and placed it on my cheek.

"Okay."

"What's your favorite flower?"

"My favorite flower? That's kind of out of the blue."

"And 'Do I believe in God' wasn't?"

She laughed, "I guess it was. Why do you want to know my favorite flower?"

"Why after all this time do you still refuse to answer personal questions?"

Her hand fell from my cheek and made a soft thud as it hit the mattress. "Oh, Ben…" She sat up and I stood, she reached for my hands and pulled me onto the bed beside her. Her fingers ran up my arms and linked around my neck, bringing my face down to hers. Kissing me. When she released me, her eyes remained closed and she pressed her forehead into my chest.

"Anemones, my favorite flowers are anemones. My grandfather grew them in his garden."

I kissed her again and started to get up to return to my bed, but she held onto me, lying down and tucking my arm around her waist. I scooted beside her and pressed my body against hers. She fell asleep in my arms.

Abby

The ceremony started at six o'clock the next evening. Anna and Ashley glided down the aisle where Derek waited at the end. Taking a deep breath and smiling at my brother, I followed behind my sisters. Once the other two bridesmaids took their place, the crowd rose and faced the bride. I kept my eyes on Derek the whole time. Tears fell down my cheeks as his face lit up at the sight of her. Pure love and happiness shone from his eyes. Ashley sniffled beside me.

I barely heard the minister as he addressed Samantha and Derek; I barely heard the vows they spoke to each other. Before I knew it, they were walking back up the aisle and I caught sight of Ben. He sat in the second row on the groom's side, right beside Will and Cain. He winked as I passed by and I almost tripped on my dress.

The band introduced the bridal party into the reception and we stood around the dance floor while the bride and groom danced their first dance to "The Way You Look Tonight." I made a mental note to tease Derek about the song choice after he got back from the honeymoon. Finally, we found our seats and the band announced dinner service would begin soon.

Ben waited for me at our table. *Damn, he looks good.* He wore a dark blue suit, with a white shirt and light blue tie that matched his eyes. I'd never seen him in a suit before and couldn't believe I once thought he looked his best in sweats. He jumped up to pull out my chair as I reached the table. I thanked him, but we didn't have much time for conversation as my sisters, their husbands, and two other couples joined us. Anna and Ashley talked non-stop about the ceremony, the flowers, the linens, the cake, etc. and frequently called on me for my opinion, so I didn't have the opportunity to talk to Ben until after dinner.

He finished telling me about the golf outing with the guys that morning as the bandleader announced, "Samantha and Derek would like to invite all of the other couples in love to join them on the dance floor." A slow and pretty tune played, and I glanced around wistfully, watching as Anna and Will, then Ashley and Cain, took a place among the happy couples. Ben tapped on my shoulder.

"May I have this dance?" He offered me his hand.

"Oh. Of course!" *How stupid you are, Abigail! You're in love, too!* He led me to the floor and we joined the other couples rocking rhythmically back and forth. He pulled me close and firmly placed one arm around my waist. I followed his lead as he twirled me around, weaving in and out of the other pairs. We locked eyes and my heart swelled to three or four times its normal size.

"I wanted to tell you before, but I didn't have the chance," he leaned in even closer, "you look absolutely stunning tonight." I blushed and laid my head on his shoulder.

When the dance ended, the band began playing a more up-tempo number and Ben whirled and spun me like crazy. I couldn't help but laugh at his goofy attempt at dancing and soon he was laughing at my ungraceful attempts, too. We stayed on the dance floor for the next hour.

"How come I've never seen you in a suit before?" I asked when we took a break to watch Samantha and Derek cut the cake and be toasted by the maid of honor and best man.

"You haven't? Well, I guess I haven't needed to wear one before now."

"You should wear one every day, you look incredible."

"I'll keep that in mind." His eyes twinkled as he leaned over to kiss me. "Now, back on the dance floor, young lady!" We danced until we were ready to fall over from exhaustion.

Once the guests sent Derek and Samantha off in their limo, Ben grabbed my hand and led me away. Alone in the elevator, he pressed me against the wall and kissed me. It took me off guard: we'd spent such a romantic sweet evening, but now the passion flowing between us threatened to explode. My hands groped his back and shoulders while his ran through my hair and down my arms. When the doors opened on our floor, I slipped beneath his hold and jumped out, practically running to our room and dragging him along after me.

It took a few minutes to get the key in the door because we couldn't keep our hands off each other, but when we finally managed to get inside, I pushed it shut with my foot, keeping my mouth locked on Ben's and letting him lean me into the door. The knob pushed into my spine, but I didn't care.

Every touch sent me spiraling closer to a vortex of pleasure I'd never known. *It's been long enough. You're both ready. Just go for it*, my mind screamed and my body listened. I reached around to unzip my dress, but Ben stepped away from me.

"I've got to take a shower," he mumbled before throwing himself into the bathroom and slamming the door. The lock clicked into place a second later and I fell face-first on the bed. I knew this room wasn't such a good idea. *It's a good thing one of us can control ourselves.*

Chapter Twenty-Two: Christmas

Abby

We spent Christmas Eve with Ben's family. His parents bought me a stationary set, with monogrammed paper and a fountain pen. I laughed at the "A" on the header and Ben chuckled as well when I showed him.

"I guess I forgot to tell them about your initial."

"I'm glad you didn't and please don't now. It's nice to be in a family where I'm the only A." I didn't want his parents thinking I didn't like it. I could just imagine myself sitting at my desk, writing the next month's article with it.

When Joey and Hannah began to fall asleep, everyone said goodnight and Ben and I drove back to his house holding hands and singing Christmas carols. My heart was full as we walked into the house together, put our newly acquired gifts under the tree, and cuddled on the couch watching *A Christmas Story*. We'd both seen the movie so many times we laughed before our favorite parts and he imitated Ralphie in every other scene. Life was perfect. I wanted to spend every Christmas with him.

As the movie ended, Ben kissed my neck and let his lips rest below my ear. "You can stay over if you want."

I did want to. We'd been walking on eggshells since Derek's wedding. Ben's self-control that night shocked me. I wouldn't have stopped him, I wanted him, but I'm thankful he did stop. I still wanted to wait. But tonight was different somehow. There was nothing sexual in his invitation.

I only hesitated for a second. "Okay."

He fell asleep before me. Lying in his bed, feeling the warmth from his body, I looked around his bedroom. Moonlight streaming through the window fell on a picture hanging on the wall: the two of us, in Florida, candles lit on his birthday cake, him kissing my cheek. I didn't remember it hanging there, so he must have put it up in the last few days. The box I gave him sat on his dresser, its lid open, and I knew he put his wallet and keys in it when we came home. My purple scarf hung on the closet door, a pair of my shoes occupied the corner. I didn't wear either that day. Pieces of me were there, in that room, in that house. I couldn't believe how safe and secure the thought made me feel.

Waking up on Christmas morning with Ben's arms wrapped tightly around me, I thought I was still dreaming. It was a kind of happiness that couldn't be real.

"Merry Christmas," he whispered in my ear.

I rolled around so I could see his face, but he kept his hold on me. "I love waking up beside you."

"I love waking up beside you, too." We kissed and lay together for another hour before he announced he wanted to make us breakfast. I stayed in bed, pulling his pillow over my face and breathing in his scent, until the smell of pancakes and bacon invaded my nostrils. Reluctantly throwing off the covers, I made my way to the kitchen.

I convinced Ben to eat breakfast in the living room so we could watch *It's a Wonderful Life*. We sat cross-legged on the floor in front of the tree, balancing our plates on our knees and sharing in George Bailey's joys and sorrows. We both remained in our pajamas. He wore green flannel sweatpants and a white t-shirt while I sported a pair of his boxers and an old baseball jersey. I loved it. I loved being so comfortable with him I didn't care how my hair looked or if I wore the right makeup or the right outfit. I could just be me.

When we both had our fill of breakfast, Ben started handing me presents. "I think you spent too much money on me," I scolded him as the pile of gifts in front of me grew larger and larger.

"They're just little things, honestly, I didn't spend that much."

"Mmhmm." I didn't believe him, but opened the gifts anyways. The first several contained books or DVDs I had mentioned wanting.

"This one I think you're really going to like." He handed me a large, flat, rectangular present.

I tore the paper apart and gasped, "Oh my god, Ben. This is beautiful. I can't wait to hang it up." I held a black wooden frame containing my first published article. "Thank you, thank you, thank you."

I gently set the frame aside and stepped over mounds of wrapping paper so I could sit in his lap. I draped my arms around his neck and kissed his cheek. "Thank you." I kissed his lips. "Thank you. I love it. I love you." He parted his lips and I kissed him again. When he pulled away, I let my cheek rest on his, and noticed he hadn't opened any of his gifts yet.

He must have realized where my gaze rested, because he said, "I got distracted watching you open yours. Your reactions are so cute. Your eyes get all wide, and you get this goofy half-grin when you really like the gift. It's so cute I wish I'd gotten you more."

"You got me plenty. I love every single thing, and my article looks so beautiful in that frame - I couldn't have asked for anything better."

"Well, I have one more for you, but it's really for both of us, so we can open it last. I'll open these first." He gestured to his small pile of gifts and I slid off his lap to give him more room. He opened a CD and DVD first.

"That's your real gift," I said as he picked up the next package. He flashed me a smile while ripping the paper off.

"A digital camera, wow, thanks! Mine broke over a year ago, did you know that?" He slid the camera out of its box and turned it over in his hands, examining every detail.

"No, I didn't. But you're always taking pictures with your phone, so I thought a good digital camera would be something you'd like."

"It is. I've been meaning to replace mine forever. Thank you." He kissed me again. "Let's try it out!" He pulled me into his lap and held the camera out with his left arm. I kissed his cheek as he snapped the photo.

"Perfect," he said, looking at the image. "Now for *your* real gift." He slid a large box out from behind the tree and placed it in front of me. Buried beneath what must have been four or five packs of tissue paper, I found a bright pink parka, ski boots, and another thin box.

"Pink?" I crinkled my nose and held the parka to my chest, looking down to scrutinize the effect.

"You look good in pink. Besides, it's the only color they had in your size."

"I thought you agreed not to buy me anything pink."

"Oh, be quiet. Open the little box."

I smirked at him, pulled the lid off the second box, and found plane tickets and a brochure to a ski resort. A piece of paper tucked inside the brochure confirmed a reservation for two in Ben's name starting on December twenty-sixth.

"We're going skiing!?" I threw my arms around his neck.

"We leave first thing tomorrow! And I've got a whole fun week planned for us. We'll stay until New Year's."

"I'm so excited! I've never been skiing before. I'll probably be terrible at it, but it looks like so much fun."

He laughed. "It is fun."

"I'm going to need to go home and pack!"

"No need. Ashley conspired with me and went to your apartment a couple of days ago. She's going to bring your suitcase tonight."

"You think of everything. What did I do to deserve you?"

"I don't know. You must be lucky."

"I think you're right." I kissed him deeply, but pulled away as a horrible thought occurred to me. "Wait, Ben. How can you afford this? You can't go spending all of your money on me when your business is in trouble."

"It's okay."

"No, Ben, it's not. We can't go on a trip right now."

"It's fine. I paid for it out of my savings."

"But what if you need that money for the business later on? No, we can't." I pushed the tickets into his hands, but he let them fall into his lap.

"Abigail, if you don't want to go, we don't have to go. But the tickets are non-refundable and I'm really not worried about the money. I always manage."

"Ben…" I pleaded; I couldn't stand the thought of being responsible for taking money away from Inner City Sports.

"Abby, you're making a big deal out of nothing." But he couldn't look me in the eye.

"You're sure?"

"I'm sure."

There was nothing left to say. He wasn't going to back down. And if he insisted on taking the trip, I couldn't stop him. "Okay… well, then of course I want to go."

"Good." He picked up the tickets and put them in the pocket of my parka, then pulled the coat open and wrapped it around me. He grinned. "See, you look good in pink."

Christmas with my family in the evening passed uneventfully. Dad made a turkey and Mom baked cookies. We all opened presents and my father gave Ben a brand new red stocking, a bright green "E" stitched on the toe.

"I guess we both got a new initial this Christmas," he joked as the eight of us posed for a picture, each proudly holding our initialed stockings.

Anna nudged Ben with her elbow. "You're part of our family now."

"I like the sound of that," he fired back, putting his arm around me.

Chapter Twenty-Three: Numbers 19, 14, and 12

Ben

Abby held my hand as we boarded the plane and found our seats in the back. "Aisle or window?" she asked.

"I can't look out the window, it'll make me want to hurl."

"Window for me, then!" She scooted into the row and sat, buckling her seat belt and, since her hand still held mine, forcing me to follow and take a seat as well.

She unlatched her fingers and took my arm in her hand, bringing it across her lap. She pushed my sleeve up to my bicep and lightly ran her nails up and down, starting at my fingertips and scratching gently up to the crook of my elbow. I closed my eyes and let her soothing touch wash over me.

When the plane landed, Abby woke me.

"Did I sleep through the whole flight?" I looked around to see the other passengers gathering their carry-on bags and preparing to exit the plane. *How is it possible I slept the whole time? I've never been able to sleep on a plane.*

"Yep!" she said, her face lighting up. "See, I'll get you over your fear of flying yet!"

I leaned over and kissed her, our lips melted together and her fingers instantly moved into my hair. With her by my side, I knew I could conquer anything. I hoped the week I had planned meant as much to her as the last few hours meant to me.

After checking into our room and changing, I led Abby to the slopes and found Rob, our ski instructor. Well, her instructor. I learned how to ski when I was eight. He complimented her pink parka, causing my "I told you so!" face to come out, which she laughingly rolled her eyes at.

She couldn't stand up straight for the first hour. It was adorable. Every time Rob got her to her feet she inevitably went right back down. He glared at me as I snapped pictures and laughed my ass off, but Abby was still smiling so I ignored him for a while. When she started looking frustrated, I decided I should probably take Rob's advice and get out of the way.

"I'll meet you in the lobby for dinner." I kissed her cheek and thanked Rob, confirming we had his time reserved for the next day as well.

"Yeah, I'm looking forward to it," he grinned, "now, back to my student."

My gut told me the guy was strange, but Abby appeared to be enjoying herself again, so I shook it off and made my way to the Black Diamond run. Every once and a while, I'd sneak back over to watch her. Rob placed his hands on the small of Abby's back to help her posture. He moved them to her hips when showing her how to turn. After her knit hat and goggles slipped off, he brushed the wet strands of hair out of her face. It hit me why the instructor was weirding me out. He was flirting with my girlfriend!

I moved forward, with every intention of stepping in and giving him a piece of my mind, but Abby swatted his hand away and adjusted her hair, goggles, and hat herself. She didn't seem to be upset by his gesture, but she also wasn't inviting more. My guess is she didn't even realize he was trying to come on to her. And she was having fun. I didn't want to ruin that. That's why we were there. So I went back to the Black Diamond and tried to forget my jealousy. At the end of the day, I knew she'd be coming back to me.

Abby

"Your husband's already scheduled a lesson for tomorrow at ten. I'll see you then," Rob said as we parted ways in the lobby.

"Okay, great. Thanks. See you tomorrow." I didn't realize until he was out of earshot, but I hadn't corrected him. Hearing Ben called "my husband" felt so natural, I blushed at the thought of it.

Ben wasn't in the lobby yet, so I plopped into an armchair by the fire and grabbed a book from the coffee table to peruse while I waited. I read the first page four or five times before giving up and putting it aside. Knowing I couldn't focus on anything else, I stared into the flames and imagined what our life together would be like.

A blue-eyed little boy sat on Ben's lap, playing with a sandy blonde puppy. His chubby arms reached out to me and I lifted him out of his father's grasp. His hands clamped around my neck and the sound of his childish laughter filled my heart with love. Ben wrapped his arms around me, enveloping both of us in a hug, kissing the top of our little boy's head, then meeting my eyes. The adoration living in his gaze had only intensified in the intervening years.

Ben's voice roused me from the daydream, "Did you miss me?"

"I did, actually. Unlike Rob, I found your laughter encouraging."

"That's good to know. Are you hungry?"

"Starving."

"Restaurant or room service?"

"Room service, please. I want to change out of these clothes and go to bed ridiculously early."

"Sounds like a good plan to me." He grinned and we headed up to our room. I insisted he take the shower first because I wanted to completely unpack my suitcase and see what Ashley provided for me. Once the water started running, I unzipped the case and found several sweaters and a couple pairs of ski pants right on top. I shook each one out, refolded, and tucked them away in the wardrobe. Underneath the standard outfits she had packed several pairs of tights, panties, bras, socks, and pajamas, plus one little black dress and a pair of red heels. I hung the dress up and discovered a white garment box beneath it. Lifting the lid, I spotted a note on top of the tissue paper. Folded in half, a large "B" stood out on the front.

B- I know how much you hate the color, but from my personal experience, men LOVE pink lingerie. Have fun- be safe! Love, S.

I immediately pushed the tissue paper aside and held up a pink silk nightie with matching panties. Condoms filled the bottom of the box. I couldn't believe it. I thought my family knew how I felt about sex, but apparently not. At least she hadn't gotten me anything too risqué. Stuffing it back in the box and throwing it in the suitcase, I finished unpacking.

I grimaced at the lone bed in the room. We hadn't discussed it yet. I didn't want to. Christmas Eve proved we could sleep in the same bed without it being uncomfortable. Why'd my stupid sister have to go and ruin it with such a tacky gift?

When the water shut off in the bathroom I began preparing my normal pajamas and toiletries so I could use it when Ben finished, pushing all thoughts of the white box and its ridiculous contents out of my head.

* * * *

By the third day, I was master enough of my skis that we went on the slopes without an instructor. I absolutely loved skiing! A similar sensation to riding a motorcycle overtook me as I flew down the hill. We were still on the beginner's slope, but I was going faster than I had ever gone on my own two feet before.

"You're actually pretty good. You picked it up a lot quicker than I thought you would," Ben admitted as we rode the lift to the top of the hill.

"I bet you thought it'd take me the whole week to be able to stand up without falling."

"Pretty much. But you're doing so well, maybe Wednesday we can try out the next slope."

"Why not tomorrow?"

"I have something else planned for tomorrow."

"What?"

"It's a surprise." He wriggled his eyebrows up and down.

I tried my best to pout, hoping he'd cave and spill the beans. "I hate surprises."

"No, you don't. You love them."

Apparently I needed to work on my pouting skills. "Damn it, you're right. I hate it when you are right."

"No, you don't. You love it."

I rolled my eyes at him, but once again, he *was* right.

* * * *

"Make sure you dress warmly," Ben instructed, pulling a wool sweater over his t-shirt.

"More warmly than I've been dressing all week?"

"Yes, and don't be a smart ass. It's cold out."

"You like it when I'm a smart ass," I teased happily.

"I do, actually. But I'm serious: extra socks, extra gloves, hat, two sweaters- as much clothing as you can possibly put on." He tossed me a pair of tights hanging in the bathroom. "I'm going downstairs to get us a couple bottles of water. I'll meet you in the lobby."

"Okay."

He left the room and I followed his instructions, putting on the tights, a pair of pants, a camisole, a t-shirt, a sweater and a sweatshirt, three pairs of socks, my parka, a scarf, a wool knit hat, and stuck two pairs of gloves in my pockets. I looked like the Marshmellow Man from *Ghostbusters.*

Sexy, I thought, laughing and checking my reflection in the mirror.

Ten other people were standing around the lobby by the time I located Ben. "This is our group," he said.

"Where're we going?"

He didn't answer, but pointed at a man by the fire, who started to speak.

"Hello, everyone. My name is Dave and I'll be your hike leader today. Before we leave, I want to go over our safety procedures: First - always remain with the group. Second - always remain with your hike partner. Third - if at any point you feel dizzy, lightheaded, or find breathing difficult, let me know immediately. Fourth - if at any point you lose feeling in any of your extremities, let me know immediately. If you haven't eaten anything today, please do so now. We'll be leaving in fifteen minutes. Thanks everyone!"

I stared at Ben, puzzled. "We're going on a nature hike, with six inches of snow on the ground?"

"Not exactly. We're hiking up the side of the mountain."

"Are you kidding me?"

"No, I'm not. It's a once in a lifetime experience. Don't worry," he must have seen the terror spreading across my face, "it's completely safe. They take groups up every day all winter."

"Really?"

"Really. That's why I chose this place."

"What happens if you get dizzy or lightheaded or lose your breath or can't feel your legs?"

"They have medic stations along the trail, you stop hiking and get warmed up at the closest one."

"I guess it could be fun."

He smirked, knowing he'd won me over. "Of course it will be, and I hear the view from the top is amazing." After he helped me put on my backpack, we followed the group out into the snow.

He was right. Again. *Damn it.* The hike was incredible. The path was a little steep, but we could see a view of the valley from every possible angle as we journeyed upward. We stopped at several of the medic stations to rest and at each stop Dave told us stories about the history of the mountain, the types of trees surrounding us, and the animals who lived there.

The snow-covered hills and peaks of the valley took my breath away when we reached the top. It looked like a picture from a postcard. We could see for miles in every direction, there was no end to the world from where we stood. The pine trees, sprinkled with white powder, glistened in the sun; a frozen river snaked through the valley, sunlight bounced off its glassy surface and illuminated its frosty banks. The entire group was silent for at least ten minutes; no one wanted to disturb the serenity living there. When Ben finally spoke to me, it was in a whisper.

"Totally worth it, huh?"

"Absolutely. I've never seen anything so beautiful before."

"I have." He said it so quietly, I wasn't sure if he meant for me to hear. When I looked into his eyes, I forgot for a minute we were standing on top of a mountain. He leaned in to kiss me, warmth spread throughout my entire body and sweat built up beneath my layers of clothing as his tongue wrapped around mine. A strange clicking noise interrupted the peace and I remembered we weren't alone. But as I pulled away, I realized no one was watching us, Ben had just pulled out his camera and taken our picture.

"Way to ruin the moment," I teased, slapping his arm.

"Sorry, I couldn't resist." His grin was so goofy, I had to laugh.

A few minutes later, a helicopter touched down. Two at a time, it flew us back down the mountain. Ben gave me his camera and I took a thousand pictures of the valley from the air; he kept his eyes closed the whole time. Being on top of the mountain reminded me of looking at a postcard, but from the helicopter the valley seemed more like a huge snow globe. The frost-covered treetops looked so perfect they couldn't be real.

"That was absolutely the coolest thing we've ever done," I whispered to him as we lay in bed that night.

"I'm glad you enjoyed it."

"What made you think to plan something like that?" I laid my head on his chest and he stroked my hair.

"Well, the resort offers it."

"But you said that's why you choose this place."

"Oh, right. I guess I must've read about it somewhere."

"I wish you would've looked at the view during the helicopter ride. It was spectacular. Like I was looking down from heaven."

He sighed. "I saw enough of it from the mountain."

"I'm supposed to be helping you get over your fear of flying. You've helped me conquer so many of my fears."

"I feel better flying when you're beside me. I think that's the best you can do." He continued playing with my hair and I fell asleep listening to his heart beating.

Chapter Twenty-Four: New Year's Eve

Abby

The days flew by so quickly, it was New Year's Eve before I was ready for it. The resort crawled with guests and employees preparing for the huge bash happening in the evening.

Unable to contain my excitement, I left the slopes early to get ready for the party. I showered, wrapped myself in a towel, and went to get my black dress out of the wardrobe. I grabbed a pair of panties and was about to slip them on when I remembered the box in my suitcase. Something compelled me to pull it out and put both pieces on.

Glancing in the mirror, my reflection caught me off guard. It was ludicrous, but I looked and *felt* sexy. The pink silk blended in with my skin and clung to my curves, my cleavage looked incredible against it. I'd never really thought of my body as sensual before, but looking in the mirror, seeing myself in the lingerie, every secret desire and fantasy I'd ever had came rushing at me. I imagined Ben's face looking at me wearing only the nightie and suddenly felt intensely hot all over. I threw the dress on to block those thoughts out and spent the next half-hour curling my hair and putting on makeup. I slipped on the pair of heels and clasped my jewelry just as Ben called from the slopes to say he'd be another couple of minutes.

I decided to go ahead to the party; I didn't want to be in the room while he got ready, anyways. I left a note on the bed.

Ben, I'm downstairs. I can't wait to ring in the New Year with you. ~Love, Abby

I made my way to the bar, where a crowd of people pushed and shoved to get closer, all waiting for drinks. After standing in line for several minutes, annoyed and ready to give up, someone near the bar called out, "Abigail!"

I searched for the source and saw Rob waving at me. I waved back and he motioned for me to join him.

"Good evening, Abigail. You look nice in normal clothes."

"Ha, thanks. These aren't my normal clothes, though. You look nice, too." And he did, he wore black slacks and a red button-down shirt that showed off his tight biceps. I felt a blush rising to my cheeks and couldn't believe I was admiring this random guy's arms. I shook my head and smiled at him, hoping he hadn't noticed my temporary embarrassment.

"Where's your husband?" he asked after acquiring a drink for me.

"I'm not sure. I left him on the slopes a while ago to get ready and haven't seen him since. And he's actually not my husband." I took a sip of the martini and Rob took a sip of his beer.

"Really?" A smile spread across his face and he leaned in closer to me. "So how's your skiing coming? I was disappointed not to see you the past couple of days."

I took a step back and casually answered, "Ben thought I was doing well on my own. Plus, we took the hike up the mountain on Tuesday. But yesterday and today we were out on the slopes. I actually moved up to a more difficult course. Ben says I'm a natural."

"Does he?"

"Yeah, and he's been skiing his whole life." I scanned the crowd, but didn't see Ben anywhere.

"How long have you two been together?" He motioned for the bartender to bring me another drink, even though I'd barely made a dent in the first one.

"Since April, about nine months." *Wow, has it really been that long?* I thanked the bartender then turned back to Rob. "I should go find him. Excuse me."

He stepped in front of me, cutting off my path. "I'm sure he'll find you when he's ready."

Shit, did I give him the wrong impression? How do I get out of this? "All the same, it's getting a little crowded in here for me. I'd rather wait in the lobby." I tried again to leave, but he continued blocking the way.

"Just have one more drink with me. We didn't really get a chance to talk on the slopes."

"I didn't realize I was supposed to be making small talk with my ski instructor during our lesson."

"Come on Abby, just one drink." He put his hand on my shoulder and slid it down my arm to my elbow. Chills ran through my body.

"Do *not* call me Abby. And get out of my way." Hearing him use that name for me caused bile to rise up in my throat. I pushed him out of the way, spilling my drink on his shoes, and stumbled out of the restaurant. He cursed, but I didn't look back or apologize. I was so angry. Only Ben was allowed to call me Abby.

The whole village appeared to have come to the resort to celebrate the New Year; there were people everywhere: cramming into the restaurant, slamming the bar, filling the dance floor, and milling around in the lobby. The crackle of the fire from the lounge called to me and I went and stood in front of it. The flames warmed my bare arms and legs, and ironically, cooled my head. A waiter passed by with a tray of champagne and I took two, hoping to find Ben soon.

"Abigail," Rob said, walking towards me, "hey, look, I'm sorry if I offended you."

"It's fine," I responded through clenched teeth, setting the glasses on the mantle.

"Can I make it up to you? How about a dance?"

"No, thank you. I'm waiting for my boyfriend."

"I'm sure he won't mind."

"Well, *I* mind." I glanced around again, searching for Ben. *Where is he?*

Ben

I adjusted my tie and dabbed on aftershave; Abby loved the smell of my aftershave. Slinging my jacket over my shoulder, I made my way out the door and to the staircase. From the top, I could see down into the lobby. It was packed. I put my jacket on, craning my neck, and slowly descended the stairs, searching for Abby and wondering if she'd already gone into the restaurant.

I spotted her as I hit the bottom step, she stood facing the roaring fire; its flames danced behind her and highlighted the caramel pieces in her hair. The black dress she wore clung to her curves and an urge to take her in my arms and make love to her swept through me. I closed my eyes and took in several deep breaths, trying to calm my mind and body.

Once I'd regained control, I opened my eyes and directed them back to her. She wasn't alone anymore. Her ski instructor stood in front of her and reached his arm out, trying to take her hand. She shoved it away and I immediately jumped into the crowd, knocking people out of the way, trying to get to her.

Rob grabbed her wrist, pulling her against him, and kissed her. *Oh hell no! Get your hands and lips off her!* I wanted to rip his head off, but I didn't have to. She pushed him off with force, slamming him into the couch. Her hand drew back and swung forward, slapping him across the face with a sharp *thwack.*

By the time I reached her side, Rob had regained his feet and was rubbing his jaw.

"Get the fuck away from her," I growled at him.

"I was just trying to keep her company." Rob held his hands up and stepped back.

"That's not what it looked like to me." I lurched towards him, fists clenched by my side and he backed further away, nearly tripping over the group of people who had turned to watch the confrontation. I spun and took my place back at Abby's side. "Are you okay?" I carefully took her hand and examined her wrist, a faint pink line where his fingers had dug into her skin caused my rage to boil over.

"I'm going to kill him!" I spat out the words, ready to wring his neck with my bare hands. I turned to follow him into the crowd, but Abby's touch on my shoulder stopped me.

"Leave it, I'm fine." She tugged on my sleeve and my eyes forgot to look for the scumbag as they turned to hers.

"Where the hell were you?" She punched my right arm with anger in her eyes, but no force behind the blow. Then, just as quickly, she wrapped her hands around my waist and hugged me tighter than she'd ever hugged me before.

"I was trying to get to you," was the only answer I could manage.

I held her for a few minutes while the crowd gawking at us dispersed. She let go and handed me a glass of champagne as we went into the party.

Abby

We managed to find a table quickly and ordered dinner and dessert. We didn't talk about Rob, but Ben refused to leave my side as we danced the night away. I loved him for wanting to protect me, even though I handled things fine on my own. The whole episode seemed ridiculous now that it was over and I was back in Ben's arms. It reinforced yet again how much I loved him; it assured me he was the only man for me.

A slow song began just before midnight and Ben drew me close to him. We swayed back and forth with the music, our hearts beating in time with each other. The countdown began. The crowds around us chanted:

"Ten
Nine
Eight
Seven

Six

Five…"

Ben didn't wait for one. We ended the old year and started the new, lips and hearts joined together as one.

When we finally released each other, it was well past midnight. The music picked up and people danced drunkenly around us. "Let's get out of here," I said, leaning into him.

Wordlessly, he took my hand, led me out of the restaurant, and up to our room. As soon as the door was locked, he took my face in his hands and kissed me again. A fire rose in me. He was the one, I knew it. I'd known it for months. I didn't want to wait anymore.

He pulled away when it started getting intense, but I kept my arms around his neck and he rested his forehead on mine. The pause cooled me down and I tried to clear my head. Did I really want it? The thought of making love to him sent heat through every vein in my body.

Yes.

I was ready. I was more than ready.

I don't know what he'd been thinking, but he staggered away and turned his back to me. Sitting on the edge of the bed, he put his face in his hands. I didn't say anything, but stepped quietly into the bathroom.

I brushed my teeth, re-applied my lip-gloss, and slipped off my dress. Shaking out my hair, I looked into the mirror. Somehow, I was still the sexy woman from earlier in the evening. I adjusted the nightie so it hugged my body in all the right places, but paused before opening the door. I'd told myself yes twice already, but this was something I needed to be sure about.

Closing my eyes, a thousand images flooded my brain. A stranger knocking on the window of my car door, the first time his blue eyes pierced mine, a light blue shirt, his face as he leaned in to kiss me, a rare book behind a glass case, a man on a motorcycle, candles flickering on a birthday cake, white knuckles clutching an armrest, waking up beside him, running towards him at home plate, the letter "E" on a stocking, my grandfather's box, snow-covered mountain, the look on his face when I said "I love you."

I twisted the handle and walked out into the room. He was facing away from me, hanging his jacket in the wardrobe. I waited for him to turn around, but he must not have heard the bathroom door, because he loosened his tie and hung that up as well, then slipped his pants off, carefully folded them in half, and placed them on a hanger. Standing alone in his white cotton boxers, he started to unbutton his shirt.

Softly, I called out, "Ben."

Chapter Twenty-Five: Beloved

Ben

I jumped, her voice came out of nowhere. "Abby, you startled me. I was just changing."

Turning, I reached towards the bed for my pajamas. Gripping them, I straightened up and took a step forward when my eyes fell on her. *Oh my God.* I stopped, unable to continue moving. *What the hell is she trying to do to me?* The pink nightgown blended with the rosy tint of her skin and her hair fell in luscious waves over her shoulders. She ran a hand up her thigh and rested it on her hip. Arousal dizzied me, but I tried to keep my composure.

"Abby, you're killing me."

"What?" Surprise flashed in her green eyes. "That's not exactly the reception I was hoping for."

"I'm struggling to control myself, but you're going to have to wear something else." I covered my eyes with my hand and rubbed the temples of my forehead, but the image of her, almost naked, seemed painted on the back of my eyelids.

"I don't want you to control yourself anymore." Her voice floated towards me, huskier than normal, definitely not helping me in the self-control department.

"Abby…" *You don't mean that. Why are you doing this?* I wanted to ask, but the words didn't come out.

"I'm ready. I don't want to wait anymore. I love you." Her presence by my side filled me. Her vanilla scent made its way to my nose while her hands grazed over my chest then locked around my waist. Torture. Absolute torture.

You don't really know what you're asking. Just walk away, Ben.

"I love you, Benjamin Harris." Her lips pressed into my Adam's apple. "I want you more than I've wanted anything in my life." She continued her assault, lips now on my collarbone. My breathing hitched as I tried to clear my head, tried to decide how to tell her no, but all I could think about was grabbing her and throwing her on the bed.

"I love you so much." She persisted, kissing down my chest. "I want this." Her lips landed on mine and gently coaxed, but I refused to open my mouth. She was a good seductress, but I couldn't go through with it, no matter how badly I wanted to. She'd regret it. I knew she would regret it.

I kept my eyes closed, but couldn't help myself as I moved my hands up and down her bare arms. Feeling goose bumps form on them at my touch, all my plans of stopping her seemed to vanish.

"Ben, look at me," she demanded.

I obeyed. Big mistake.

"I don't know how to do this, so you're going to have to participate."

I stared into her eyes and saw her desire. She was serious. At least, she believed she was. But I knew better. This couldn't happen. Not like this. And yet, my brain, and my heart, and my other body parts couldn't seem to agree on anything.

Abby

His jaw loosened and he parted his lips to speak, but I went for them immediately, cutting him off. His hands clutched at the fabric of my silk teddy and mine moved to his shoulders, tugging at his sleeves until the shirt lay on the ground and my fingers touched his smooth skin. He gave in and kissed me back passionately. I let my fingers dig into his arms and could feel his pulse speeding up.

Yes… I pushed my hips into him and recognized his excitement growing rapidly. It should have scared me, but it didn't. *Yes…* His lips left mine and caressed my neck and shoulders. *Yes…* The silk straps fell and pulled tight against my upper arms, barely keeping the garment from falling off my body. *Yes…* My fingers groped every inch of his back, chest, and arms I could reach and then went for the waistband of his boxers. He flinched and leaned back.

"Abby, wait. We can't. I can't."

No! "Why? What are you talking about? I told you, I'm ready." I reached for him, but he took another step back.

"You don't want this."

"Yes. Yes, I do. I'm in love with you."

"I'm in love with you, too."

"Then what's the problem? Don't you want to make love to me?" *Please, I want you to, more than anything. I want you to make love to me.*

"Oh God yes. That's not it." He took a deep breath and continued, "You told me you were waiting until you got married and I'm prepared to wait with you."

"I don't want to wait anymore."

"I don't want you to regret anything." He crossed his arms over his chest and took another couple of steps back. My eyes followed his.

"How could I possibly regret sleeping with you?"

"I can't take that moment away from you. When we get married, I want you to have that magnificent wedding night you've been waiting for. I won't ruin that."

I opened my mouth to speak, but no words came out. *Oh my goodness. He's planning on marrying me someday.* Sitting on the bed, I lifted the straps of the nightgown back into place. I couldn't believe he loved me that much, so much that he'd deny himself what he obviously wanted. What we both wanted.

"I love you, Ben."

He breathed out in what seemed like relief. "I love you, too."

I pulled a tissue out of the box on the nightstand and dabbed my eyes. Cleared my head. Looked at his face and saw his concern for me. But I didn't change my mind. "I know you do. And I know you'd sacrifice all of your own wants and needs and dreams for mine."

He nodded.

"Do you remember what I told you about why I wanted to wait?"

"Yes. You said you wanted sex to mean something. You wanted it to be about love, not just pleasure."

"I wanted to feel beloved."

He nodded again.

"I do, Ben. Feel beloved. It was never about the wedding night. I thought it was, but that's because I was young and naïve. Or just plain stupid, I don't know. Subconsciously, I think I thought a man would have to marry me for me to believe that he really loved me. But I'm not so young now. You've helped me grow up and I've realized that isn't true. I have no doubts left. I know you love me and are committed to me. And I know that because you've been so amazing about respecting me and my boundaries and convictions."

"But Abby…" He walked towards me and I stood to meet him, taking his face in my hands and locking his gaze to mine.

"No regrets. I promise. If you don't want to, if you still want to wait until we get married, I respect that. But we aren't waiting because of me any more. Okay?"

"Okay." He smiled, finally, and rested his hands on my hips. "I don't want to wait. But I think we're going to have to for at least a couple of minutes. I need to run down to the lobby, to the gift store, I didn't plan for this."

"Luckily for us, my sister did." I let go of him and bent down to pull my suitcase out from under the bed. When I showed him the box of condoms, laughter flitted across his face. He took it from me, setting it on the nightstand, and picked up a handful from the bunch.

"How much sex did she think we'd be having this week?"

I shrugged. "A lot, I guess."

"Remind me to get her a really big gift when we get back."

"Absolutely." I draped my arms around his neck again and he drew me close to him, our lips meeting almost instantly in a soft, delicate kiss.

Ben must have felt my hands trembling because he pulled back and whispered, "Are you sure? Are you scared?"

"Yes, I'm sure, just a little nervous, I guess. But, I'm absolutely positive I want this." I kissed him again and together our bodies moved towards the bed.

I never knew how much love I was capable of feeling until that night. It was weird, afterward, knowing – realizing - that I wasn't a virgin anymore. Laying on Ben's chest, feeling it move up and down quickly as he tried to catch his breath, I wondered if I'd be a different person with such a huge chunk of my identity gone.

But then he stroked my hair. And whispered, "I love you, Abby," so many times I lost track. That night didn't make me different. Ben crashing into my car nine months before did. I didn't regret it and I wouldn't have had it any other way.

Do I need to say it was worth the wait?

Ben

Abby fell asleep before I did, which didn't surprise me; it had been a huge night for her. Huge for me, too, obviously, but in a different way. A great way, just different. Laying there, holding her, I loved her more than ever before. More than seemed possible.

Her cheek rested against my chest, slightly above my heart, and for hours I listened to her softly breathing while running my fingers through her hair and across her shoulder. I couldn't bring myself to go to sleep. What if it had been a dream? What if we hadn't been that close? What if I woke in the morning to find she no longer trusted me to love her and care for her and respect her?

Around four-thirty she woke and wiggled out of my arms carefully, thinking I was asleep, I guess. She closed herself in the bathroom and I held my breath, watching and waiting, wondering if things had changed for her. After the flush of the toilet and a couple minutes of faint running water, she opened the door and began tiptoeing back to the bed. She hadn't put any clothes on, yet, and she was so beautiful walking towards me that I sat up and reached for her.

"Ben! I'm sorry, did I wake you?"

"No, I haven't been to sleep yet."

"Oh." She climbed into the bed, pressing herself into my arms. She yawned and snuggled even closer into me. "I'm sorry. Insomnia?"

"Yeah." Holding her as tightly to my body as possible, I lay back down and resumed caressing her hair.

"That feels nice," she murmured against my neck. "Love you."

"You, too." I brought one of her hands to my lips and kissed it, then settled into the pillows and pulled a blanket over us. I don't know who fell asleep first, but I woke up six hours later and she was still in my arms.

Chapter Twenty-Six: New Opportunity

Abby

Helen called me into her office about a month after the ski trip. Three *Facing Your Fears* columns had been published and I assumed she wanted to talk to me about the next one.

"Sit down, Abigail." She motioned to the armchairs facing her desk as I entered the room.

"Good morning, Helen." I sat, crossed my legs, and waited.

"How are you liking your office?"

"It's wonderful. I'm just happy to be out of the mailroom."

"We've been getting great response from the articles. Our readers like you. The New York office has authorized a twelve-issue series." She folded her arms across her chest and leaned back in her chair.

"That's fantastic! Thank you!" I could barely stay seated. I'd always wanted this; I found it hard to speak.

"There's something else I wanted to discuss with you. There's an interview process going on right now for a new column. I think you have the right voice for it. Would you like me to get you an interview?"

"A second column? Yeah, I'd love to try for it. What's the angle?"

"*An American in Europe*, basically the columnist would spend a year doing the tourist thing throughout Europe and writing a blog about it: your perspective on all the major sites, reactions from locals to American tourists, the best sites no one knows about, etc."

"That sounds like a lot of fun. And it sounds like me. But I don't understand how I could do both columns. I'd be flying back and forth all the time."

"No, you'd be living in London and reporting to the editor-in-chief of the UK edition. You would email me or New York your current column, or you could write several in advance before you left."

I was sure the surprise must have read all over my face, but Helen didn't seem to notice, "I'd have to live in London?" Maybe I'd heard her wrong.

"Yes, like you said it would be impossible to do both living here."

"I've always wanted to live in London." Again, she didn't appear to detect the disappointment in my voice.

"Great. I'll set up the interview for next week and have my assistant let you know the details."

"Thanks, Helen. This is an amazing opportunity for me. It means a lot that you thought of me."

"Like I said, I think you have the right voice for it. Don't get your hopes up, though. There are a lot of writers interviewing for this." She gestured to the door, and I realized she was through with me.

"Right, I won't bank on it. Thank you again." I left and made my way down the hall to my new office. Well, it wasn't exactly new anymore; I'd been in it for a month now. The article Ben framed for me hung on the wall beside the door, so I could see it from my desk. Beside my computer a seashell picture frame his niece and nephew gave me for Christmas stood in contrast to the snowy photo it held of Ben kissing me on the mountaintop.

A job in London was a dream come true, but I felt sick to my stomach looking at that photo as I sat down behind my desk. I tried to remember Helen's words: "Don't get your hopes up." It wasn't likely I'd get the job, but the thought of having to move thousands of miles away from Boston made me dizzy. I pushed the idea out of my head and focused on the article in front of me. Helen had bled it to death again, so there was plenty of work to keep my mind off the interview.

At twelve o'clock sharp, someone knocked on my door. "Come in," I called out, eyes still glued to the papers in front of me.

"How's my girl doing today?" Ben cheerfully asked, poking his head in. I looked up and couldn't help but smile as soon as I saw his handsome face.

"I'm great. What're you doing here?"

"We had lunch plans, remember?" He walked in and came around the desk to kiss me.

"Oh yeah, of course. Sorry. I've had a busy morning." I pointed at the article and he grimaced at the red ink.

"I didn't realize the editing process was so gruesome."

"This isn't the worst one." I closed the folder and grabbed my purse out of the bottom drawer of the desk. "Let's go, I'm hungry."

Ben

"You're quiet today." I took a sip of my beer, studying Abby's grave face. She looked so downhearted, but I had no idea why. I hated that. I hated when I couldn't figure her out.

She looked up from her plate and attempted a smile. "Sorry, I have a lot on my mind. Helen told me this morning the column is going to appear in at least twelve issues."

"Abby, oh my God! That's wonderful. Congratulations!"

"Thanks. I'm excited." Her eyes dropped back to the table.

"You don't seem like it."

She shrugged her shoulders. "It's a lot of pressure."

I knew she was holding back, but why? What? When I didn't respond she took the cue and changed the subject.

"Have you ever thought about living somewhere else? Besides Boston, I mean."

"Where did that come from?"

"I've just been thinking about it lately. All this talk about the future, I guess. We've never said where we're going to live."

Does she want to move? Is that what this is about? "We both live here. I never thought about living anywhere else. Do you want to? Your job is here."

"Yeah, I know. I was just thinking about the possibilities."

"I would love to try some other places, but right now, I'm pretty settled here. I can't leave my business and my family is here."

"Right, of course." She nodded and pushed her salad around the plate with her fork. I realized she hadn't eaten any of it.

"Abby, what's going on?"

"Nothing. My food's really good, how's yours?"

"Don't lie to me. Something's wrong and you haven't even touched your food. You think I don't know you well enough to know when you're hiding something?"

"You're right, I'm sorry. I'm distracted because Helen asked me to go to New York next week to meet with an editor."

"Well, that sounds like a good thing." I shook my head. Only Abby could see meeting with the New York editor as a problem.

"Yeah. It does sound like a good thing. You're right again." She laughed and took a huge bite of her salad.

"I don't know why you can't accept the fact that I'm always right!"

"I don't either, I guess I'm holding out for that rare occasion when you won't be and I can mercilessly rub it in your face." She crumpled up her napkin and threw it at me. It hit my forehead and bounced to the table. Laughing, she took another bite of her salad. Things were back to normal.

Abby

The interviews were running behind when I arrived at the New York office the following week, but I didn't really mind the delay. It gave me time to think. I wanted the job. I didn't want to leave Boston. I really didn't want to leave Ben. But every time I thought about living in London, touring through Europe, my heart screamed how amazing it would be. I couldn't help but think I deserved it. I'd paid my dues for *years* in that damn mailroom and now things were finally happening for me. First the *Fears* column, then the interview. It could be my shot to do something truly great. If it were only for a year, Ben and I could handle the long distance, right? Before I could answer that question, the receptionist called my name.

"Ms. Bronsen, please have a seat." A short, squat woman with curly blonde hair and thin mouth waved to a chair opposite her desk.

"Please call me Abigail." I reached to shake her hand before sitting down.

"It's nice to meet you, Abigail. My name is Elizabeth Brewing and I'm the editor-in-chief of *Intuition-UK*." Her handshake was firm, her accent dry. "The column you are interviewing for will be running in the American edition, but since I'll be the initial editor of the piece, I'm conducting the first round of interviews."

"It's an honor to meet you." I handed her a folder containing my resume and the first three *Facing Your Fears* columns. She flipped it open and glanced at the pages.

"Tell me about yourself."

I started with basic information, "I'm twenty-five years old. I live in Boston. I went to Boston College and graduated summa cum laude with a degree in journalism. My family means everything to me. I have two sisters and a brother, and they're my best friends in the world."

"Are you married, Abigail?"

Not yet. "No, ma'am."

"Any children?"

Someday, hopefully. "No ma'am."

"What made you want to be a writer?" She closed the folder and her eyes focused on me.

"I wanted the world to hear my voice. I love my family, but it can be hard growing up with so many people around, sometimes you aren't heard at all. I think I have something to say to the world. I'm not always sure what that something is, but I know if given the chance, it would be worth hearing."

"I see." She was smiling now. "How do you feel about the premise of this column?"

"I love it. I've always wanted to see Europe, London and England especially. I've been a big reader since I was four and most of my literary heroes are English. Jane Austen, Charles Dickens, George Eliot. I want to see the places they saw and wrote about. And I've never had the opportunity. There are so many Americans who never have the opportunity to experience the history and culture Europe has to offer. America today tends to set itself apart from the rest of the world, we only dream of going to Europe, or Africa, or Asia. I think I can provide a medium for women like myself to see what we're missing."

She continued to smile as I rattled on. I couldn't tell if she was impressed or suppressing laughter, but it really didn't matter. I was just being myself and being honest. She could like me or not, I was proud of my answers.

"I've read these articles," she held up the folder, "tell me, what inspired you to write them?"

"The friend I talk about in the articles told me once that I was too young to be so afraid and the words stuck with me. Anytime I was scared to do something, he pushed me, told me that I could do anything. I realized I hadn't gotten published because I was too scared to write about anything I cared about, so after giving blood, I just started writing from my heart, not caring whether or not it was what my boss wanted to read, and luckily, she liked it. But it was her idea to turn the article into a series."

We chatted for another twenty minutes. Her questions ranged from "What places would you want to write about?" to "How do you like working for the magazine?" The interview went well, but a line of women was waiting to speak to her when I walked out of the office. Who knew what she was looking for?

"Don't get your hopes up," I muttered to myself as I drove back to Boston with the radio blaring.

Two weeks later, I found out Elizabeth recommended me for a second interview. And she only recommended a total of three people. And they were now planning on the column lasting for at least two years, maybe longer.

Another week after that I turned twenty-six years old and Jeanette Maneheim, the New York Editor-in-Chief, called and offered me the job.

Chapter Twenty-Seven: The Best Gift Ever

Abby

"Abigail, I know you don't like your birthday, but for me, and for your parents, can you at least pretend to be happy?" Ben looked over from the driver's seat and I quickly put a smile on my face.

"I'm sorry. I'm very excited about my birthday dinner." I perked up in my seat and tried to cheerfully participate in the conversation. He seemed pleased with my attempt and focused on the road once more. I hadn't told him about the job offer yet. I hadn't even told him about the interviews. It was stupid and selfish of me, but at first I didn't think I'd get the job and when the idea that I might crept into my head, I pushed it away, unable to imagine living with an ocean between us.

When we reached my parents' house, the entire family was already there, crowding into the living room. After hugs and "Happy Birthday's" all around, I sat down with Samantha to look at her wedding album while Ben began debating spring training with my dad.

The album was pretty standard: pictures of the bride and groom getting ready, the ceremony, the highlights of the reception. I "ohhed" and "ahhed" in all the right places, told Samantha how beautiful she was, and pondered loudly why she married such a troll. Derek responded by throwing a pillow at me. On the next to last page, a picture of Ben and I caught my eye. Dancing, my eyes closed and chin tilted up towards him, he smiled, blue eyes focused happily on my face. He was so beautiful, I wanted to cry. I turned the page promptly and told Samantha I needed to help with dinner. Ben followed me into the kitchen, taking drink orders from my family on the way.

"Abby, what's wrong?"

I hugged him tightly around the neck, burying my face in his chest. "Ben, I love you so much." *I don't ever want to leave you.*

"I know. I love you, too." He seemed to realize that was all I wanted to say and shouts of impatience from the living room caused him to let go of me and grab a few beers from the fridge. "Are you ever going to tell me what's been going on with you lately?"

"Yes. But not here."

"Tonight? When we get home?"

I merely nodded, I knew that by "home" he literally meant his house, but he actually meant *our* home.

I ate silently, listening to my brothers and sisters talk about me, reminiscing with stories from our childhood. Ben paid close attention, asking questions and laughing boisterously at the tales.

When dinner ended, my mother carried over a cake with white icing and twenty-six candles blazing away. After a rousing, and extremely tone-deaf, thanks to Ben, version of "Happy Birthday," I blew the flames out in one breath.

Everyone started handing me presents, but Ben was squirming in his seat so much, I could tell he wanted me to open his first. I pushed the pile to the side and held my hands out to him. His mouth looked like it was going to stretch permanently into a Cheshire cat grin.

"Before you open it, I want to say something." He set a box wrapped in light blue paper in my palms. "I know you hate for me to spend money on you. I had to spend a little, but for the most part, I made the entire gift."

He looked so proud, I leaned over and kissed him. I didn't need to know what was in the box. For what must have been the first time in my life, the phrase *it's the thought that counts* honestly meant something to me.

"Hey, save that until after you open the present," he said, pulling away and glancing at my father.

I turned back to the gift in front of me and ripped the wrapping paper off. When I removed the lid from the box I was surprised to find a photo album inside. Lifting it, I threw the empty box on the floor behind me. One look at Ben told me his excitement was increasing. I opened the book to the first page and nearly dropped it when I saw a familiar sheet of paper that had been folded and smoothed out several times. I didn't say anything, I couldn't decide if I was angry or happy or excited, so I just turned the page.

#25 Cut Off All My Hair (At least once!)

was scrawled across the top in Ben's handwriting and he'd pasted in several pictures of me with a short pixie cut.

"Your mom gave me the photos," he explained. I didn't know what to say, so instead glanced at the opposite page.

#24 Sing Onstage

"I didn't have to do anything at all for this one. You planned the karaoke night!" He laughed, pointing to the photos of me dancing onstage with a microphone held to my mouth.

This one? I flipped the page and read the next heading.

#23 Learn How to Cook

Pictures of me at the stove and a recipe card for lasagna matched the title.

"She's really good, too," Ben told my dad.

#22 Learn How to Develop Photographs

"I got those pictures out of a book in your apartment. I hope you don't mind," he said as I ran my fingers over the flowers, landscapes, and other random subjects I'd shot for my photography class in high school. I turned the page, still unable to decide how I felt about what was in front of me.

#21 Learn a Foreign Language

This page was blank except for the header. I hadn't learned a foreign language, yet. Ben took my free hand. "There are classes we can sign up for," he pointed out. I nodded and looked at the next heading. A gasp escaped my throat.

#20 Learn How to Surf

I glanced at the photos of Ben and I in the waves then turned my face to meet his. Had he been planning this that long ago? *Holy shit.* I couldn't form any words as his smile stretched even wider. He squeezed my hand and I lifted the page without saying anything.

#19 Learn How to Ski

My heart beat faster as I looked at the pictures. He'd created an evolution across the page, showing me as a beginner, barely able to stand, but with each successive picture my skill improved. At the bottom of the page, I crouched low in the photograph, poles held straight behind me, my face and body a blur as I whipped past the camera. I looked to the next page, trying to hold back the emotions building inside me.

#18 Go Scuba Diving

"Did you plan that trip for me?" I finally spoke. Looking at the pictures of brightly colored fish and Ben in full scuba gear, I remembered Matt saying *he* hired the instructor.

"Yes and no. I planned it to celebrate my birthday. But I thought while we were there we could cross a few of your list items off."

"Ben…" I couldn't find my voice anymore; it caught in my throat as I tried to say something else, anything else. But he understood. He flipped the page for me and pointed to the next heading.

#17 Give Blood

I remembered the picture he'd taken of me with his phone that day as I looked at it in front of me. I proudly showed off my hot pink band-aid while holding a cup of juice. I looked so happy.

#16 Get a Tattoo

This page was blank, too.

"Now that's one I can't *wait* to do!" Ben exclaimed. "I almost tried a couple times, but I didn't want to give away that we were checking things off and I thought this one would be a little too obvious." He beamed at me as I turned the page again.

#15 Visit all 50 States (And Washington, DC)

He had carefully written in the name of each state, alphabetically, over several pages. I scanned them quickly. The states I'd visited had pictures under them.

"Anna, Ashley, Derek, and your parents helped me gather the pictures for this one. Well, except Florida and Colorado." I looked at those states, he'd chosen pictures from his birthday weekend and our ski trip to place there.

"We'll fill in the rest together." He squeezed my hand again and I flipped to the next new heading.

#14 Climb a Mountain

A tear splashed on the page as I took in the pictures of Ben and I hiking and kissing on top of the mountain. *So that's why he chose that resort.* My father handed me a handkerchief and Ben dropped my hand so he could put his arm around my shoulders.

#13 Ride a Motorcycle

The only picture on the page was one of Ben's bike parked in front of his house. "I didn't have any actual pictures of you riding it, but we can take one if you want," he explained.

"I hope you didn't get the motorcycle because of my list," I whispered, unable to speak louder without sobbing.

"No, my parents knew I've always wanted one, that's why they got it for me. They didn't know anything about your list."

"Okay." I flipped the page again.

#12 Ride in a Helicopter

Before I could look at him, Ben said, “Sorry I couldn’t get one of you.” The pictures on this page were ones I’d taken of the valley from the helicopter, along with one of Ben, his eyes squeezed shut. I wanted to laugh, but was too close to losing control of my tears to attempt it.

#11 Own a Real Diamond

This page was blank, too. Ben leaned in close to me and whispered in my ear, “Soon.”

By now, my entire family stood around us, looking over our shoulders, enjoying the journey. Ben lifted the page.

#10 Own a Brand New Car

“Your mom gave me those pictures, too.” Ben smiled as I looked over the pictures my mother insisted on taking when I bought my Nissan two years prior.

#9 Go to Disneyworld

Pictures of me with my college roommate and Mickey Mouse covered this page. “Anna got me those. And I realize it’s already crossed off, but we have to go there together. I’ve never been and I hear it’s the happiest place on earth!” He laughed, but the request was serious.

“Actually, it’s ‘Where Dreams Come True.’ You’ve never been to Disneyworld?” With all his parents’ money, they didn’t take him there as a child?

“Nope, so can we go?”

“Um, yeah, someday, definitely.”

“Awesome!” He turned the page again. There were no pictures on the next page either, but Ben left a hand-written note.

#8 Teach Someone Something of Value

Abigail,

You have taught me the most valuable lesson of my life. I searched for years for the right woman and then I crashed into you. I went through bad relationship after bad relationship and could never understand why I didn't feel about anyone the way my father feels about my mother, the way Matt feels about Trish. Then I met you and I learned sometimes the best things in life are worth waiting for. You intrigued me. You made me work hard for your affection and trust. You taught me that love doesn't just fall into your lap, that love must be earned. You taught me how to love. And it's the best lesson I've ever had. I love you, Abby, with my whole heart.

Yours Always,

Ben

I couldn't hold back the tears any longer. They poured down my cheeks and my eyes were so full I could barely see. I put my face in my hands, still clutching my dad's handkerchief, and Ben had to read the last few lines to me. He rubbed my back and waited patiently. When I finally lifted my head, he wiped away the streams on my face and spoke softly, "Don't stop now, there's only seven left."

I nodded and looked at the opposite page.

#7 Buy a House

Another empty one. Ben took my hand and placed a picture of his house in it. "Just say the word and your name is on the deed."

I stared longingly at the photograph for a few seconds, tucking it in the binding of the album before moving on.

#6 Visit Jane Austen's Home & #5 Go to Europe

Both pages were blank. Ben tightened his grip around my shoulders. "That's what vacations are for." It would have been the perfect time to tell him about the job, if we were alone. Fresh tears escaped as I flipped the page once again.

#4 Have a Column in a National Magazine or Newspaper

He had cut out and pasted my first published article onto the page, along with a post-it note from Helen: *Keep up the good work.*

I smiled briefly, thinking of all the rejection notes that preceded it, hoping I'd never see another one.

#3 Get My Journalism Degree

I skimmed over the pictures of me in a cap and gown, posing with my diploma. Ben didn't say anything, but I assumed my mother provided those photos as well.

I knew what was next. When I turned the page it would be blank. Empty. I couldn't do it. Ben saw my hesitation and moved his hand to flip the page himself. I stopped him.

"Wait. Just a second." I took in a breath and exhaled slowly. I wiped away the few stray tears still on my cheeks and gripped the edge of the page.

#2 Get Married

I wanted to move on quickly, he'd left the opposite page blank as well, but he wouldn't let me turn immediately.

"I promise." He took my chin in his hand and nudged it so I was looking into his eyes. His beautiful, perfect, wonderful, blue eyes. "I promise," he repeated, then turned the page for me.

#1 Fall in Love

He filled four pages with pictures and little mementos: movie tickets from our second date, a receipt from Nancy's bookstore, plane tickets, notes I'd written to him. Tears flowed freely again as I examined every detail.

Ben brushed a few strands of hair off my forehead. "I know we didn't get to everything, but it's a start."

I realized as he spoke we were the only two left in the kitchen. I had to tell him. "Ben…"

"Hey now, stop that crying. It hurts me to see you cry." He wrapped his arms around me, like he had so many times before. I buried my face in his chest, like I had so many times before. I couldn't control the surge of tears. He didn't say anything else, just held me while I cried.

"Thank you," I finally managed, "it's the best gift anyone's ever given me."

"Do you wanna go home?"

I nodded. I wanted to go home with him every day for the rest of my life.

Chapter Twenty-Eight: The Hard Truth

Abby

Ben talked through most of the ride home. He was so excited to finish the list.

"We can go and get tattoos sometime this week, if you want, and learn a foreign language, well, I'm fluent in Spanish, I can start teaching you whenever you want. I'm not sure about visiting every state, the complex still isn't doing great, but we could probably work in little weekend trips here and there…" He had a plan for every blank page in the album. I let him talk. I loved him. I loved hearing his plans for us, even if I was going shatter them.

The drive to his house seemed shorter than normal, probably because I couldn't stop thinking. I thought about Ben and our future. I thought about London and the new column. I thought about how great it would be to have both, but how impossible that was. In London, I wouldn't truly have Ben. If I turned down the job, I'd always wonder what if.

He held my hand as we walked into the house together and I knew I had to tell him, knew we had to discuss it. I didn't want to. The thought of me living in London would hurt him and I didn't want to hurt him.

"Ben, we need to talk," I said as soon as he plopped down on the couch.

"Sure thing, babe." But he didn't seem to actually want to talk. He pulled me onto his lap and kissed me, hard. I instantly forgot about London and the job as I ran my fingers through his hair. How could I think about anything else while his arms were wrapped around me?

But eventually he pulled away, dropping one last light kiss on my mouth and letting his forehead rest on mine.

"Happy birthday."

"Thanks." I took a deep breath. "You know, a lot of big things happen on my birthday."

"Oh yeah?"

"Yeah. I was in a pretty bad car accident on my fifth birthday. I broke my right arm. That's kinda where my fear of blood comes from."

"I was wondering about that after your first article."

"And on my twenty-fifth birthday I was in another car accident and met the most amazing man."

"Wait - the car accident we were in was on your birthday? You never told me that."

"Yeah, so we met one year ago today."

"Wow. Well, happy anniversary then."

"We didn't start dating until a month later, so it's not exactly our anniversary."

"Still."

"Yeah."

"What big thing happened on your twenty-sixth birthday?" He grinned, I guess he was expecting me to say his gift was the big thing. And it was. But the job was a little bigger.

"Well… I got a phone call today, from the New York editor. She offered me another column."

"Oh my God! Abby, that's amazing! So, you'll have two columns?"

"Yeah, if I take it."

"Why wouldn't you take it? I mean, that's just awesome."

"I'd have to move," I said quietly.

"Move? To New York? That's not that far away. We'd still see each other every weekend and when we get married we can find someplace in between and commute. You shouldn't let that stop you from taking it." He smiled at me, so eager to be happy and supportive. God, I loved him.

"It's not in New York."

"Where is it?"

I gulped and tried not to look into his eyes, I didn't want to see the confusion in them when I answered. "London."

"London? London, England? You'd have to leave the country?"

I nodded, incapable of elaborating further.

"What about your column here?"

"I'd still write it. Helen said I could finish several pieces in advance and we would teleconference and email during the editing process."

He seemed to brighten at this idea, his voice sounded happier as he asked, "Why can't you do that with this new column?"

I finally brought my eyes to his. His face was hopeful until I started to speak. "Because the concept is *An American in Europe*. Basically I'd be traveling all over the continent and recording my experiences. I'd be reporting to the UK Editor-in-Chief, in London."

He stood up now and walked to the window, keeping his back to me. His voice was strained, "Are you going to take it?"

"I don't know. I have to tell them by Friday."

"When does it start? When would you have to move?"

"I'd need to be there by the end of March."

"Less than a month," he said quietly, his back still to me.

"Ben, I…"

He interrupted me, "This is a great opportunity, Abby, and I'm happy for you, really I am. But you don't have to take it, you know. You've got your column here and your family is here and I'm here. Don't worry about money, I can take care of you."

I wasn't expecting that. I thought he'd encourage me to take it. I didn't know what to say at first, but he waited for me to answer. "Ben, I love you. I appreciate that you can take care of me, that you've been taking care of me, but is that really fair to either of us? Do you really want to have to take care of me for the rest of your life? Shouldn't I be able to stand on my own two feet?"

"What? Of course I want to take care of you forever. And you *can* stand on your own two feet."

"No, I can't. I thought I could, but you've been holding me up this past year. I need to know I can do things on my own. I've been trying my whole life to be independent and this is my chance. I know you can't understand that."

He turned around so quickly I expected him to fall over. "Why can't I understand that?"

"Because you've never had to work for anything in your life!"

"Oh really? Is that what you really think of me?"

"No, Ben, no, I'm sorry..."

But he cut me off, "Why are you even with me then, if you think I'm some spoiled, pampered, brat?"

"Ben, please, I didn't really mean it..."

"Don't think I haven't worked my ass off to get the complex where it is - that I'm not working my ass off to pull it out of debt, or that I didn't work my ass off for you, to get you to love me. I can't even believe we're having this conversation."

"Ben..."

"What about our life? Didn't we have plans? Are those just going up in smoke now? Did you mean it when you said you wanted to marry me?"

"Yes, of course, I still do."

"Then you're right, I don't understand." He crossed his arms over his chest and moved back to the window.

"Don't you see? Don't you see why this is so important to me? You're living your dream. The complex, helping the community. This is my dream, to be a writer, a real writer."

"What're you saying? That you've already made up your mind to go?"

"No, I haven't decided yet. But I can't just stay here for you. No matter how much I love you. And I do, I love you so much." I got up and walked to his side, taking his hand. He wouldn't turn to look at me. We stood like that for a long time, looking out the window at the bleak night, the starless black sky matching the pain in our hearts. Why did it have to be so hard?

"What happens to us if I go?" I finally asked.

He squeezed my hand and pulled me into a hug. "I don't know."

I began crying, his hold tightened. As he held me, I hoped he'd support whatever decision I made. *He may not like it, but he'll support it, won't he?*

I went home instead of staying over, the first night since New Year's we didn't spend together. Why was it such a big deal? Was two years really such a long time? Maybe we could handle it together.

But what if we couldn't? What if the distance destroyed us? I'd never done a long distance relationship before, but Ben had. Jennifer. It didn't work. She broke his heart. He waited around for her his freshman year when he could have been happy with someone else. I didn't want to do that to him. Plus, he said he'd never do it again, didn't he?

I never really deserved him anyways. He had always been too good for me. He came from money. He was successful, handsome, funny, and intelligent. He deserved someone better than me. Someone who knew how to live, who didn't need to be tricked into doing the activities she'd always wanted to do.

Realizing I'd left the album at his place, I curled up in my bed and closed my eyes, desperately trying to picture it in my mind. The words he'd written haunted me, *You made me work hard for your affection and trust. You taught me that love must be earned.* What he said as we discussed the job tortured me, *don't think I didn't work my ass off for you, to get you to love me.*

He gave everything for our relationship, for me. What had I ever given him? He earned my love, but what had I done to earn his? Nothing.

Maybe me leaving was the best thing for him.

Ben

She left a little before midnight. I walked her to her car, kissed her goodbye, and watched her drive away. A sick feeling in my gut told me a bigger farewell was coming.

I walked into the house and immediately went to bed, hoping sleep would block out the questions and thoughts spinning around my head. But once again, I found myself wide awake.

She said I couldn't understand. Damn right I don't understand. I don't understand how we can go from being so in love to this. To me wondering if she'd rather take a job she doesn't even need than stay here with me. She already has a job she loves. Isn't that enough? Aren't I enough?

Chapter Twenty-Nine: Tough Decision

Abby

The week was hell. How was I supposed to choose between the two things I wanted most in life? It didn't seem possible to have both the career I'd been working towards the past four years and the man I loved more than life itself. I couldn't concentrate at work. I burned everything I tried to cook. There was a distance between Ben and I that never existed before. It was the toughest decision of my life, but by Thursday I'd made up my mind.

As soon as he opened the door, tears welled up in my eyes. His face was vacant, his eyes dead. Was he trying to hide his anguish? Make this easier for both of us? Nothing could make what I was about to do any easier. He stepped back wordlessly, inviting me in. Neither of us spoke for a full minute.

"I love you," he said, the blank mask disappearing, his eyes searching my face for a sign of hope I couldn't give.

"I love you, too." I felt like I had been kicked in the stomach; all breath seemed to escape me at once. I wanted to reach for his hand, feel the warmth of his touch, but I knew if I did, he would put his arms around me, he would comfort me, and that wasn't fair to him. It was my choice; I had no right to be comforted. I searched my brain, looked into his eyes; *is there anyway I can do this without hurting him?*

"No," he said, as if reading my mind. He turned away and walked to the window. "It's raining," he threw out, "only fitting, I guess. We've come full circle."

I wiped my face with the back of my hand and followed his gaze out the window. Thunder clapped, interrupting our silence. *Would it be better now if I just left, without saying another word?* It broke my heart to say goodbye - maybe if I didn't say it I wouldn't regret the choice I'd made. I heard the jangle of my keys, heard my footsteps as I walked towards the door, but didn't feel the motions. My heart remained where it was: standing in his living room, watching him.

"Don't leave." He turned with pleading eyes and made a step towards me.

"I don't want to," I admitted, hand on the door.

"Then why?" Another step.

"Because I have to. This is my chance to do something special, to be someone special."

"But you're special to me." Another step.

"But not to myself. And you don't deserve that, and I don't deserve you."

He crossed the room, his hand touched my face, wiped away my tears. I reached up and grasped his hand with mine, gently removing it. I kissed his palm and guided it back to his side.

"Don't make me say goodbye," I pleaded, my eyes focused on the doorknob.

"Goodbye?" His voice suddenly stronger, deeper. "Is that what this is?" His hand closed around mine, preventing me from turning the handle. I didn't answer.

He grew angry, "If that's what this is, then you can't pretend we aren't breaking up. You don't get to have it that easy. If you're going to end this, you have to do it. If you don't say goodbye tonight, then you better be planning on coming back tomorrow."

His stare pierced my heart. "I meant it when I said I was ready to spend my life with you. I'm not the one giving up. If you don't want me, you have to say it!" The blue eyes I fell in love with sparked with fire, I couldn't look away, even though I wanted to.

"It's not that I don't want you."

"Then why?" He almost screamed the words, but his volume didn't change.

"I don't want to leave you, I don't want to end this." I placed my free hand on my heart then on his, like so many months ago in Florida when I told him I was finished doubting his feelings for me.

"If there was a way to have both… But I don't think it's fair of me to ask you to do long distance, to ask you to wait for me when I have no idea when I'll be coming back." I paused, waited, hoped he'd tell me I was wrong, that we could handle anything together. But he said nothing. His free hand clutched at mine, still pressing against his chest. His silence strengthened my resolve and shattered my heart.

"I've been waiting my whole life for this. I've worked so hard, my entire life, and I've never gotten anywhere. I've been stuck in limbo, struggling to move forward. If I don't take this opportunity, I'll regret it forever. I'll always wonder what if. You and I, well, I never thought this was in the cards for me. I went so long without caring for anyone, without anyone caring about me, I imagined I'd never get that opportunity. And then you came along and you are so perfect. I couldn't have dreamed you any better." My hands trembled and the words shook coming from my mouth.

"I love you in a way I never thought I could love anyone. I don't want to say goodbye, because I don't want it to be over. This can't be the last conversation we have, the last time we see each other, the last time we touch. Don't wait for me, move on with your life, but don't ask me to say goodbye. I don't want to end it like that, I don't want to think it's over." My lip quivered as I finished, I bit down to stop the tremors.

"You can't do that to me. You can't have it both ways." Tears formed in his eyes.

"I'm sorry. But, I need to know that I can do this. I need to know I can do it on my own. I don't want to live without you, but I need to know I can. Then someday, if I have the chance and I choose to be with you, you'll know it's not because I need you, but because I want you."

He didn't answer, but his eyes clouded over, a tear broke out and streaked his handsome face. I hated myself for the agony I was causing him.

"I'm so sorry." The words were so pathetic I wouldn't let my voice get louder than a whisper. I leaned forward to kiss his cheek, but he moved swiftly, suddenly, and our lips met before I was aware of what he was doing. His hands released mine and moved to caress my face. They grew firm, holding me to him. Instinctively, I threw my arms around his neck, pulling his body closer to mine.

And that moment became my past, my present, and my future. His arms moved again, now clasping around my waist. We felt like one person: no beginning, no end. My eyes closed tight, but I could see his face - smiling at me, eyes focused. No pain, no tears. We could have stayed there forever; I could have stayed there forever. But I knew it was only making the separation more excruciating for both of us.

I tried to pull away, but he drew me closer. I let him. A few more seconds wouldn't kill me. But what about him? The thought of extending his pain hurt worse than my own, so I broke free.

"I love you." I turned the knob and walked out the door. Rain fell on my hot skin, but it couldn't cool down the fever raging inside me. I didn't look back. I already regretted leaving and knew if I saw his face again, I wouldn't be able to resist him. I prayed this wasn't the end. I prayed someday circumstances would change and one of us would find the other. I knew in my head I was doing the right thing for me. I knew in my heart how selfish it was. And I hated myself for it.

Ben

As I stood on my front porch, watching her walk out of my life, I couldn't distinguish between the drops of rain pelting my face and the tears falling from my eyes. My whole heart, my whole soul ached; the pain intensified with each step she took.

I knew I couldn't stop her. I knew she had to leave, but I couldn't prevent myself from running down the stairs and following the path of her taillights as they glided down the road and eventually disappeared.

She was gone. Out of my life as quickly as she had entered it.

When there was no longer hope of her headlights reappearing, I went inside. The house I planned on being our home felt completely empty. Glancing around the living room, a scream built up inside me.

Why, why would she do this to me? Doesn't she know how much I love her? Doesn't she remember all of the things we did together, all of the fears I helped her face? My anger rose and I slammed the door behind me, trying to close out the world. *What now?*

My cell phone rang, and I lunged for it, knocking it off the arm of the couch and sending it clanking to the floor. Scrambling to pick it up, I tripped on my own feet and fell headfirst into the hardwood. I didn't care.

"Hello? Abby?" I answered, breathless and wincing.

"No, it's Matt. Didn't you look at the caller id?"

"No, I was just hoping."

"Geez, man. You are soooo whipped."

"Not anymore," I muttered.

His voice lost its sarcasm. "What do you mean?"

"She broke up with me. She's moving to London."

"No shit!"

"Yeah."

"I'll be right over."

"No. Don't. I want to be alone tonight. I don't want to see anyone." I covered my eyes with my hands and massaged my forehead. I couldn't stand being around Matt right now. He'd be really supportive, but his idea of support would be trashing Abby for hours and goading me into telling him all the reasons I was better off and I couldn't take that right now. Because I wasn't better off and nothing would convince me that I was.

"What about tomorrow, you want to go shoot some hoops?"

"Maybe. Hey, what were you calling for?" I wanted to talk about something else. Anything else.

"Oh, um. Well, it can wait," his voice cracked.

"Spit it out, Matt."

"I don't think now's a good time."

"For Christ's sake. Just tell me."

He was silent for at least a minute. I was about to hang up when he blurted out, "Trish and I are engaged."

"Oh my God." I tried to say more, but I couldn't speak. My best friend needed me to be excited for him, but all I felt was emptiness.

"I know you'll be happy for us when you wake up tomorrow, so you don't have to say anything. Are you sure you don't want me to come over?"

"Yeah, I'm sure. Um, congratulations."

"Thanks. I'll talk to you tomorrow."

"Okay. " I hung up without waiting for his reply. *Matt and Trish are getting married and Abby and I are broken up. What the hell is going on in the universe?*

Chapter Thirty: Aftermath

Ben

I woke up the next morning and immediately reached for her. I don't know why I had that reflex. I guess the habit developed quickly after New Year's. But it didn't matter, because she wasn't there.

The first hour of the day was spent clearing my house of her things. She would be moving soon, if I didn't pack her stuff, she might leave without it, and I couldn't bear the thought of constant reminders.

She left a couple pairs of shoes and a few sweaters hanging in my closet. Taking a familiar lavender one off its hanger, I caught a whiff of her scent. Vanilla. Tears came to my eyes. *God, what a pansy you've become.* Stuffing the sweater into a box, I grabbed the rest of her clothes and went into the living room. The album I'd made sat on the coffee table, glaring at me. I flipped through it one last time before putting it in the box with the rest of her things. *Now what?*

I dialed her sister's number.

"Hello?"

"Anna, hey, it's Ben."

"Ben? Oh my goodness. Are you okay?"

"I've been better. Listen, I know she's going to be leaving soon and she left stuff at my place. I don't think I can see her again. Do you mind picking it up?" I coughed into my hand to hide the despair in my tone, but I knew I wasn't fooling her. *Get a grip, man!*

"Of course. I'll come by after work tomorrow. Ben, listen…"

I cut her off, "Thanks, I'll see you then." I hung up and moved the box, setting it beside my front door so I would have easy access to it when Anna stopped by. It wasn't going to be easy seeing her, either. She looked too much like Abby. *God, you're pathetic.*

I went back to my room for my wallet and keys, realizing as I walked in the door they were in the box she gave me for my birthday. I snatched it and dumped the contents on the bed. Picking what I needed out of the pile, I left the remains scattered on top of the comforter and took the box to put with the rest of her things. No way I was going to leave that memento lying around.

I locked the house and made my way to the complex. Matt planned to meet me at noon. We were going to play basketball and I was going to forget about Abby. She was gone. I wallowed. It was time to move on.

And I tried, I really tried to move on. I tried not to think about her when Anna stopped by to pick up her stuff. I tried not to think about her every time I sat down to dinner or went to bed alone. And if I'd had more time, maybe I would have succeeded.

Two weeks after she dumped me, I was still in the process of forgetting when, toweling off after a long, hot shower, I noticed my phone glowing: one missed call, one new voice mail. Flipping it open, Abigail's picture and name stared at me. Why hadn't I deleted her from my cell yet? I threw the phone on my bed and got dressed, then went into the kitchen to make myself dinner. I wasn't interested in what she had to say.

Oh, who was I kidding? I was *extremely* interested.

I tried to eat my dinner calmly, but my thoughts kept wandering back to the phone. *Fine. I'll listen to the message.*

"Ben, hey, it's me. I'm at the airport, waiting for my flight, and I just, I just wanted to hear your voice. I know I don't deserve it, but if you could call me back in the next hour… well, no, I'm sorry. Okay, Anna gave me the stuff I left at the house, your house, and um, I just wanted to let you know…" the message cut off, ending my brief moment of bliss. Her voice had been shaky and full of pauses. I hated listening to the pain in her words, but still, it made me feel a little better. At least I wasn't the only one going through hell. I contemplated calling her back, when the phone started buzzing in my hand. Her again.

"Abigail?"

"Ben!" Neither of us spoke for several seconds, I couldn't think of what to say to her.

Finally, she broke the tension, "I'm sorry I called, but I got cut off on the last message and part of me was hoping you'd call back, and well, I just couldn't imagine leaving the country without talking to you…" her voice trailed off. I still didn't speak.

"I know you're upset, angry with me. I won't push you; if I were in your place I wouldn't talk to me either. I just wanted to tell you I left my grandfather's box, your box, with Trish. I understand if you don't want it right now, but it's yours, I gave it to you, and maybe someday you'll be able to look at it and remember the good things about me, about us." Her voice broke, and muffled sobs made their way to my ears. I hated to hear her cry.

"Thanks, Abby. I'll get it from Trish when I'm ready. Hey, good luck, and have fun."

"Ben, I…"

"Yeah, me too. Bye." I hung up before she could say anything else. The pain in my heart deepened as I stared at the now-silent phone in my hands. Tossing it back on the bed, I grabbed my keys and headed to the complex, to my bar. Six tequila shots later and I felt much better. For the first time in my adult life, I enjoyed the taste of liquor as it slid down my throat, helping me block out the last month, helping me forget.

Abby

He hung up without letting me say I love you. Probably a good thing. Why make it more difficult on either of us? I snapped my phone shut and let it fall into my lap, tears flowing freely down my face. My sobs grew louder and I struggled to take air into my lungs. People stared as they walked by, but I couldn't control myself.

With every sob another memory flashed before my eyes: our first kiss, the first time I said 'I love you,' meeting his family, Ben holding his own against my father. I could barely see through my tears, but pulled the photo album out of my carry-on bag and opened it to the last page. Still unable to see the pictures before me, I hugged the book to my chest, closed my eyes, and tried to remember the warmth of Ben's arms holding me.

It didn't work.

Oh God. What have I done? He's never going to forgive me for this, is he? Is it too late to take it back? To run back into his arms?

Yes.

"Ladies and Gentleman, we are now boarding for flight number BA0238 Boston to London," a woman's chipper voice came over the loudspeaker.

I let a few more sobs out as I repacked the album into my carry-on and gathered the rest of my things. Taking a final look at what would be my last view of Boston and the US for several months at least, I breathed in deeply and stepped towards the gate. My hand shook as I gave the attendant my boarding pass, I.D., and passport.

"Welcome to British Airways, enjoy your flight," she said, smiling and giving my license and passport back. I gulped and followed the passengers ahead of me onto the plane. *No turning back now.*

I cried throughout the entire trip. All six and a half hours. The flight attendants stopped asking what was wrong by hour two. I knew I was being ridiculous. I broke up with him. The pain in my heart was my own doing. But it still hurt.

Chapter Thirty-One: Picking Up the Pieces

Ben

With Abby gone, I had no choice but to get back into the swing of things. When we started dating, I'd neglected the other people in my life. Mainly my family. I wanted to make it up to them.

Tracy hugged me quickly as she ushered me into the house. "Ben, thank you so much for taking Hannah and Joey today. Ike was supposed to be home, but he had an emergency at the hospital."

Joey came running into my arms and I squeezed his little body to my chest.

"No prob. You know how much I love hanging with my little buddies." I tickled my nephew's stomach and he squirmed and squealed, giggling and begging for more. I obliged for a few more minutes before setting him on the ground. He ran out of the room and Tracey grabbed my arm.

"How are you holding up?" She gave me the same sympathetic, I'm-here-for-you look she'd given me after every major breakup in my life, but then she did something different. She pulled me into a hug and rubbed my back, "You know I'm here for you if you need anything."

"Geez, Trace. It's not like she died. She broke up with me. I'm fine." Pushing her away I went in search of Joey and Hannah.

She called after me, "I'll be home at two. Call if you need me."

I didn't need her. Finding Joey and Hannah in their playroom, I sat down and began building a tower of blocks that my niece promptly knocked down. I built it again, she knocked it down again. If it hadn't been such a metaphor for my life, I would have enjoyed playing the game with her.

"Hey, do you guys want to go see a movie?" I asked when I couldn't stand to build the tower again.

"No!" Hannah cried.

"Yes!" Joey shouted.

"Hannah Banana, I think you're outnumbered, because I want to get out of the house!" After getting their shoes and jackets on, we went to see the newest animated film. I felt better almost instantly. With Joey and Hannah I didn't have to endure the constant stream of sympathy I got from everyone else. They just had fun with Uncle Ben.

The movie was actually funny. Abby would have liked it. She liked all kinds of movies. *God, I can't believe now I'm the one bringing her up.*

It had been so easy, at the beginning of our relationship, to learn the little things about her, to put her wants and needs before my own. I didn't even hesitate. I enjoyed making her happy, my heart soared when her face lit up, when she smiled, when she laughed. But I needed to retrain my brain to remember how I reacted to the world before her. I could do that. Hannah and Joey's laughter brought me out of my own head, somehow managed to get me in a positive mood, and after the credits, I took them to Chuck-E-Cheese for lunch and games.

A single parents' group was gathered around a table nearby and several of the young mothers smiled at me as I cut Hannah's pizza into bite-size pieces. I tried to ignore them, but the constant stares finally broke me. I bowed my head and smiled back.

"Hey, would you like to join us? We usually have a couple other single dads in the group, but they couldn't make it today," a pretty blonde said, catching my eye.

"Oh, thanks. But I'm not a dad. These are my sister's kids."

"Well, that's okay, you're still welcome to sit with us if you want." Her grin widened and I swear she actually batted her eyelashes at me. *Great, I must be wearing a sign that reads "Back on the Market."*

"We're leaving soon. But thanks." I turned to Hannah, and made sure to keep my back to the group the rest of the time we were there. The blonde was cute and friendly, but I wasn't ready to flirt and date again. I needed time to think about what I wanted.

"Uncle Ben?" Joey asked as I strapped him into the car.

"Joey?"

"How come Aunt Abigail didn't come with us?"

My heart sank. I'd been doing great since the movie, *where'd he get the idea she was his aunt?* "Abigail isn't your aunt, Joey."

"Mommy says she's going to be, so I should call her that."

"When did Mommy say that?" I put Hannah in her seat.

"I don't know. Where is she? She likes trains, like me." He made choo choo sounds to make sure I knew what he meant.

"She had to go away. She had to move because of her job. I don't think she's going to be your aunt, so you probably shouldn't call her that."

"But I like her."

"I like her too, buddy, but sometimes that isn't enough. Now, let's go home. Mommy will be back soon." He didn't argue, so I got in the driver's seat and drove back to their house. Tracey's car was already in the garage.

"Hey guys! I missed you!" She gave each of the kids a kiss and hoisted Hannah up so she rested on her hip. "Thanks again, Ben. I got a lot of work done."

"Yeah, no sweat. Can we talk for a minute?"

Her face immediately transformed back into the pity-party from earlier. "Of course. Let me put Hannah down for her nap and pop a video in for Joey." I followed them into the house and helped Joey pick out his DVD while we waited for Hannah to fall asleep. A half hour later, I was alone with my sister in the living room.

"What's up?" she asked, putting her hand on my arm.

"When did you tell Joey that Abigail was going to be his aunt?"

"What? Why, did he call her that?"

"Yeah. When did you tell him?" I tried to keep my voice steady. I shouldn't have been angry about it, after all, it's what I planned on for the past six months at least, but my emotions seemed to have minds of their own.

"I don't know Ben. Not that long ago, I guess." She removed her hand and tucked her arms across her chest, refusing to meet my gaze.

"Before or after the break up?" *It was after, I just know it.*

"After, I think." She paused, but continued, "We all know the two of you are going to end up together."

"Yeah right." I rolled my eyes and got up from the couch. I grabbed a foam football from where it lay in the corner of the room and squeezed and pounded it in my hands, trying to beat out my frustration.

"I saw the way she looked at you, Ben. She loves you. She only broke up with you because she felt guilty for leaving and didn't think it was fair to you to continue the relationship when you could find someone here."

"If she knew me at all she'd know that was crazy."

"Really? You mean you wouldn't have done the exact same thing if you'd been in her shoes?"

"I would've chosen her," I spat the words out and realized for the first time why I was really upset. Given the choice, I would've always chosen her. I wanted to scream, to purge myself of the anger, pain, and betrayal clogging my heart. I wanted everyone else to feel as miserable as I did.

"I gotta go. I already tried to explain the situation to Joey. I'd appreciate it if you'd back me up and not continue telling him that Aunt Abigail is coming back to play with him."

"Don't leave angry."

"I'm not angry." I grabbed my jacket and stormed out of the house. But yelling at Tracey didn't make the continuous ripping of my heart heal itself. Guilt spread through my conscience for taking my resentment out on her, but she went over the line. *Ugh! Can I just get out of here? Find a place where no one knows me or knows about Abby and me? I'm sick of the whole damn thing!*

* * * *

My bike hummed beneath my thighs as I tore down the highway. The wind rushed at me in currents and the cautious recklessness of the ride comforted me. I hadn't mapped out a plan or selected a destination. I just rode into the night, ready for whatever fell my way. It was almost midnight and I started getting sleepy, *man, you're getting old,* so I decided to stop in the next town and get a hotel room.

It didn't take long to find a motel and check in. Dirty and run down, the place was perfect for a man of my circumstances. I found my way to room twenty-five and locked myself in for the evening. The queen size bed had a broken leg, with newspaper stuffed beneath it to level the frame. The faded floral comforter and pillows smelled musty, but it was something different. I threw myself on it and fell asleep within minutes.

This can't be the last conversation we have, the last time we see each other, the last time we touch. Don't wait for me, move on with your life, but don't ask me to say goodbye. I don't want to end it like that, I don't want to think it's over.

Abby's last words to me tortured my sleep that night. No matter how far away I got, my subconscious wanted to think of her. Wanted to hold on to her. I woke up several times and tried to push the words away by watching television, reading the magazines stacked on the nightstand, even playing games on my cell phone. But each time I closed my eyes again, her green stare met me. I gave up sleeping in order to get away from it. My heart bled enough in the daytime, I couldn't take the grief in my dreams, too. Wasn't the idea to get away from her memory, not get more acquainted with it?

When enough light shone through the windows to make it acceptable to be up and about, I checked out of the room and found my way across the street to a small diner. The breakfast special consisted of three eggs cooked to order, bacon, sausage, and whole-wheat toast. Sounded pretty good to me.

"Would you like coffee, honey?" The waitress set my plate and silverware before me.

"Ugh, no. Just another glass of orange juice, please."

"Sure thing, sweetie. You going to the baseball game today?"

"Baseball game? Sorry, I'm not from around here." Salting my eggs and unfolding my napkin, I waited for her to leave, but she continued standing beside me, staring out the window.

"It's going to be a good day for a game. You should check it out. You look like a sports fan." She nudged the rim of my baseball cap and finally walked away. I watched her go. A baseball game actually sounded like fun. I hadn't seen anyone other than the Red Sox play in months. When she returned with a glass of OJ, I asked her how to get to the game.

It didn't take long to find the field and the bleachers were already half-full when I took a seat on the highest bench. Kids ran back and forth in front of the crowd, playing a no-rules version of "Tag" and mothers laughed and snapped photos as the audience waited for the ump to start the first inning. The teams looked like a hodgepodge of characters and I instantly thought about my friends in Boston and longed for the feel of the ball in my hand.

As the teams stepped onto the field, the now-full bleachers stood, howling and applauding. Several players were called out by name, many waved to acknowledge their family and friends in the stands. As play began, I turned to the person closest me, a teenage boy, and asked him if the game was part of a tournament of some kind. He laughed at my ignorance.

"Nah, just a couple of rec teams playing a rematch. It was rained out a few days ago."

"Why is everyone making such a big deal about it?"

"Whaddya mean?"

"Well, the stands are full, everyone's clapping and cheering like they're at a major league game."

"We just like to support our people, I guess." He turned to his friends and made several, not-so-quiet, jokes at my expense. I had to chuckle along with him. My knowledge of small-town life was restricted to stereotypes from movies and television.

I got caught up in the game. It didn't feel like two small-town teams battling for bragging rights at the local bar. It reminded me more of the final game of the World Series. The crowd cheered for every play, every strikeout, every homerun, every error, every bad play the ump called. They knew nothing about what was going on, but by the end of the game, I cheered along with them. Every play got the crowd excited and I found myself swept up in the energy. As the teams exited the field, I jumped to my feet, yelling and clapping with all my strength.

Rejuvenated, I got on my bike and hit the road again, heading back to Boston. My life before Abby hadn't disappeared. I longed to get back on the softball field, to get to the complex and begin new plans for advertising and create new projects for the kids, to spend time with friends, to hang out with my sister.

I pulled into Matt and Trish's driveway at a quarter til six. The look of surprise on Matt's face was priceless when he opened the door.

"Ben! What are you doing here?"

"I came over to celebrate."

"Celebrate what?" He stepped aside to let me in, confusion replacing surprise in his features.

"Your engagement, of course!" I pulled him into a hug and he slapped a hand on my back.

"Thanks, man. Trish!" he called, "Ben's here!" Trish came out of the kitchen and immediately hugged me. I squeezed her and offered my congratulations again.

"I'm sorry I wasn't a better friend when you first told me. I needed some time for the shock to wear off. I'm really happy for both of you."

"That's good, because we've already set a date." Trish smiled warmly at me, happiness diffused over her face.

The bride-to-be glow suited her. Why had Matt waited so long?

"Oh, yeah? When's the happy day?"

"September eighteenth." Matt slung his arm around my shoulder. "And I'd like you to be my best man, whaddya think?"

"Of course! Of course I'll be your best man!" We hugged again and Trish laughed at us.

"Am I going to have to start warning you two about PDA?"

"Haha, very funny." I took a few steps away from him. "Wait, September, that's only five months away."

"My parents' country club had a cancellation and my dad really wants to throw the wedding, so we didn't have much of a choice," Trish explained.

"Well, whatever you guys need me to do, just let me know. I'm really thrilled for you. I know you guys are going to be happy together for a long time. At least until Trish realizes the mistake she's made." I jabbed Matt in the stomach.

"Dude, you're my best man now, save those kind of jokes for your toast."

"Don't you worry about that. I've got enough dirt on you to toast your second and third marriage, too."

"Hey, now, I don't find that particularly funny." Trish wrapped her arms around Matt's waist and lightly kissed him. Suddenly, my happiness for them drained out of me. Seeing them so blissful brought memories of Abby rushing to my head. How many times had she held me like that? Countless. Bracing myself, I forced my smile back into place and told them I'd interrupted their evening for too long.

They walked me to the door and Trish gave me one last hug before I left. They stood, arms around each other's waists, in the doorway as I revved my engine and flew down the street.

It will only get easier with time, I thought to myself. *I really am happy for them. I'd be happier if Abby were here to celebrate with us, but that's not going to happen.*

As I entered my silent house it felt like days since I'd been there, but I'd only left the afternoon before. Immediately, I went to the calendar hanging on the fridge and marked September eighteenth. My dreams were peaceful that night; I woke the next morning ready to reacquaint myself with my former life.

Chapter Thirty-Two: Starting Over

Abby

Everything in London was different.

I found Kaffeine my second week in the city. It was nothing like Starbucks: the music was always fresh, I never heard the same song twice, and the employees knew every customer by name and their order by heart. I wrote my columns there, usually. I'd sit in the shop, or just outside on a wooden bench, with a latte and my notebook and watch the Londoners around me. I got to know the barristas pretty well, they always laughed when the quiet American came in and were constantly trying to get me to drink tea. One of them looked a lot like Ben. Same height, same light brown hair, broad shoulders, and amazing forearms and biceps. I was tortured by the resemblance every time I walked through the door, but for some strange reason, I felt compelled to come to the shop every day.

"Why are you so nice to everyone but me?" he came to my table and asked after a couple of weeks.

"Huh?" I stared down at the notes for my column, looking into his face hurt too much.

"You smile and say hello to everyone when you come in, but whenever you see me behind the counter, you take a seat and wait for someone else to take over before ordering. You might as well have a sign that says 'Piss off' on your forehead."

"Are you allowed to speak to customers like that?"

"Yes."

His matter-of-fact manner and the seriousness of the question caused me to look up from my notebook. His eyes were brown, not blue. *Thank God.*

"I'm sorry, it's nothing personal."

"Bloody well feels that way."

"Listen, um…" I glanced at his nametag, "…Austin, it has nothing to do with you, not really. You just look a lot like my ex-boyfriend." Ex-boyfriend. It was the first time I'd said the word out loud. When I started crying, Austin teetered back and forth on his heels, looking like he wanted to run away as fast as humanly possible. But he didn't. Instead, he pulled a napkin out of his apron pocket and handed it to me.

"Hey, I'm sorry. What'd the bloke do? Shag someone else?"

"No, no, nothing like that. It's my fault. I took a job here and he…"

"…lives in America?"

"Yeah."

After that, Austin avoided me whenever I came in.

My apartment, well, my flat as everyone kept correcting me, seemed huge compared to the broom closet I called home in Boston. I even had a guestroom. And it came fully furnished, so nothing looked like it belonged to a broke college student.

I only went to the *Intuition* offices once a week, to update Elizabeth on the progress of my column or to teleconference with Helen or Jeanette back in the States. I didn't have an office and wasn't expected to keep a nine-to-five schedule. Mostly, I traveled, visiting as much of the United Kingdom as I could, and never having enough time to see everything I wanted to see.

At night, alone in my flat, I'd pull out my photo album and look over the blank pages. Sometimes I added a picture to it. My first week I visited the home in Chawton where Jane Austen spent the final eight years of her life. Walking through the drawing room, imagining her sitting there, writing and editing and playing the piano, I knew I'd done the right thing in coming. But as I placed photos from the outing in the album, I thought of Ben. I thought how proud he'd be of me for fulfilling that dream.

I thought about him all the time. But I never saw him or talked to him. The loneliness should have been familiar, I'd been alone for twenty-five years before him, but it was the most different thing about my new life.

Ben

"Ben! Hey Ben!" Matt yelled as I pulled my motorcycle into the parking lot. It didn't take long for me to get in the habit of riding it everywhere. The freedom and independence of the ride countered the memories of Abby that arose whenever I got on.

"Hey, man. What's up?" I slapped his shoulder as I approached and gave Trish a quick one-armed hug.

"Not much. We've been waiting for you, let's play!"

Teams formed and my excitement increased as I took the lead and began assigning positions. We were in the field first, so I claimed my spot at shortstop and heckled Trish as she stepped up to bat.

She struck out and so did the next two batters. Our team scrambled to the dugout. I was sixth in the batting lineup and wasn't sure if I'd get the chance to hit that inning, so made myself comfortable on the bench with a bottle of water.

"Hi, Ben, you're looking good today," Madelyn trilled as she sat beside me.

"Oh. Thanks, Madi. You look nice, too." And she really did. Her long blonde hair was swept off her face in a ponytail and tiny red shorts showed off tan, muscular legs that went on and on. She wore less makeup than usual, allowing her natural beauty to shine through.

"Thanks," she giggled, slapping my knee. "Do you have plans for after the game?"

"I thought everyone could come back to my bar and hang out for a bit. The Sox are playing tonight."

"That sounds like fun. I'll definitely be there." She let her hand graze my arm as she spoke, then got off the bench and grabbed a bat, "I'm up next, wish me luck!"

"Good luck." I watched her walk away. *God, she's sexy*, I thought. I hated to admit it, but it was true. Every move she made was deliberate and the graceful swaying of her hips as she walked caught every guy's attention. *Why haven't I been interested before?* There seemed to be so many reasons I stayed away from Madelyn and her twin sister, Carrie, in the past, but I couldn't think of any of them. *Geez, Ben, keep your head in the game!*

I went up to the plate in the bottom of the second inning and a surge of adrenaline rushed through me as I gripped the bat with both hands and released a few practice swings to warm up my muscles.

Matt was pitching and gave me his most evil grin; he had no intention of going easy on me. The first pitch sailed over the plate. I knew from the windup it would be a curveball and decided to wait for his fastball, he was just cocky enough to throw it last.

"Strike one!" the umpire called.

Next pitch, another curveball. Again, I let it fly by me. Again, the ump called a strike.

Matt's smile disappeared as he furrowed his brow and clutched the ball inside his glove. Kicking up his leg, his shoulder swung forward and the ball came hurtling towards me. *Wait for it...* I grasped the bat tighter, preparing for impact, then swung with every ounce of strength I could muster.

THWACK!

The ball went zooming over the heads of the outfielders. The bat was still vibrating in my hand when I flung it aside and ran to first base.

"Homerun!" the ump cried out. The ball had crossed over the fence and lay somewhere in the next field over. Rounding second and third, I winked smugly at my teammates then strolled across home plate. They waited for me in the dugout with cheers and slaps on my back.

"Way to go, Ben!" Madelyn threw her arms around my neck. I just barely registered she was there, when she backed off and went to take a seat on the bench. Grinning, I joined her, and we spent the rest of the game talking and laughing at the expense of our friends.

"Madi, do you want to ride with me to the bar?"

"I'd love to! Where's your car, I don't see it." She hooked her arm around mine and tossed a glance back at her sister. Carrie shot her a nasty look and rolled her eyes, but shrugged her shoulders and turned her attention to one of the other guys.

"I didn't bring my car. I drove the bike over."

"Oh. Never mind, I'll get a ride with my sister." She dropped my arm and walked away. *Great. I put myself out there and she doesn't like the motorcycle. I thought this girl would do anything to get in good with a guy she liked. Maybe that's my problem. I misread the signs. She's not interested in me. God, what an idiot I am!*

I made it to the bar at least ten minutes before the rest of the team and prepared the staff for the ambush about to burst through the doors. Luckily, a few tables sat open in the back corner and I kept them clear while waiting for the group.

"First round is on me!" I announced as everyone filled the seats and raucously shouted orders at the waiters. They cheered for me and turned their attention to the big screens playing the game. I took a chair next to Trish and enjoyed the chaos for a few minutes, until Madelyn maneuvered her way beside me.

"Hey, sorry 'bout not riding with you. I just don't like motorcycles. They're so scary."

"Have you ever ridden on one?"

"No."

I nudged her shoulder. "Maybe they wouldn't seem so scary if you tried it."

"No, I couldn't. I can't even do roller-coasters," she giggled and placed her hand on my arm as the waiter set a pitcher of beer on the table. I poured her a glass and she sipped quietly for a few minutes. "So, what's up with your girlfriend? What's her name? Anabeth?"

"Abigail. And she's not my girlfriend anymore." *So, she is interested.* I knew Madelyn knew we'd broken up and

I knew she knew her name. The games girls play don't make any sense to me.

"Oh, I'm soooo sorry." She let the "o" drag out and moved her fingers down my arm to rest on top of my hand. "Can I do anything for you?"

What the heck, I'm not getting any younger. "Yeah. How about dinner tomorrow night?" *If I'm serious about moving on, that means dating someone new, right?*

"Yes! I'd love to have dinner with you. You wanna pick me up around six? In your car?" Her face broke into a megawatt smile while a momentary sense of dread washed over me. I shook it away and returned her enthusiasm.

"Six sounds great."

Abby

Walking into the tattoo parlour, my blood ran cold. I wanted to do it. I needed to do it. But I couldn't do it alone. Who was I kidding? I needed Ben to hold my hand. Plus, he really wanted to get a tattoo. *I should wait until we can go together,* I thought. But reality reared its ugly head. *You're not going to be able to go together. You aren't with him anymore. He probably hates you.*

I turned to leave, but a tall man with dirty blonde hair and tattoos running up the entire length of his arm stepped forward before I could make it out the door.

"Can I help you?"

I looked around the shop again before answering. It looked clean and more cheerful than I was expecting, with bright white walls, stainless steel tables, and red chairs. Not dodgy in the least, like several of the ones my neighbor recommended to me. I'd passed it several times on my way down Great Portland Street to and from the *Intuition* offices, before finally summoning the courage to walk in. "Um, I'm not sure. I was kinda thinking about getting a tattoo."

He looked startled for a second and I couldn't understand why until he asked, "Yank?"

"Huh? Oh, am I American?"

He nodded.

"Yeah. Just moved here a little over a month ago."

"I like your accent." He grinned and motioned for me to take a seat at a table near the door.

"I like your's too." I blushed as he sat opposite me and pulled out a couple of design books. He had a beautiful smile, with pink full lips and straight white teeth. He looked like he came straight out of a toothpaste ad.

"I'm Billy," he thrust his hand out and I took it to shake. There were calluses covering his fingers, but the roughness of his skin only gave him a more manly quality.

"Abigail."

"What were you interested in getting done?"

"Oh, I don't know. I'm not even sure I want a tattoo."

"Then why'd you come in?"

"I'm trying to live more."

He laughed. An earthly, round laugh. It had a soothing effect to it. Suddenly, I felt safe in his hands. "Then you definitely need a tat. Look at some of these books and tell me what you think. Or we can always design something for you." He flipped through a couple of pages and pointed to a few options. "I take you to be a hearts and stars kinda girl, whaddya think?"

I looked over the cupid's hearts and cheesy shooting stars and crinkled my nose. Did I look that frilly? "I don't think so. Actually, I was thinking maybe a tribute to my grandfather. We were really close, but he died ten years ago. He grew anemones in his garden. Do you have any of those?"

"Anemones? Never heard of them. Is that a flower?"

"Yeah."

"Let's look it up." We walked to another table with a computer and he googled some images. I pointed to a few and he sketched them on a blank pad. When I choose the one I liked best, he ripped it out and drew it on a fresh page.

"Where do you want it?" he asked, preparing the needles and ink he'd need to impale me with the design.

"Oh. I don't know. What's popular?"

"Hang what's popular."

I laughed. "What about right here?" I held my left hand out and pointed to the outside of my wrist, right above where the arm met the base of my hand.

"Looks good. I hope your boss won't mind such a visible tattoo."

"I'm a writer, I think the editors will be okay with it."

"Then that's where we'll put it."

My hand shook as he descended upon it with the needle. I had to press down with my other hand to control the tremors, and even that didn't work. I yelped the first time he pierced my skin, but after that, I kept my eyes closed tight and bit down on my bottom lip to stop from screaming. Billy chuckled gently to himself, but would stop and ask if I was okay any time my arm tensed up. Which happened every five seconds.

At one point he paused and asked, "Does your boyfriend dig tattoos?"

"What makes you think I have a boyfriend?"

"You're too fit not to have one."

I swear flames erupted on my face. "Well, be that as it may, my ex lives in the States, and yes, he does like tattoos."

"Ah. Must be a real prat to let you get away."

I was too embarrassed to respond further, partly because I was flattered and partly because it didn't matter how cute and charming Billy was, he wasn't Ben and I didn't want to continue the flirtation.

Two hours later, he cleaned up the artwork with a damp paper towel and placed a white bandage on it. I stared at my wrist in amazement. I'd done it. I'd gotten a tattoo. All by myself. *Holy crap!*

"Come back in a couple of days and I'll touch up any areas that need it and get a photo for my portfolio." He was still holding my wrist, examining the bandaged area, but he brought his brown eyes to mine as he spoke. My stomach did a little flip.

"Okay, sure. Thanks so much. You made this really easy."

"It was my pleasure." He smiled at me and my cheeks reddened once again.

I paid him and left quickly, anxious to get back into the spring air, to cool off my head. There was something so familiar and comforting about him, but it made me uneasy. I reached the corner and heard footsteps behind me.

"Abigail!"

I turned and Billy headed straight towards me, that brilliant smile radiating as he held out a slip of paper to me.

"I think you left this in the shop," he said.

"What? I don't think that's mine." I took it without thinking and he grinned before turning on his heel.

"It's for you," he called over his shoulder.

I opened the paper as he disappeared back into the parlour and couldn't believe my eyes.

Call me sometime--- (020) 1050 5690
-Billy-

Chapter Thirty-Three: Ugh, A First Date

Ben

At five o'clock the next day I scavenged my closet for a shirt suitable for a first date. *Shit, a first date. I planned on never going through this again.* Grabbing a light blue one off its hanger I started to pull it over my head, when Abby's voice rang in my ears.

How about that pale blue button down shirt you have? The one you wore on our first date. It matched your eyes.

Immediately, I took it off and threw it on the bed. It was stupid, but I couldn't wear that shirt, Abby's shirt, on a date with Madelyn. Abby didn't like Madelyn.

I tried to get excited. I wanted someone who was completely different from Abby. Someone who wouldn't remind me of everything we had. And Madelyn was definitely different. I needed this. I needed to feel like a woman wanted me. And Madelyn always treated me like she wanted me.

I grabbed the closest shirt and threw it on. A black, collared, button down, it fit nicely over my thick biceps. I checked the mirror and decided to skip shaving. I could pull off the rugged look. Putting a jacket on, I headed out the door, ready to eat and laugh with someone new.

When Madelyn came to her front door, my jaw nearly fell off it dropped so quickly. She was wearing an extremely low cut, short, tight, black dress. I wasn't prepared for the overt sexiness she exuded.

"Um, uh, you look great," I stammered, trying to keep my eyes above her neck. I don't think she would have cared if I let them wander, but I was determined to behave like a gentleman.

"Thanks," she crooned. "I'm so excited. Where're we going?"

"I was thinking that little French bistro downtown."

"Sounds great. Let's go." She took my hand as we walked to the car, shocking me with her confidence. I attempted several topics of conversation on the drive to the restaurant, politics, baseball, family, etc. but she was more interested in laughing at my book of CDs.

"Don't you have any dance music? Britney Spears? Rhianna?"

"I'm not really a big dancer."

"Oh." Silence. My excitement began to wane. Did we have anything in common at all?

The conversation at the restaurant was even more torturous. She chatted non-stop about pop culture gossip and *Grey's Anatomy*. I tried to occasionally offer a sentence or two in response, but she didn't really seem interested in anything I had to say. *Who the hell is McDreamy?* I wanted to ask, but I'm glad I didn't. That might have led to thirty more minutes of a conversation I cared even less about. When she started running her foot up my leg, I excused myself and went to the restroom.

Splashing water on my face, I tried to psych myself up for the rest of the evening. *She's pretty. She's good at sports. She's friendly. You can do this, Ben!* Luckily, the food arrived by the time I got back to the table and we ate quietly. When she finished her salad she picked up where she left off, describing last year's Season Finale.

"And so, at the end, you see both Izzie and George. Izzie's in the elevator, in the same dress she wore the night Denny died and George is waiting for her when the doors open and he's dressed in some kind of military uniform…"

Who the hell is Izzie? George? Denny? Does she honestly think I'm interested in this show? God, this is a disaster.

"Um, Madelyn, why don't we talk about something else? Like your job. I don't even know what you do." I continued working on my steak, taking a bite as she stared at me incredulously.

"I'm a model, silly."

"A model? Really? What kind of modeling do you do?" *You've got to be kidding me.*

"Well, I haven't had any jobs yet. I'm still waiting for my big break."

Ah ha. "Oh. What do you do for money? I mean, don't you have bills and stuff?"

"Nope."

"No?"

"My parents pay for everything."

Seriously? Does she know how pathetic that is? I cleared my throat, "Oh. Um, how old are you, Madelyn? I thought you were in your twenties."

"I am. I'm 23."

"And your parents still pay all your bills?"

"Of course." She frowned at me, like she didn't understand what I was trying to say. I decided it would be best to change the subject.

"I'm sorry, why don't you finish telling me about, um, Izzie, was it?" Her face lit up again and she spent the next half-hour rambling on about the Season Premiere. *I* spent the next half-hour trying to quote the entire script of *Office Space* to myself. When the bill finally arrived, I paid and tipped our waiter and gave her my hand to help her up.

She was just as chatty on the drive back. *Office Space* continued playing in my mind. When we reached the house, I walked her to the door and said goodnight. She grabbed my face and planted a kiss straight on my lips. Instinctively, I kissed back for a few seconds, but ended it just as quickly.

"Night, Madelyn. I'll talk to you later."

"Wait, do you want to come in?" She smiled coyly and took a step inside the house, gesturing with her finger that I should follow.

"Sorry, I don't think I should. Thanks for going to dinner with me." I turned and walked away without another glance. I didn't want to hurt her, but she was crazy if she thought I was interested in going any further that night. Or any night. The whole thing was a huge mistake.

* * * *

A week later, Madelyn had sent me a dozen emails and called at least once a day, not to mention the hundreds of texts I received, all asking when we were going out again. I was as polite as possible, but started getting annoyed. So, when I sat in my office on Friday afternoon, preparing to go home for the weekend, and my phone rang, I braced myself to tell her we would *never* be going on a second date.

"Madelyn, I'm sorry, I'm just not interested," I spat out immediately upon bringing the phone to my ear.

"Excuse me, I may have the wrong number, is this Benjamin Harris?" a man's voice responded.

Good going, Ben. Please don't be an investor, please don't be an investor. "Oh, I'm sorry. I thought, never mind. Yes, I'm Ben Harris."

"Oh, Mr. Harris. I'm Henry Clayburn of Clayburn's Jewelers. The piece you ordered is ready."

The phone fell out of my hand and landed with a thump on the carpet. I could hear Mr. Clayburn's voice on the other end, asking if everything was all right. It took every bit of self-control I had to retrieve the phone and ask calmly, "Can I pick it up today?"

"Yes, sir. We're open until eight this evening. I'll let the sales staff know you'll be coming. Are you prepared to pay the balance?"

"Oh. Yes. Of course. I'll be there shortly." I hung up and grabbed my keys off the desktop. *How could I forget about that?*

Traffic was crazy, but I managed to weave my bike around the jammed intersections, and parked in front of Clayburn's within fifteen minutes of leaving the complex. The woman behind the counter jumped as I hurried into the store and shrank back as I approached. I must have looked like a crazy person. I felt like a crazy person.

"Excuse me. My name is Ben Harris and I placed a custom order a few months ago. Mr. Clayburn called to let me know it's ready. I'd like to pay for it and pick it up, please."

"Of course, Mr. Harris. I'll get that for you right away." She scampered through the door behind her and I looked down into the glass cases framing the room. Hundreds of necklaces, earrings, bracelets, and rings stared back at me. Gold, silver, big, small, elaborate, simple. Each design unique.

It seemed like years since I first came into the store, but it was only late February. I planned on resetting my grandmother's diamond from her engagement ring into a new setting and proposing to Abby on her birthday when she looked through the album. But, when we finished the design, Mr. Clayburn informed me it wouldn't be ready by March.

"That's okay," I had said, "I can wait another month or two. I've been waiting my whole life for her."

Henry Clayburn swept out of the backroom and extended his hand over the glass case to me. I shook it, but immediately turned my eyes to the velvet box he held. "Ah, Mr. Harris. Welcome back. I didn't expect you so soon." He placed the box on the counter and nudged it toward me. Never taking my eyes off it, I gently picked it up and popped the lid.

There it was. Abby's ring. It was absolutely perfect. My grandmother's one-carat diamond surrounded by sapphires and set in platinum. My eyes filled with tears as I imagined slipping it on her beautiful hand. I should've told him I didn't need it anymore. That he could sell it to someone else. But, my mother would've killed me if I sold her mother's diamond and the thought of anyone but Abby wearing it made me sick. I clutched my stomach and set the box on the counter, pulling out my wallet to hand Mr. Clayburn my credit card.

"Put the balance on that, please." I gingerly lifted the ring out of its cushion and looked at the engraving on the inside of the band, *With My Whole Heart*. Tears splashed on the counter, but I wiped them away with my sleeve and replaced the ring by the time Mr. Clayburn returned with my receipt.

“Thank you, Mr. Harris. And congratulations. I’m sure she’ll be thrilled with it, it’s beautiful.”

“Yes, it is. Thank you for all of your help, Mr. Clayburn.” I turned and left the store, the ring heavy in my pocket. I had to wait a full ten minutes before my eyes were clear enough to drive home.

I stuffed the ring and its box into the sock drawer of my dresser as soon as I entered the house. Was God trying to punish me? For what? For taking out Madelyn, for leading her on? For letting Abby leave without putting up a fight? Why couldn’t I get her out of my life?

Chapter Thirty-Four: All Work and No Play

Ben

By June, I resigned myself to the fact that dating wasn't an option. I hated how pathetic it was, but I needed to get to a point where I didn't compare every woman I came in contact with to Abby. The ring in my sock drawer haunted me; I could sense its presence every time I walked into my bedroom. I considered selling it, but my heart raced and waves of nausea came over me anytime I attempted to remove it from its hiding place. The only option I had to get away from it was to stay out of the house.

I started spending twelve hours a day at the complex. Lord knows it needed the extra attention. School was out and kids crowded the fields and courts on a daily basis but the financial difficulties hadn't improved. Steve constantly reminded me how surprised he was I hadn't gone bankrupt yet.

Meetings consumed my daily life. Meetings with accountants and financial planners. Meetings with current investors and potential investors. Meetings with suppliers and city officials. Meetings, meetings, meetings.

It was hell, but it was better than sitting at home alone.

One Monday morning I was working on payroll and taxes when the phone rang. "Ben Harris," I answered.

"Mr. Harris, I'm Gwyneth Jones with *Sports Illustrated*. I was wondering if you would have a few minutes to meet me for coffee today."

"I'm sorry, who did you say you were with?"

"*Sports Illustrated*, the magazine." Her voice possessed a sing-song quality to it that didn't quite seem to match the magazine she worked for.

"And you want to meet with me? Benjamin Harris?"

"Yes. If you are the Benjamin Harris who owns and operates Inner City Sports in Boston, Massachusetts."

"Yeah, that's me."

"Great. Can you meet me for coffee? If you can't do it today, I'll be in Boston for a week."

"No, no. Today is fine, what time? Where?"

"Two o'clock, I believe there's a Starbucks across the street from your business, is that right?"

"Yeah, that's right. I'll see you then."

"Have a good day, Mr. Harris."

"Thanks, you too." I hung up the phone, stunned. What could she possibly want with me? I brought my hand to my face and massaged the tension along my jaw, unable to remember what I'd been working on before Ms. Jones's call. A knock at the door roused my attention and Dejuane poked his head in.

"Hey, come on in! I feel like I haven't seen you in forever!" Immediately standing, I went around the desk to meet him.

"Hey man. I know, but with school and basketball, things have been crazy. I'm glad it's finally summer." He flopped down in one of the comfy armchairs in the corner of the office and I leaned against my desk.

"Yeah, me too. It's good to see so many people down there," I gestured out the window and smiled at the view of kids of all ages, races, and sizes connecting on the tennis and volleyball courts. "So, what's up?"

"I was wondering if I could take some time off from the store. My coach set up some meetings with different college coaches and they're all over the country."

"Of course, you can take all the time off you need. That's amazing, Dejuane! What schools?"

"It's a long list. But I'm really excited about Wake Forest. They're not the best team in the country, but it's my dream school." He got up, walked over to my bookcase, and looked over my own college memorabilia.

"I want that," he pointed at my diplomas, "more than I want to play."

"You'll get it. And you know I'll help in whatever way I can."

"Yeah man, thanks." He started making his way to the exit.

I stopped him. "Hey, how long are you going to be around today?"

"Don't know. I just came to lift weights."

"If you're still here around quarter til two, I'm going across the street to have coffee with some lady from *Sports Illustrated*, you wanna come with me?"

"Seriously?!? What're you doing meeting with someone from *SI*?"

"I have no idea, she called a little bit ago and wanted to meet for coffee."

"It would be so awesome if she wrote an article about this place!" Dejuane enthusiastically punched me in the shoulder and headed out the door.

It would be awesome. It would be incredible. There weren't enough adjectives in the universe to describe what an article in *Sports Illustrated* could do for my business. Not only would it attract investors and possibly help pull ICS out of the economic sand trap, but it would also open up a whole new world of opportunities for the kids. My imagination went wild as I dreamed of professional athletes running training camps, tickets and box seats to major league games, more funding for upkeep and free transportation.

Shaking my head, I got back to work, but every few minutes a new dream would pop up. I couldn't be that far off base. An article seemed the only possible reason anyone from *Sports Illustrated* would want to talk with me in person; surely they didn't handle subscription issues face-to-face.

At 1:55, Dejuane and I sat sipping drinks and discussing his college tours at Starbucks. It was weird being in the same shop where Abby and I ran into each other for the first time after the accident. I could almost picture her in her favorite armchair, by the fireplace, reading a dictionary-sized novel. *Why, of all places, did Ms. Jones pick this one?*

"You must be Ben." A lanky woman with cropped brown hair approached us. She held out her hand and I shook it.

"Yes, it's nice to meet you Ms. Jones."

"Ah, Gwyneth, please," she waved off my formality with a flick of her wrist. "Or Gwen. Whichever you prefer."

"Well, Gwyneth, this is Dejuane. He's a friend and he also works at the complex. I hope you don't mind that I invited him along. If it's possible, he's a bigger sports fan than I am and he reads your magazine religiously."

"Dejuane! I'm so happy you are here, because actually I wanted to speak with both of you. Ben, did Abigail spill the beans on me?" She took the empty chair at our table, pulling a notepad and pen out of her bag.

I was sipping my coffee when she said Abby's name and nearly choked on the hot liquid. Sputtering into a napkin, I looked up and barely managed to speak, "I'm sorry, do you know Abigail?"

"Oh, I guess she didn't tell you. Yes, we went to college together. I was in Europe last week and we had lunch. I told her I'm relocating to Boston and looking for a human interest story for the magazine to help get myself reacquainted with the area and she suggested I contact you."

"Wait, what? Abigail told you to contact me?"

"Yeah, she told me about how you were a Big Brother in college and how Dejuane inspired you to open Inner City Sports. So, if the two of you are willing, I'd love to get more of the story. I can interview you now, or we can set up another time."

"I'm game!" Dejuane enthusiastically shook her hand again, but I still couldn't believe what was happening. *Abby told her to contact me. Abby created this wonderful opportunity for me.*

"Um, yeah, of course. Now is good. But the story shouldn't just be about the complex. You should watch Dejuane play. He's amazing. He's meeting with college coaches this summer."

"I'd love that. I'm sure when the article comes out, even more scouts will be coming after you." Gwyneth squeezed Dejuane's hand then began firing questions at us. The first several were directed at me, so I had to pay attention, but I kept wandering back to the nagging question on my mind, *Why? Why did Abby do this for me?*

I looked to the complex as an escape. There were no Abby reminders at ICS. Yet, she linked herself to my job from halfway around the world. It wasn't fair. I'd left her alone. Why couldn't she leave me alone, too?

Two hours passed and Gwyneth filled at least twenty pages of her notepad. When she ran out of questions, she stood to leave. "Thank you both for your time. I'll call you to follow up and of course to schedule a time to come see you play." She smiled at Dejuane.

"Oh, and I'll be sending a photographer to the complex sometime in the next week or so. I'll call with that information as well." We both shook her hand again and she headed to the exit.

"Dejuane, hang here for a minute. I need to ask her something." Without waiting for an answer from him, I leapt from my seat and bolted out the door. "Gwen, wait!"

She turned around, pausing in the middle of the parking lot. "Did I forget something?"

"Oh no. I just… Well, I needed to ask you, I mean, um…" fidgeting with my hands, I couldn't seem to form the words.

"Yes?"

"What exactly did Abby, er, I mean Abigail say, um, about me?" *Geez, how old are you? Twelve? It's not like she passed her a note in study hall.* I could feel my face getting pinker by the second and dropped my eyes to the ground, but Gwen's calm tone as she answered gave me courage and I lifted my eyes to see her smiling.

"She said if I were looking for human interest, I couldn't do better than you. I told her that her being in love with you didn't make you interesting," she paused and my cheeks blazed red, "and then she told me about the complex, how you created the business plan while you were in grad school, broke ground only a month after graduation, how Dejuane was at the opening with you, and how you gave him his first job in the memorabilia store. She went on and on, even though I was hooked once she described the complex itself."

"Oh. Okay. Thanks." I turned to go inside as she got in her car.

I don't know what I'd been hoping for. Maybe that Abby realized what a mistake she'd made leaving me. Or that she wanted to call me but was too afraid I'd blow her off. I wanted some indication that I still meant something to her. If I was wasting away in Boston, I wanted her to be wasting away, too, and I didn't really care how selfish and petty that made me.

I opened the door and went back to the table where Dejuane waited. Finishing our coffee, I let him talk non-stop about the article and his excitement.

"My mom is going to be so proud of me! And Coach..." he yammered on, but I only caught pieces of it. My excitement over the article was mixed with confusion over what to do about Abigail's hand in it. I mean, I was grateful to her, even while pissed she'd weaseled her way into my work-life, but I didn't know how to handle it. *Should I find a way to thank her? Or pretend I don't know?* She hadn't given me a head's up; maybe she didn't want me to know the article was her idea.

Gwyneth said Abby loved me, but I'd never really doubted that. Well, yeah, maybe I did. She chose her job over me. If she really loved me, she would have chosen me, right?

Gwen called a few times in the two weeks after our meeting to ask follow-up questions and set a time for the photographer to come to the complex as promised. She told me her editor loved her notes and looked forward to reading the finished article.

"Oh, and I heard from Abigail last week. She emailed me to see how the article was coming along. I thanked her for recommending you and told her you were doing well. I hope that's okay." She threw the information in as an afterthought, but I knew she was trying to gauge my reaction. I don't know why she cared about my relationship with Abby, but I chose my words carefully anyways.

"Yeah, of course that's okay. If you happen to talk with her again, please thank her for me, for suggesting the complex." That was good. It couldn't be taken for anything other than indifferent gratitude.

Not long after that conversation, I received an email from Gwyneth saying the article would run the third week of August, to coincide with a set of articles showcasing the nation's most promising high school athletes. "Dejuane might even make the cover!" her email exclaimed. I couldn't wait to tell him when he got back from his college visits, she told me she'd let me deliver the good news.

She didn't mention Abigail again.

Chapter Thirty-Five: Emotional Rollercoaster

Abby

I never called Billy. I couldn't. I didn't even want to. He wasn't Ben. My neighbor thought I was crazy for not giving him a shot and constantly reminded me how dull I was. But I still loved my kooky new friend. One of the first people I'd met since moving to London, Charlotte (Lottie for short), made it her mission to befriend and school me in the ways of the English.

"Ab, you've got to do something else while you're here besides being a tourist. You're so pretty. If you would just come to the pub with me once in a while, you'd be able to take a delicious British man back with you to the States next year. Way better than bloody snow globe souvenirs from the Tower of London." Lottie grimaced at the box of gifts I'd collected for my family. I was working on a column, trying to decide which photo would work best with the article, and she refused to leave my flat, convinced that no twenty-six year-old single woman should spend a Friday night alone and working. I'd never explained to her that the real reason I didn't want to go out was because I'd already found the perfect guy.

"Thanks, but no thanks. I have no interest in British men right now." *Or ever, really.*

"At least come and get pissed with me, then."

"My columns are due Monday. They aren't ready yet."

"Can I read them?"

"They aren't ready."

"I'm sure they're good. You're a perfectionist."

I put down the photos and stood up. "Very true. Which is why I'm not going out with you tonight. Have fun though." Forcibly steering her towards the front of the apartment, she sent a few choice British curse words my way until finally she was on the other side of my closing door.

Instead of exploring the nightlife and social circles of Westminster that night, I finished my articles.

My days kept to the similar theme of focusing on work. In addition to exploring the United Kingdom, I strolled down the Champs Ellysees and window-shopped stores I'd never be able to afford to shop in. I smoked my first, and last, cigarette sitting at a sidewalk café in Bordeaux and listened to the beautiful strains of La Bohéme seeping out of the Opera House as I rode gondolas through the watery streets of Venice. Me. Abigail Bronsen. I visited libraries and museums in every city and experienced more culture than I ever imagined existed. It was way better than getting sloshed at a stupid pub.

Words flowed smoothly from my head to my pen.

Luckily, Elizabeth was easy to work with, her editing and feedback style more verbal than Helen's, and she didn't seem to think I'd only been acting like a tourist. Even Jeanette in New York praised me for being so open and vulnerable in the new articles.

"The readers love it! Letters are coming from all over the country. People are rooting for you, Abigail. It's phenomenal. Though, I'm guessing you probably won't want to keep the article going for two years like we planned," she said during a teleconference at the beginning of July.

"I don't know. I don't have any reason not to at this point, but I'll let you know. I'd never leave you hanging."

"That's good to hear. We'll talk in a couple of weeks when I get your next submission. Enjoy Spain."

"Thanks." The conference ended and I left the office immediately to head to the airport. Whenever I boarded another plane, I thought about Ben, wondered if he had tried any flying since I'd been gone, and hoped that if he had, he wasn't afraid anymore.

Ben

By mid-July *SI* announced Dejuane and seven other high school seniors from across the country would be on the cover of the magazine, representing a variety of sports: basketball, football, baseball, soccer, volleyball, track, and swimming.

"This never would have happened if it weren't for you, Ben," Dejuane said as we hung out on the courts one afternoon.

"You're crazy. You got here through hard work and determination. You set your eyes on a goal and you're the one getting yourself there." I shot from the 3-point line and watched as it bounced off the rim and fell back to the ground. Dejuane grabbed the rebound and jumped, performing the perfect layup.

"Nah, man. If you hadn't come along, if you hadn't encouraged me to focus on my schoolwork, I probably would've given up, dropped out of school. Shit, I would've been lost." He tossed the ball back to me; I caught it and just stared at him.

"Your mom would've kept you straight." I swallowed the lump in my throat and arched the ball towards the net again. It tapped the backboard before plopping neatly through the goal. Dejuane grabbed the rebound again, grinning as he dribbled to half court and showed me what a real shot looked like.

SWISH!

Showoff, I thought.

"Yeah, she would've killed me if I dropped out. I guess you both have my back."

"And always will." Slapping him on the shoulder, I retrieved the ball and we played one-on-one for another hour or so, until his shift at the store started and I made my way over to Matt and Trish's for dinner.

They took pity on me after Abigail left. I spent more time with them than with anyone else. It hurt seeing their unfettered and unabashed devotion to each other, but it also gave me hope that someday I would find that again.

I agreed to help them stuff their wedding invitations. Why? I don't know. Because they'd been there for me without question, without hesitation, I guess.

"Okay Ben, it's really simple. The invitation and an RSVP card and an RSVP envelope go in this envelope." Trish held up an ivory rectangular envelope.

"Then, I'll address that envelope, and Matt you'll put it in the outer envelope." She held up a second ivory rectangular envelope. They looked absolutely identical to me.

"Then I'll address the outer envelope, stamp it, and put it in the completed stack. Once they're all complete, we'll sort them by address. There are some people living out of the country and we'll have to send theirs earlier than the others." By this time, both mine and Matt's eyes were glazed over, but I started assembling the packages as fast as I could.

"I thought bridesmaids were supposed to help with this kind of thing." Stretching my back and arms, I got up from my seat on the floor and did a walking lap around the room.

"Ugh, men. You think everything to do with a wedding is the responsibility of women." Trish glared at me, looking up from the envelope she was working on.

"Sorry, Trish, I'm happy to help." I regained my seat and resumed my task with fervor. Matt chuckled from his corner, so I punched him in the shoulder.

"Hey, man, no violence around the stationary. My little woman will kill me if I get blood on the invitations."

"That's not even funny, Matt." She pursed her lips tightly and Matt and I just grinned at each other. We made a silent pact to stop antagonizing the bride. We finished addressing and stuffing after an hour and moved on to the next step.

Flipping through the already-assembled envelopes to determine which new stack they should go in was a piece of cake. Trish lightened up when she saw Matt and I focused on the job.

In state. Out of state. Out of country. In state. In state. Out of state. The piles grew until only a handful of invitations were left. I picked up the last one in my stack and glanced at the address before tossing it on the "Out of country" pile. But something registered in my brain and my hand shot forward to scoop it back up just as Matt tossed an invitation on top of it.

"Trish, you're inviting Abby?" My heart lodged in my throat as I stared at her name on the envelope. Surely it was a mistake. They wouldn't invite her without talking to me about it first.

"Of course. Didn't Matt tell you? He said you didn't mind."

"Matt?" My voice came out in a harsh snarl and a red flush crept its way up my neck.

"Oh, yeah, um Ben, do you mind if we invite Abigail to the wedding?"

"I can't believe you didn't even consider asking me, Matt! What made you think I wouldn't mind?" Already on my feet, I headed for the door.

"Don't leave. Look, I'm sorry. I guess I thought if she came, you guys could talk. I didn't ask because I thought you'd say no and you obviously have some stuff you need to deal with."

"Really? Are you my therapist now? Fine, invite her. I don't give a damn. But put us at separate tables on opposite sides of the room. I don't have anything to say to her. She dumped me, remember? If she wanted to talk to me, or see me, she's had plenty of opportunities." My hands shook as I crossed my arms across my chest.

"Ben, what're you talking about? She's been…" Trish started, but Matt cut her off.

"I'm really sorry. You're right; I should've considered your feelings. I'm sorry." He came to my side and placed his hand on my shoulder. "I didn't realize you'd be so upset. I thought you'd want to see her again."

"It's not that I don't ever want to see her again. I just, I don't know. It's hard to describe. I can't get away from her. Every time I think I've moved on, something comes up, her name, something we did together. I need some distance, some space." Silence sank around us. Matt's hand on my shoulder tightened. He was a good friend. His heart was in the right place.

"I don't have to send this." Trish held up the envelope bearing Abby's name and address in London. "I don't know that she expects an invitation. I mean, we've been emailing, so she knows about the wedding, but I don't think I've ever said we're going to invite her."

"No, you should invite her. She's your friend and I'm sure she'll want to be there for you. I'm sorry I made a big deal about it. Just took me by surprise. We're done with the invites, right? I want to head home."

"Yeah, we're done. Thanks for all your help." Trish smiled.

I nodded and left.

* * * *

With events like these, it's not surprising I almost forgot my birthday. I didn't realize it was approaching until Matt called to tell me he and Trish wanted to throw a party. I agreed, reluctantly.

I finally understood why Abby hated her birthday. I was not where I should be at twenty-nine. My business was floundering and the rest of my life was empty. The previous year, my birthday seemed like a fresh start, a new beginning. Abby and I spent our first weekend away together. She opened herself up to me. I introduced her to things she thought she'd never do. But she was gone and my birthday felt like just another day. Nothing special, nothing worth celebrating.

My family was already at Matt and Trish's when I arrived for the cookout. Tracey and my mother hugged me and Hannah and Joey ran at me, almost knocking me over. Handing me a homemade card, Hannah wished me a "Habby birfday!"

Our softball team showed up with beer and gifts. Dejuane and his teammates came, too, and took over the hoop in the driveway. People sat on the porch steps, crowded the couches, played games around the dining table, chatted on the back lawn. Everywhere I looked, I met a friend. The chaos surrounded me and I thanked Matt for insisting on doing something. It felt normal for a change.

After the group gathered to sing "Happy Birthday" and watch me blow the twenty-nine candles out, Trish tugged on my arm and asked me to follow her. She led me to the guest room and motioned for me to sit on the bed. Going to the closet, she pulled out a present wrapped in neon green paper. Handing it to me, she smiled and walked to the door.

"I think you'll want privacy to open that. It's from me and Matt. We love you, Ben. Happy Birthday."

I watched her leave before glancing at the gift. Shaking it, I tried to guess the contents, but it made no sound. Something was familiar. I couldn't put my finger on it.

Shouts seeped through the crack under the door, including more than one "Hey, where's Ben?" and I wanted to get back to the party. But instead, I ripped the wrapping paper off and threw it on the bed. A note taped to the top of a cardboard box read:

Ben,
I think it's time you had this back. Your gift from Matt and I is inside.
Love, Trish

I found the flap on the side of the cardboard and lifted. Tilting the package, a handcrafted wooden box slid out. Abigail's grandfather's box. I smiled in spite of myself. Looking at it, I remembered our last phone call and she was right. I remembered all the good things about Abby, about us. Her smile. Her laugh. The feel of her hand in mine. Her beautiful heart. Her love for me. I remembered our first date, how she double-checked herself in the mirror before getting out of her car. The flight to Florida, how she wouldn't let me be afraid. The way my breath caught in my throat every time I saw her. My reaction to the invitation suddenly seemed utterly ridiculous.

Ten minutes passed before a glance at my watch brought me to my senses. Shaking my head, I lifted the lid and pulled out a thin envelope. An open-ended plane ticket to London. Of course.

Tucking the box under my arm, I made my way back out to the party and gave Trish a hug. "Thanks."

* * * *

The next morning, I woke up and kissed my twenty-eighth year goodbye. Abby's box sat in its old place on my dresser and it was like she was there with me. I still hurt, I was still angry with her, but seeing that box made me admit I was also still in love. I couldn't get away from Abby because I didn't want to get away from her.

My cell phone rang while I cooked breakfast for myself. The caller id didn't recognize the number.

"Hello?"

"Happy birthday, Ben." Abby's voice. My heart sang, anger and pain melted away. It had been too long since I'd heard that sweet voice.

"Abby!"

"I didn't call too early, did I? I've been counting down the hours all day, just waiting until I thought you'd be up."

"No, your timing is perfect. I was cooking breakfast."

"I miss your breakfasts." Her tone lost its sparkle and sadness crept in.

"How's London?" I thought a change of subject would help her sound like herself, but it didn't.

"It's great." Her answer was flat. She didn't elaborate. "How are you?"

"I'm okay. I've been spending most of my time at work."

"Me, too."

We both paused, unsure where to go from there. She spoke again first.

"I got you a gift. Well, I tried to anyways. My sisters assembled it for me. I asked Ashley to drop it off this evening. Is that all right? If you have plans, she can bring it to you some other time, or if you don't want it I understand."

"No, tonight's fine. I don't have plans. We had a party last night."

"Oh. Great." Another pause. I wanted to tell her I missed her, I still loved her, I wanted her to come home. But I didn't say anything.

"Um, I guess I should go. My calling card doesn't have much time left on it and I don't want to get caught up in a conversation," her breathing hitched, "we can't finish."

"Oh. Okay. Thanks for calling." *Lame, man. You can't think of anything better than that?*

"Happy Birthday. I, well, I… oh God. Goodbye, Ben."

"Goodbye." I listened to her breathing for another few seconds before she disconnected. She wanted to tell me she loved me, but she didn't. I knew why, she didn't want to hurt me anymore. But then why call at all? The happiness that filled my heart while her voice sounded in my ear faded, replaced by a dull ache. Was she ever coming back to me?

Ashley rang my doorbell at a few minutes past seven. I was glad it was her and not Anna. I liked both of Abigail's sisters, but Anna looked the most like Abby. It still pierced my heart to see Ashley, but it wasn't as bad as seeing Anna.

"Happy birthday, Ben!" Ashley gave me a hug as she stepped in the door. It took me by surprise and I stiffened at her touch. She sensed my discomfort and backed off quickly.

"I'm sorry, Ashley. It's just, um, you smell like vanilla."

"Huh?"

"Never mind. Come on in."

She stepped inside, bringing with her a flat, rectangular package wrapped in brown paper. "This is it. I think you're going to like it." She beamed at me and it shattered my heart. Her smile looked so much like Abby's.

"Thanks, Ashley. If you don't mind, I'd like to open it privately." I took it in both hands and set it on the couch.

"Of course. Happy birthday. Bye." She waved walking out and I waited until her car disappeared around the corner before shutting and locking the door. This package looked familiar, too. A warm sense of déjà vu swept over me as I tore the paper off and held the frame up. On either side, pictures of the complex and of Dejuane and myself surrounded a mock-up of the article that would be appearing in *Sports Illustrated.* A note was attached to the corner of the frame.

Ben, Happy Birthday! Gwen sent me a mock up, but you can replace it with the actual article when it comes out. You always gave me the courage to go after my dreams and I hope this gives you the courage to continue chasing yours. I know you have what it takes to keep the complex going. I am so proud of you. Love, Abby

Her handwriting covered the page. Her signature. I looked over the frame, the pictures, and the article. Folding the note into a square, I pulled my wallet out of my pocket, and slipped it inside.

Picking the gift up, I walked to my bedroom, and propped it on my dresser, taking the airplane ticket from Trish and Matt out of her box and placing it face up in front of the article. I ran my fingers over the destination, then reached down to my sock drawer and pulled out the velvet box. I cracked the lid open, set the box on top of the plane ticket, then backed up and sat on my bed, keeping my eyes glued to the trio in front of me.

Chapter Thirty-Six: An Invitation

Abby

Three rapid knocks on my door alerted me to Lottie's arrival.

"Door's open!" I yelled from the kitchen, where I was busy chopping vegetables for the stir-fry we planned to make that evening.

Lottie danced into my flat, carrying a couple bags of groceries, and floated into the kitchen. It always amazed me to watch her walk. For an extremely tall woman, she was over six foot, she possessed more grace than the most poised ballerina and always appeared to be gliding rather than taking steps.

"How's it coming?"

"Good so far. Would you mind grabbing the bag on the couch? I bought a new wok the other day and forgot to bring it into the kitchen."

"Sure." She disappeared, singing to herself.

When she came back into the room, she was carrying more than the wok. "Ab, who is this *gorgeous* man?" She held out my photo album, open to the *Fall in Love* pages. I didn't realize I'd left it on the coffee table the night before until I saw her holding it. I always tried to hide evidence of Ben before someone came over. It was too painful to explain why we weren't together anymore.

I set the chopping knife down to reach for the album, but Lottie moved away before I could take it from her and sat on a stool on the opposite side of the counter. She flipped to the beginning of the album and laughed at my list.

"Oh, Ab, this is priceless! Have you done all these things?"

I shrugged and continued chopping. "See for yourself." I wanted to snatch the book out of her hand, close and hide it away forever, but Lottie would see that as an excuse to hound and torment me about it for the rest of my natural life. Probably a little beyond my natural life, too. Rather than deal with the heckling, I let her look.

"I officially forgive you for not going out with tattoo man. This guy is divine. That's it. If you ever move back to America, I'm coming with you. They don't make men like this here."

"They don't really make them like that in America, either. He's one-of-a-kind," I said without thinking. I'd planned on keeping silent on the whole thing, but that opened it up for discussion. *Damn it.*

"Wait, is this E?" she blurted out after reading the note on the page with list item number eight.

"How do you know about E?"

"Please, hun. As soon as you told me you wrote for a magazine, I looked it up online. You didn't think that just because you won't let me read your drafts that I haven't read the published ones? I've read all your articles since you've lived here."

"I didn't know that. Why didn't you say something?"

"You seemed to want to keep it private. I mean, as private as you can when you go splashing it around an international magazine. You've never talked about him." She pushed the album towards me and I set the knife down again. Picking up the book, tears developed and pooled in my eyes, but I blinked them away.

"Ben. His name is Ben."

"Ben? Then why do you call him E?"

"It's an inside joke."

"Explain it to me! I want to know everything!" She leaned towards me, propping herself up on her elbows, craning her neck forward to see the album.

"Everything would take too long. You can ask five questions, then we're moving on to different topics."

"Okay. Last name?"

"Harris. I can't believe you wasted one of your questions on his last name."

"When I go to Google him, it won't feel like a waste."

"Do *not* Google him."

"Please!"

"No! Come on, the poor guy has been through enough. He doesn't need some crazy woman on the other side of the world cyber-stalking him. Besides Ben Harris, it's a pretty generic name. I don't think you'll find much."

"Don't underestimate my powers in the art of snooping."

"Please Charlotte…"

"Uh oh, pulling out the whole name. I know you're serious when you call me Charlotte."

"Really? That's funny. I think I actually get that from Ben. He calls," I stopped, the word didn't seem to fit our situation, "he called me Abby usually, except when he was serious about something or mad at me. Then he called me Abigail." A tear slid down my cheek as I tried to bring his voice into my head. Lottie walked over to me, hugging my shoulder.

"Okay, I won't Google him."

"Thank you." I wiped away the tear and she sat back down.

"Alright, so question two, when's the last time you spoke to him?"

"July seventeenth, his birthday."

"You spoke to him on his birthday? Did he mention the articles? Did you? When's he coming to see you?"

"Yes, I called him to wish him a happy birthday. He didn't mention the articles, neither did I. As far as I know, he's not coming to visit me. And I believe that made six questions, so we're done talking about Ben." I snapped the album closed and took it to my bedroom.

I missed him all the time. All. The. Time. I wanted to pick up the phone every day to call him, but knew I couldn't. It wouldn't be fair to him. I wrote to him every day. The letters stacked up beside my computer, but I never sent them. Part of me was afraid he'd tear them up and throw them away without reading them, even though I knew Ben would never do that. I guess I just felt like that's what I deserved.

I only took a minute to look at the last pages of the album before shutting it again. Lottie stood at the sink, washing chicken breasts, when I came back into the kitchen.

"What's next on your hit list?" she asked.

"Oh, um, Germany. At the beginning of September."

"I love Germany. Want company? I can take a few days off work."

"Actually, yeah! That would be great." I turned the stove on and poured a teaspoon of olive oil in the wok before adding the vegetables. Lottie cut up the chicken and tossed it into the mix.

After dinner, we loaded junk food and margaritas onto my living room coffee table and watched the BBC version of *Pride and Prejudice*. We'd both seen it about two hundred times, but part of the fun was quoting the lines to each other.

"Ah, if only I could find a man like Mr. Darcy," Lottie sighed as the first part ended.

"Yeah, if only…" I agreed, knowing I'd already found, and lost, one.

"Oh! I almost forgot, Ab!" She jumped up from the couch and flew out the door. I was too accustomed to her flightiness to be surprised.

She came back a few minutes later carrying a stack of envelopes. "They delivered your letters to me yesterday." She dropped them on my lap and snatched the remote, hitting play and starting part two.

"Thanks." I thumbed through the pile while the credits rolled, most of it was junk, but one thick, ivory envelope stood out.

"Oh my God." The return address read: *Patricia Martin, 125 Trenton St., Boston, MA.*

"What's wrong?"

"Nothing. Nothing's wrong. This is from my friend, Trish. I think it's her wedding invitation."

"Why do you seem so surprised?"

"I didn't expect to be invited."

"You aren't that close, huh?"

"No, that's not it. The groom is Ben's best friend."

"Oh."

We watched the second part of the movie in silence, but when it ended, Lottie turned off the television and faced me. "Are you going to go?"

"I don't know."

"I think you should. What better place to kiss and make-up than a wedding?"

"Maybe. But I don't know if he feels the same."

"Ask him."

"How?"

"Whaddya mean, how? Ring him, email him, write him a letter. There are a million forms of communication nowadays. Or if you're too chicken to directly contact him, you could just do what you've been doing the past couple of months."

"I'm not chicken! I just don't want to pressure him."

"Ab, I know I don't know him, but judging by that album, that boy is seriously in love with you. Love like that doesn't disappear overnight. I bet he'd be ecstatic if you came to the wedding."

"Maybe."

"You know I'm right. Where's the response card?" She found it amongst the scattered pieces of mail on the table and checked the *Yes* box.

"Chicken or steak?"

"I think I should think about it for a few days. Maybe touch base with Trish and see if she or Matt talked to Ben about it."

"Okay, chicken it is." She checked the entrée box, stuck the card in its small envelope and sealed it. "Alright, love, I'm going to bed. I'll put this in the letterbox for you tomorrow on my way to work and we can finish *P&P* next weekend!" She floated out the door before I could object, but despite her mailing the card I wasn't going to the wedding unless I got the okay from Trish or Ben.

I went into my bedroom and dug around in my purse for a calling card and my cell phone. Finding them, I sat on the bed and punched in the code, but when it came time to put in Ben's number, I froze. Our conversation on his birthday went well, but he hadn't acted like himself. He didn't seem happy to be talking to me.

I hung up the phone and lay back on the bed, deciding to email Trish in the morning and going for the "chicken out" method Lottie suggested. If he still cared, he'd be reading the magazine, right?

Chapter Thirty-Seven: Angel in the Outfield

Ben

July faded into August and the collection of artifacts on my dresser grew to include Abby's pink Red Sox hat, which I found a week after my birthday hiding under my bed.

When I couldn't sleep, which was pretty often, I'd take her note out of my wallet and re-read the words I'd already memorized. Some nights the audacity of her phone call and gift would make me livid. My fists would ball around the paper and throw it, crumpled, on the dresser along with the other souvenirs.

Inevitably though, the next morning, I'd smooth out the wrinkles, neatly refold, and put it back in my wallet. On those days, I'd seriously consider booking myself on the next flight out of the country, but even the thought of seeing Abby again wasn't enough to get me through six and a half hours on a plane alone. At least, that's what I told myself. Then, thinking of the distance, fire would rise in my chest and head until I was so pissed off at Abby for leaving, I couldn't think straight.

I repeated the same pattern over and over again, but couldn't bring myself to dismantle the shrine in my room.

* * * *

"Ben? Ben! Man, snap out of it!" Dejuane had to clap his hands in front of my face before I registered that he was in my office.

"Oh, sorry. When did you come in?"

"A few minutes ago. God, you've been outta it lately. Please tell me it's not still about your woman."

"Says the boy who came to me blubbering like a baby when Sarah broke up with him."

"Man, that's cold. That was different, she was already hookin' up with one of my teammates."

"Yeah, I'm sorry, that was a low blow. What's up?" Swinging my legs until my feet were propped up on the desk, I folded my arms across my chest and leaned back in my chair. Dejuane held out a slip of paper.

"I need letters of recommendation for my college applications. You mind?"

"Not at all. When do you need them by?"

"End of the month?"

"Sure, that's no problem, but why so soon? School hasn't even started yet." I looked over the list; he was applying to twelve different colleges, all over the country.

"I wanna get the applications done and out of the way, so I can focus on my game and getting scholarships. I won't be able to send them in until after first semester, but they'll be ready to go."

"How did you get such a good head on your shoulders?"

"I don't know, I guess I had some pretty cool people to look up to." He laughed, heading towards the door. "Hey, the magazine comes out tomorrow! I can't believe I'm going to be on the cover of *Sports Illustrated*!"

"I know, it's crazy. Who'd want to put your ugly mug on the cover of a magazine?"

"Ugly? Shoot, you wish you were half as good looking as me." He strutted out the door, swinging it closed behind him. I chuckled, feeling blessed to have the kid in my life.

I paused after writing the first draft of his letter to check my email and noticed a new one from Gwen.

Hey Ben- the article comes out tomorrow. I've messengered over some advance copies for you and Dejuane. They should arrive this afternoon at the complex. Let me know what you think! Gwen

Hitting reply, I thanked her, promising to write again as soon as I read it.

When the package arrived an hour later, I dropped everything to rip it open. Gwen sent ten copies, five for me, five for Dejuane. My mouth stretched into the biggest grin I've ever worn as I examined the cover. Pride. It was the only word to describe the emotion building in me. Pride in Dejuane, pride in myself.

I scanned the table of contents and found the page with the article. A picture of myself standing on the baseball field filled two pages with the headline, *Angel in the Outfield: Boston's Athletic Philanthropist*. The title was new. Gwen tossed several around, but I'd never heard this one. My face flushed and my palms grew slick as my fingers fumbled with the corner, trying to separate the pages.

Benjamin Harris (29, Boston, Massachusetts) is not your typical philanthropist. He doesn't donate millions of dollars every year to numerous charities supporting a wide range of causes. He doesn't attend benefits or openings of new medical facilities. Instead, he spends his days on a baseball field, a basketball court, a golf course. He spends his days providing a safe haven for the kids of Boston.

Not exactly the life most children of privilege choose for themselves. And that's exactly how the humble Harris describes himself: a child of privilege. Growing up in Brookline, a wealthy suburb to the west of Boston, his parents held important roles in the community. His father was a successful prosecutor-turned-judge, his mother a respected pediatrician. He attended Tufts University, then Harvard Business School. "I wanted for nothing," he explained.

With MBA in hand, Harris could have followed in his parents footsteps and gone to medical school or law school. Instead, he used his trust fund to build Inner City Sports, an athletic complex situated just north of Dorchester that houses basketball, tennis, and volleyball courts, swimming pools, golf course, and baseball field in addition to fitness center, ticket office, sports bar, and memorabilia store.

While the complex itself is an amazing achievement, the real story lies in Harris's motivation for building it and the way he chooses to run it.

At the age of 17, Harris joined the Delta Tau Delta fraternity, and volunteered for the Big Brother program at the local YMCA to fulfill his required philanthropy hours. "I had no idea what the meaning of compassion, or charity, was before I joined Big Brothers," Harris smiled as he described his first year at Tufts. "I just wanted to party and have fun, and the frat said I had to do volunteer hours." Don't let his modesty fool you, though. He put in more hours in his first year with the Big Brothers than the entire senior class of Delta Tau Delta combined.

It was while working with Big Brothers that Harris met Dejuane Jackson, then a five year-old kid living with his mom in Roxbury. With no funds for childcare, and no father at home to provide Dejuane with a positive male role model, Mrs. Jackson signed her son up for the program at the Y, hoping he would find a better way to spend his time than the other kids on their street. She was in constant fear that one day her son would join a gang and throw away any chance at a future outside of their neighborhood. Though Boston has seen a reduction in crime since the 1990s, Mrs. Jackson witnessed first hand what the youths of the city were capable of. Dejuane's father was killed in a drive-by shooting when Dejaune was just two years old.

With Harris as his Big Brother, Dejuane was encouraged to follow his dream of becoming a professional basketball player (see page 80 for more information on Dejuane's hoop dreams). But, as Harris's school demands grew, he had less time to transport Dejuane back and forth from the Y. It was during his second year of business school that he came up with the idea of the complex. He wanted to create a place where Dejuane and others like him could go to "play, have fun, and be kids." Where kids without a privileged background could learn to love sports, just like he had as a child. And in order to ensure that every kid had that opportunity, he arranged van rides from all over the city to the complex, absolutely free of charge to anyone who wanted a ride. Use of the facilities is free as well.

Throughout the building and construction of the complex, Harris still mentored Dejuane and ensured that his schoolwork was his highest priority. When Inner City Sports opened in 2006, Harris was 25, Dejuane was 13, and they played the first game on the new basketball court together. When Dejuane turned 16, Harris gave him his first job, as a part-time employee in the complex's memorabilia store.

Today, the two friends still play one-on-one and Harris still looks out for underprivileged youths. The complex is open seven days a week, 363 days a year (it closes only on Christmas and Thanksgiving), and the vans run from 8:00 AM until 10:00 PM during the summer, 8:00 PM during the winter.

While Harris does make a profit from the non-gratis functions of the complex (the ticket office, gym, sports bar, and memorabilia store), he is constantly exceeding it to improve the free programs; often taking pay cuts to make up the difference. He also lets investors in, giving the complex even more options for expansion and success.

When asked how he feels about being a hero in the community, Harris just laughed and waved the label off. "I'm no hero. I'm just a friend. I'm the lucky one to have these kids in my life. They show me what true joy is, what a free spirit is. My love of sports led me here, but I've stuck around because of the kids. Every child deserves the opportunity to play."

And the kids of Boston have embraced the world of sports he provides for them. When SI visited, every court and field was full. Children and adults of all ages, races, and backgrounds share the complex, filling it with the joy and spirit that keeps Harris going.

He may not consider himself a hero, but Dejuane certainly does. "Ben was a true brother to me. He's been there for me every step of the way. I'm going to graduate high school in ten months and I'll be the first person in my family to go to college. That never would have happened without Ben."

And the city of Boston wouldn't be the same without its athletic philanthropist. Sure, he doesn't flaunt his generosity and sure, he'd rather play softball than admit his growing impact on the community, but that's what makes Inner City Sports, and Harris, so special.

My emotions and brain were in hyper drive by the time I got to the end of the article. I couldn't make sense of my own feelings. Gratitude, disbelief, overwhelming happiness. I sat staring at the last page, a cheesy grin spread across my face, the muscles in my cheeks actually hurting.

Picking up the phone, I started to dial Abby's number, but quickly hung up. I wanted nothing more than to share this moment with her, but I couldn't bring myself to finish dialing. She should've been there, it should not have been up to me to figure out the time difference to make the overseas call to experience it with her. *She should be here for this, for me.*

Chapter Thirty-Eight: Regret

Abby

I slumped into my apartment after a long day at the *Intuition* offices. I met with Elizabeth for two hours, going over my September and October itineraries and editing my current piece. She loved the personal information, but had a lot of comments on my coverage of Spain. After that, a teleconference with Helen to go over the same piece produced similar results.

With the column finally given the green light to be sent to New York, I hailed a cab, too exhausted to walk, and made my way home. Well, as much home as my flat could be without Ben.

I flung my body onto the couch, not bothering to take off my jacket or shoes, and settled in for a nice long nap when Lottie's familiar knock sounded on my door.

"Ugh, go away," I called half-heartedly.

"No chance of that!" she sang as she glided through the door. "They brought me your letters again. Since when do you read *Sports Illustrated*?" She dropped a bundle of bills and magazines onto my lap, *SI* right on top.

"Oh my God! I can't believe it's here!" I squealed, unable to answer her question. I ripped the plastic wrap off the cover and sat up at the same time. Lottie slid onto the couch, taking the space where my head previously rested.

"What's so exciting about a sports magazine?"

"Him for one thing." I pointed at Dejuane on the cover, but didn't really give her time to look before flying through the pages and reaching the article on Ben's business, "and him, for another."

Lottie gawked at the picture of Ben filling the left hand side of the page and turned her eyebrows up at me. "Your man's an athlete?"

I sighed. "He's not my man anymore, I don't think. And not exactly. He owns this athletic complex. Well, here, read the article with me, you'll see what it is."

She shrugged her shoulders and scooted closer to me on the couch. I flipped the page and started at the top. Each new sentence, each new paragraph filled my heart with a deep sense of pride. Ben was such a good man. He'd done such a wonderful thing with his life. And I had been lucky enough to be loved by him, even for just a little while, even if I'd ruined it by leaving.

By the time I reached the end of the article, I imagined Ben, sitting in his office, reading the same words. I wanted to call him, congratulate him. Tell him how wonderful he truly was, how the article couldn't even capture half of his generous spirit and kind heart. I actually attempted to find my phone in my purse, before realizing I was probably the last person he would want to hear from.

Lottie finished reading a few minutes after me and tugged the magazine out of my hand to get a better view of the pictures. "Why'd you break up with him again? He seems fantastic," she asked, never lifting her eyes.

"I don't know."

Ben

Two weeks after the article came out, it was still all I could think about. I got calls from dozens of new investors once the issue hit newsstands and the owner of the Red Sox called me personally to congratulate me. He even wanted to come to the complex and take a tour. Money came pouring in and for the first time in over a year, all Steve had to say was "Congratulations." I was elated, to say the least, but tried to remember my duty to my friends as I approached South Street and the restaurant where I was meeting Matt and Trish for dinner.

"Matt, what do you want to do for your bachelor party?" I asked, joining him at a table. As far as I could tell, Trish hadn't arrived yet. It was a weeknight, but most of the tables were full and the lights had already been dimmed.

"I don't know. I hadn't thought about it."

"You haven't thought about your bachelor party? I thought that was the reason you're getting married!"

"Very funny. I guess I don't really feel like a bachelor. We've been together forever." He scanned the menu and sipped a beer, looking as if he could care less about the end of his bachelorhood.

"We gotta do something. I'm your best man, it's practically the law that I throw you a bachelor party."

He continued looking over the menu, ignoring me.

"We don't have to do the stripper, cigar, get-drunk-off-our-asses bachelor party, but we should do something." I grabbed my white cloth napkin off the white tablecloth and put it in my lap, looking around for the waitress at the same time. I really wanted a beer.

"Whatever you want, man. But definitely no strippers. Trish would kill me."

"Now who's whipped?" I snorted.

"Yeah, yeah. Laugh it up. Tell me where and when and I'll be there, but seriously, no strippers."

"I think you know me well enough to not worry about that. Strippers aren't really my thing."

"Yeah, I know."

Trish walked up at that moment and bent over to kiss Matt before sliding into the chair beside him. "What're you boys talking about?"

"Oh, just the usual, strippers, getting wasted," I teased.

"Riiiight. Ben, I saw the article. It was fantastic. Congratulations!"

"Thanks. I think it turned out pretty good. Did you see the page on Dejuane?" Picking up the menu, I perused the entrees, and tried to mask my true excitement. I didn't want to monopolize the conversation, but I also wouldn't have minded talking about it all night.

"Yeah. It looked good, too. We're so proud of you, aren't we Matt?"

"Of course. Good job, man."

Shaking my head at Matt's disinterest, I thanked Trish again. I knew he was happy for me; he just wasn't the type to show it. Trish moved on to discussing the wedding and my article seemed forgotten, until the check came and she insisted on paying for me to celebrate it.

We were leaving the restaurant when a familiar laugh caught my attention. My heart skipped and I whipped my head around quickly, trying to find the source. Scanning the candlelight tables, I found it, in the back corner of the restaurant. Anna.

My brain couldn't stop my feet from carrying me over to the table where Abby's siblings were having dinner. Anna's laughter stopped as soon as she saw me, but her smile remained plastered to her face.

"Ben! Oh my goodness, it's so good to see you!" She hopped up from the table and I couldn't help but stare at her protruding stomach. She hugged me firmly, and I actually felt a little punch in my abs.

"Anna, you're pregnant! Congratulations!" I grabbed her hand and squeezed it tightly, trying to wrap my brain around this new information. It seemed like something I should have already known, but Abby and I hadn't talked in months, so how could I have?

"Yeah, thanks! I'm due in November. You should see Will, he's so excited. He keeps coming home with baby shoes and shirts and toys. This little girl is going to have him wrapped around her little finger." She patted her belly and grinned at me. She was glowing. *A little girl.* My stomach lurched. At that moment, there was nothing I wanted more in life than a little girl with my throwing arm and Abby's green eyes. *Snap out of it, Ben.*

"I'll bet. Man, I can't believe it. I'm so happy for you." I hugged her again then turned to greet Derek and Ashley. Both got up from their seats, Ashley hugged me, and Derek shook my hand.

"It's good to see you," he said, griping my fingers, "how are you?"

"I'm alright. How are you guys?"

"We're blocking the aisle, let's sit down," Ashley motioned to the server trying to get around us and I took the empty chair beside her. "Ben, we've missed you."

My face grew hot, so when a waitress passed I asked for a glass of water. "That's nice of you, Ashley, but we don't need to go there. What's new with you all? Other than Anna's pregnancy?"

"Not much," Ashley answered. "We were actually just talking about Abigail. She was right about this place, the food is delicious."

As she spoke, alarms went off in my head. I looked around and realized this was the restaurant we'd gone to on our first date. The waitress who set a glass of ice water in front of me looked familiar. Had she been our server that night?

Ashley didn't seem to notice my anxiety attack, because she kept right on talking, "Oh, and her latest article came out yesterday, did you see it?"

I gulped the liquid down before responding, "Um, no, can't say that I have. I guess I'll have to pick it up." *Yeah right.*

"You should. I think you'd find it interesting."

"Yeah, well, um, I think I've interrupted you long enough. I know your siblings' dinner is kinda private." Hastily standing up, I gave a half-hearted wave and headed for the door. I barely heard their cries of "goodbye," as I joined Trish and Matt. They had paused to wait for me.

"What was that all about?" Trish asked as Matt held open the door.

"Abby's family."

"Ah."

"Matt, I'll call you about plans for the bachelor party." I turned away from them and hopped on my bike.

"What bachelor party? Wait, were you guys serious when you said you were talking about strippers?" Trish shot daggers at me with her eyes, but I just chuckled and revved my engine.

"Not completely. Good luck, Matt." Pressing my helmet over my head, I kicked into gear and zoomed out of the parking lot.

On the way home, I thought about what Ashley said about Abby's article. I realized I hadn't read a single one since she'd been gone. A momentary sense of guilt came over me, soon replaced by resentment. How could anyone even imagine I'd want to read those articles? They were the reason she left Boston, the reason she left me. Vowing to never look at them, I turned into my driveway and went inside the house exhausted.

The last six months had put me through every conceivable level of hell. Anger, pain, betrayal, guilt, remorse, love, and even more pain. The muscles in my neck and shoulders strained against the stress and I tried to work out the knots with my knuckles.

Six months and I couldn't get over her. Six damn months. Fury kept growing inside me until I was so frustrated I balled up my fist and punched it through the wall. The plaster gave way as stinging jolts rushed through my fingers and blood trickled onto the floor. Pulling my t-shirt off, I wrapped it around my bleeding knuckles and stretched out on the couch, thankful to the physical pain replacing the ache in my heart.

Chapter Thirty-Nine: Another Wedding

Ben

"How the hell did you get these seats, Ben?" Matt asked, sipping his second beer and looking around our private box in amazement.

"It's the article. The owner read it and offered me use of the seats anytime I wanted for the rest of the season. I brought a group of kids last week."

"If I'd known I'd get to watch the Sox from box seats, I wouldn't have given you such a hard time about the bachelor party."

"You'll know better next time," I joked, punching him in the shoulder.

"Nah, this is it for me. I've found the woman I'm going to grow old with."

"*Going* to grow old with? You're already there, man!" Everyone laughed, myself, his coworkers, and the guys from our softball team.

Matt and Trish were the epitome of the old married couple, desperately in love, and prone to bickering when they thought no one was watching. Trish had been an extension of Matt for so long, it was hard to remember what my friend acted like before she came into his life. Oh right, a smart-ass. I guess he hadn't changed much.

As the guys turned their laughing into mocking of Matt and the state of marriage, he turned to me, and said quietly, "You remember when Trish and I broke up, after I graduated from law school?" His eyes were serious and his jaw pulled tight; probably what he looked like in a courtroom.

"What? You and Trish never broke up."

"We did, for a couple of months. We were so young, like twenty-four or so, I think it was around the time you started building the complex."

"Oh. Yeah, I do remember now. I guess, I mean, you guys seem like the perfect couple, I just forgot."

"I try to, too. I was working constantly, trying to prove myself at the firm, and I neglected her. I canceled plans all the time; I never told her how much she meant to me. I forgot about us." He stroked the stubble on his chin, lost deep in thought.

"Why are you telling me this?"

"Because she forgave me. She gave me a second chance. And it's time for you to do the same."

"Come on, this is a bachelor party. We're supposed to be getting drunk and having fun, not talking about such deep stuff." My face grew red. His situation and mine were completely different.

"I've known you all my life, I'm telling you this because I care. You need to man up. Forgive her. That doesn't mean you have to get back together with her, maybe you don't want to give her a second chance, but you're never going to be able to move on, with her or without her, if you can't forgive her."

My heart was full as I listened to him. Forgiveness wasn't that easy. It should be, but it wasn't. My love hadn't been enough, how do you forgive someone for that?

Instead of responding, I left my seat and grabbed two beers from the cooler in the back of our box. As I sat back down, I handed the extra one to him, but kept my eyes focused on the game. My silence said, *Thanks for the advice. I'll think about it*, and he understood.

We didn't speak throughout the rest of the game, but Matt cheered or yelled along with the rest of our party whenever the Sox made a great or lousy play.

After the game, Hunter, Matt's friend from work, took over the reigns and forced us to barhop all over the city. I dropped him off with Trish around two in the morning. He was completely trashed as I helped him through the door.

"Thanks for bringing him back in one piece," she snapped.

"Hey, I just planned the baseball game, blame Hunter for the inebriation."

"I'm sure he didn't do any drinking at the game." Her tone tried to convey anger, but a smile threatened to expose her true amusement at the situation. "Will you try and keep him sober next week? I can't have a sick groom on my wedding day."

"Don't worry, we're all bachelor-ed out."

"All right. I guess I'll see you at the rehearsal. Be there at five."

"Yes, ma'am. Night, Trish."

"Goodnight, Ben. And hey, thanks for planning this for him. I'm sure he had fun."

I waved at her as I walked backwards to my car. She smiled at me from the porch, then made her way inside to her drunken fiancé.

* * * *

On the morning of the wedding, I got up and went to the complex to exercise. My muscles had been aching sorely for weeks and nothing loosened the kinks like a strenuous work out. Stretching my arms high above my head, I thought about what Matt said about forgiveness being the key to moving on. The more I thought about it, the more convinced I became he was only partially right. I needed closure to move on, not forgiveness. Closure might take the form of forgiveness sometimes, but not always, and in this case, what I really needed was to tell Abby to leave me alone for good. I needed to get her out of my head.

The ceremony started and I followed Matt down the aisle, involuntarily scanning the crowd for Abby. Part of me hoped she was there and part of me prayed she wasn't. I didn't see her. My heart calmed its beating and I focused on waiting for the bridesmaids to file in. The audience rose and I craned my neck, searching for a glimpse of Trish, but couldn't see over the heads of the guests, so instead, I looked at Matt. His eyes brimmed with tears and he had the biggest, dorkiest grin plastered across his face. When Trish came into view, he sucked in a breath and held it for a few seconds before slowly letting it out and forming the grin again. I'd never seen him so happy.

She glided down the aisle, looking so serene and beautiful I felt wrong being in her presence. Her father kissed her cheek then shook Matt's hand before sitting in the front row.

"I love you," Matt whispered as he took her hand and they turned to face the minister.

"I love you," she whispered back.

"Family and friends," the minister began, "we are gathered here today to witness the marriage of this man, Matthew Jacob Poole, to this woman, Patricia Brooke Martin…"

He gave a short message on the importance of marriage, then instructed Matt and Trish to face each other and hold hands. I couldn't see Matt's face anymore, but Trish was just beaming as she repeated after the minister,

"I, Trish, take you, Matt…"

"I, Matt, take you, Trish…"

"With this ring, I thee wed…"

"With this ring, I thee wed…"

"Ladies and Gentleman, it is my privilege to announce that Matt and Trish are now husband and wife. Matt, you may kiss your bride!" With the minister's permission, Matt took Trish's face in both hands and planted the steamiest wedding day kiss on her I've ever witnessed. I put two fingers in my mouth and let out a loud whistle; the rest of the crowd followed suit. Applause broke out and continued to grow as Matt and Trish's unfettered kiss went on.

When they finally released Matt yelled out, "Hell yes!" and grabbed Trish, lifting her off the ground and spinning her around. I laughed so hard, tears came to my eyes, and the rest of the crowd hooted and hollered until the newlyweds finally decided to walk back up the aisle.

The group of people clamoring around the couple, trying to express their good wishes was so dense, I couldn't even make out Matt's big head. Sighing, I planted myself in a corner and waited until the last of the non-family, non-bridal party guests were ushered to the cocktail hour. Finally, a clear path was open to the bride and groom, and I hugged Trish as tightly as I could manage.

"Ben, I can't breathe!" she choked out, pushing her hands against my chest.

"I'm sorry," laughing, I released her, "I'm just so happy for you guys!" I repeated my bear hug with Matt, who crushed me back.

A half-hour of pictures later and I finally made my way to the bar to grab a drink. I scanned the crowd again. A tingling in my arms told me she was there, but I couldn't find her.

The DJ announced, "Ladies and gentlemen, friends and family, I am happy to present, for the first time, Mr. and Mrs. Matt and Trish Poole." They burst through the doors to the ballroom and charged through the crowd of people clapping for them, then waltzed onto the dance floor effortlessly. As their first dance played, I tried to relax. The tingling in my arms faded; *maybe she's not here after all.*

As soon as the bride and groom took their seats, dinner service began, and I turned all of my attention to the prime rib in front of me. I knew after dinner, I'd have to give my toast, so I pulled out the index cards I'd prepared over the last week and silently reviewed them as the plates were cleared around me.

"Ladies and gentleman, the father of the bride would like to toast the happy couple and then we'll be hearing from the Maid of Honor and the Best Man."

My hands shook as I waited for my turn. Public speaking was not my favorite thing. Finally, the DJ announced my name and I took the microphone from him.

"For those of you who don't know me, I've been friends with the groom here for as long as I can remember," grinning at Matt briefly, I then turned to face the tables full of guests.

"You see, Matt and I played little league baseball together and the very first thing he said to me was 'You better not suck, because my team always wins.' I think if I had sucked he would have hated me for the rest of my life." A few chuckles broke out and one in particular struck me; I turned towards it, but couldn't see in the dim light.

"As we grew up, and I got better at the game, and Matt got worse," another laugh, but I still couldn't see the source, "we began sharing more than baseball. He's been my best friend through everything: high school, college, grad school for me and law school for him, the opening of my business, good times and bad. I couldn't have asked for a better friend." I nodded in his direction, he nodded back.

"Somewhere along the way, he met Trish. I say somewhere, because to me it feels like they've always been together. They have a love that is truly constant. When I think of that cliché, 'soul mates,' they come to my mind. Matt's whole face lights up when Trish enters a room, he'd lay down his life for her, and I know he's going to spend the rest of it doing everything in his power to make her happy. And I, as his best friend, will do everything I can to ridicule and humiliate him as he becomes more and more whipped over the years."

A clear, sparkling laugh broke out over the subdued chuckles sounding throughout the room, and I couldn't deny it anymore. Abby was there.

"So, here's to Matt and Trish, the world's most sickeningly happy couple. I love you guys!" I raised my champagne, heard the clinking of glass spread throughout the room, took a gulp, and headed to their table. They both stood to hug me and thank me for the toast, Trish kissed my cheek.

"What's wrong?" she whispered before pulling away. "You're as pale as a ghost."

"It's nothing, just don't like public speaking."

"Oh, well, you did great! You didn't seem nervous at all."

"Thanks. And really, congratulations. I love both of you, very much."

"We love you, too." She squeezed my hand before sitting back down and I made my way to my table. A slice of cake was waiting at my seat, but instead of sitting, I headed for the exit. I needed fresh air.

I was only a few feet outside when I heard the clack of heels hurrying behind me. Bracing myself, I spun to face her. When she stepped out of the building, I involuntarily held my breath. Her hair was swept off her face and pinned back, loose strands danced on her shoulders as she moved towards me. She wore a long, strapless, navy dress that swished with each step, hugging her hips and showing just the slightest hint of cleavage. Her neck and shoulders were bare, smooth and tanned.

"Ben." She stopped a few feet in front of me and looked straight into my eyes.

"Abigail." I stared back, not willing to show her my pain by avoiding her eyes, but her gaze nearly broke me.

"It's so good to see you!" She rushed forward and threw her arms around my neck. My entire body stiffened and I wouldn't let myself hug her. She quickly let go and took a step back.

"It's really, really good to see you," she repeated.

"I wish I could say the same."

She took another step back, looking like I'd slapped her. She wrapped her hands around her arms, rubbing them up and down to warm the goose bumps forming in the chilly autumn air.

"Look, Abigail, I'm sorry. That came out a lot more severe than I meant it to." I took off my jacket and handed it to her. Attempting a smile, she took it and pulled it on.

"I understand. I'm not really happy to see me most days."

"Don't start with that. I don't need to play your self-esteem coach tonight." Again, she winced at my words, and again I felt guilty for being so rough, but I didn't apologize this time. "Why are you here?"

"Matt and Trish invited me."

"Yeah, I know that. But why did you come?"

"Isn't that obvious? I wanted to see you."

"Why? Can't you stay away from me? Every time I turn around, there you are. Your name, your family, your baseball hat. I can't take it anymore. How am I supposed to forget you if I can't get you out of my life?" All of the resentment inside me seeped out as I yelled at her, unable to control any longer the anger she'd created.

"You want to forget me?" she asked through sobs.

"You didn't seem to have any problem forgetting me. You left me and you haven't even glanced back, except for one phone call on my birthday. What's that about? Were you trying to ruin my day?"

"No, Ben, I didn't think, I…"

"Yeah, you didn't think. You've only thought about yourself. Did you even consider I wouldn't want to see you here?"

"Yes, I did, but I hoped you would. I thought, well, have you been reading my articles?"

"Yeah, sure. A poor substitute for you being here." I don't know why I lied. What difference would it make if I'd read the articles? For some reason, my anger wouldn't let me wound her in that way.

"Ben, I had no idea you were so upset, please, let me explain." She could barely speak through her tears, but still I ranted on.

"Explain what? That I wasn't enough to keep you here? That your job means more to you than I ever did? How can you explain that? You can't explain it and I don't want to hear it. I'm done. I needed closure and this feels pretty final to me. Don't call me again. I don't ever want to see you again. I'm done." I stormed past her into the hotel and didn't look back. I left her crying, just like she left me.

My victory was short lived. As soon as my feet hit the ballroom entrance, I was racked with guilt. No matter how badly I hurt, no one deserved to be treated like that. I turned on my heel and followed the path I'd just taken. She wasn't there anymore, but I found my jacket folded neatly on a bench near the entrance to the hotel. Putting it on, I caught her scent, probably for the last time. My body slumped backward and the bench caught me. Putting my head in my hands, I let myself cry until I was completely drained and exhausted.

I knew I had to go back into the reception, but celebrating the happy beginning of Matt and Trish's marriage seemed like the absolute worst idea in the world. How could I act happy for them when my heart was broken and bleeding? When I knew Abby was somewhere weeping and devastated? Wasn't confronting her supposed to make me feel better? Why did I feel worse than ever?

Matt's voice startled me from my thoughts. "Hey, Ben, we've been looking for you."

"I'll be right there."

"Dude, you okay?"

"No, I'm really not. But don't worry, I'll be fine. I just need a few minutes alone." I kept my eyes focused on the ground and waited until the patter of his footsteps ceased before standing and wiping my eyes with the back of my hand. Finding a bathroom on the way to the ballroom, I splashed water on my face to cool the red heat threatening to give me away. *Get it together, Ben. For Matt and Trish. This is their day.*

The DJ announced the garter toss as I entered the ballroom for the third time. I didn't join the other single men on the dance floor. Abby was across the room, leaning against a wall. Even from the distance, I could tell her eyes were red and her cheeks splotchy with tears. When our eyes met, she turned her head immediately. I watched as she walked over and spoke to Matt and Trish. Then she gathered her bag from her table and left from a side door. My heart beat wildly in my chest, until I clutched at it, afraid it would literally break.

It was really over.

Chapter Forty: Broken

Abby

I went straight to the airport. My flight didn't leave for another twenty hours, but I couldn't stay at the hotel. Ben was there, hating me. I couldn't be in the same building with his hate, I couldn't be in the same country as that hate.

"Please, are there any flights that leave sooner?" I begged the attendant at the ticket counter. He furiously typed into his computer, trying to help, but we both knew there was nothing he could do.

"I'm sorry Ms. Bronsen. All the flights to London are booked this evening. If anything opens I'll be sure to let you know. Where are you staying?"

"It doesn't have to be a flight to London. Any flight towards the European continent will do. Please, I have to leave the country tonight."

"There is one flight leaving in an hour and a half to Lisbon and there are a few seats left."

"Great, can I exchange my ticket? I'll figure out how to get to London once I get there."

"Yes, ma'am, I'll take care of it." He printed out and handed me a new ticket and I headed to the terminal. The plane wouldn't be boarding for another forty-five minutes, so I called Lottie, hoping she could make arrangements for me to get home.

"What the hell are you calling me so late for?" she asked.

"What, what time is it there?"

"Three in the morning!"

"Oh, Lottie, I'm sorry, I wasn't even thinking. It's ten here, I forgot about the time difference."

"Ten? Why aren't you dancing the night away with your hunky man?"

Waterfalls flooded from my eyes and down my cheeks and Lottie's tone changed from annoyed to concerned.

"Ab, what happened? What's wrong?"

"He hates me. He never wants to see me again. I'm coming back tonight. Well, I'm trying to. I can't get a flight to London, so I'm flying to Lisbon. Can you help me get home?" I couldn't speak anymore, I bawled into the phone while Lottie tried to calm me down.

"It's okay, Abigail, it's fine. If he can't get over himself then he doesn't deserve you." Her comforting words didn't help, but I gulped in several large breaths in an attempt to gain control of my emotions.

When I could finally speak again, I said, "Listen, can you get online and find me a flight from Lisbon to London? I'll email you my flight information when we hang up."

"Yeah, I can do that. Call me as soon as you land in Lisbon."

"Okay, thanks." We hung up and I let myself weep into my hands until the flight started boarding. *Why? Why am I back here, crying at an airport after leaving Ben alone in Boston?* That wasn't how it was supposed to happen. I was supposed to run into his arms, feel his warmth and love. He was supposed to kiss me and tell me all was forgiven.

The plane ride was torture. I couldn't stop replaying everything that happened between us. It didn't make sense.

My eyes followed as Ben hugged Matt and Trish then made his way to his table. He lingered for just a moment but didn't sit. Instead, he turned abruptly and headed for the ballroom doors. Jumping up, my water glass tipped over, splashing liquid all over the table. I dabbed at the tablecloth hastily with my napkin before traipsing after him, knowing it was now or never.

Only a few steps ahead of me, he threw open the doors and walked outside into the cool autumn air. God, he looked good in that tux. His pictures didn't do him justice. I'd been staring at photographs of us together for months, but damn he looked good in person.

He kept his face away for only a few seconds, then turned and focused his eyes on me. I noticed that he glanced up and down, taking in my entire body, and a fever rose into my cheeks.

"Ben."

"Abigail," he responded.

Abigail. Not Abby. Not a good sign, but wait… He met my eye and I got lost in those deep blue pools of his.

"It's so good to see you!" I couldn't stop my feet from rushing forward, or my arms from finding that familiar position around his neck. His eyes said it all, he still loved me. But for the first time since I'd known him, his body didn't respond to my touch. Well, it did, but not the way I wanted it to. He usually melted into me, our bodies molded together like clay. But now, his arms stiffened and the muscles in his neck tightened. He didn't put his hands around my waist.

Releasing my hold and taking a step back, I tried again, "It's really, really good to see you."

"I wish I could say the same." His voice was cold, distant, unfamiliar. Where was my Ben?

I took another step back, unsure what to say. I didn't want to cry, but felt the beginning of tears behind my eyes. Goosebumps erupted over my arms and instinctually I wrapped them around my chest and rubbed my hands up and down, trying to hold in the pain in my heart and warm my body at the same time.

"Look, Abigail, I'm sorry, that came out a lot more severe than I meant it to." He handed me his tuxedo jacket. The simple act reminded me of the Ben I knew, but also made me feel guilty, I don't know why. And still, he didn't call me Abby.

"I understand. I'm not really happy to see me most days."

"Don't start with that. I don't need to play your self-esteem couch tonight." The coldness returned and his words hit me like a bullet to my heart. The assault continued, "Why are you here?"

What did he mean? Didn't he know why I was here? "Matt and Trish invited me."

"Yeah, I know that. But why did you come?"

"Isn't that obvious? I wanted to see you."

"Why?" he screamed. "Can't you stay away from me?" His voice got louder and louder as each word hit me like a punch in my stomach. "Every time I turn around, there you are. Your name, your family, your baseball hat. I can't take it anymore. How am I supposed to forget you if I can't get you out of my life?"

I couldn't hold back the tears any longer. They poured down my cheeks in currents and I sucked in huge breaths to try and control my voice, "You want to forget me?"

"You didn't seem to have any problems forgetting me. You left me and you haven't even glanced back, except for one phone call on my birthday. What's that about? Were you trying to ruin my day?"

Ruin his day? Did he really think I wanted that? "No, Ben, I didn't think, I..."

"Yeah, you didn't think. You've only thought about yourself. Did you even consider I wouldn't want to see you here?"

"Yes, I did, but I hoped you would. I thought, well, have you been reading my articles?"

"Yeah, sure. A poor substitute for you being here."

He's read them and he's still angry? What have I done? Have I really lost him for good? "Ben, I had no idea you were so upset, please, let me explain."

"Explain what? That I wasn't enough to keep you here? That your job means more to you than I ever did? How can you explain that? You can't explain it and I don't want to hear it. I'm done. I needed closure and this feels pretty final to me. Don't call me again. I don't ever want to see you again. I'm done." He swept past me without a second glance, cheeks red with anger, mouth drawn into a tight, thin line.

Rivers of tears streamed down my face and I clutched his jacket, wrapping it tightly around me. It smelled like him, like his delicious grassy, minty scent. The scent was too much to take. I stripped it off and folded it in half as I walked back inside, dropping it on a bench outside the doors. He was upset, but I knew him. He'd feel bad for blowing up and come looking for me to apologize. I didn't want to hear it. He was right. I deserved every word he screamed at me. An apology from him wouldn't change anything. He'd still hate me, I'd still hate me.

We were over.

I cried myself to sleep an hour into the flight, but my dreams were just as cruel asleep as my thoughts were awake. Ben yelled at me over and over, always with pain in his eyes. I couldn't figure out what had gone so wrong, why he wasn't expecting me, or why he hadn't told me not to come.

The plane touched down with a jolt and woke me from my nightmares. I turned my phone on as soon as the "Turn Electronics Off" sign went dark. Lottie had emailed me my new flight information; my connection would be leaving in two hours.

The intervening time between those flights was a blur. I can't remember exactly what I did or said or thought about. I called Lottie, but I don't know what our conversation consisted of. I pulled my notebook out on the second plane ride and started writing everything I could remember about the beginning of our relationship. I don't know why. I guess I thought I could purge it from my memory. Maybe the memories would heal a little of the broken heart barely beating in my chest. But like everything else, it made the pain worse.

Lottie met me at Heathrow, she folded me into her arms and let me cry.

"It's going to be okay, Ab, it's going to be okay." She patted and rubbed my back for a good fifteen minutes before putting me in a cab and taking me home. She helped me out of my dress, the dress I wore to the wedding, the dress I wore on both plane rides. Then she tucked me into my bed and I cried myself to sleep again with Ben's words ringing in my ears.

I don't ever want to see you again. I'm done.

Chapter Forty-One: Realization

Ben

"Ben, we need to talk," Trish said as soon as I answered the phone.

"Sure thing Trish, what's up?"

"In person. Can you meet me across the street at Starbucks in like twenty minutes?"

"I can meet you, but not there, anywhere else is fine."

"No, Ben. Starbucks, twenty minutes. I'll see you then." She hung up without waiting for my protest. Shit. That was the last place in the world I wanted to go.

My outburst at the wedding had the exact opposite effect than I intended. Instead of feeling better and being ready to move on, I felt so much worse. The constant stinging in my chest told me I was still in love with Abby, I still wanted her more than anything in the world and I ruined any chance at reconciliation that may have existed. My anger may have been righteous, but it wasn't right.

No, Matt was right. Forgiveness was the only option. *But I don't think there's any way she can forgive me now.*

Approaching the building, my heart leapt into my throat. It was just wrong. *I shouldn't be here.* It was her safe haven, where she went to relax, read, and feed her coffee addiction. I was violating her memory by being there after the way I'd treated her. Putting my hand on the door handle, I paused and took a deep breath. I really had no choice but to go in.

Trish was already there. She was sitting in Abby's favorite armchair by the fireplace, flipping through a magazine. I couldn't see the cover, but had a sneaking suspicion it would be *Intuition.* A cup of coffee sat in front of her on a table and she bent down to pick it up as I flopped into the chair beside her.

"How was the honeymoon?" It felt weird that I hadn't seen her yet; they'd been back for a week.

"It was great. Rome is absolutely breathtaking. Have you ever been?"

"Nope."

"You should go someday."

"Yeah, sure." Running my fingers through my hair, I turned and faced the fire. It wasn't really cold out yet, but the flames still comforted me.

"Ben, what happened at the wedding?"

"What do you mean?" I didn't want to discuss it with her. If she and Matt had stayed out of it in the first place, it never would have happened.

"I got an email from Abigail saying she couldn't be friends with me anymore. That she was done torturing you by being so present in your friends' lives. And she left the wedding crying, she came up and hugged me, tears streaming down her face. What the hell happened between the two of you?"

"I asked her why she came and yelled at her for putting me through hell."

"Ben…"

"I was a jackass. I know I was. I feel completely horrible about it, but it's too late now. I can't take it back."

"Why not? Ben, it's not too late for you guys."

"Why do you even care? It's none of your business."

"You're like a brother to me and Matt. We love you and want you to be happy. And she makes you happy when you aren't too busy being a proud asshole."

"She made me happy, then she broke me. Then I broke her. Doesn't exactly sound like a great foundation for a relationship. Besides, it's too late. I told her I never want to see her again."

"You act like the first person in the world with a broken heart. It happens to everyone. You guys had what, like a year without a single fight, and you're going to give up because you've had a rough couple of months? Get over yourself Ben. Matt and I are sick of you acting like a wounded puppy all the time." She was fuming now, chastising me like my mother. Folding my arms across my chest, I continued staring into the flames.

"Have you even read her articles?"

"What is it with the damn articles? No, I haven't read them. Why the hell would I want to read about what a fabulous time she's having thousands of miles away from me?"

"Oh Ben. If I had known you were thinking that," she stopped short and shook her head. Reaching down beside her, she lifted a stack of magazines and placed them in my lap. "If I had known you weren't reading them, well, I would have done things differently."

Staring at the stack before me, I grimaced. I couldn't read them. My heart was already torn in pieces. I tried to lift them and hand them back to her, but she pushed my hands away.

"No, Ben. You *need* to read them. I marked the pages after I heard from Abigail." She stood and wrapped her arms around my neck, cradling my head, "Call us when you get to London." Releasing me, she walked out the door and I was left alone with nothing but my curiosity to keep me company. What could the articles possibly say that would change things?

I looked around the shop at the other customers. A couple of teenagers sat in one corner, holding hands and kissing. The sight tugged at my heart. I wanted that again. I wanted Abby's hand in mine, her lips on mine. I glanced at the stack of magazines in my lap and remembered the first article she ever had published. She quoted me as an inspiration, called me a friend. *Now what am I? Nothing.*

And that's when it dawned on me. *How could I be so stupid?* If she wanted to communicate with me she would use the magazine. Knowing her, she was afraid email or a phone call would force me to respond even if I didn't want to. And she didn't want to force me to talk to her if I didn't want to. Of course she'd use the magazine.

"I'm such an idiot!" I said. Several customers looked at me from their place in line, but I didn't acknowledge their stares. Instead, I grabbed the top issue, checking the cover for the date: May 2010. It would have gone on newsstands in April, not long after she left. Flipping through the pages, I searched for the place Trish marked. There it was.

Facing Your Fears, by Abigail Bronsen

This month's column was supposed to be about Ophidiophobia, or the fear of snakes. Since this column first began, hundreds of letters have poured in from readers who want me to tackle this phobia with them. A couple of readers, anxious to conquer it, went with me to see a zoologist to learn how to handle a python, but I've decided to save that account for next month. Instead, I have a much more personal story to share with you.

A little over a year ago I met the man I've referred to in previous columns as my friend, E. Most of my avid readers have probably realized E is more than just a friend. He's so much more. He's the man of my dreams, as cliché as that is, it's true. I am deeply in love with him.

So why am I telling you this? What does E have to do with this article of facing fears? For one thing, if it weren't for him, I wouldn't be telling you anything at all. It's because of his support and encouragement and adventurous nature that I was given the opportunity to write this column and it's because of his love and faith in me that I was given another opportunity as well. Last month, I was offered a second column that will be debuting in the June issue of this magazine. For the next two years I'll be traveling and documenting my adventures as "An American in Europe."

What does the new column have to do with E? What does it have to do with "Facing Your Fears?" Well, for me, accepting this column is my way of facing my fear of the unknown.

Writing this column means moving to London and spending the next two years in Europe. It means turning my world upside down and staring ahead into the black abyss of the foreign and unfamiliar. What scares me most is being away from E. I'm scared leaving him now means losing him forever. I seriously considered turning the job down, staying in America to get married and have a family with him. Even now, I wish I'd made that decision, but if I had, I would have been giving into my fear.

The thought of him at home, in pain because I'm gone, tears my heart into pieces. But then, other thoughts creep into my brain. I think maybe he's okay, moving on to someone new, and I'm torn between happiness for him, anger against myself, and pain that he isn't missing me. I know how selfish the last feeling is, and yet, it's still there.

Ever since I met him, my biggest fear has been losing him. I was so afraid that taking this column would mean he'd break up with me that I broke up with him first. I fled. I should have known better. It was the wrong way to deal with my fear. Learn from my mistakes. Cut and run is not the way to deal with tough choices in life. If I included him in my decision, we would have worked something out, together. I'm thoroughly ashamed of myself for ending things the way I did and I hope with all my heart he will forgive me someday.

This leads me back to facing my fear of the unknown. I have no idea what's going to happen this year. I could fail horribly with the new column. I could lose the love of my life, forever. I could have amazing and life-altering experiences visiting countries and cities I've always dreamed of seeing. I have no idea what's coming, but I'm trying my best to face it head on.

I stared at the last paragraph for ten minutes, trying to comprehend what I'd read. When she left, my heart knew she didn't want to leave me, but I didn't care about her pain. I only thought of my own. I should have forced her to talk to me, to make long distance work. Both of us only considered two options: either she stayed with me or she left me. But there was a third option and I felt like an ass for not even trying to make her consider it.

Yes, she made the choice to leave me, but would she have been capable of making that choice if I hadn't encouraged her to spread her wings? Suddenly, all of my anger melted away and a surge of pride rushed through me. I was proud of her, for once in her life, she hadn't taken the easy way out. If I hadn't been wrapped up in my own desires, I would have persuaded her to take it, to not be afraid of how it would change her life, to be excited about the chance for a fresh start in a new place. That's who I'd always been for her. I couldn't believe I was so mad with her for being the person I'd always encouraged her to be.

I put May aside and picked up June's issue. The first earmarked page was the "Letters to the Editor" section. Two responses to Abby's column were printed.

Abigail, don't worry girl. If he loves you, he'll support your decision and wait for you. Good luck in Europe, I'm rooting for you!

I can't believe you have the nerve to complain about breaking up with your boyfriend in your column. You chose your job over him, you shouldn't expect him to be okay with that. Would he have done the same thing if the roles were reversed?

The first response stung. She, whoever she was, was right. I should have been supportive. The second response stung even more, because it's exactly the attitude I took when she left. I flipped quickly through the magazine and found her "Fears" column. It was about snakes, just as she promised. I laughed reading her description of draping a python over her shoulders and feeling it slither in her hands. The picture it created in my head was priceless: Abby, holding a snake, stiff as a board and trying not to scream. At the bottom of the page, a single sentence was placed on its own:

E - I miss you.

I continued flipping through the pages until I found the new column. The heading took up half a page and was imposed over a picture of Abby at Buckingham Palace, arms crossed over her chest, staring down one of the infamous guards. The article described her visits to several of

London's famous tourists sites, Parliament, Big Ben, and Westminster Abbey, and the culture shock of meeting Londoners and getting to know the city. Her excitement popped off the page, but the tone of the article became bittersweet at the last line.

My whole life I've dreamed of visiting London and I can't believe I actually live here now. It's surreal. It's nothing like I imagined it would be; but it's great. There's only one thing I would change. E - I wish you were here with me.

I didn't stop to think, I picked up the next magazine. More letters to the editor asked Abby what the status of her relationship with "E" was. I flipped to "Fears" to find out, but there was no mention of me this time. I frantically turned to "Europe." The left-hand page was a picture of Abby in front of the Eiffel Tower, holding up a sign that read "Happy Birthday, E!" Turning to the cover, I realized I held the July issue. The article detailed her first visit to Paris and her happiness was contagious. I found myself wanting to be in Paris, wanting to see the Mona Lisa at the Louvre and look up at the gargoyles of Notre Dam. She talked about wistfully window-shopping the world's most fashionable stores, only to be heartbroken when she finally went in one and looked at a price tag.

The magazine certainly picked the right girl for the job.

In August's "Fears" column, Abby helped two readers tackle their fear of heights by taking them skydiving. Abby, skydiving. It was unbelievable. Again, there was a message for me at the end:

E - Skydiving! Can you imagine? It wasn't even on my list. I want to go again with you. You would absolutely love it.

The "Europe" column was about Italy: Venice, Rome, Milan, and Florence. She rode in gondolas, stared up at the

Sistine Chapel, listened to opera, went to fashion shows, and threw a few coins into Trevi Fountain.

E - I don't want to jinx it, but I wished for a second chance with you. Am I crazy to hope? I feel like there's more to our story.

September was the last issue Trish gave me. This would be the issue that Ashley mentioned when I ran into her, Anna, and Derek in August. The "Europe" column was first this month and Abby described her journeys through Spain. There was no mention of me, but the article was so beautifully written, I read it twice before turning to find the "Fears" column. The bulk of the column was about the fear of public speaking, but the last couple of paragraphs were dedicated to me.

E - M & T's wedding is next month and I want to come. I want to see you. I miss you so badly it feels like my heart has been put through a paper shredder. I told you I needed to try and live on my own two feet and that's what I've been doing since I've been here. I've been crossing things off my list. I visited Jane Austen's home. I got a tattoo. I've been learning French. There's only a few things left. Things I want to do with you. And I've added two things.

#26 Have children with you. #27 Grow old with you.

I said before that staying in America and starting a family with you would be giving in to my fears and at the time I left that was true. But it's not true anymore. I faced that fear. I told you I needed to see if I could face my fears on my own and I did. Now I'm ready to face the world with you. Please can you forgive me? I love you.

I'll be waiting for your answer at the wedding. If you don't love me anymore, I'll never bother you again, I promise. More than I want you back, I want you to be happy. If you are happiest without me, then I'll fade out of your life forever.

That was it. She put her heart out there and I stomped all over it. She wouldn't try again, there'd be no more messages for me in the magazine. She was staying true to her word: fading out of my life. My stomach rolled and my arms began to shake. I couldn't lose her. I'd spent seven and a half months trying to get her out of my head, out of my life, but she wanted me back. I'd never stopped loving her. There was no other woman in the world who could make me happy. The depth of my misery while she was gone had been nothing compared to the depths of my joy when we were together. What the hell was I waiting for?

Gathering the magazines in my arms, I sprinted out the door and headed for my house instead of the complex. Three hours later, I was on a plane.

Chapter Forty-Two: Reconciliation

Ben

My fingernails dug into the armrests as the pilot announced we were clear for takeoff. Closing my eyes, I replayed the scene from Matt and Trish's wedding. What if I had just hugged her back? Things would be so different.

"Ben." She stopped a few feet in front of me and looked straight into my eyes.

"Abigail."

"It's so good to see you!" She rushed forward and threw her arms around my neck. Grabbing her around the waist, I pulled her tight to me and squeezed, inhaling her vanilla scent.

"Oh God, Abby, I've missed you so much." I whispered in her ear, nuzzling her neck with my mouth. She buried her face in my chest and it was like we'd never been apart.

"Ben, I'm sorry for everything. Can we try again?"

"Yes, absolutely." I lifted her chin with my index finger and covered her lips with my own. We became one person for a few seconds and love spread through me, starting at my toes and working its way up through my legs and into my chest and arms and brain.

"Abby, I love you more now than I ever thought possible. I want us to be together forever."

Shaking my head, I turned and looked out the window. I expected fear to overtake me, but instead of dread, calmness claimed my body as I peered through the dark clouds and let the night engulf me.

There's nothing to be afraid of. Think about the thing in life that makes you happiest. Abby's words from our trip to Florida played in my head. I tried to take her advice again.

Closing my eyes, I thought about her face as she looked at me. The love that always lived in her smile.

My fingers relaxed their grip on the armrests and the tension drained out of my shoulders. I was on my way to Abby. She could turn me down, refuse to listen to my apologies, tell me I lost my chance, but I felt more alive just anticipating seeing her, than I'd felt in the last eight months.

The woman seated next to me was writing in a spiral notebook and an idea came to me. "Can I borrow a sheet of paper and something to write with?" I asked hopefully.

"Um, sure." She ripped a sheet out and dug in her purse for a pen. I thanked her, pulled down my tray table, and began to write.

The plane touched down seven hours later and the pilot announced our arrival at Heathrow Airport. Unbuckling my seatbelt, I could barely contain my desire to exit the plane, only for the first time in my life I didn't want to get my feet on the ground because of fear. I wanted to get to Abby as fast as humanly possible.

It took over an hour for the plane to taxi to the terminal and allow passengers to exit. I wanted to scream at the flight attendants, find out what was causing such a long delay. My fidgeting caused concerned stares from the other passengers, but I couldn't restrain my nervous energy. Getting off, I was thankful I hadn't checked any luggage. I couldn't wait at baggage claim, customs was bad enough.

A group of taxis was lined up outside and I tossed my bag in the backseat of the nearest one. Snatching a scrap of paper out of my back pocket, I read off the address Anna gave me before I left the States. We sped off.

It took forty-five minutes in traffic to get to the street I wanted. Along the way, the cabbie made small talk, pointing out different sites and instructing me to look out the window. I only heard half of what he said; my mind was swimming with the events of the last year and a half.

"Here you go." The cabbie stopped the car and I gave him his fare. A flower shop faced me as I stepped out of the cab and I could imagine Abby going in once a week to buy fresh flowers for her apartment.

Opening the door, floral scents overwhelmed my nostrils. Lavender. Roses. Lilies. There were plants and flowers everywhere. I brushed them out of my face as I walked to the counter. After making a selection, I left the store feeling hopeful. Abby's building was only a few steps away.

My palms were sweating and the hairs on my arm stood up as I climbed the stairs to the landing. A call box at the entrance listed the occupants and I scanned the names, searching for the one I'd know. There she was. Flat #52. I touched my finger to the button and pushed. And waited. And pushed again. No answer. She wasn't home. Damn it.

I sat on the top step and put the flowers beside me on the landing. It was the middle of the week, why had I thought she'd be home? Oh well. A couple more hours of waiting wouldn't kill me. I really didn't have a choice.

* * * *

My watch wasn't right. I didn't adjust the time when we landed, even though the pilot had informed the passengers of the correct time. Was it seven AM when we landed? Or eight? I couldn't remember, but I kept checking my wrist every five minutes, knowing the time it stated meant nothing here in England. At least I could count the hours as they passed. Three, so far.

I rummaged in my bag and pulled out the last copy of *Intuition* Trish gave me. It was already opened to Abby's article. Reading the beautiful words again, I felt empowered to wait on the steps all night, all week. However long it took for her to come home.

Two women walked past me on the steps. Their confused expressions diffused into grins as they saw what I was reading. Smiling sheepishly, I explained, "My girlfriend writes for this magazine."

"Abigail?" The taller girl asked, just a hint of an accent coming through.

"Yeah, do you know her?"

"She lives across the hall from me. You must be the elusive E she's always writing about."

"Yep."

"You look like your pictures, but different." She stared at me, studying me, her arms crossed over her chest. "Oh, I'm Lottie."

"Nice to meet you, Lottie." I stood up and extended my hand, but she didn't take it.

"Did you come here to make her cry again?"

"What? No. Absolutely not. I came to beg her forgiveness."

"Oh, good. What took you so long?" She laughed as she put her key in the door and moved inside. Watching her leave, I sat back down and shame overcame me.

What took me so long? Anger, pride, pain. Resentment, pride, grief. Pride. Pride. Pride. I was too proud to admit to her that I missed her, too proud to admit I loved her, too proud to admit she never wanted to hurt me. Sitting there, damning my miserable pride, I prayed I wasn't too late.

Two more hours passed. I reread the articles so many times each line was memorized, torturing my subconscious with my pigheadedness. I thought about going to find something to eat, it was well past lunchtime, but was too afraid to leave her steps. What if she came home and I missed her? I was contemplating this when a whisper broke through the sounds of tires and engines on the road in front of me.

"Ben?" Her voice reached my ears and a smile spread across my face. I didn't look up immediately; I needed to make sure I wasn't dreaming. Pinching my arm, I felt the sting of my fingers twisting my skin. Definitely not dreaming. I looked up.

She was beautiful. Her brown hair hung down her shoulders in loose waves, bangs swept off to the side. Light blue shadow played up the aqua tones in her eyes and her cheeks were flushed the most gorgeous pink I'd ever seen. I jumped from my seat and picked up the flowers. Taking a step down, I held them out to her. Wordlessly she took them and stared into the bouquet.

"Anemones," I said.

"Yeah, I know. Thank you."

"You're welcome." I couldn't stop staring at her. She wore a soft yellow sundress, spaghetti straps showing off her tan shoulders and neck. A cream-colored cardigan was folded over her arm but she nearly dropped it when she reached for the flowers, revealing a tattoo on her wrist.

"Ben," she breathed after a minute, "I can't even tell you how happy I am to see you. But I don't understand. Why are you here?" Her eyes looked back and forth from me to the flowers, confusion spread across her face.

"Matt and Trish got me a plane ticket for my birthday."

"Your birthday was months ago."

"Yeah, I know, I couldn't bring myself to get on the plane."

"But, you said you were done. You said you never wanted to see me again, I thought I'd never see you again." She turned her eyes to the ground and guilt rushed through me. I hated myself for yelling at her, for doubting her all these months. I'd deserve it if she turned and walked away and never looked back.

"I can't even begin to tell you how sorry I am for how I acted at the wedding." I took a step closer to her. "I didn't know about these." I held up the magazine.

"But you said you read my articles."

"I lied. I was so hurt, and I didn't want to admit it to you. I'm sorry. I'm so sorry. I had no idea what you were writing. I should never have yelled at you like that, you didn't deserve it, even without these, no one deserves that." Another step forward.

"I didn't mean to hurt you. I never wanted to hurt you. I'm sorry, Ben." She still refused to look up.

"Abby, please look at me." One more step and she was only a foot away. Her eyes remained fixed on the ground.

"I know you didn't want to hurt me. Deep down I always knew that. But I *was* hurt. And I couldn't deal with all of the reminders of you in my life. I couldn't bring myself to read the articles because they were just another reminder that you chose your job over me."

This caused her eyes to meet mine. Her mouth pulled into a frown and her bottom lip trembled.

"Ben, please," her eyes pleaded with mine, "I hate myself for leaving. There's nothing in this world more important to me than you. But how could I give this up? I just couldn't. I thought if I left, you'd find someone new. Someone who could make you happy, make you realize that I wasn't good enough for you."

I tried to interrupt, but she held up her hand, "Don't. I know I should've known better. And when Trish told me how miserable you were, it broke my heart. I was so angry with myself. And then I was even angrier with myself because I started to feel hopeful. Hopeful I hadn't lost you for good. That's when I decided to write to you in the articles. I thought if you still loved me, maybe you'd be reading. I didn't want to force myself on you. And when we talked, on your birthday, I thought maybe you'd forgiven me, but I wasn't sure, you didn't sound like yourself, so I didn't push you then, either. Maybe I should have."

"No, you were right. It just would've made me resent you more."

"Will you ever forgive me?" A single tear slid down her cheek and I lifted my free hand to wipe it away, letting my fingers linger. The tears swimming in her eyes melted away as her skin absorbed my touch.

"I already have. Will you ever forgive me?"

"For what? You haven't done anything to need forgiveness for."

"Yes, I have. And not just at the wedding. I should've supported you. I shouldn't have let you end us. We could've done the long distance and neither one of us would've had to endure the last eight months of torture."

"Oh, Ben, I'm so sorry." She brought her hand to where mine rested on her cheek and covered my wrist, her eyes now burrowing into mine.

"Abby, I came here because I want us to move forward, together. You told me in March to move on with my life and I tried to without you, but Abigail, my life isn't worth living if I can't talk to you. If I can't know what's going on in your life. When you left, you said you needed me. Well, I wanted you then. Now, I'm letting you know I need you, too. Do you want me?"

"More than anything."

My heart soared and lungs constricted, I took a few shallow breaths and let my mouth stretch into a broad smile. Letting the magazine fall, I pulled the paper I wrote on the plane out of my pocket.

"I made you a list." She took it from me and turned her eyes from mine. A toothy grin broke out across her face as she read the items.

What I Want to Accomplish Before I Die, by Benjamin Harris

1) *Go to London*
2) *Find Abby*
3) *Beg her forgiveness*
4) *Tell her I love her*
5) *Kiss her again*
6) *Hug her again*
7) *Make love to her again*
8) *Marry her*
9) *Have beautiful children with her*
10) *Show her every day how much I love her*

As she finished reading the list, her green eyes made their way back to mine and I knelt before her, pulling the velvet box out of my pocket. Her eyes shone as she watched me, but they never left my face to look at the box.

I took her hand, "I know it will be tough at first and I don't want you to leave your job here, but I need to know you'll be mine for the rest of our lives. If that means we do long distance for a little while, or if that means I move here to London, I'm willing to do whatever it takes. I can't lose you again. Abby, I love you. I don't ever want to go another day without hearing your voice."

Tears fell from her eyes, but she stayed connected to me.

"Abigail Bronsen," I lifted the lid on the box, "will you marry me?"

I realized as the diamond and sapphires sparkled that a crowd had gathered around us, watching, waiting for her answer, but I didn't break my focus on her beautiful eyes. I took the ring out of the box and slid it on her perfect finger.

Before I knew it, the flowers and list were on the ground, her fingers closed around the collar of my shirt, and she pulled me onto my feet. Our lips met and eight months of dormant passion awakened and surged between us. Her soul bonded to mine, our bodies dissolved into one another, and her hands slid around my neck, pulling my face even closer to hers. I latched my hands around her waist and lifted her off the ground.

Clapping and cheers from the people surrounding us faded into the distance at first, but now erupted into a deafening roar, and Abby pulled away, laughing as she heard the shouts around us.

"I'm sorry," she started. "The normal response is yes, absolutely, I'll marry you."

"I liked your response better." I pulled her back to my mouth and stroked her hair, intoxicated by its silky softness against my fingers. I was never going to let her go again.

Chapter Forty-Three: The Wedding

Ben

I beheld an angel gliding towards me. Sunshine seemed to come from her very soul and her skin was glowing. The love in her eyes as she looked at me drove joy into my heart and my mouth expanded into a smile. My blood pumped faster and my hands quivered as she came closer.

Finally, she was before me, clinging to her father's arm, but never taking her eyes from mine. The minister addressed the crowd.

"I feel honored to be in the presence of Abigail and Ben's love today. I think we all do. Watching them together, I'm reminded what true love is. They think of the other with every move they make. Abigail can't say his name without a twinkle in her eyes, Ben lights up when she laughs. Their love is unending. We are all here today to show our support and love for them and I know they are thankful that each of you is here to celebrate with them." He paused and smiled at the crowd, then turned to Abby's father.

"Who blesses this woman in marriage?"

"Her mother, brother, sisters, and I do," Phil answered. He kissed Abby's cheek, and reached for my hand.

"Take care of her, son." After our handshake, he took Abby's hand and placed it in mine.

Abby

Ben's fingers closed around mine and the warmth of his skin actually sent tingles down my arm. "I love you," he whispered as I stepped forward to face him.

"I love you, too."

We stared into each other's eyes while the minister continued, "Abigail, Ben, you are starting on a never-ending journey. Your two paths are becoming one, and the road you travel will be filled with hope and love, but also tragedy and grief. Let your love for each other guide you in both the good and the bad times. Ben, do you take this woman to be your wedded wife, to live together in the covenant of marriage? Do you promise to love her, comfort her, honor and keep her, in sickness and in health, and forsaking all others be faithful to her as long as you both shall live?"

"I do." He pressed his hands over mine.

"And Abigail, do you take this man to be your wedded husband, to live together in the covenant of marriage? Do you promise to love him, comfort him, honor and keep him, in sickness and in health, and forsaking all others be faithful to him as long as you both shall live?"

"I do."

Ben

The minister smiled as he again spoke to our friends and family. "Ben and Abigail have chosen to recite personal vows that they have written themselves. Ben, keep your eyes on Abigail and tell her how much she means to you." The crowd chuckled, they knew my eyes weren't going anywhere.

"Abby, I promise to love you with my whole heart forever. I promise to stay by your side and hold your hand through all the ups and downs of life. I promise to be your Mr. Darcy," I paused as she laughed and took the opportunity to rest my palm against her cheek.

"I promise to be your Mr. Darcy and to let you keep my pride in check. I promise to continue showing you how amazing you are, and to never let you be afraid of trying anything new. I promise to spend the rest of my life making you happy." I raised the hand I was still holding and kissed it.

"Abigail, tell Ben how much he means to you."

She placed her hand over my heart and began, "Ben, I promise to never take this beautiful heart of yours for granted. I promise I will support you and hold your hand every day for the rest of our lives. I promise to learn from you and grow with you as life throws its lessons at us. And I promise to cherish every moment I spend with you, to always remember that you love me, and to love you more with every passing day."

Abby

I felt tears forming, but held them back as I vowed to spend my life with Ben. His beautiful blue eyes shone down on me as we promised to love each other unconditionally.

The minister turned to Matt, "May I have the rings please?" Matt pulled my ring out of his pocket and placed it on the officiant's Bible. Then, Anna slipped Ben's off her thumb and placed it beside mine on the open pages of the book.

"Ben, place the ring on Abigail's finger and repeat after me." Ben picked the ring up and slid it halfway down my fourth finger and mimicked the minister's words.

"In token and in pledge of our constant faith and abiding love, I give you this ring as a reminder of the love, happiness, and contentment you have brought to my life. As this ring has no end, neither shall my love for you." He slid it the rest of the way and kissed my hand again.

"Abigail, place the ring on Ben's finger and repeat after me." My hands trembled as I grasped the ring between my index finger and thumb and placed it on his finger.

"In token and in pledge of our constant faith and abiding love, I give you this ring as a reminder of the love, happiness, and contentment you have brought to my life. As this ring has no end, neither shall my love for you." I slid it to the base of his finger, then laced my fingers through his, never taking my eyes off his face.

"Ladies and Gentleman, you are all witnesses today to the miracle of this couple's love and I am proud to announce that by the exchange of vows and the exchange of rings they have pledged to live for and love each other throughout all the days of their lives. I am happy to proclaim that they are husband and wife. Ben, you may kiss your bride."

My insides grew warm as Ben wrapped his arms around my waist and lifted me to meet him. He lightly kissed my lips, letting his breath wash over me. I wanted to make this moment last forever, so I refused to let him pull away.

Ben

Our lips touched for the first time as husband and wife and a spark ran through my body. I didn't want to go too deeply and embarrass her in front of our family, but luckily, she turned our soft kiss into a passionate one. I heard the eruption of applause from our friends and family, but couldn't tear myself away.

Abby and Ben

We pulled apart at the same moment and stared into each other's eyes for a split second before joining hands and walking back up the aisle, beaming at the friends and family who cheered for us. Our love flowed in and around us, and we knew our adventures together were just beginning.

~ The End ~

ACKNOWLEDGEMENTS

I have so many people to thank for supporting me: Mom, Dad, Theresa, Amanda, Danny, Adam, Stephen, and Addison – thank you for being an amazing and loving family. Grandma, thank you for being my first investor! Ashley, Charles, Gracyn, and Lane – you truly are my second family and I love you as much as my first.

Brooke – thank you for always supporting my writing, even when the genre isn't quite your favorite. I promise the next one will be right up your alley!

Jaclyn – without you and our monthly (now bi-weekly!) sessions, I never would have written a second book, and I probably wouldn't have thought to publish this one. I can't wait to keep writing with you. A million thank you's for the gorgeous cover.

My fabulous friends at TNBW (Charity, Jason, Ang, Ann, and April, especially) – without you, *Twenty-Five* would have never made it past first draft stage. The book is better because of you and your diligence and insightful questions/thoughts.

And a huge thank you to all of the following, I know you have my back: Brad B., Christine D., Keith H., Megan D., Barbara J., Anthony L., Sarah K., Nicholas R., Steve D., Jean D., Myron B., Serena K., Matt B., Lindsay M., Jessica P., Phillip L., Jayson V., Kathy S., Mary L., Megan E., Samantha D., Joseph H., Sarah C., and Dan C.

Made in the USA
San Bernardino, CA
28 September 2013